After Mrs Hamilton

by

Clare Ashton

After Mrs Hamilton

By Clare Ashton

Credits:
Editor: Diana Simmonds
Cover photograph: CURAphotograph/Bigstock.com

For Jayney

Part 1. Friday Meetings

1.

Marella was having a bad day at work.

She sat in the lounge of one of her favoured Mayfair hotels. Mrs Hamilton, the only name the client would give, sat on the other side of the coffee table. She looked calm, assured and measuring. She sat elegantly cross-legged in the armchair, lit by the low autumn sun through the window. She held a cup of coffee above a saucer and appraised Marella from behind a pair of sunglasses.

Marella assumed the same look with difficulty, spending too much effort on stopping herself from leaning forward, crossing her arms or tucking and hiding her legs under the chair.

'You're not from England are you?' Mrs Hamilton said. This was the wrong way around. Marella should be the one asking the questions, to elucidate the client's needs.

'No. Poland.' She paused. She felt drawn into replying in the woman's silence. 'But I've been living in London for ten years now.'

'Do you like it here?'

Marella didn't want to answer and nodded, limiting the conversation. She avoided divulging too much about herself with her clients. It clouded the impression they gave her if they started to tailor their personalities towards her. She needed to see their fresh, instinctive responses.

The first five minutes were the most important for watching the client in the raw. First Marella watched their responses to the doorman, the receptionist, the waiter. The first-timers often looked uncomfortable and kept interaction to a minimum. They thought this made them less noticeable. But underneath the predictable furtive behaviour, they still gave away their inclinations, background and expectations. Did they look the doorman in the eye? Did they thank the doorman? Did they choose the male or female receptionist? She was already building a picture before they reached her table.

Marella dressed neutrally, business-like, to deter the client's inclination towards her. She allowed them to settle and watched their reactions to their surroundings while she procrastinated and chose from the menu. Her choice of waiter was purposeful, made to give more detail to some impression already gained from her client.

But Mrs Hamilton had ignored the doorman and had waited to be attended by either receptionist. She had offered no second glance to the Australian waitress who took her coat, or to the young Spanish waiter who brought the menus. She had glanced around before sitting opposite Marella and had hardly removed a gaze that was half-hidden beneath her sunglasses.

She had been forward and asked confirmation of her identity. 'Marella. No?'

Marella tried to determine Mrs Hamilton's accent. There was a hint of European flavour beneath an English accent that tripped and drawled over the odd American phrase.

She was tall, perhaps a little overweight, with a figure that would have been athletic in her youth. Her dress was made from fine-woven, soft, cream fabric, cut elegantly and held by a narrow belt round her waist. She wore a little jewellery and makeup and her perfume smelled like a lighter Chanel No 5.

Every detail about the woman suggested sophistication, confidence and money. She was perfectly turned out for a morning appointment.

'You are very beautiful,' Mrs Hamilton said, as a matter of fact. 'To be expected, I guess. I suppose.'

Again Marella felt disarmed and under scrutiny. 'Thank you,' she said, trying to gain the upper hand by accepting the compliment.

Marella was naked in front of this client. Her stomach muscles were clenched with tension that radiated out to her shoulders and arms. She felt cornered and unable to shake off her rigidity without giving away her discomfort. She sipped her coffee and released her tension under the guise of appreciation.

'They serve very good coffee here,' she said.

Mrs Hamilton shrugged. 'Passable, I suppose,' she said, but she refused to be diverted from her study of Marella. 'Have you always done this kind of work? Were you always, ah, an escort?' Her voice had an edge.

Marella tensed further. She was tempted to walk away. If the woman had not been referred by a trusted, long-term client she would have left.

'Not always,' she said. 'I do very little now. This...' she spread her arms in front of her, 'assessing people's needs and matching them is what I do.'

'So you do not attend clients yourself?' Mrs Hamilton had spoken quickly and looked uncomfortable for the first time.

'No. I don't take new clients, and I never take female clients. I have a number of colleagues who I can recommend. If I can, I will match you with one of them. I'm sorry if this arrangement wasn't clear to you.'

Mrs Hamilton did not shift her gaze from Marella's eyes. Marella was not sure if she had understood. She opened her mouth to repeat her terms but the client stopped her with slight raise of her hand. 'How long ago did you stop taking new clients?'

'A few years now. I'm surprised you didn't know. Finding the perfect escort is my speciality. That is what you are paying for. Your acquaintance, he didn't tell you this?'

Mrs Hamilton was silent and looked away. She did not fidget or touch her face, but Marella could see her chest move with rapid deep breaths. She waited for the client to compose herself, taking the opportunity to survey her unhindered.

Even distressed, Mrs Hamilton looked refined, covering her emotions with good breeding or training. Marella could not decide if she would describe her as beautiful. She guessed that she was in her fifties. Her hair was long and neatly tied back, streaming the streaks of iron grey from her forehead back over her head and the rest of her dark hair.

She had enviable bone structure, high cheek bones and an intelligent forehead. She had a strong jaw, but not so strong as to be masculine. From the side, no longer hidden by the glasses, Marella could see that she had long eyelashes and dark eyes – perhaps hazel, she could not quite tell. Perhaps it was just the colour of her face that detracted. Mrs Hamilton had a Mediterranean complexion, but she seemed drained somehow, sad.

Marella was beginning to be more at ease and in control. She offered, 'Would you like me to assess your needs?'

Mrs Hamilton still looked away. Her expression was receding, her face becoming blank as her thoughts took her away.

'Madam. Mrs Hamilton....'

The client came to, smiled with resignation and made a sharp exhalation through her nose.

'Why not,' she said. 'Let's see what you can arrange for me.'

2.

Laura looked into her small terraced house behind the tube station in Wood Green. She kicked away a burger wrapper that had blown into the front garden from the street and stepped closer to the window. The back garden was glowing green in the sunlight through the patio doors. The kitchen-diner and small living room were dim and the sagging sofa that divided the rooms seemed to be a uniform dark shape. She looked to each side of the room, her eyes focussing on the canvas photos of flowers, but she couldn't see her husband.

One last time she checked behind her and reached into her doctor's bag for her keys. She stepped through the front door, letting her eyes adjust to the darkness, and closed the door to seal out the noise from the street. She waited in the hallway, listening. The house was quiet.

She dropped her bag onto the cracked Edwardian tiles and ran up the narrow stairs to the front bedroom. With no time to shower, she started to tug her jumper over her head. Her chest heaved, out of breath, under her crossed arms, and she pulled off her top and slip and threw them on the bed. She unhooked her skirt and let it drop around her ankles. She took the first pair of jeans from a shelf in the cupboard and pulled them up, jumping up and down to squeeze the tight white material over her hips. The jeans were creased and she smoothed the thin folds with her palms, catching her wedding ring on the plastic crystals that made a heart shape over the front pocket.

Clothes hangers rattled in the cupboard as she searched for her favourite pink blouse. She flicked through the casual tops she wore at weekends and, with less hope, through the duplicate skirts and jumpers she wore for work that varied only by colour.

She turned to scan the bedroom. The bed was unmade, the duvet turned over on Josh's side. Her pillow beside his was still puffed full. Her eyes flicked up at the mantelpiece to their framed wedding photo that looked over the marital bed. Josh stood proud in his hired morning suit beside his bride. His smile took over his whole face, all his teeth on show and his eyes creased. He had too much hair. Dark wisps were brushed over where he was now receding, and his skin was smooth where deep horizontal lines had recently crinkled his forehead.

Laura recognised that she had changed less in the eight years since their wedding at university. She stood beside him in the picture, stooping a little so that she did not match his height. She was smiling, with her lips shut, and her eyes did not meet the camera lens. Her long bleached hair was tied in a plait and drawn back over her dark roots. She wore it loose today, over her thinner face. Her cheeks, which still had puppy fat in the picture, were tighter across her cheekbones. She looked again at Josh, smiling at her from the photo, blushed under his gaze, and left the room.

The air smelled stale in the spare room at the back of the house. Her sleeping bag lay curled up like a maggot on the bed. She unzipped the bag and folded it out to air. From the corner of her eyes she saw her top, crumpled on the chair in front of the computer desk. She lifted it to her face and breathed in, wrinkling her nose at its mustiness.

A key scraped in the front door lock and she stiffened. She felt vulnerable, standing in her bra. She pushed her arms down the sleeves of the dirty blouse and struggled with the buttons. The door latch clicked open and the noise of cars and footsteps in the street flooded into the house. Shoes scuffed the hallway tiles and another doctor's case was dropped to the floor. The latch clicked shut and the house was silent once again.

Laura stood still, repressing her temptation to turn and look out down the stairs. She hoped he would look for her downstairs first. If he searched for her through the living room, into the kitchen and garden, she might be able to escape.

The stairs creaked in the hallway and she heard his shoes scrape on the wooden steps. She counted twelve steps and then his shoes were quietened by the landing rug and he appeared in the doorway.

He looked tired. A deep crow's foot was stamped on his forehead and the skin around his eyes was grey. Sweat patches darkened his poly-cotton shirt beneath his armpits and his arms hung heavy by his sides. He looked at her, taking her in, and then his shoulders sagged.

'You're not going out are you?' he said.

Laura's insides tensed and she clenched her jaw. She tried to sound neutral. 'I told you I was going out tonight.'

'Can't you cancel?' His eyes seemed sad and his face pleaded with her. 'We really need to talk.'

'We talked last night,' she said.

He turned away and breathed out noisily through his nose. He opened his mouth ready to talk, but closed it again without saying a word.

'I need to get ready,' she said. She made a step forward out of the room and waited for him to step aside. He reached forward though, and lifted her hand from by her side. She could feel his large fingers stroking inside her palm. It was a familiar sensation, her caring husband reaching for her hand, but it made her shudder. She twitched her hand away, crossed her arms and kept her hands out of his reach.

'This is getting serious Laura. Can't you give Clo a miss tonight? For once? We really need to sort this out.'

'I don't know what more I can say,' she said. 'I'm just not ready and no matter how much we talk it over, I'm still not ready.'

'But you've always said you wanted kids. I can't believe you've changed your mind.'

Laura breathed in, taking a moment to calm herself and think. 'I still want kids.'

The image of Josh running around in the garden, kicking a ball with a small boy, flashed in her mind. She could see Josh smiling, concentrating on the ball by his feet and kicking it to the boy who was turned away from her. She heard the boy laugh as the ball rolled by his feet, and he turned around towards her. He was still giggling, but his blank face had no mouth to laugh. It was featureless. His features moved and writhed under stretched white skin, but she couldn't see who he was. Her stomach curdled.

'I can't do it Josh'. She rubbed her temples with her fingertips trying to massage the image in her head. She shook her head. 'I can't picture them.'

'No-one can,' he said quietly. 'Nobody knows what their kids are going to be like. That's part of the fun, having a whole unpredictable little person in your life.' He was trying to catch her eye.

'But at least people know where they've come from. They know that their ginger hair's from their granddad. They know that they're great at maths just like their granny. What am I going to be able to tell them?'

She stared at him, questioning. 'I don't know what illnesses they'll inherit? I could be carrying some horrible genetic diseases.'

'Oh come on Laura.' He tilted his head to one side, ridiculing her worry. 'Lots of people carry genetic diseases. When people only have one or two kids you've no idea what traits you might be carrying.'

She stared at him and could see him deflate as he realised that he had only harmed his case. He stared at the floor and she started to feel sorry for him.

'Let me find them,' she said.

He shuffled from foot to foot and crossed his arms, but still looked at the floor.

'I can't see how you're going to get any further than last time,' he said.

'Let me at least try.'

'But it could take years.' His jaw was clenched and he squeezed his fingers into his biceps. 'You could be too old to have children by the time you find them.'

Only she would be too old for children? She wondered for the first time whether he would leave her. She looked at his tense profile and wondered how far she was pushing him. She saw her devoted friend from school, the person she used to confide in, the person she told about every girl she had loved and slept with. He had followed her to Oxford University, supported her when she had broken down and persuaded her to marry him. But was she worth all of this?

'You know why I don't want you to try again,' he said.

She blushed. 'I was younger then. I was behind with my studies and trying to find my parents, and then when Clo left university as well…. I just think I would be stronger this time.'

'Why? What's changed?' he said, irritated. 'You still pile pressure on yourself at the surgery, Clo's still completely unpredictable.'

'That's not fair. It wasn't Clo's fault. She would have been there if she could.'

'Really?' he said raising his eyebrows. 'I mean really? The only thing you can rely on Clo being is completely unreliable.'

She felt sick at his red face and the sneer on his lips. 'It's not about Clo anyway,' she said.

'Good. Because you really can't count on her this time either.'

'I didn't think I'd need Clo's support this time…' Her voice faltered. 'I thought I wouldn't need it, because I'd have you.'

He blushed and looked down and stepped from foot to foot, hugging himself with his crossed arms. She waited for him to look up and say some reassuring words, but they didn't come. Anger swelled in her stomach and she no longer wanted him in her sight. She brushed past him roughly and ran down the steps.

'Laura!'

She grabbed her coat from the hooks in the hallway, squeezed the pocket to check her phone and purse were inside, and opened the door.

'Laura, of course I'm here for you. I'm desperate to start a family. I'm just angry.'

She stepped out of the front door, letting it go behind her, not caring whether it shut. She marched into the street eager to get away from him, but then stopped and looked back. Josh's shout was muffled inside the house. She turned around and ran in the opposite direction, along the street away from her usual bus stop, not slowing until she was out of sight.

She lifted her phone from her coat and pushed out a text message with her thumb: 'Can you meet up earlier? Need to talk'. She stroked her finger over the screen, scrolling through her contact list, and selected Clo.

3.

Mrs Hamilton, the client thought, had been an odd choice of name. She had taken it from her Republican sister-in-law. It amused her to think of her husband's sister, who she usually met at the golf club, waiting for a prostitute in an expensive London hotel. It was almost as amusing as standing there herself. Did they call male prostitutes, prostitutes? Did hooker only refer to women? She had spent very few of her fifty-four years thinking about male prostitutes for women.

What would he look like? She pictured a man at the door, playing with shining cuff links at the sleeves of a crisp shirt beneath a dark suit. He was white with light brown hair and blue eyes. Maybe he would be black. He changed to a black, muscular man with dark eyes and beautiful perfect teeth. Or Asian. Again the image changed.

She had no idea what to expect. She was not sure what she wanted. Marella the madam was famed for her ability to pick the perfect escort, but had she given her enough of a chance to decide? After all, it was not what she had seen Marella for.

Partner for her evening was the phrase Marella had used. This calmed her. The phrase implied a couple of hours of company beyond the.... She did not even know what to call the act she had paid for.

Again, she tried to guess who would come to the door. Young, she decided. And by young, she meant approaching middle age: old enough to have been married and have a young family and an established career, but still young enough to have full cheeks and laughter dents rather than her sharp creases.

She drew back the curtain to the balcony window and gazed out into the square. The light was starting to fail and fewer people criss-crossed the square below. City people had gone home, tourists were retiring for the day and it was still too early for nightlife to begin.

She raised her hand to her neck and felt her soft but no longer taut skin move as she gulped. She turned from the window to check her appearance again and went to the bathroom.

She examined her reflection in the heated mirror, devoid of steam from her second shower. The light was flattering; the soft pink favourable to pale, aging skin, mottled with blemishes that could not be avoided after fifty odd years of sunshine, laughter, grief.

She stroked her dark eyebrows smooth. It was annoying that even eyebrows had to be brushed these days. Still, they were one of her best features, arched above darkest brown eyes that were still clear, on a good day.

She was frowning again. She had been frowning for the last ten years. She wiped her brow hoping to smooth away the lines. A lock of grey hair loosened and curled across her face, a strand of almost black hair falling behind it. With an ingrained habit, she flicked it back behind her ear. She preferred it tied back, but all the grey that sprung from her hair line would stream over her head, hiding the dark hair.

She smoothed her cheeks back to experiment with the effect of plastic surgery. Wrinkle free but the permanent grin scared her. She let the loose jowls flop forward, pale for a moment before the blood could flow again. She'd had a beautiful bone structure once, still did, she guessed.

Her figure was firm with almost daily swimming, but again hidden under a layer of looser flesh. She thought she hid it well with her choice of clothing: a skirt that was tight enough to show her still shapely legs and hips, but not so tight to reveal any irregularities and dimples; a tailored shirt, drawn in to suggest more of a waist than she had, and which pressed up her still enviable chest.

Yes, a good sensible choice, her outfit.

All confidence drained away. A sensible suit, covering an old lady's body waiting for a nubile young man to make her forget her husband's infidelity. Stupid. She felt old and stupid.

She sat on the side of the bed. Tears threatened to come as she slumped forward, rocking over her feet. What the hell was she doing?

Meeting Marella had not been as painful as she had imagined meeting your husband's whore would be. The woman was stunning. She could not fault his taste. She was intelligent, respectable looking even. And young. How did she think that she could compete with that?

But Marella was a businesswoman. A businesswoman an ocean away who seemed to have no inclination to give up her lucrative profession and steal anyone's husband. He was just a long-term client of Marella's. Longer term than she had hoped for. And that had hurt, the discovery that while she thought they had been still in physical love, he had already engaged Marella's services.

She pictured them both half clothed and half in bed. Odd, she was not even feeling jealous now. Disgusted she wondered? Not even that. Numb perhaps and little embarrassed for her husband – comparing his wrinkly behind with the perfect curves of Marella. It had been so long since they'd had sex, she found it difficult to picture him accurately.

She was reassured, however, that her husband was safely pleasuring himself far away from their backyard and with someone who was very little threat to their daily routine. She could go back to her life, relaxing in California, accompanying her husband to New York, entertaining his clients, colleagues, partners. Going out to the theatre. Sailing with their friends. No-one knew of her husband's London arrangement. He had several old clients here, that was all. No London-based colleagues to snigger behind her back. No-one else in the know.

It was a strange relief. She would no longer have to feel any guilt at refusing her husband's groping hands. It hardly ever happened, now that she had moved into a separate room. But the thought that she no longer had to worry about fulfilling her marital obligation post-menopause was, quite frankly, a relief. The thought of Malcolm's advances had made her nauseous for over a year now. She could safely and guilt free think of Malcolm as her asexual friend. Nice and asexual Malcolm. Grey Malcolm.

Marella had left Mrs Hamilton with few feelings of jealousy. Her desire for revenge had dissipated. Her marriage felt surprisingly secure. So why on earth was she choosing to have sex with someone else?

Panic started to rise again, gripping her chest around her heart. It shocked her that she had let it go this far. The thought of a strange man appearing at the door, undressing and fucking, chilled her.

She snatched her bag from the bedside table and pulled out her phone. It was nearly eight o'clock and he would be knocking on the door any moment.

She fumbled Marella's number into the phone and urged the phone to connect. The phone rang, lapsing into long silences between rings. She strained forward in her head, trying to will the distant Marella into answering her phone.

'Hello,' came an answer, quite calm, bathed in a background of silence.

'Hello. It's Mrs Hamilton.' She sounded collected. 'I'm sorry, but I'm going to have to cancel my appointment.' Training had automatically kicked in. Her voice came out slower than her thoughts and lower than her mental scream.

'Is there a problem that I can help with?'

'No, no problem. Thank you. More a change of mind. I'm sorry for the lateness of the cancellation.'

'That's quite all right. Although I need to contact my employee straight away.'

'Yes of course. Good night.'

'Good night. Please call again if you change your mind. I will keep the offer open until tomorrow.'

She pressed the button to end the call and breathed out. She snorted a small laugh, releasing the tension, and shook her head in disbelief. 'Stupid,' she said. She stood up and eased off her shoes and un-peeled her tights, rolled them into a neat ball and put them in a drawer. She strolled around the room, trying to relieve the tension that had built up in her shoulders, arms and legs.

In the bathroom, she un-tucked her hair that had caught in her shirt collar and pulled back her greying strands over her head into a pony-tail. She dabbed out her contact lenses and reopened her heavy varifocals from her washbag.

Her glasses covered half of her face, hiding her eyebrows behind thick tortoiseshell frames, shrinking her beautiful eyes to unremarkable clams that winked beneath her eyelashes. She laughed out loud at herself. She had several more elegant pairs, even glasses to match particular outfits. But she always liked these, last thing at night, when she was no longer on show.

A sharp knock on the door interrupted her come down. She drew in a sharp breath, fearing that she had cancelled too late. Peering through the spy hole, she was relieved to see a waiter carrying a tray of Champagne with two glasses. The wine was unopened and she considered sending it back. But she did have things to celebrate: a new job, a new role, and perhaps a saved marriage after all.

Besides, she loved fizzy wine. It did not need to be Champagne. Just a dry, yeasty, floral wine like they made at home. This home was not home in the California hills. Or home in her husband's New York apartment. It was not even the homes she had occupied in England, before she moved to the States and remarried.

English memories threatened to bubble out of control and she stopped leafing through her old homes. She took a generous gulp of Champagne. The memories had been threatening all day. Images rushing vividly into her head like water into blotting paper, threatening to overwhelm. It had taken a real threat to her marriage and lifestyle to bring her back to England and risk stirring up the past. It was not a visit she had ever thought she would make again.

She took another mouthful, causing bubbles to leap up her nose and make her eyes water. And another. She refilled her glass to accompany a secret cigarette that she'd had the forethought to buy.

Evening was descending faster outside now. The air was cool against her face out on the balcony. The sky blended from blue twilight to orange city glow above the square. She inhaled a long first drag on her cigarette. She had smoked for too many years in her youth for it to make her cough now, but she still experienced the light-headed hit after a long break. She leaned forward onto the railing to steady herself and flicked the ash into the bathroom glass she had brought outside.

There were only a handful of people passing through the square now. The noise was mainly contributed by an American couple standing, twirling and pointing in the middle of the square, searching for some landmark. The elderly couple both wore baseball caps, polo shirts, trainers and bum bags. They looked tired. The man had sweat marks in his armpits and a damp stripe down his back.

A young couple, dressed in long dark coats and carrying brief cases crossed the square, oblivious to the plight of her compatriots, and a burst of English business speak rose towards her as they hurried down a side street. The American couple stood open-mouthed, trying too late to gain the attention of either.

She could see one other person in the square. Opposite the hotel, a young woman stood beside a lamp post with two shopping bags from a clothes store on the ground beside her. She was staring towards the hotel doors and seemed to be waiting, checking her watch carefully. She did not seem to fit either the tourist or city mould.

She was dressed in a matching light jacket and trousers, but wore so low cut a top that it appeared she was naked beneath. It looked good on her. She was young enough to reveal as much neck and chest as she wanted. She was lightly tanned, her skin glowing against the light suit, and her hair was short, floppy and blond. She was too far away for Mrs Hamilton to see her eyes. Shadows fell across distinct cheek bones and around full lips. She was slim, but with hips and breasts large enough to curve out into a woman's figure.

The young woman's waiting was over. With a last glance at her watch, she picked up her bags and started to walk across the square towards the hotel.

'Miss. Miss?' Mrs Hamilton's spying was interrupted by the American couple trying to ambush the young woman. 'You don't know the area do you?' The young woman smiled, shaking her head, pressing on towards the hotel.

'Oh.' Mrs Hamilton could hear the couple's disappointment and the first signs of becoming disheartened. The two glanced at each other, but neither had any more ideas. Maybe she should go down and see if she could help.

'I'm sorry. I do know the area well. Can I help you?' The young woman had returned to help the couple. The man grinned and pressed his hands together in prayer. The young woman took their guidebook and frowned at the open page.

'I'm sorry, you're quite a way from there,' Mrs Hamilton could hear. It was a soothing voice, deeper than she'd expected for a young woman in her late twenties, early thirties.

'I can recommend somewhere nearby, if you're after an old English pub and some proper food?'

The American couple looked overwhelmed, their fatigue turning into relief. They ambushed the young woman with hugs and thanks. Mrs Hamilton smiled and felt a small sense of gratitude towards the stranger.

'Come here then, I know one just around the corner.' The young woman picked up her bags in one hand and scooped the arm of a surprised American wife in the other, and swept the couple out of sight across the square. Mrs Hamilton, under the fizzy influence of Champagne felt a wave of elation rise through her chest and lifted her glass and smiled after the trio.

The square was quiet. The orange glow was starting to take over and pigeons shuffled, crapped and cooed under the yellow leaves in the plane trees, getting ready to settle down for the night. Mrs Hamilton's cigarette glowed hotter and redder in the fading light.

The hum of the city and cars way beyond the square were punctuated by rapid steps; not quick enough for someone running, but a very swift walking pace. The young woman reappeared around the top corner of the square, looking ruffled in her haste. She paused in sight of the hotel and dropped her bags to the side and smoothed her hair, jacket front and sleeves. She took several deep breaths and then continued her approach to the hotel at a more relaxed pace.

Her face wore an expression of a mix of pleasure, interest and politeness. The woman disappeared into the building beneath Mrs Hamilton and a little while later, just long enough to take a lift to the second floor, Mrs Hamilton heard a light knock at the door.

'Oh,' she exclaimed out aloud, as she realised Marella's mistake. 'Oh,' again. She smiled, covering her mouth with her hand, as she let the turn of events settle over her. 'How funny.'

Eyes wide with surprise, she stepped back from the window and contemplated receiving her visitor. She left the balcony and slid back into her shoes and smoothed down the front of her shirt. She straightened her spine and pulled her shoulders back, just enough to lift her head and chin and to feel the confidence that the movement always gave her. She called out, 'Come in. It's open.' As the door opened, her hands betrayed her and sprang out and clasped together.

A bright wedge of light from the corridor widened on the wall and then was gone again. The door clicked shut and they stood silent while their eyes readjusted to the dimness of the room. It was only lit from the street lights, although Mrs Hamilton, with her back to the window, had the advantage over her guest. Her visitor was an inch or two shorter than her and she was more petite than she had appeared from the balcony. Fresh and light perfume extended towards Mrs Hamilton and she regretted having the cigarette.

Her guest put down her bags. She squinted in the darkness and stepped forward to introduce herself. At a distance close enough to shake hands, she tripped as she caught her shoe in the rug on the floor, making her stumble forward. She put out her arms to stop her fall and her open hands encountered Mrs Hamilton's ample bosom as a soft landing.

'Oh!' the young woman said. She looked down at her hands holding Mrs Hamilton's breasts in her palms. 'Oh, I'm so sorry. I tripped.'

Mrs Hamilton laughed, steadying her guest. 'Yes, I can see.' She had shot out her arms to catch her falling guest. They stood facing each other, holding each other's forearms.

'Are you OK? I didn't mean to. I'm very sorry,' the guest said.

'Are all English escorts this polite?' asked Mrs Hamilton. She noticed how American she sounded compared with her guest's English accent.

Her guest giggled and replied 'Perhaps not.' It was a lovely sound and sight. An unguarded youthful giggle and smile directed towards her.

'Hi,' her guest said. 'I'm Clo and I am really sorry.'

'Hi,' Mrs Hamilton replied, and they stared at each other's blurred faces in the darkness.

4.

Laura sat in Beck's, Clo's favourite Soho bar. Laura leant on a table, spinning her glass of white wine by its stem, the condensation running down the glass, cold onto her fingers. She stared at her phone as it lay on the table, willing Clo to respond to her text.

The autumn sun was low in the sky and shone through the large open doors, warming everything in an orange glow. She squinted in the light and tried to see into the street, her mind primed to spot Clo. Her short, floppy blond hair would shine in the sun and Laura listened out for her mellow voice that would shout out her name.

Laura held her hands tight together, her interlocking fingers pale. Clo would know something was wrong. She would see straight through her, the way she had when Laura said she was going to marry Josh. Despite all those girlfriends that she had loved, sweated and writhed with, she was going to marry her best male friend. 'Won't you crave being with a woman?' Clo had said. Laura had turned away, the question unanswered and Clo had held and kissed her, apologising and blurting out her congratulations.

Laura bounced her legs on her tiptoes beneath the table, her thigh muscles shuddering. She stopped. Within moments her calves, then her thighs, began to cramp. The tension wound itself up her legs to her tummy, pulling the knot in her stomach tighter. Where the hell was Clo?

The bar was nearly empty. The woman serving was talking to the only other person in the room - a woman with short hair who looked down the front of the bar maid's vest. The woman had tried to chat to Laura when she'd ordered her drink, but Laura had been distracted and abrupt. Now the woman half-turned towards her every so often, with a disapproving look on her face.

Laura's phone vibrated on the table in front of her. It buzzed, fell silent and buzzed again, creeping across the surface. It glowed with a photo of Josh and she snatched it up, not wanting to see his face. She tapped hard at the red button beneath his photo and his image was wiped away into darkness. She put the phone back on the table and checked towards the door, screwing up her eyes.

A person entered the bar. Laura opened her mouth, ready to call out to Clo, her legs tensing to rise from her chair. The blurred shape walked in a relaxed sway, the halo of light obscuring Laura's view, until the sun became blocked behind the body and the person became distinct and sharp. A woman, with long hair and too tall for Clo, approached the bar.

Again, Laura's phone buzzed on the table. She glanced over to see Josh's picture light up and tapped her finger on the red button.

She heard an American accent ask for beer and Laura looked up to see the tall woman watching her. The woman smiled a generous wide smile, with perfect teeth, and winked.

The woman with the short hair beside her muttered something. 'I wouldn't bother mate,' perhaps. And the tall woman turned back to the bar. They talked more quietly and Laura frowned, unable to hear what they said. She was about to look away when the tall woman leaned over the bar. Her tailored shirt rose up her back as she bent over and rested on her elbows. Laura could see her skin tanned and warm under the crisp white material. Her dark hair flowed and swung across her back as she talked to the other women. It had a coppery sheen, which flashed in streaks as she turned her head.

Laura was startled when all three women burst out laughing and the tall woman put her arm out to squeeze the other customer around the shoulders.

'You bet,' the tall woman said, patting the other's back, and she turned towards Laura with her drink. She left the bar with warmth but finality and strode towards her.

Laura's mouth opened as she approached.

'Hey,' the woman said. She said it with such ease and confidence.

Laura eyes widened as the woman approached, panicking at the thought of the woman intruding on her time with Clo.

'I'm sorry, I'm waiting for someone', she said. She flicked her eyes from the woman, to the doors and back, to emphasise her point and blinked quickly with nerves.

The woman laughed. 'Yeah, me too.' She set the bottle of beer on the table and dragged a chair across to join Laura. She sat down and crossed her long legs, resting the ankle of a heavy boot on her knee.

'No sorry,' Laura swallowed and frowned. 'I'm waiting for a friend…'. The woman stepped forward and put out her hand.

Laura pulled away from her. 'I'm married,' she said.

The woman did not reach any further, but she did not withdraw her hand either. Laura held up her left hand and pushed it towards the woman. Her engagement and wedding rings came unstuck from her skin and slid down her finger.

The woman sat back in her chair, with her mouth open, the words halted by Laura's outburst. She laughed and shook her head.

'Well of course you are,' the woman said.

'Of course?'

'Sure.' She made the word last and raised her palms shrugging. 'Want to know what else I can tell?'

Laura couldn't answer.

The woman reached out her hand to inspect Laura's wedding rings. 'May I?' she said.

Laura glanced towards the door willing Clo to appear, but she did not come. She turned back to the woman and held out her hand, letting the woman hold her fingers and examine her rings. Her touch felt odd. Her hands were large for a woman's, like Laura's, but smaller and smoother than Josh's. They lacked the tufts of dark hair that that sprung from the back of each of his fingers. These hands were tanned and soft. Her nails looked pale and pink on her brown skin, the white half moons clear, and Laura was tempted to reach out and trace her finger around them.

'Well for starters, your engagement ring is tasteful, but not the most expensive. I'd guess you were married young. Right?'

The woman stared at Laura waiting for confirmation. Laura nodded and let the stranger continue to hold her hand. The woman held her gaze. It was difficult to look away. Her irises were a saturated dark green and lined by long lashes that glinted the same copper as her hair. The woman smiled, her lips curling up on one side.

'Let's see what else….' The woman turned her fingers over and studied her palm. She traced a finger slowly along the lines, sending a gentle tingling sensation up Laura's arm into her chest. The feeling radiated out, warming the rest of her body, and the knot in her stomach began to loosen.

'I'd say you are one bright lady, office job, perhaps lawyer? No wait. I'd guess you are a doctor.' The woman grinned at her. 'Am I right?' she said raising her eyebrows.

Laura nodded with her mouth open.

'What else?' The woman frowned and returned to examine Laura's palm. 'Of course I see you're younger than me, I'd say by six years.' The woman frowned and concentrated on a particular line for a moment. 'Yeah, definitely twenty-seven years old.'

'I'm twenty-eight,' said Laura. She took her hand away, pleased to correct one of the woman's remarks.

'Shit, yeah. You just had your birthday didn't you.' The woman sat back and tapped her head with her fingertips.

A shiver agitated Laura's insides. She took her hand away from the table.

'And if pushed,' the woman said, 'I would have to say your name's Laura. Laura Edeson if I really had to.' The woman grinned at her and put out her hand. 'Susan. Susan Miller.'

Laura stared at her.

'Clo's friend? From the States?'

'God, I'm so sorry,' Laura breathed out. She rubbed her forehead and brushed her hair back awkwardly. She stood up at the same time as Susan. 'I completely forgot Clo said you'd arrived. I didn't realise you were coming out tonight.'

Laura felt her cheeks heat and the blush spread down her neck and chest. Wanting to hide it she drew Susan towards her into a hug.

They were almost the same height and Susan's breasts pressed gently into hers as her shoulders wrapped around her. The other woman's warmth filled her through their joined chests.

'Couldn't help myself,' said Susan by her ear. She pulled away and Susan grinned at her as they parted. 'Just can't stop kidding around and flirting with straight girls.'

'I was being an idiot. Sorry, I'm just a bit distracted. But, I wasn't always…'

Her phone buzzed on the table beside them. She looked down at the table and drew away from Susan when she saw Josh's photo looking up at her.

5.

Where was Clo? Susan had gone to buy another round of drinks and Laura stared towards the bar doors. The sun had gone down behind the buildings and she could see clearly into the street. Several times Laura jumped half out of her chair thinking she had seen her. She thought she saw Clo amble into the bar, but as she came closer her face changed into someone else and Laura sank back into her chair.

'Did I freak you out earlier?' Susan said, a half smile on her lips, holding a glass of wine and bottle of lager in her hands.

'No, no. Sorry, I was just miles away.' She collected herself and smiled. 'Well, you did freak me out. I didn't realise Clo had told you that much about me.'

'Oh, she talks about you the whole time,' said Susan, sitting down.

Laura knew a little about Susan from Clo, but she hadn't known what she looked like or detail like her age. She wasn't what she'd expected though. She'd imagined a sharp-tongued New Yorker. The laid-back woman before her couldn't be more different.

'I'm sorry. Clo hasn't told me as much about you,' said Laura. 'Although I've been a bit distracted recently and perhaps haven't taken it in.'

Susan shook her head. 'Don't worry. I think it's different if you see each other the whole time. We've been writing pretty long emails since we got back in touch online. She sends me photos, the odd video, sometimes we Skype. She sent me pictures of your twenty-seventh birthday party'

Laura's cheeks flickered almost into a smile, realising how Susan had guessed her age so well.

Susan took a drink from her bottle and Laura didn't resist the opportunity to peek at her phone. It was nearly eight, the time they had originally planned to meet. She picked up her phone and clicked through to her messages, to check that she hadn't missed a text from Clo. The latest message was a reminder that she had a voicemail message. She knew it would be from Josh and put the phone back down.

Voices and laughter passed by the doors and into the bar. Two women walked in, but neither was Clo. She looked past them, into the street. Couples, men in suits, women in dresses, all sliced past each other, but no-one else entered the bar.

Susan was smiling at her when she turned back. 'I'm sure Clo'll be here soon,' she said.

Laura nodded and tried to smile back. She breathed in and forced her brain to think of a polite question.

'When did you arrive in the UK?'

'Oh, just yesterday. Flew in from Hawaii, so my body clock is still all over the place.' Susan took another swig from her lager and looked at her.

Laura tried to think of another question. 'Is that where you're from? Hawaii?'

'God, no. I was on vacation. Although that's one of the few states I haven't lived in. No, I'm from pretty much all over.' Susan folded her arms on the table. 'My dad was in the army, training posts mainly, so we moved every year or so. I loved it - meeting new kids on the bases, new places to explore, but it was kind of strange not having some place I thought of ....'

Laura checked her phone. Another two minutes had passed and she allowed herself to glance towards the doors again. A group of four women were hanging around the entrance. She tilted her head but couldn't see around them. Panic clawed at her stomach. She didn't want Clo to peer into the bar and miss them and Laura shuffled in her seat, tempted to stand up and walk to the doors to stay in clear view.

'...Baltimore is probably the place I stayed longest - I was in med school at Hopkins.'

Laura's mind was brought back into focus on Susan.

'Med school? You're a doctor too?'

'Yeah. I work in paediatrics. I'm just about to start a new post at Charing Cross. Clo says you're a GP right?'

'Yes. That's right.'

Laura's phone beeped twice. She snatched up her phone to read the new text. It was from Clo: 'So, so, so sorry. I have to work. Speak tomorrow?' Laura had to read it twice before it registered and the disappointment began to seep in. Her face dropped. Another last-minute order at the patisserie, she supposed. That was the usual excuse. She deleted the text and put the phone down, stared into the room and felt her body deflate.

'You OK?' Susan was frowning at her.

'Clo cancelled.' She managed to get out the words over the lump in her throat.

'That's a shame. I was really looking forward to seeing her again.'

Laura gulped two mouthfuls of wine, trying to wash away the lump. 'Have you not seen her much?' she tried to say evenly.

'She met me at the airport when I arrived. She gave me a lift. And before that it was like years and years ago when we were kids.' Susan laughed. 'She was my teacher's kid at primary school. I mean she was younger than me. I guess she was not much older than a toddler.' Susan turned more intently to Laura. 'But I just remember she had these incredible eyes. Recognised her straight away from her photo online.'

Laura nodded.

'They were this weird pale blue-green. Like the water you see in photos of tropical seas. You couldn't help stare at them.' Susan looked at her with an inquiring expression.

'I know what you mean,' she said. 'People get mesmerised by them all the time.' Laura's insides churned, disappointed that Susan would be enchanted by Clo, like so many others, and feeling the letdown by her friend more keenly.

Clo wasn't coming. It was beginning to sink in. The tension, from arguing with Josh for days, wouldn't find a release. She sat up in her chair, cleared her throat and tucked her hair behind her ear. She would give her full attention to her companion and try to ignore her rising hysteria.

'Sorry, you were saying your dad was in the army....' Laura said.

Susan laughed. 'Yeah, a little while back. I can stop talking, it's all right.'

'I really wanted to speak to Clo. Sorry I've been so distracted. Please, please keep talking.'

She needed Susan to keep talking now. She didn't know how she would get through the next minute, hour or evening if she stopped.

'OK,' Susan nodded slowly.

'How long are you staying in the UK?' Laura forced out.

'Three years at least. That's my contract. Hopefully longer. I've been wanting to come to England, well, since we left.'

Laura blinked and tried to think of what to stay. She strained to remember what Susan had been talking about.

'Your dad was in the army.'

Susan laughed again. 'Yeah, that's right.'

'Is that why you moved back to America? Was he reposted?'

Susan paused. Her face fell into a neutral expression, her features aligned horizontally across her face.

'No. Mom died when I was six.' She said it in a well-practised way, as if she'd had to say it all her life, but in a way that still hinted at something deeply painful.

'She was from Oxfordshire. They met when Dad was stationed there. I think he found it too painful to stay when she was gone and he wanted to go back home.' Susan raised both palms. 'I mean, he could hardly talk about her and England. There were so many times I wanted to talk to him about Mom and our house in Middle Heyford, but he would just clam up.' She shook her head and frowned. 'He died last year and I never really got to talk to him about Mom and why she died.'

'I'm so sorry,' said Laura. She blushed as a memory gnawed at her. 'I think Clo did tell me.'

Susan looked away, the first ripple across her calm surface. She looked serious and Laura's stomach tightened, feeling Susan's loss as her own. She wanted to lean across the table and hold the American's hand, comfort her like Laura wanted to be comforted.

Susan shrugged and twirled her glass in her fingers.

'It's why I've come to England now. I didn't feel I could come back while my dad was alive. It would have been too painful for him. But Middle Heyford is the only place I remember being home.'

Laura opened her mouth, but the back of her throat was closed with a lump and she couldn't speak. She breathed in, opening her chest wide, trying to clear her throat.

'I know what it's like', she managed, before her throat closed again. She tried to blink her tears thin across her eyes. She wanted to say that she knew what it was like, the not knowing. She knew what an insatiable hunger it was, yearning to know about your parents, when no-one could or would tell you. The knot in her tummy was wrung so tight her muscles started to ache. She held her hands, curled into painful fists on the table.

Susan was turned away. 'I'm staying with my aunt in London. She used to talk to me about Mom when I was a kid. I'm kind of hoping we'll visit Middle Heyford and talk about old times….'

Tears were flowing down Laura's cheeks. They brimmed and trickled warm down her face. Her mouth hung open, taut in a silent cry, and her nose ran, joining her tears to drip from her top lip.

She felt Susan's warm fingers over her fist, stroking the back of her hand. Laura slumped in her seat, giving in to her tears and dejection. Her shoulders sagged and her hands sprung open. She felt Susan's soft fingers slide inside her own and her arm curl around her shoulder.

Sobs clutched at her belly until she was empty and her muscles ached. She drew in a strangled breath that caught and whined in her throat. Out again, the cry juddered and she inhaled a wheezy breath. She let her cry take over, released by Susan's warmth and sympathy.

'Can I take you home?' Susan whispered.

Laura shook her head. Her tears flowed across her cheek and dripped from her jaw.

'I can't go home.'

Susan's hands held her arms and encouraged her to stand up. Laura couldn't see through the film of tears. The bar, the people, the tables and chairs all blurred and flowed in her eyes. She stood up to let Susan take control and lead her out of the building.

6.

'Please, would you like to sit down?' Mrs Hamilton gestured towards the table and two chairs by the hotel room window. Clo smiled and sat down, crossing her legs to point in Mrs Hamilton's direction.

'Would you like some Champagne?' Mrs Hamilton offered, adopting her hostess role.

'I'd love some, thank you.'

Mrs Hamilton smiled, listening to the young woman's voice. She wondered if it was her own accent and soothing natural tone, or one that she had cultivated for her clients.

'Are you celebrating?' asked Clo.

'Yes, I suppose I am,' Mrs Hamilton said, pouring a glass of Champagne for them both. She paused, wondering how much she should give away about herself. She hesitated. 'I was offered a new job today.'

It had been a long time since she had last worked. More than ten years and that had not been real work, as she would like to think of it. She had not been serious about competing for the job. It had only been an excuse to come to London, so that she would not feel so foolish, travelling half way around the world to investigate her husband's mistress. It had turned out to be an attractive prospect though, far better than she deserved having spent so much time away from the business.

The young woman was watching her, a neutral expression on her face, inviting Mrs Hamilton to speak as much or as little as she wanted.

'It's been a long time since I've worked. A very long time.' Mrs Hamilton stood the bottle of Champagne on the table and sat next to Clo. 'I am actually thinking of taking this role though.'

She turned to the young woman. They were close together. She could perceive the warmth of the other woman's body, their legs a fraction of an inch apart.

'Is it based in the States?' Clo asked, taking a sip of wine. 'Marella thought you were from the States,' she added.

Mrs Hamilton nodded. 'Yes, I think so. Well that's the plan anyway. It depends on my co-...' she cleared her throat and turned again to Clo. 'It depends on a co-worker, who they haven't hired yet. But, yes, it should be in the States.'

'Are you looking forward to it?' Clo asked, leaning forward, reducing the distance between them.

'Yes. I think I am.' Mrs Hamilton smiled. 'It's only just beginning to sink in you know.'

It would be strange to start work again, but a perfect excuse to cancel several engagements with her husband's colleagues and wives and further withdraw from her marriage.

Mrs Hamilton noticed Clo's glass was empty. 'Another glass?' she said, amused at the young woman's indulgence.

'Oh dear, that went down a bit quickly,' Clo admitted. She sat back and checked her glass. 'I'm afraid I drink Champagne a bit like pop.'

Mrs Hamilton raised an eyebrow at Clo in jest. Clo smiled back at her with her whole face in response, eyes wide and engaging. She had an open, expressive face, which showed every flickering emotion, even more so after the Champagne.

*

'Is Clo your real name?' asked Mrs Hamilton.

'Yes, it is actually.'

'Do you use it normally when you're working?'

Clo hesitated, perhaps wondering how much to reveal. 'It depends on the client. It depends on what Marella thinks the client would like me to be called.'

Mrs Hamilton realised she would have been referred to as the client, in a conversation discussing the appointment between Marella and her employee. It made her feel odd, as if she were someone else. She wondered about Clo's other clients. Were they like her, well off, older women seeking comfort and company? She felt uncomfortable at an image of herself, in a line of well-dressed clients.

'So,' she said distracting herself. 'Are you usually called things like Madam Dominique the Dominatrix, Seductive Sandy the Sex Slave?' she said, teasing.

'No. I was thinking something more like Rachel.'

They both laughed at the mundanity.

'No really,' Clo said. 'A lot of regulars of Marella's want something fairly traditional. It's better to have a name that doesn't remind them that they're with an escort,' she said shrugging, 'so the less made-up it sounds the better.'

Mrs Hamilton considered Clo's reply. 'What else do you change?' she asked. 'I was guessing dress style? Don't you wear those leather outfits with straps everywhere? Bondage gear? I hope you're not going to tell me that you're more likely to wear something from Marks and Spencer's?'

'More M&S than S&M,' said Clo laughing. 'Again, sorry to disappoint you, but if it was appropriate for the client then yes.'

'Are you wearing M&S this evening?'

'No,' said Clo, shaking her head and smiling. 'Marella chose Nicole Farhi I think. Touch it. It's amazing.' Clo pinched the material covering her arm and offered it towards Mrs Hamilton. The material was soft to her fingertips. She could feel the shape of Clo's arm beneath it, slim but with youthful, firm flesh. She could feel her warmth through the material, could feel that she was really there.

'It's lovely,' Mrs Hamilton said, smiling.

Mistaking her comment as a surprise in the quality, Clo continued. 'In general, if in doubt, don't out-dress the client, that goes for women clients at least.'

Mrs Hamilton frowned. 'Do you have men as clients?'

'No, women only,' Clo said, looking directly at Mrs Hamilton, almost reassuringly. She must have detected the hint of distaste in her voice.

'Marella tells me the opposite is true for men. If in doubt, overdress. Men like to think they've got something more special than they deserve. Of course, the client may be after something different, something out of their social group.'

'Trashy or posh,' Mrs Hamilton said bluntly.

'Trashy or posh,' Clo grinned.

'Tell me more,' said Mrs Hamilton. 'What else do you vary?'

'Hair colour sometimes, makeup style. Perfume's important, although very difficult to predict. Working out what scent is going appeal to someone else is really difficult if not impossible. Of course, the general perfume style is usually a matter of fashion and the person's age, but the right one, very difficult.' She paused, and then went on. 'You have a nice perfume,' she said smiling and gazing into her eyes.

Mrs Hamilton was mesmerised by the way Clo had said it. She had offered the sentence to her, almost a question. She was drawn in by a gaze that did not leave her. She managed to stop herself swaying towards her, and straighten up.

'How much do you change the way you act?' she asked.

'Quite significantly,' Clo said, tipping her head to one side to think. 'I find I very much play a role and that role can vary enormously.'

Mrs Hamilton wondered how good an actress this young woman was. She was very appealing to her. She would have to congratulate Marella on her choice.

'Is it Marella who decides how you should behave for each client?' Mrs Hamilton asked.

'Yes, to start with at least. After the consultation she usually has a broad picture of the type of person required, and preferences of course. It's easiest when the client is explicit about what they want. But then it's up to us to act it out and fill in the detail. So it's not all dependent on Marella, although a lot of it is.'

'Does she always get it right?' Mrs Hamilton wondered out loud, increasingly surprised how well Marella had matched her to Clo.

'She's incredibly good actually. I couldn't do what she does.'

'So what did she say about me?' Mrs Hamilton braced herself for the answer.

Clo didn't respond immediately. 'Well. That's the funny thing. It's the first time I've seen her at a bit of a loss. I really shouldn't be saying this.' She raised her wine glass and looked at it accusingly, and stopped speaking.

'That's OK,' Mrs Hamilton said. 'I know it's not fair to ask.' She sat back and stared out of the window. 'I was also unfair to Marella,' she said as a confession. 'You see, I didn't really go to arrange an appointment.'

She was finding it difficult to talk out loud and her chest filled with rising emotion. She tried to swallow the feelings away and clenched the arms of the chair to force out her confession.

'I wanted to see Marella because she's fucking my husband.' She breathed out noisily and breathed in and out for a few moments before carrying on.

'I found out from a London friend of mine. He's actually another client of Marella's. Well not of hers. He likes boys.' She paused again, recollecting her friend's painful admission to her. 'He saw my husband, having dinner with Marella when he was meant to be visiting his London office. And my friend supposed, correctly, that he was a client of hers.' Mrs Hamilton took a long swallow from her glass. 'Then, this opportunity to come to London came up and I couldn't resist seeing who she was. I don't know what I expected. But I still wanted to see her.'

Clo left a few moments' silence before responding. 'That can't have been easy,' she finally said. She reached across and squeezed Mrs Hamilton's hand that still gripped the arm of the chair. She maintained the touch long enough to make it known that her sympathy was real and then withdrew her hand.

'No it wasn't easy,' Mrs Hamilton said. 'You know, I thought I would be more angry with her, but I'm not. She was too professional, too detached for me to feel anything that violent against her.'

Mrs Hamilton sank back into her chair, deflated by the revelation, and they sat in silence. She continued to stare out of the window. The wine had made her numb, but also more indignant about Malcolm's infidelity. Funny how emotions took such twists and turns. She wondered how long it would take her brain and heart to process what she felt about it all. It was the humiliation that was demanding attention now, humiliation and sadness.

A beeping interrupted their silence and Clo turned around to locate its source. 'Sorry,' she said. 'That's a text message on my work phone. Do you mind? It will be Marella and she wouldn't contact me unless it was important.'

Mrs Hamilton nodded as Clo went to retrieve her phone from her bags.

She heard Clo return and could feel the warmth of her standing behind her.

'I'm sorry, I had my phone switched to silent for calls and I missed two from Marella. You wanted to cancel the appointment?'

Mrs Hamilton had forgotten her cancellation.

'It's OK, I can leave,' Clo continued. 'I've had a glass or two of Champagne and it's been very nice.' Mrs Hamilton could hear that she was smiling from her voice and the way she spoke. It was soft and warm and gentle, flowing out and around her, comforting.

'Would you mind staying?' said Mrs Hamilton, still staring out of the window. 'I would like the company'. She turned around. 'I would like your company.'

'I can stay until dawn,' Clo replied, smiling. 'Otherwise I'm here for as long as you want me, for whatever you want me for.'

7.

Mrs Hamilton had ordered another bottle of Champagne. They lay on the bed in the dimly lit room, facing each other. Mrs Hamilton leaned on her elbow, resting her head on her hand, and twirled her glass on its stem. Clo mirrored her.

'Do you mind me asking questions?' asked Mrs Hamilton.

'Not at all,' said Clo smiling. 'It's nice to talk about it actually. I don't talk about this to anyone apart from Marella.'

'Do your other clients ask many questions?'

Clo grinned, 'No, they're more interested in their own appointment,' she said 'and there's a great deal more sex.'

Mrs Hamilton laughed. 'Do you enjoy the sex?'

'I usually get something out of it. I can usually make myself get something out of it.'

'I don't understand,' Mrs Hamilton said. 'How did you get into this...' She found she did not want to say the word anymore.

'Prostitution,' Clo finished for her. 'You can call it what it is.'

Mrs Hamilton nodded for her to continue.

'I met Marella at a bar and after talking a while she asked if I would come home with her, have sex, stay until she was asleep and then leave, all for a generous amount of money.' Clo shrugged. 'I'm afraid the arrangement suited me. Marella was impressed that I could follow her instructions, listen to what she wanted without becoming too emotionally involved and offered to find me more clients.'

She paused and stared at Mrs Hamilton, switching from eye to eye as if deciding what to admit.

'I live with my Gran,' she said, looking away. 'She has had arthritis for the last few years, very bad in her hands. I've always tended to take care of the house, do the cooking, cleaning. But she also had cancer at that time and it was quite tough when she was going through treatment. She was very ill and I'd given up my job to care of her. Working the odd evening as an escort paid more than I'd ever earned before. It was convenient and it suited me.'

Mrs Hamilton frowned and reached out to Clo's forearm. 'I'm sorry, I shouldn't have asked.'

'Don't get me wrong,' said Clo, holding up her hand. 'That's a real sob story isn't it?' She smiled. 'I could have stopped a long time ago. Amelia, my Gran, has been well for the last four years with no sign of the cancer coming back. It just turned out that I was good at the job. I get enough money to keep us going with very few hours work and I like being able to spend time with Amelia, if she wants it. She's amazingly busy, has more friends than I do.'

'Doesn't it make it awkward for you to have a girlfriend though?' Mrs Hamilton asked.

Clo looked surprised by the question and inhaled, trying to think of a response. 'Well I suppose it would,' she said. 'I don't know how the others' partners cope with it. But I don't have girlfriends. Relationships don't suit me it turns out.'

'Oh, really?' Mrs Hamilton said, raising a mocking eyebrow. 'Are you quite the Lothario, or scared of commitment?

Clo seemed troubled by the joking accusation. 'I never thought that I was, but I just don't seem to fall in love as quickly as other people,' she said, looking at Mrs Hamilton to see if she understood. 'I don't understand how people become so keen on me before they really know me.'

She sat up and put her hands out in defence. 'I'm not being arrogant, saying that people fall for me all the time. Just, it scares me how intense they are, before I even get a chance to find out who they are.'

Mrs Hamilton nodded in understanding.

'And then, me being that step behind, being that little bit less keen, seems to do terrible things to people. They become...' She was searching for the right phrase.

'Needy,' Mrs Hamilton said.

'Yes!' Clo said emphatically. 'And it's horrible. It seems to turn them crazy. They end up hating you, but still wanting you at the same time. And then they hate themselves because they can see themselves doing it and can't stop....' Clo swallowed the last of her drink.

Mrs Hamilton sat up, took Clo's empty glass and turned round to grab the bottle of Champagne. She slowly poured her another glass and offered it back to her. Clo took a sip and stared at the quilt. Mrs Hamilton looked down her face, admiring its symmetry and beauty.

'It doesn't help that you are very attractive you know,' Mrs Hamilton said. She could empathise with Clo. Mrs Hamilton had been beautiful when she was younger. She had watched strangers approaching her with that lustful look in their eyes, convinced they already knew who she was, reacting with indignation when they realised she did not feel the same way.

Mrs Hamilton nodded. 'It is unnerving when someone you hardly know seems to be in love with you, before you've barely exchanged a few words.'

'Yes! Finally, someone who understands,' Clo said, enthusiasm lifting her expression. 'I've tried explaining this to people before,' she said quickly. 'And they think I'm being arrogant, moaning about people being attracted to me. But it's not like that. It's so frustrating when people won't give you a chance to get to know them. They just want to steamroller you into a relationship. You're quite right. They just don't give you enough time to feel the same way.'

This time they both stared down at the quilt.

'You don't think that we're just a bit slow, do you?' Clo ventured. 'I mean that perhaps we're just a bit thick.'

Mrs Hamilton's laughed out loud. 'Maybe,' she said, still smiling. Then she shrugged in defeat.

*

'So how did your husband seduce you? What did he get right?' Clo asked.

'Oh,' Ms Hamilton said, trying to give herself time to respond. She had been surprised at her own thoughts. When Clo had mentioned her husband she had thought of her first husband. Her second had receded a long way in her thoughts.

She was in England, in Oxfordshire, a long time ago. The sun, not at its highest in the sky, was shining with the warm golden light of late summer. The leaves on the trees were at their darkest green and the garden was full of berries and apples hanging over long grass. She was waiting for her husband to come home. She was in a state of despair she had never felt so acutely again. She breathed in sharply at the memory. 'Out,' she willed, pushing out the picture. She tried to pull in scenes from her early life in California with Malcolm.

Their home in the hills filled her head. She mentally searched the house, through the hallway, into the large sitting room with wide glass doors through to the garden and swimming pool. She could not find Malcolm here. But these pictures were too late anyway; they were already together. She strained to uncover earlier memories. She searched his apartment in New York, but could not find their first meeting there either. He turned up in her memories as an existing fixture.

'I can't remember,' said Mrs Hamilton. 'I can't remember. It's just gone. I know I can recall it, I just can't think right now.' She pressed her fingers into her forehead, pressing the lines across her brow as if this would squeeze the memory loose.

'I can't remember,' she said in shock, turning towards Clo, scared of how faint Malcolm was becoming in her mind.

*

'Come on,' said Clo. She nudged her arm. 'Would you like a massage to relax those shoulders? I expect they're in knots after today,' she said smiling.

Mrs Hamilton shook her head.

'Right, I'm going to be Dominatrix Dominique now and you are going to have a massage,' Clo said, kneeling in front of her on the bed. 'Come on. If you're going to hire an escort for the night, you might as well get some physical pleasure out of it.'

Mrs Hamilton smiled, coming round.

'Now let's see. Perhaps not lying down with those breasts hey?' Clo said, looking down at Mrs Hamilton's chest. 'How about you lean forward on the table with your head on your arms?' Clo got off the bed and walked over to the table and chairs.

'Do you have a problem with my breasts?' Mrs Hamilton said, arching her eyebrow as she accompanied Clo to the table.

'Not in the slightest.' Clo reached up to Mrs Hamilton's collar and started to undo her shirt buttons, careful not to touch her skin as she passed her chest. Clo removed the shirt which stroked over Mrs Hamilton's skin as it was pulled free. Clo guided her round to sit on an ottoman stool and gently encouraged her to fold her arms and place her head on them.

'No, I'm quite a fan of your breasts you know,' Clo continued. 'Falling into them was the highlight of my week, but I suspect you haven't lain on your front since the 1960s,' she laughed.

'And now you have a problem with my age?' Mrs Hamilton tried to protest, but she was half-muffled by the pillow of her forearms.

'Again, not in the slightest. If anything I have a thing for older women.'

'Oh really? When you get to my age, you won't have a thing for older women, because older women will be geriatric.'

Clo laughed. 'I'm sure when I'm your age there'll be plenty of attractive pensioners for me to run after.'

'When you get to my age, believe me, you won't be running anywhere.'

'Not if I had those breasts,' laughed Clo, and she kissed the crown of her head.

Mrs Hamilton twitched at Clo's first touch on her shoulders, unused to another human touching her bare skin. Clo left her hands in the same place, letting Mrs Hamilton relax again, and sat on the chair behind her, legs either side of Mrs Hamilton's. It was reassuring, being surrounded by her, in safe, experienced hands.

Clo stroked down Mrs Hamilton's back with a light pressure, letting her skin get used to the touch in preparation for working on deeper muscles. Clo pressed at her lower back first, pushing in circles either side of her spine.

She worked her way up slowly, feeling for knots of tense muscle and worked on them until the tightness dissipated. Mrs Hamilton felt her pinch a handful of flesh around her collar as she worked her thumbs into the shoulders.

Mrs Hamilton could feel herself unfreezing beneath Clo's fingers, her muscles being oiled. She was used to the hard, muscular fingers of men. Clo's fingertips were small and soft.

She allowed herself to moan with enjoyment as Clo freed her aching muscles, working out the tension over the whole of her upper body. Clo ran warm palms up both sides of her neck and Mrs Hamilton's whole scalp tingled as her fingers massaged the base of her head.

Clo was winding down now, massaging more gently, covering her back with sweeping soft movements, warming down her muscles. She felt Clo run her fingers down her shoulder, almost coming to a halt, and then trace her outline from her neck, along her relaxed shoulder muscle, to the bumpy bony top of the arm.

'You have lovely shoulders,' Clo said quietly.

Mrs Hamilton felt Clo run her hand down her right shoulder. She could feel her admiring with her fingertips, pressing at the shape of the muscle and feeling its definition.

The change in her tone and the way she touched her made Mrs Hamilton's skin become alert. She was aware of every inch of her exposed skin and how it waited expectantly for Clo's hands to caress it. It tingled as Clo let her hands explore down her back, taking in the shape of the muscles that ran down either side of her spine.

How long had it been since anyone had touched her like that? She was aware of her whole body coming alive again with the admiring caresses. She could feel the shape of herself. Her body was no longer a cold, numb vessel that carried around her brain. She felt painfully, fluidly human again.

'Are you OK?' Clo had stopped moving her hands. She held the top of Mrs Hamilton's arms, squeezing them in comfort.

Mrs Hamilton sat up. A tear ran down her cheek. Embarrassed, she wiped it away and sniffed. She breathed out, trying to stop her tears from taking hold of her.

She coughed to clear her throat. 'I'm sorry,' she said. 'It's just been a long time.' She stopped, having to quell a wave of self-pity.

Clo's fingers gently squeezed her shoulders and then her soft lips touched the top of her back. Clo kept her mouth pressed against her skin for a few moments and the warmth and comfort spread through her.

The consoling kiss almost made Mrs Hamilton choke again. She shook her head. Clo was being paid to care, she reminded herself. She was a professional at this kind of physical reassurance.

Clo held up her shirt. She pushed her arms into the sleeves and covered herself up from further exposure.

*

They were silent and gazed towards the window and out to the sky. The indigo horizon was bleached by the still low but rising sun.

Clo reached out to hold her arm. 'I'm sorry. I should go,' she said.

Mrs Hamilton turned to look into Clo's eyes. 'I know. Thank you for staying. It's helped me through what would have been a long and very lonely night. I doubt Marella thought you would have to stay this long.'

'I offered,' Clo said, and she smiled.

Clo got up and retrieved a coat from one of her bags. She pinched her shirt cuffs and pulled the arms straight beneath her coat sleeves. Mrs Hamilton walked around to her and they stood apart for a few seconds. She wondered how she should say goodbye.

Clo broke the impasse and stepped forward to embrace her, sliding her arms beneath hers and pulling her close. Clo's breasts fitted neatly beneath hers and her cheek rested in the softness of her neck and chest. Clo's breath was warm and moist on her skin. Her coat was still undone and Mrs Hamilton could feel Clo's chest, stomach, and thighs mould into her own, and the warmth seep through their clothes to her own skin.

A wave of lust, bursting from her thighs, flowed up instantly and through her body. It seemed to knock her head back. The strength of it had the potential to overwhelm any civilised thought or restraint. Had the shock of it not paralysed her whole body, she wouldn't have trusted herself not to savagely kiss Clo with little thought as to whether Clo wanted it. She stood frozen in fear of what she might do to the young woman clinging to her. She could hear her blood pounding. Her whole body seemed to pulse.

Clo stirred and raised her face. 'Goodbye,' she said quietly. She lifted her hand to Mrs Hamilton's face, and pressed tender lips to her cheek. Clo picked up her bags and started towards the door. She turned the handle and eased it open to let in the dim night light of the corridor.

Still stunned Mrs Hamilton watched Clo walk away, unable to comprehend her own feelings. Confused, all she could say was a question she had not had the courage to ask earlier. She called out 'What instructions did Marella give you? About me? How did she tell you to act?'

Clo paused. 'She didn't,' she replied without turning round. 'She told me that I would have to be myself.' She shut the door behind her.

With the click of the latch, Mrs Hamilton's heart sank at the prospect of being left behind.

*

She had not given a thought to what she was doing. Her shoes were on her feet and she grabbed her coat. She swept her key from the table and left her room. She punched the lift buttons in the corridor, but seeing it was on the ground floor, spun around and took the emergency stairs, clattering down the concrete steps in her heeled shoes.

She felt the shock of cool damp morning air on her face as she burst through the hotel doors into the square. She turned, casting her eyes around beneath the trees. No-one was around, but she could hear footsteps receding, becoming muffled, to her right. Pulling her coat close around her neck she set off in pursuit.

The streets of Kensington were grey and quiet at this time of day. The few cars still had their lights on, and the only people awake were emptying bins or opening service doors on the less frequented sides of shops and restaurants.

Clo had sped ahead and Mrs Hamilton breathed heavily as she tried to keep up. The streets became unfamiliar as they moved away from Kensington towards Hammersmith and the huge meander in the river.

More residential now, Clo jinked away from the main road and into side streets. Mrs Hamilton increased her pace, afraid she would lose her. Her heels jarred painfully on the pavement and sent sharp waves up her legs. The streets of white, four-floored houses narrowed, looming over her, as she pursued Clo.

Turning left behind Clo, she entered a wider street. A couple of cars screamed by, drowning out any other sound and blasting a wave of dusty air at her. She squinted and covered her eyes. When she could see again, she had lost Clo. The street was long. She couldn't understand how she had disappeared, unless she had gone into one of the houses near by.

She checked up and down the nearest houses trying to spot any signs of activity – a light switched on or the sound of a door shutting. Nothing. Nothing but the sound of her breathing and her heart beating with the exertion.

Turning around she saw an archway, and through it, the facing rows of smaller houses that made up a mews. After one last look up and down the street, she headed towards it.

Her heels echoed on the cobbles. They must have been audible to anyone living in the tightly enclosed street. She felt too exposed and stepped back, retreating under the archway while she searched from house to house. All the ground floor windows had curtains drawn or blinds turned down in front of unlit rooms. She cast her eyes higher. In the middle of the left terrace, a second floor window was lit and a shadow moved behind the curtain. Then above, on the third floor another light came on, shining out of an attic room.

She stepped into view, surveying the house. The curtain on the second floor twitched open. She found herself in full view of an elderly woman who clung onto the folds of material and stared out, straight at Mrs Hamilton. She stared back at the woman, unable to flee or respond in any appropriate way. Fixed there, she had time to study her.

It was an alert, intelligent face that looked at her. It was puffy with age and looser, but it did not disguise what was a familiar face to Mrs Hamilton. She had not seen her for more than twenty years, but her face and name, Amelia, now vividly flooded back into her consciousness. And the memories that had threatened all day came crashing through.

Part 2. Saturday Morning Hangovers

1.

Laura stirred. Her legs twitched, feeling uncomfortable in the rough folds of her jeans. She opened her eyes and saw the blurred outline of the door from the landing light outside. She shuffled, half asleep, half dreaming. Her tongue stuck to the roof of her mouth, and she swallowed with difficulty before turning over on the large double bed. Susan's hair tickled her face. She opened her eyes, registered the back of Susan's head and fell asleep, breathing in the smell of her hair.

Laura snapped her eyes open. She breathed in hard and her breath rasped. She'd forgotten where she was. The morning light glowed around the edges of two windows, but the room was kept dim by the thick long curtains.

She sat up and the hangover exploded in her head. The pressure inside her skull made her forehead ache, threatening to push out through her eyes and nose. Her stomach reeled and nausea hit the back of her throat. She swallowed it down and closed her eyes to stop the room spinning.

She felt across the wrinkled sheet and remembered Susan had been there when she'd stirred earlier. She opened her eyes, beginning to focus in the grey light, and looked down at the imprint Susan had left. Laura stroked across the bed, smoothing the wrinkles, enjoying the soft sheet against her palm. She gathered the material in her hand, and rubbed the folds between her fingers, her skin sensitive in her hung over state. She smiled at the pleasure the soft material gave her. Perhaps she was still drunk.

She hadn't phoned Josh. He wouldn't know where she was. Her insensitivity made her blush and she drew her phone from her back pocket. She expected to see dozens of missed calls and text messages. But there were none. Irritation tickled her insides. Why hadn't he called? She put the phone away, annoyed at being unreasonable.

She swung her bare feet out of the bed onto smooth floorboards and the tassels of a woven rug. With her shoulders hunched from the pain of the hangover, she pushed her hand and head through the gap in the curtains and squinted in the sunlight. She was in Susan's aunt's house, on the first floor of the three-storey Kentish Town house. The square walled garden below was beginning to turn with autumn. Yellow leaves dotted the lawn and she could see old swings at the back of the garden through the skeleton of a large plane tree.

She pulled the curtains open and turned around to the revealed room. There was a sofa at the end of the bed and next to it a wine bottle with two glasses swirled with red wine stains. Susan had comforted her last night as she poured out her heart. Susan had held her hand and drawn her close into her chest. Laura felt lighter today, emptied of her worries and supported by her new friend. Her cathartic outburst and consuming hangover made her feel careless.

She bent down to pick up the glasses and bottle, wanting to avoid kicking the remnants onto the Persian rug, but the blood rushed into her head and made her lurch into the sofa. She sat for a moment while her head settled. The smell of the souring wine made her want to gag and she closed her eyes, trying to control the reflex that constricted her throat. Her head thumped with her strong pulse and her heart raced in her chest. She waited for her insides to quieten, her whole body relaxed.

A familiar, woman's laugh echoed outside the room, and another woman spoke.

'I can't believe you have someone in your room already,' the woman said.

'Quiet. She's still asleep. And it's not like that. She's a friend.' Laura recognised Susan's American accent.

The voices passed the door and became quieter, muffled by their footsteps on the stairs.

Laura opened her eyes and slowly walked to the door. She stepped out onto the wide landing and peered down the stairs. Susan was wearing running gear and stopped inside the front door. Light filtering through the stained glass above the front door coloured her hair with greens and reds. She talked to an older woman with long greying hair, dressed in a dark grey suit.

'Don't look at me like that. She is just a friend,' Susan said.

The woman laughed, loud and confident.

Susan continued to protest. 'She needed someone to talk to and we were up late. She didn't want to go home and she stayed.'

'Really?' The woman sounded unconvinced.

47

'Seriously, if she's up before I get back, go easy on her. She was really upset last night. She's been thinking about trying to find her folks again and was a bit cut up about it.'

'I'm sorry. I'm just pulling your leg. Yes, I'll be well-behaved. I assume she was adopted?' the woman said more seriously.

'Yeah, and a string of foster homes for a while.'

'All right. Don't worry. I'll be gentle.'

'And don't go interrogating her. She is just a friend.'

'No grilling? Where's the fun in that? ' The woman's tone was lighter.

'Let her settle in for at least a minute.' Susan laughed. 'You'll have plenty to talk about though.' Susan turned to the front door. 'She's really nice and she's a doctor.'

'Oh good. Another doctor.' The woman laughed.

'I'll see you in about a half hour.'

Susan opened the front door and stepped out into the sunshine. The older woman turned into the passageway beside the staircase and disappeared from Laura's view. The sound of crockery on a hard surface and a cutlery drawer being opened echoed up to her.

Laura grabbed the smooth wooden banister and stepped carefully down the stairs. The ground floor hallway extended further back than upstairs. Bright light shone through a doorway at the end of the hall that blinked as Helen passed back and forwards across the kitchen.

Laura walked slowly along the hallway, passing the sitting room doorway. She peered inside. Three leather sofas sat around a fireplace. The walls were covered in floor to ceiling bookcases and original paintings whose familiarity nagged at Laura. A grand piano stood on tiptoes between the two windows and she looked enviously at the instrument.

It was covered in photo frames containing family pictures, a mix of black and white and colour. A photo of a younger Susan in graduation robes stood at the front, but it was a large sepia print that caught her eye and drew her into the room. The woman in the photo resembled Susan, except how she might have been in another era. The woman had the same thick hair, flowing in waves around her shoulders, and long eyelashes around slightly larger, more feminine eyes. The smile was exactly the same, that wide generous mouth and lips, and even teeth. Her eyes creased in the corners in the same way that Susan's did, and Laura started to reach forward to stroke around her cheek.

'They look so alike don't they?'

Laura clasped her hands together, stepped away from the picture and turned round.

The woman who had been talking to Susan came towards her with a hand and friendly smile on offer.

'Helen,' she said. 'I'm Susan's aunt.'

Laura took her hand and squeezed it gently. 'I'm sorry,' she said. 'I couldn't help coming in when I saw the photo.' She turned to study the picture, her concentration drifting with her hangover, and then remembered herself.

'I'm Laura, by the way.'

Helen smiled and nodded.

'It is Susan's mother isn't it?' Laura said.

'Yes. Isabelle. She was my sister.'

The similarities became clearer still with the confirmation, the way she held her head and the mouth open in a half-laughing smile.

Helen looked at Laura, as if trying to hold back, then exhaled through her nose and smiled. 'It's frightening sometimes,' she said. 'When I see Susan from behind and she flicks her hair I think it's Isabelle, just for a second.'

Helen was tall like Susan but had lighter hair that was streaked with grey. Laura could see the same bone structure though, high cheek bones and a wide mouth.

Helen smiled at her. 'Oh we looked similar as well. It was more apparent back then.' She reached behind Isabelle's photo and held a family portrait in front of her.

'This was me and my husband, we've split up now, and my twin boys when they were two.'

The family were sitting on a beach, their bare legs too orange and the blue sky tinged with brown from the old colour-processed picture. Helen sat with one twin on her knee and her husband with the other in his arms. She was smiling, her head to the side, the kind of expression that showed she knew how lucky she was to have that moment.

'You look very happy,' Laura said smiling. 'Such a lovely big family.'

49

'They're about your age. They've got their own children now.' Helen opened her mouth to continue, but remained silent and looked away, clearly remembering Susan's instructions and refraining from asking the polite question.

But Laura guessed Helen's thoughts. 'I was adopted,' she owned. 'So I always envy people who have large families.'

Helen pursed her lips tight in sympathy. 'Yes, Susan said. She also said you were a doctor. I think that's very admirable given your background.'

Laura laughed. 'I had very supportive foster parents. I wouldn't say I had a disadvantaged upbringing.'

Helen shook her head. 'Sorry, that's not what I meant to imply. Susan said you had a number of foster homes and that must have been very disruptive.'

'I was lucky,' said Laura smiling. 'My last foster parents cared for me from when I was eleven. They had lots of time for me and were very encouraging. And I had fantastic science teachers at my local comprehensive.'

Laura shrugged and reached out to the piano. She ran her finger along its smooth edge. She could see her reflection in the black veneer, her bleached hair running up into the silver frames and into the photos.

'Do you play?' asked Helen lightly.

'Yes, but not on something like this,' Laura laughed. 'I had a second-hand Yamaha digital keyboard when I was at school. I was so happy when I unwrapped it – it was a present. I still play it.'

Helen reached down and opened the fallboard. She pressed middle C and grimaced.

'Oh dear. I haven't played for a while. It desperately needs tuning.' She turned to Laura. 'I play a little. It was Isabelle's forte though, not mine. She loved this instrument.'

'She used to play here?'

'Yes, this was our family home. We grew up here,' Helen added. 'Isabelle spent hours playing in here. This music book is one of hers I think.' She picked up the blotched cream book and flicked through to the front. 'Yes, here it is.' She pushed forward the inside cover to show her the large, looped handwriting.

Laura shivered, the thought of Susan's mother's presence tangible to both women. Helen put down the books and closed the keyboard.

A photo at the back of the piano caught Laura's eye. It was a colour picture of Isabelle sitting in a garden on a cast iron chair painted white.

'That was the last photo taken of Isabelle,' Helen said.

Laura looked more closely, leaning over to peer at the photo, her medical curiosity asserting itself. Isabelle appeared well. Her cheeks were flushed with health and her crossed arms were plump. But she stared away from the camera, her eyes disconnected, the same look Laura recognised from her own wedding photo.

She heard Helen breathe in. 'I can see you trying to look for symptoms. But you won't find any physical ones. She committed suicide.'

The heat drained from Laura's face and a chill shuddered through her. Her stomach turned with the mix of hangover and emotion.

'I'm so sorry,' she said. 'I didn't know.'

But the older woman just stared at the photo of her sister.

'It hurts every time I see it,' she said after a few moments. 'But I can't bury that photo away in a box.'

Laura blushed, the heat rapidly filling her body and face, and the change in temperature made her head reel and nausea swell. She felt dizzy, trying to recall what Susan had said last night. All she could remember was pouring out her feelings about her own parents, at how she longed to know them and how it had eaten away at her all her life. She wondered at Susan's confidence, how such an undermining event had failed to dent the American's robust personality, and was embarrassed by her own fragility.

2.

'You don't look well,' said Helen.

Laura stumbled back, feeling faint, and cold sweat broke on her forehead and body. She put her hand out to support herself on the sofa and her head spun the room around.

'I'm sorry. I didn't know,' Laura said.

'You look really quite rough though,' Helen said peering into her eyes.

Laura blushed, feeling inadequate and stupid. 'I had too much wine,' she admitted. 'I don't remember how much we got through.'

Helen took her arm and smiled. 'Let's get you a coffee.'

She led her along the hall into the kitchen. The back of the house had been extended into the garden. A large skylight and long single patio door let the morning light into the large room.

'Sit down. I'll get you a cup,' Helen said and she guided Laura gently into a seat by a long oak table.

Laura put her hands flat on the table and stared at the grain, waiting for her head to become stable. She relaxed her shoulders, which had hunched in tension, and breathed out. The nausea began to subside.

She winced at the rattle of coffee beans and the head-splitting racket of the coffee machine grinder. She glanced up to watch Helen moving around the kitchen.

'Sorry.' Helen laughed above the noise. 'It'll be worth it though.' She placed two cups beneath the twin spouts of the machine, which began to steam and gurgle; she leaned back against the island in the middle of the kitchen. She folded her arms and smiled at Laura.

'I'm sorry I shouldn't have surprised you with that. Susan did warn me to hold back.' She tutted. 'I could tell you were trying to diagnose her though. It's a difficult practice to break isn't it?'

Laura nodded.

Helen continued. 'I sometimes wish I could look at my friends without seeing what mineral deficiencies they have, who's prone to diabetes or a heart attack. It would be nice just to see people like everyone else sometimes.'

'I know what you mean,' said Laura.

'What do you practise? Susan didn't say.'

'General,' said Laura. 'I'm still training though, on rotation at St Jude's, Finsbury Park at the moment.'

Helen nodded. 'I used to know a doctor there. Retired now though.'

'How about you?' Laura asked.

'Cardiologist. Harley Street.'

'Wow,' said Laura, 'I'm very envious.'

Helen waved her hand in the air as if dismissing the difference between Laura's lowly post and Helen's prestigious position. 'It's the same job. I think you get used to wherever you end up. I've done it for more than twenty years. Isabelle was a doctor too. A GP. Although she'd given it up when she died.' She frowned and brought their coffees to the table. She slid a cup over to Laura and squeezed her shoulder.

'This should help,' she said.

The scent of fresh coffee filled Laura's nose. She closed her eyes and hugged the cup in her hands, breathing in the smell, the steam condensing on her nose.

'I usually only have instant,' she said.

'Perfect for a hangover,' Helen grinned. She paused for a second. 'Let me be nosey,' she said. 'Where did you grow up?' She looked at Laura kindly and sat down opposite.

'It's complicated,' Laura said. She felt purged of her past this morning, having talked through the night with Susan, all through her long history of adoption, loss and fostering. 'After eleven I grew up in Loughton though.' She shrugged.

'Over in Essex?'

'Yes,'

Helen smiled. 'I thought I could hear a slight accent. Not much, but it is still there.'

Laura laughed. 'I think going to Oxford knocked that out of me.'

'You went to Oxford?' Helen was surprised.

'My teachers were very encouraging of me and my best friend and we both made it to Oxford.' She opened her mouth, ready to explain that her best friend was now her husband.

'That's very impressive,' said Helen. 'I think you must be a very bright and determined young woman.'

Laura blushed at impressing the successful consultant and at the real reason for her determination to get to Oxford. She looked away into the garden.

She recognised the garden furniture on the stone patio outside, some chairs and a table, the same as the Victorian iron chair that Isabelle sat on in the photo. The patio was surrounded by a raised herb bed and beyond that a large lawn extended to the brick wall at the back of the garden. The garden glowed in the low autumn light, with the vivid greens of the lawn and evergreen border shrubs, and reds and yellows of the dying annual flowers and deciduous plants. The colours deepened and brightened, changing in waves, as a cloud passed overhead.

'Would you like to go outside?' Helen said. 'Fresh air will probably help.'

Helen took her by the hand. She opened the heavy patio door and sound flooded in. Laura expected the rush of traffic, footsteps in the street and people shouting that she heard at home, but there was only the quiet noise of the city that hummed far away. She stepped out onto the patio, holding Helen's hand, and looked up into the tall trees at the back of the garden.

'I can hear birds,' she said. She listened out and heard a scratching noise and then a pair grey squirrels caught her eye, chasing each other around a large tree trunk. 'It's difficult to believe I'm still in London,' she said, grinning.

Helen smiled. 'It's lovely isn't it? I was so glad that we managed to keep the house after my parents. I loved growing up here and loved bringing up my children here too.'

Helen led her across the patio and up the steps onto the lawn. She pointed to the swings and a pole for swing-ball. 'My grandchildren play with these now. I can't believe they've lasted so well since the twins.'

'It's a wonderful place to raise a family,' Laura said. She imagined the small boys from the photo running and kicking a ball on the large lawn and laughing and screaming. She tried to imagine Susan as a young girl playing the same game.

'What was Susan like when she was younger?' Laura found herself smiling trying to imagine it.

Helen stared at her with an analytical look. 'She was a bit of tomboy actually. Although that may not surprise you.'

'Do you have any photos?'

'Yes, somewhere. I should dig them out really. She was such an energetic little girl. Always running around, keen to explore, or help cook or dig in the garden. But so loving too. My boys stole my heart, of course, but they weren't like Susan. I think girls are more affectionate in some ways. More interested in people.'

'She's so confident and outgoing, isn't she,' Laura said beaming.

'Yes. And I'm glad she is,' Helen said. 'I suppose I should give credit to her father for that. He gave her a lot of self-belief and confidence I think. He needed to.' Helen trailed off.

'Did she stay here often?' Laura asked.

Helen smiled. 'Yes. Every couple of weeks before the twins were born. We used to visit them in Middle Heyford and they would visit us the following weekend. They were very happy times.' She fell silent.

'Do you know Middle Heyford well?' Laura asked, her enthusiasm for her own small Oxfordshire connection getting the better of her.

'I did yes,' Helen said. 'But I never go back now.'

Her jaw tensed and she remained turned away. Laura's excitement receded again. She imagined Isabelle's home and the memories were too painful to revisit. Did Isabelle kill herself there?

She looked around the lawn at Isabelle's family home, imagining a younger Helen hosting the family and Susan running around in shorts. She wondered how someone would want to give up a life that included such people.

'I'm sorry. I really need to leave for work. I have an emergency clinic this morning.' Helen glanced at her watch and she set off back towards the house again taking Laura's hand. She stepped briskly into the kitchen and gathered up a handbag, scarf and pair of gloves.

'It's been lovely to meet you,' she said. 'I hope I have the pleasure again.'

She extended her hand towards Laura and smiled that big family smile.

'Yes, so do I,' Laura said, beaming at her welcoming host.

'Help yourself to another coffee. Make some toast.' Helen waved a glove over her shoulder as she walked out of sight into the hall and Laura heard her shoes tap down the corridor. The front door clicked open and Helen's footsteps stopped.

'Hey, you off out?' Susan's voice came through.

'Yes, running a bit late actually. I've been talking to Laura.'

'I hope you were good.' Laura heard Susan's laugh echo down the corridor and into the kitchen.

'Yes of course I was. She's lovely. I can see why you encouraged her to stay in your bedroom.'

'Will you stop?' Susan laughed. 'She's married.'

'Oh,' Helen's voice became quieter. 'She didn't mention that.'

'Was she meant to? Did you grill her on all aspects of her personal life?'

'No I didn't. You're quite right. But,' she hesitated. 'Be careful. She likes you.'

'And I like her, but that's it.'

Laura couldn't hear what Helen said next and the door shut a moment later. She rushed over to the table, sat down and cradled the dregs of her coffee as Susan's footsteps squeaked down the hallway.

3.

Susan entered the kitchen with a glowing face and a newspaper under her arm.

'Hey. How you doing?' she said.

'I feel awful.' Laura laughed.

Susan rolled her eyes. 'God, me too. I was going to go for a jog on Hampstead Heath, but went to buy a paper instead.' She laughed and dropped the paper onto the table. She unzipped her hooded top and poured herself a glass of water from a jug in the fridge.

'You survive Helen's questioning?' she asked over her shoulder, smiling.

'She seems really nice.' Laura sat forward on the edge of her seat, rocking it on the front legs. She opened her mouth, wanting to apologise to Susan, but not knowing how to. 'We looked through some of the family photos...'

Susan turned around and looked at her seriously.

'I'm so sorry about your mum,' Laura said. 'I didn't realise.'

'I wondered if that would come out. There's not much holding back Helen.' Susan shook her head. 'There's no reason to apologise though and I guess it's no secret.' She sat down opposite Laura with a glass of water and took large gulps, draining half the glass.

'I've known she committed suicide all my life. I was with my dad when he heard.' She looked away out into the garden. 'It was weird. We were in a hotel room somewhere. It was a huge room, although I was only six and everything looked bigger back then I guess. It had a large bed and lots of swirling carpet around it.' She looked at Laura. 'He was on one of those old dial phones, a beige one. He was sitting on the bed and I could hear Helen's voice on the other end. She was really upset. I'd never heard her cry before. I don't remember what she said other than "She's dead."'

Laura wanted to stand up and hug her friend. She didn't know what to say. It was such a devastating thing to happen to a six-year-old, she knew that well. But telling Susan how cruel it was wouldn't help her.

'I didn't see any pictures of your dad,' she said instead.

Susan breathed out noisily through her nose. 'No, I guess you wouldn't have. Not here.'

Laura didn't understand and frowned.

'Dad and Helen didn't get on,' Susan said. 'I don't know why. When she came over to the States, she always used to stay at a motel. Frustrating when the two people you love most can't get on.'

Susan shrugged. 'I suppose they were completely different types of people. Dad was a clear-cut, black and white kind of guy. Brought up in Chicago, went straight into the army from school. Bright guy though. Whereas Helen sees things in a whole load of colour, not even greys.' Susan laughed. 'But Mom would have been the same and they got on.'

'Which are you like?' Laura said smiling.

'Me? Oh, a lot of my dad's attitudes rubbed off on me, although we had our fights when I was growing up.'

'Was he strict?' Laura asked.

'Kind of. He wanted to be.' Susan smiled. 'Hard not to be after being an army instructor all day long, but he made himself hold back with me. Used to teach me the way to do things, but then left the choice up to me, whether to do the right thing or not.'

'He sounds like a decent bloke.'

'Yeah, he was.'

Susan looked away and they fell silent.

Laura fidgeted. 'By the way, I'm sorry about last night,' she said. 'I really dumped everything on you. I'm afraid I was really wound up and needed to talk.'

'Oh, don't be sorry. I completely get where you're coming from. I don't think you could have picked a better person to unload on.'

Laura shook her head, squeezing her hands tight in a knot on the table.

'No, I'm really glad you talked to me when you needed to,' Susan said smiling. 'That's not something you can let lie. You've got to try to find your folks or it's going to eat you up. If there was a chance I could speak to my mom again, I wouldn't let up until I found her. And god help anyone who tried to stop me.' She laughed.

Susan reached forward and held Laura's wringing hands, rubbing her thumb over her fingers until Laura began to relax, her fingers parting, arms relaxing and shoulders falling in a breath.

Laura nodded. 'Thank you,' she said. 'It's nice to have some support.'

Susan took away her hand and smiled at her. 'Good. You can definitely count on me for that.' She stretched up in the air and yawned. 'You mind if I get a quick shower?'

Laura shook her head.

'I've got a few photos of my dad upstairs if you want to take a look.'

*

They walked up the stairs side by side.

Laura could smell Susan's fresh sweat. It wasn't unpleasant and it surprised her. It was like her own, not the astringent smell of Josh after he'd been playing football. She had grown used to living with a man's odour over the past nine years. Susan wore her hair tied back, revealing her slim neck and her chest, and the v-necked T-shirt cut a view over her breasts. Laura looked at the way they curved up out of her bra.

'Did you get a text from Clo inviting us to lunch?' Susan said.

Laura nodded. 'Yes. I think she's feeling guilty for cancelling last night. She's always cancelling.'

Susan hooked her arm under hers, and Laura felt the warmth against her chest and along her breast. Her nipple tightened with the contact and Laura held her arm tense, embarrassed at the pleasure it gave her. She tried to relax, but that pulled Susan's arm closer, massaging her breasts as they climbed the stairs.

'You going to come along?' Susan said.

Laura blushed. They stopped on the landing by Susan's room. The temptation to stay in Susan's company was too appealing.

'I should go and talk to Josh,' she said, shaking her head. 'I'm surprised he's not been ringing constantly this morning.'

Susan held her hand. 'I answered your phone last night. After you crashed out on the bed? I thought I'd better put his mind at rest and I promised I'd get you home safe.'

Laura didn't look up.

'Was that OK?'

Laura rubbed her hands together, uncomfortable about her thoughts of Josh. She could feel the anger beginning to rise again, reminded of her argument as she left the house. She nodded her head, knowing it had been the considerate thing for Susan to have done.

'He sounded like a nice guy,' Susan said. 'After he'd calmed down.' She was smiling, her dark green eyes looking intently at her.

'He is a nice guy,' Laura nodded. 'Thank you for talking to him.'

Susan lifted her hand and held it in hers. Laura liked the sensation of being enveloped by her. She could feel her pulse, and the warmth from Susan's hands spread up Laura's arm. The sensation glowed and radiated through her chest. It lingered warm and pleasant in her belly and flooded down her body.

'How about we see Clo, then we'll head over your way and I'll drop you off?'

Laura licked her lips, ready to speak. She realised her face was flushed and her lips were full in response to Susan's touch.

'I can lend you some clean clothes,' Susan said.

Laura nodded, unable to resist.

*

Laura stepped into the free-standing bath and drew the shower curtain along the ceiling rail around her. The shower was generous, tens of fast-flowing streams, not the dribble she wriggled beneath at home. She stood still, letting her hair soak and the water run over her scalp, warming her face and her back. She bent her head forward letting the shower tickle her shoulders and gently massage her stale skin with running water.

She picked up the soap and began to lather under her arms. She stroked firmly down her arms, awakening her hungover flesh that was receptive even to her own touch. Her fingers slipped around her breasts, her firm nipples tickling her palms as they circled over. A stream of bubbles ran down her belly, rushed around her pubic hair and poured down her legs. She was tense and conscientiously relaxed her lips and let herself enjoy the warm running water over them.

The temptation was overwhelming to stroke down her belly, slide her hands across her skin and slip her fingers between her legs. She knew who she would think of. She would put a face to those breasts and the body that she usually fantasised about. She clutched down at the bath rim, her fingers hovering over her hair, paralysed and refusing her own thoughts.

An image of Josh flickered in her mind. She saw him waiting for her at home and she shuddered, her arousal turning to revulsion. Her insides clenched and she snatched her hand away from her body.

She roughly washed, dousing her pubic hair where it was slick, and stepped out of the bath. She grabbed a crisp clean towel from the chair, where Susan had piled her clothes, and rubbed hard down her limbs so that her skin turned pink.

She slid into the boxer shorts, letting the wide elastic waist snap around her hips. The soft cotton hugged around her buttocks and she blushed at the feeling it gave her to be in Susan's underwear. She shook her head and pulled on a pair of faded blue jeans and quickly buttoned up the tailored shirt.

The sound of water splashing came from the ensuite as Laura entered Susan's room. The bathroom door was ajar and Laura consciously looked away and turned to look in the mirror on the wardrobe door. Her image was a shock. She looked more like Susan than herself. Her damp hair was darker and she looked different in the clothes. She ran her fingertips over the arm of the shirt, admiring its thick weave, and traced around the outline of the modern floral print. She pressed the fabric flat down her sides and looked disappointed at her reflection. She didn't fill the chest and shoulders as Susan did. She was hunched over, her belly appearing larger than it should.

Standing straight and pushing her shoulders back, she pretended the same confidence Susan had. She stretched her arms out and filled her chest with air and pushed her breasts out. When she relaxed she filled the shirt and looked more comfortable.

'That fits you great.'

Laura turned round to see Susan coming out of the bathroom. She wore a white towelling dressing gown, her hair in dark ribbons around her shoulders. Laura blushed and turned back to her reflection.

'I like it,' she said, stroking the material under her breasts and enjoying the confidence that the new clothes gave her.

She saw Susan, in the mirror, kneeling on the bed behind her. Susan sat back and stretched her legs out in front of her, before pulling her ankles back to sit cross-legged. For a moment, the dressing gown lifted up and Laura glimpsed Susan's dark hair. She stared at the lips that were parted and gaping. Susan held an album in one hand and flipped the bottom of the dressing gown over her leg so that Laura's view was blocked.

'I've got a photo of my dad in here,' Susan said, looking up.

Laura turned around slowly, wishing her red cheeks would cool.

Susan flicked through the album.

'Here we go,' she said. 'This was when he took me on a tour of the base when I was about ten.' She held the album cradled between her legs.

Laura tried to concentrate on the faded Polaroid picture. A man with broad shoulders and short hair stood stiffly. Beneath his arm, a child version of Susan leaned, her long thin legs bent in ways that defied adulthood.

'See,' Susan said. 'A bit different to Mom and Helen huh?'

Laura nodded, but all she could think of were the lips that were hidden behind the photo album.

4.

Clo blinked, squinted and blinked again. Her attic room was filled with a diffuse yellow glow through the curtains. Lying with her head to the side, she eased her eyelids open. They were stiff with salt and it was an effort to open them.

She lay motionless, heavy, as if pressed into the bed. Her face was drooping, the muscles still relaxed from sleep. She didn't have the energy this morning to lift them up and gnash her features awake.

Her stomach and heart sank as she became more conscious. 'Fuck.' Her early morning return to the house was dawning on her, and she lifted a lethargic arm and hand to her forehead. She rubbed the sleep and dried tears from her eyes and massaged her face awake. 'Fuck.'

Clo had opened the front door slowly, trying not to wake Amelia who slept on the ground floor. Her grandmother had a bedroom and bathroom in the converted stables, easy and accessible for when her joints were bad. They shared the living room and kitchen on the next floor with Clo in the attic.

But Amelia had been awake when she had returned home. Her grandmother's bedroom door had been open and the landing was lit by a beam of light from the sitting room. Tears glazed Clo's eyes as she despaired at being caught by Amelia in her emotional state. She had tried to stop them, but she hadn't been able to hide the tears from Amelia.

Clo rolled over on the bed and saw her suit hanging over the chair. It looked incongruous. Her room contained few possessions: a wardrobe held T-shirts, white shirts, several pairs of skinny jeans; there was a bookcase, with a collection of French and English classics next to a section of lesbian crime; her iron-framed bed; a wooden desk with a secondhand laptop; and a dirty clothes basket.

She usually got ready for work at Marella's, where she applied suitable makeup, dressed in what Marella chose and returned there after the appointments to shower, washing every inch of her body, squeezing clean every strand of hair and scrubbing under her nails.

She reached out to the pale suit and drew it to her face. The material was soft and started to feel warm where she breathed.

She could still smell Mrs Hamilton's fragrance from their embrace. Clo gathered the material in great handfuls, trying to make the cloth substantial and hugged it to her chest. She breathed in the scent, closed her eyes and filled her head and arms with the memory of Mrs Hamilton.

She remembered resting her head on her chest, the soft skin of her neck against her own face. She wanted to lift her head and gently kiss up the neck, across the cheek and take in the full lips with hers. Her whole body warmed with the memory, her chest, tummy, thighs almost feeling Mrs Hamilton's body against hers.

She squeezed her fingers into the suit. The material was flat and empty in her hands and cold sorrow and loneliness washed over her as it had done on the walk home. Chilly grey London mornings after the night before could lend themselves to loneliness and isolation, but Clo had never felt so despondent as after leaving Mrs Hamilton.

She pushed herself up in bed and rubbed her face again, trying to stop the tears. She couldn't cry again. She needed to get up and reassure Amelia, not indulge in misery. Clo listened out to see if she could hear Amelia downstairs.

She thought she heard a cup, and then another, clinking on the granite worktop in the kitchen. She imagined them being placed by the kettle on the breakfast bar. There were two voices she thought; women's voices but muffled.

'Bu huh muh gu wu nurrr'. That was Amelia's clipped voice.

Then another responded. The tone, rhythm and intonation suggested a comfortable familiarity with Amelia. 'Huh huh huh. Buh oo eally ood,' came the reply. Clo's reassurances would have to wait until the company had left.

It was a beautiful day outside. The autumn sun had climbed above the terrace on the other side of the mews and beamed through the thin curtains of Clo's attic room. It must be late morning.

She swung her legs out from under the bed clothes to the floor. She stretched up her arms, trying to enjoy her nakedness in the sun-warmed room. It did not feel as good as it should this morning. She dropped her arms, flexed her shoulders and twisted her neck, trying to shake off the weighty sensation depressing her.

She stood up, crossed the room and peered through the curtains to check that the house opposite was unoccupied. Friends of Amelia's lived there, but should have left for the South of France early in the morning. Their main bedroom was opposite Clo's and a mirror dormer window peeked out of the sloping slate roof. The curtains were drawn back, but it was dark inside. She peered down to see if there was any activity on the floor below. No-one was sitting in the bay window seat at least.

She drew back the curtains and let the full force of the sun in through the window. She closed her eyes and saw the sun glare in red and orange pulses through her eyelids. With her arms open wide holding back the curtains, the sun warmed her naked body and tempered the chill of loneliness.

She could hear the voices from the kitchen more clearly now. Sounded like Barbara after all. Clo frowned. She concentrated, twisting her head towards the door. Definitely Barbara. They were around after all. She couldn't hear Bernard. No male baritone interrupted the women's conversation.

She opened her eyes and her heart leapt, attempting to escape through her throat. A beige and grey man in a blue pullover passed by the window opposite. Catching sight of Clo, he threw up a large, pale, bony hand in recognition and receded into the bedroom.

A red flush bloomed on Clo's face. She snatched the curtains across her chest and slowly raised a cheery wave in reply. 'Bollocks.' Exposing herself and giving her elderly neighbour a heart attack was not how she wanted to start the day.

She walked back to the bed, let herself drop and bounce on the mattress and curled up into a foetal position to wait for the wife of the exposed to leave the tête-à-tête with Amelia.

5.

Clo was at a party, where there were lots of other children, and she was three. Her mother made her wear a pretty summer dress with her favourite red shoes. The dress billowed out so that she couldn't see her feet, and she pulled it up around her ears, showing her knickers. Two of the other girls walked up to Clo and showed her their knickers too, but she wasn't interested. She wanted to look at her shiny shoes. So the other girls pulled their knickers down. Clo stared at them, not sure what to think.

Her mother bore down on her. From high in the air a rigid hand descended, smacking her thigh. She heard the sound of the slap before she registered the full smart of it. She turned to her mother in shock. Uncomprehending, she looked at her mother bending over her, blond hair hanging down around her deep red face. Her eyes looked wild.

'Get out,' her mother shouted. 'Go home with Amelia.' Her mother pointed to the door. Clo couldn't see her grandmother, but walked towards the door, her hands rigid by her sides and her lower lip beginning to wobble. She turned around and looked at the legs of adults in skirts and trousers, but couldn't see Amelia. She started to cry.

A woman's legs stopped in front of her. The pretty lady she couldn't understand, especially when she talked to Amelia, picked her up. Clo looked into her eyes, the deepest brown she'd ever seen, and the lady said something in a kind voice. Clo rested her cheek on her shoulder and nuzzled into her neck, as the lady hugged her and took her out the door. The lady had soft dark hair and smelled funny in a good way. Perfume, Amelia explained.

Amelia, the nice lady and her son played in the woods by the lake. Clo remembered it as the same day. It was an endless hot summer and she played in the stream while Amelia sat on a tree stump up the bank.

Clo paddled through the cool water, turning every stone, trying to find creepy crawlies, as her mother would have dismissed them. Caddis larvae Amelia told her. Clo loved their stone-encrusted homes and turned over the stones trying to count them. She waded around barefoot all afternoon and Amelia sat and watched over her.

She turned over a stone with so many caddis larvae she wasn't sure she could count them. Determined to get it right, she took the stone to Amelia. Stone in one palm held up high, cool stream water running down her arm, she pushed off from the large boulder in the stream. She crawled and scrambled up the mossy bank towards Amelia who stood up ready for the inspection.

Almost at the path, Clo pulled on the branch of one of the trees she liked. The one with the jagged diamond leaves and white ribbon strips for bark. She wrapped her fingers around a low stub of a branch and tried to pull up to her grandmother, her whole body tense. Her arms, stomach, back and legs all strained with their full strength, barely moving.

She heard a crack and all her muscles seem to snap and relax like a broken rubber band. She floundered in the air, one hand holding her precious rock and the other the small broken branch.

Quicker than she'd seen anyone move, her grandmother snatched her flailing arm. Her grip was vice-like, bruising. Steely swollen fingers wrapped round Clo's forearm, holding her hand aloft, preventing her from tumbling backwards onto the boulder below. The strength of her grandmother had surprised her, but it was the expression on her face that made her stomach churn.

Instead of her fond look, she had a wide-eyed intense expression that Clo had never seen on her. Her mouth was serious, down-turned. Her brow was concentrated, and her eyes burned with fear and concentration. The two seemed to hang, frozen, staring at each other.

Held there trying to fathom her grandmother's look, it reminded Clo of her mother's face at the party. She was scared that this was the same and she would receive another blow.

Straining together, Clo and Amelia's balance edged towards a threshold and the scene unfroze, and Clo slumped forward at her grandmother's feet. Amelia gathered Clo up. 'Oh god. I thought you were going to crack your little head on that rock. Oh god,' she kept repeating.

Afterwards Clo's whole body shook, thrilled by seeing someone act so instinctively to save her. And the physicality of the incident made her hold her sinewy grandmother in a new kind of awe.

*

Clo looked through the half-open doorway of the sitting room. The white room glowed in the sunlight shining through the bay window. The pale sofas on either side of the window were empty. Clo could hear the chink of china cups and she pushed the door open wide. Amelia was leaning on the breakfast bar that separated the living room from the kitchen. She was more fragile with arthritis and over twenty-five years older, but Clo still thought of Amelia as possessing a colossal strength.

Barbara had gone and Amelia was tidying the tea-cups and plates away. The plates chattered in her shaky hands.

'Hello darling. I didn't hear you come down.' She looked up at Clo with a sad fondness and reached towards her.

Clo put her arms around Amelia's rounded shoulders, squeezed her tight and kissed the old woman's grey curls. Amelia pulled away and held Clo's arms with her crooked fingers.

'How are you?' she asked her directly. She looked into Clo's eyes, flicking intently between them.

'I'm fine,' Clo said. She tried to smile, managing to curl her lips up, but not lighten her eyes. They refused to smile and threatened to water if she squeezed them too tight. 'I'm sorry if I worried you last night. I'd had a bit to drink,' she added. 'I was just overtired.' She swallowed, becoming tearful again, remembering how she felt returning home.

Amelia was frowning. Her eyes looked watery with fatigue and there was an undercurrent of mournfulness. Clo stared at the knots of Amelia's swollen knuckles, which did not relinquish their grip on her arms. She peeked up tentatively, apprehensive of the penetrative look. She held her breath, waiting for Amelia to ask her outright. Where had she been so late? Not at the patisserie. Not in that suit. Not with those tears in her eyes. She would tell her everything if she asked.

Amelia blinked and relaxed her grip and Clo pulled away from the opportunity to confess.

'I'll clear those away,' Clo offered. She stepped towards the breakfast bar and started to remove the crockery from the surface. 'Sit down while I clear up.' Amelia held her gaze with a frown for a moment and then looked away.

'Thank you darling. I think I will.' She smiled and lurched in small steps towards the sofa by the window.

'Have Barbara and Bernard only just left?' Clo called from the kitchen. 'I thought they were leaving early?'

'Yes, just now. Bernard was sorting a few things. They're renting out the house while they're away. Barbara popped in to say goodbye again, and of course one cup of tea led to another. You know how it is.'

Clo dried her hands and waited in the kitchen. Amelia sounded as if she was about to say something more, or was trying formulate her next sentence. Nothing came. Amelia was staring towards the window in between thought and conversation. She looked tired and drained, more than she usually did.

Amelia exhaled and turned to Clo. 'Come and sit next to me. Come and keep me company for a few minutes.' She patted the sofa beside her and Clo slid next to her and held her hand.

Amelia stared out of the window. 'Barbara invited me to stay again,' she said.

Neither of them responded.

'It's been a long time since you moved in, hasn't it?' Amelia said, head still turned away. 'Tempus fugit.' She sighed.

'It's made me think, you see, that I don't take you for granted as such, but that I've grown to expect more of you than I should.' She turned towards Clo. 'Don't think that I don't appreciate all the cooking, cleaning, and above all the incomparable company, but you shouldn't have to live with a geriatric.'

Clo stopped Amelia from going further, afraid of where Amelia was leading. 'Don't be silly. You did me an incredible favour taking me in. I will always be grateful. But it's not gratitude that keeps me here. I love living with you. I'm very happy here.'

'Are you?' said Amelia. She stared at Clo with that look that made Clo fear that she could read her thoughts. Clo wanted to close her eyes to stop her from reaching in and sifting through the scenes that Clo hid, while her heart filled and the emotion tightened her throat, wanting to spill out and confess everything to her.

'I'm not saying that I've made you unhappy,' Amelia continued. 'Just perhaps, I've held you back from getting on with your life.' She hesitated. 'It's been a long time since Sally.'

Clo twitched. Her hand wanted to curl up away from Amelia's arm. She stared at her fingers, willing them to stay still. She tried to think of nothing but the skin on her hand and her breathing, to let the brimming sadness ebb. She exhaled and looked up at Amelia.

'I don't think that at all,' she said. She tried to smile at Amelia to comfort her but Amelia looked unconvinced. She seemed torn, as if trying to reconcile some thoughts. Neither of them said anything.

At length, Amelia patted her hand. 'And besides,' she said. 'I also wondered if perhaps a few months of sunshine would be a pleasant break from the dismal British weather.'

Clo looked up to see her smiling. Amelia had let her go.

'Some southern sunshine and Mediterranean food may be just what I need,' she said.

Clo cleared her throat. 'Perhaps you could go and stay for a short while, if this winter gets very bad.'

Amelia was unmoved.

'Think about it?' persisted Clo.

'Yes, indeed. Something to think about.'

6.

There was a knock on the front door. Clo looked up from the casserole through the steam. She stopped stirring and rested the wooden spoon on the edge of the pot. Amelia was sitting by the window and she flipped down the top of her newspaper, which she held at arm's length. She peered over her glasses.

A voice came from downstairs. 'Door's open. Is it OK to come in?'

Clo recognised Laura. 'Yes, come on up,' she shouted.

She tilted her head to look through the doorway and down the stairs. She saw Laura's bleached hair shining in the darkness of the stairwell, bouncing and floating as she ran up the steps.

'Hey,' Laura said. 'That smells delicious.'

Laura beamed her wide smile. Her face looked flushed and well, like she used to look when she was happy. Clo frowned through the steam, taking in the change, and Laura spun round to see Amelia.

'Good morning,'

'Good morning my darling,' Amelia said, struggling to get out of the sofa.

Laura strode over towards her. 'Oh don't get up,' she said, and she bent down and put her arms around Amelia's shoulders and kissed her cheek.

'You look very well my dear,' Amelia said, still holding Laura's arms as she stood up.

Laura frowned. 'You look tired. Is everything OK?'

'Oh just a bad night's sleep. I'm much the same as always.'

Laura squeezed Amelia's hands gently. 'Good. Sorry, do you mind if I get a glass of water. I'm gasping.'

'Of course, dear. You know where everything is.'

Laura bounded over to Clo and filled a glass from the tap. She leaned over the casserole, drawing her hair back behind her ears.

'This does smell delicious,' she said. 'Is it your beef and Guinness stew?'

Clo nodded, stirring the bubbling stew, pockets of rich meaty steam rising to her nose.

'My favourite. Real food,' Laura said greedily.

'Amelia's right. You do look good today,' Clo said.

Laura swallowed a mouthful of water. 'Thank you.'

'Is that a Paul Smith shirt?' Clo said, looking over the familiar pattern. It was similar to one in Marella's set of outfits.

'Oh I don't know,' said Laura. She pinched behind the collar lifting it up to show Clo.

'Yes, Paul Smith.'

Laura laughed. 'It always amazes me how much you know about fashion. You seem to lounge about – looking great I know – but you do just lounge about in a T-shirt and jeans most of the time. And then you talk about, god I don't know, well Paul Smith.' She threw up a hand in exasperation.

Clo blushed and tried to ignore the comment. 'Is it new?' she said.

'No, it's Susan's. I've just borrowed it.'

Clo looked at her, silently asking for more detail.

'I stayed the night at Susan's. She'll be here in a minute, she's parking the car.'

Clo looked away and down into the pot, steam condensing on her face. Laura stayed silent for a moment and fiddled with the rings on her left hand. 'I just had an argument with Josh,' she said quietly. 'I'd already met up with Susan at Beck's when I got your text and I got talking to her. I didn't want to go home.'

'Everything OK?' Clo asked.

'I've just been freaking out a bit about my parents.'

Clo looked up at Laura more concerned. 'Why? What's brought this on?'

She didn't look her in the eye. 'Josh wants to start a family. I feel weird about it, not knowing where I came from.'

Clo stopped stirring and focused her attention on her fully. 'But you've always wanted kids,' she said. 'You're brilliant with them. I can't imagine you not having a family.'

'I know. I know.' She looked tense and unconsciously held her hand to her belly. Clo reached out and held it.

'Is there anything else?' she asked.

Laura shook her head. 'No. I just think it's brought everything up again with him wanting to start a family now. I don't think I'm ready for it, not without finding my parents.'

Clo took her hand away.

Laura looked at her. 'You don't think I should try, do you?'

Clo shook her head. 'No it's not that. I'm just sorry I wasn't there for you last time.'

Laura smiled and stepped forward, putting her arm around her shoulder. 'Please don't worry about that. It was a shitty time for both of us. I got obsessed about it, and took it too far. I wouldn't let that happen again.'

Laura squeezed her shoulder and Clo looked up at her friend, one of the most determinedly single-minded people she'd met, and doubted every word she said.

'I'm sorry I cancelled last night,' Clo said.

Laura shook her head. 'Don't worry. I'm glad I met Susan anyway. They do mess you around at that patisserie though. And I don't know how you and Amelia survive. They can't pay you very much and they're very unreliable.'

Clo saw Amelia look over her newspaper towards them. Clo blushed and the steam from the casserole inflamed her face. She looked into the pot, hoping Amelia wasn't listening. She doubted Amelia believed her claim of returning from an early-morning shift at the patisserie.

'I know someone from college at a law firm with a big European department.' Laura continued. 'They always have translation work. You could work from home. Look after Amelia. Then you might be able to come out more.'

Clo saw Laura look at her from the corner of her eye. Laura didn't move except for the pinch of her eyebrows into a frown. Clo's skin started to crawl under the scrutiny and she held her breath, wondering what she would say.

'Clo? You're wearing makeup,' she said.

Clo concentrated, trying to control her blush, which spread down her neck and up to her scalp. She could hear her pulse rushing in her ears and they felt like they throbbed. She waited, wishing Laura would move on.

'You never wear makeup?'

Amelia's voice came across to them, calm. 'I was showing her how I used to make up my face in the fifties.' She was looking at Clo and had an unreadable expression on her face and Clo couldn't look at her for long. Tears were beginning to mix with the steam, and she turned her back to Laura and Amelia and wiped her face with a tea towel.

'Really? How fantastic,' said Laura. 'Would you show me?'

Clo heard Laura's voice fade as she turned to talk to Amelia.

*

Clo looked in the mirror above the washbasin in the upstairs bathroom. She had a faint trail of eyeliner around her eyes that hadn't rubbed off on the pillow or been washed away by her tears. Her eyelids were puffy and the whites of her eyes had a hint of pink soreness.

She turned on the tap, wetting a cotton pad in the stream, and lifted it up to her face and squeezed it onto each eye. Cool water seeped between her eyelids and soothed the rawness. She dabbed over her eyes and gently drew the pad along the lashes, removing the eyeliner she never wore in front of her friends. When she opened her eyes, she saw herself.

She reached for another cotton pad and poured on a moisturising cleanser that Marella recommended for client-pleasing skin. She lifted the pad to her cheek then stopped. Her cheek had touched Mrs Hamilton's neck when they held each other. Her skin remembered how it had felt and started to warm. She closed her eyes and imagined herself back in Mrs Hamilton's arms, her face buried in her neck, her breath moist over her skin, tickling across her cheek. She inhaled through her nose trying to smell the perfume that had infused her, wafting up from Mrs Hamilton's breasts.

Her nostrils felt dry as she breathed in hard and all she could smell was cleanser. Clo gulped and a tear leaked from between her eyelids and ran down her cheek. She let the cotton pad rest on her skin, let the coolness of the lotion take away the memory, and she began to circle around her cheek.

She thought she heard a knock on the front door. Laura and Amelia's conversation from the living room below sounded unbroken. Clo looked out of the door and down the stairs. Another knock. She padded down the stairs, went unnoticed past the living room door, and down to the ground floor.

'Hey gorgeous,' Susan said, as she opened the door. She grinned at Clo with that big smile and reached for her with an enthusiastic hug. Clo stumbled back when she was released and smiled up at Susan.

'Come in. Come in. Laura's upstairs.' Clo stepped back to let Susan through, but reached out to stop her from going up the stairs.

'Is she OK?'

Susan's expression flickered into concern. 'She'd had an argument with Josh,' she said quietly. 'She wants to look for her folks again, but he doesn't want her to. I think it was driving her nuts not being able to talk about it.'

Clo opened her mouth.

'Don't worry,' said Susan. 'She's fine. We got drunk, talked a lot, she blew off some steam. Hopefully they'll sort it out.'

'I know it's been on her mind a lot recently,' Clo said. 'But I didn't realise she wanted to try again.'

Susan was about to respond, but turned to look up the stairs. Her mouth was still open, ready with her reply, but no words came out. Clo peered round to see what she was looking at. Amelia was standing at the top of the stairs, gripping the banister so tight that her misshapen joints turned pale. She was staring at Susan, her eyes wide and her eyebrows crinkled. She switched her eyes to Clo and fixed her with the same look.

Her appearance scared Clo. She had never seen Amelia looking so perturbed. She was not sure if her grandmother recognised her at that moment. She stepped forward. 'Amelia?' But she looked away from Clo and back to Susan with the same agitated expression.

The old woman grabbed the banister with both hands and stepped down the stairs, one foot down, bringing the other to join it, without taking her eyes from Susan. She stretched out to Susan's hands and squeezed her fingers with the desperate strength of an old person reaching out for support.

'Susan Miller. You could only be Susan Miller,' Amelia said, whispering up to Susan.

Susan nodded in response, looking confused and concerned for the elderly woman.

Amelia moved closer to examine her, peering beneath Susan's hair that flowed around her face. Amelia reached up with her hand, brushing the hair aside and rested her fingers on Susan's cheek.

'I'm so sorry my dear,' Amelia whispered, as she stroked her thumb across Susan's cheek.

Recognition rippled across Amelia's face and she blinked into a more familiar expression. She breathed out. 'Forgive me. Forgive me my dear. You took me by surprise.' She squeezed Susan's fingers.

'You look so like your mother.' Amelia lifted Susan's hands to her lips and gave them a dry, affectionate kiss. 'With my eyes, you could have been her.'

Clo saw Susan gulp and try to smile at Amelia.

'My dad used to tell me I was the spitting image,' Susan said. 'Used to catch him looking at me sometimes with a look of real pain on his face.'

'Yes, I was so sorry to hear about your father. I'm afraid we didn't keep in touch and I didn't realise he had been ill.'

'Oh, Dad kept it pretty quiet. It was stage four by the time he'd been diagnosed properly, and he didn't have much time left. I don't think he had the chance to say goodbye to everyone.'

Amelia let go of Susan's hands and turned towards the stairs. 'I'm sorry. You must come in my dear. Come upstairs. I want to hear everything about you.'

7.

Clo washed the dishes from lunch. Susan stood beside her, a tea-towel over her arm. She picked up a plate from the rack and spun it round, wiping it with the towel. She looked away and Clo followed the line of her face to see Amelia sitting on the sofa.

'Gave Amelia a bit of fright I think,' Susan said.

Amelia looked deflated. She sat on the end of the sofa, hunched over and sagging forward. Laura sat beside her, holding her hands, stroking gentle fingers over the swollen knuckles. They talked earnestly about her current medication.

'You know, I remember her quite well,' Susan said, turning back to Clo. 'Playing with you near the lake at the weekend or in the evening and sometimes bringing you into school at the end of the day.'

Clo frowned trying to recall, 'Yes, I suppose she did look after me a lot.'

She scanned over Susan's features, her dark eyebrows, the coppery eyelashes that flicked over green eyes, her straight nose; she checked her cheekbones and full lips. Susan lifted her hand to stroke a ribbon of hair behind her ear, and Clo felt the thrill of recognition with the action. She looked again at Susan's features, trying to make them into someone else's, but the memory disappeared.

'I'm sorry, I don't remember your mum,' she said.

Susan smiled and shook her head. 'You were real small, although I wasn't exactly old. They used to let me look after you in the summer holidays. Do you remember?'

Clo shook her head.

'Our moms would send us off down to the lake together, while they put their feet up. Can you imagine anyone doing that now?'

'That was very trusting,' said Clo, raising her eyebrows.

'I know. Not sure I'd want my kids playing unsupervised by a lake. Guess they were a bit more relaxed than I would be.' Susan laughed. 'It was great fun. I used to take you paddling in the water. You fell in once. You got a whole lungful of water and coughed for an age. You were soaking from head to toe, mud up to your knees, so we went back to your mom's early. She was so annoyed.'

Clo blushed, ashamed at inciting her mother's venom.

'I guess you don't remember Helen either,' Susan asked. 'She used to visit quite often.'

'No, I'm sorry I don't.'

'You know, you guys should come over for my birthday. Helen's organised a party - a kind of welcome to the UK and happy birthday all rolled into one. It's in two weeks. Be great if you, Laura and Amelia could come over.' She looked over to Laura and Amelia.

'What's that my dear?' Amelia said. Laura helped Amelia to her feet and they joined them at the breakfast bar.

'I would love for you and Clo to come over to Helen's for my birthday. It's a bit formal though. Helen loves to dress up.'

Laura laughed. 'Oh don't worry about that. Clo scrubs up surprisingly well.'

'I don't doubt it. She's gorgeous.'

'You wait and see,' said Laura smiling.

Amelia frowned. 'Is that Helen your aunt?'

'Yeah. Do you remember her from Middle Heyford?'

'Yes I do.' Amelia still looked serious. 'I wonder if I could trouble you for her phone number. I should like to speak to her first.'

'Oh I'm sure she won't mind you all coming. She's told me to invite a whole load of people from work too.'

'All the same. I should like to talk to her.'

*

Laura and Susan talked about the party, and Clo turned her attention to Amelia who smiled and blinked slowly.

'You look exhausted. Do you have to go out this evening?' Clo asked. She huddled up to Amelia and squeezed her hand.

Amelia nodded her head. 'Yes I'm afraid I do. Some comfort from both companionship and food is very much required.'

Clo wondered which friend was in need of Amelia's rescue, but did not ask.

'I've put a portion of stew in the fridge for you to take. I think we've got some Rhone wine to drink with it,' Clo said, thinking through the blend of flavours. She imagined the browned beef, rich tomato, the slight bitterness of the Guinness, then a comforting mouthful of the warm Syrah wine. She tapped her tongue on the roof of her mouth and gulped down the fruity liquid, smelling the earthy vapours that filled her nose and imagining the warm hit of the alcohol that would leave the brain with a pleasurable fuzziness. 'Yes I'll get a bottle to go with it.'

Amelia smiled. 'That would be marvellous. Most restorative.'

'Why don't you try to have a nap before you go. You look so tired,' Clo said.

'I think I'll have to,' Amelia said.

Clo helped her to her feet and watched her hobble across the room and out the door.

*

'I'd better get home,' Laura said.

Susan sat on a stool by the breakfast bar. 'Sit and have your coffee first,' she said, patting the stool beside her.

Laura perched on the stool and folded her arms.

'If you need more time, you're welcome to stay for the evening,' said Clo. 'Both of you. Amelia's out. We could watch a DVD, have popcorn.'

'I like the sound of that,' said Susan, raising her eyebrows and nodding. 'What kind of movies do you like?'

Laura smiled. 'Oh don't let Clo choose. She'll have you watching French films and actresses all night. It's quite a love affair she has, but I've done my time with those.'

Clo grinned. 'Who doesn't love French actresses?'

'Oh, I can't fault your taste,' Laura smiled. 'Who doesn't love Deneuve and who wouldn't want some Fanny Ardent.'

Laura laughed and Susan stared at her.

'Really?' Susan said

'Oh absolutely, but I lost an entire day of my life watching those Francoise Desmarais videos, which I will never forgive you for.'

Susan looked between Laura and Clo, confused. 'Um. Bit of a Desmarais fan are we?' she said.

'Hadn't even heard of her before university,' Laura continued. 'Clo was trying to find a scene that she thought she saw when she was little. Twelve hours of miserable French films, where bugger all happens, apart from when some ugly French chap beds a beautiful French actress, and an English World War Two film. Still didn't find the scene she remembered.' Laura threw up her hands in despair.

Clo laughed. 'I'm sure the war film was edited you know. I've tried to find an uncut version. No luck though.'

'Good,' said Laura. 'And if you do find it, stay clear of me until you've seen it.'

'What's the scene?' said Susan.

'It's definitely from *Remembrance*,' Clo said. She looked away, turning her thoughts inwards. Her eyes became unfocussed as she pictured the scene. 'Her hair's quite short and curling up in that forties style. She looks incredible, walking through a forest, towards the hero I think. She looks her most beautiful in that film. She stopped making films when she was quite young, but she looks a little older in that compared with the others.'

She looked towards Laura who rolled her eyes.

'Well she didn't do any films after that. Anyway, she's intoxicatingly aloof the whole film – like Kristin Scott Thomas in *The English Patient* – but then there's this scene where she is suddenly soft and warm. She approaches the hero with such a smile and look of joy. She comes right up to the camera and says, almost surprised, "you have the most amazing eyes in this light"'. Clo stared into the blurred living room for a few moments, remembering that look, her impression of the scene still so vivid she could almost imagine the breeze on her face and the sound of it in the forest trees.

She looked up. Susan and Laura stared at her. 'Anyway, I couldn't find it.'

'Wow,' said Susan. 'That's quite a crush you have there.'

Laura looked at her with a sad smile, her head tilted to the side. 'Oh Clo. How are you going to find someone real if you only love French actresses?'

Clo blushed and Susan looked down into her coffee.

'It's been such a long time,' Laura said. 'Not everyone's like Sally you know. You really should try opening up to someone again. Preferably someone as beautiful as you, so you don't drive them crazy.'

Clo's blush deepened and she turned away to hide.

'Never known anyone have so many women fall for them,' she heard Laura say to Susan. 'She could have had anyone at college.'

'Anyone?' said Susan.

'Yes, anyone, and she mostly did,' said Laura, laughing quietly.

*

Clo followed them down the stairs to the door. The two tall women gave her equally lung-crushing hugs, and she watched them walk away over the cobbles.

A woman entered the mews. She stopped under the arch and looked towards her. She wore sunglasses, a black dress, and held a clutch bag in front of her, behind crossed hands. Often a welcome sight at the end of an appointment, this close to her home, a chill settled in Clo's stomach when she recognised her elegant madam.

Marella turned to look at Laura and Susan as they walked under the archway. Clo stopped breathing as she saw them look up and Marella smiled. Clo gripped the door and watched the two sides of her life brushing close together. She could feel her eyebrows stretching her eyes wide and her body and limbs lighten in panic. Her stomach caved in with tension as Laura and Susan's faces panned round to Marella.

Marella flipped open her bag, and took out a petite mobile and held it to her ear. She began to stroll into the mews as she talked, and Laura and Susan increased their pace beyond the archway.

Clo breathed out and raised her palm, trembling, to her mouth. Marella caught her eye and turned back to walk under the arch.

'This is a bit much,' Clo said, frowning as she caught up with Marella.

Marella reached out to hold her arm. 'This won't take long,' she said, calmly. 'And if you'd switched on your phone, I wouldn't have had to come out at all.'

'Sorry. I didn't think you'd need to contact me.'

Marella looked at her for a moment, assessing her.

'I was surprised to see Mrs Hamilton this morning,' Marella said. 'She attended her post-appointment briefing with me. You should have told me that you went ahead with the appointment.'

Clo took a second or two to remember that Mrs Hamilton had wanted to cancel her appointment. 'Sorry. Yes I should,' Clo admitted, shaking her head.

'You know why, especially with first-time clients,' Marella said seriously. 'You must let me know exactly where you're going. She seemed a good client to me, but I don't always get it right.'

'I know, I know,' said Clo. 'I'd already arrived – had a glass of wine – when I got your text and I was, distracted.'

'Did it go OK?' Marella asked more gently.

'Yes. Very well,' she said, although she could not say it with any happiness. Her sorrow was returning and dragging at her chest.

'Did she ask to see me again?' She blushed as she said it, but couldn't stop the words coming out.

Marella hesitated. 'No. As far as I know, she's gone back to the States. She paid this morning and said I had made an impeccable choice.'

It was strange being called an impeccable choice. It felt so cold and business-like after the warmth of the night. She could not imagine Mrs Hamilton saying it.

Marella was frowning at her

'I stayed all night....' Clo tried to explain. 'I liked her more than I should have,' she said looking tentatively at Marella. She was embarrassed by her thoughts and feelings in front of her employer. If things had been different. If she wasn't an escort. If Mrs Hamilton wasn't a client. If she wasn't married. Too many ifs. She felt stupid having these feelings for a client in front of Marella. 'She was lovely though.'

Marella analysed Clo's expression. 'I'm not losing you am I?' she said. 'You're one of my best.'

Clo shook her head, trying to shake the sorrow. 'I'll be fine. It'll pass,' she said. 'Just give me a little while.'

'How about this afternoon?' Marella asked, looking uncomfortable at pressing Clo so quickly.

Clo groaned and rubbed her eyes and face. She did not want to service another client. The thought of touching another woman made her nauseous. She wanted to hide at home all day, curled up on the sofa with only Amelia for company. She dropped her hands. 'Who is it?' she looked up with heavy eyes.

'Not a new client, just Eleanor Abrahams.'

'Didn't I see her this week?'

'One last visit before she goes on holiday, I'm afraid.' Marella tried to smile.

Clo shook her head. 'OK. OK. I can do a short appointment.'

'Good,' Marella said. 'Come round at four. We'll get you ready,' Marella said, preparing to leave. 'And switch your phone on.'

Clo walked back to the house, groping in the back pocket of her jeans for her key. She stared down unfocused as she scraped around the keyhole. The key was stiff and wouldn't turn. She squeezed it harder and looked up, cursing the old lock.

She started as she caught Amelia's face in the front window. She was staring towards the archway in the direction that Marella had taken. She turned and looked at Clo, her face pale and drawn; she had an intensity in her eyes that made Clo's insides chill.

8.

She looked more like her mother today, Clo thought, catching her reflection in the passenger mirror of Marella's car. She wore heavy make-up for the appointment, her eyes big with a bold application of eye-liner, eye shadow and generous lengthening mascara.

They'd deliberated about her lipstick. With such full lips, Clo could sometimes look too swollen with red lipstick. They'd opted for a pale pink. It went well with the grey suit Marella had chosen. Clo had let her mould and paint her, dress and ruffle her hair into the image that Mrs Eleanor Abrahams desired – Rebecca the obliging and submissive call girl.

When Marella had finished, Clo stood up, straightened her back, opened her eyes in polite attentiveness and stretched a welcoming smile across her face. 'Perfect', Marella had said. Clo wished she'd stayed in character since. After the near collisions between the two sides of her life, she was distracted and agitated.

She checked her appearance again in the mirror. Yes, she looked like her mother and the top half of her sister's face. Her younger sister, Lottie, had her mother's beautiful large eyes, but where her mother's face was completed by a delicate heart-shaped chin, her sister had an asymmetrical jaw-line.

Clo didn't know whose eyes she'd inherited, but the high, sculpted cheeks and jaw and full lips were from her father's side of the family. How disappointed her mother must be in them both. Her sister too ugly, Clo too diluted by her father and too gay. Her sister was by far the most approved of, though. Seven years younger than Clo, she'd settled with a husband and had already provided the first grandchild.

Clo and her sister had grown up in different generations in their Oxfordshire cottage. They'd never overlapped at school and had different dispositions. Her sister liked pink. Clo didn't mind pink, but didn't see why it should appeal above all other colours. Her sister liked dolls. Clo had played with her dolls as part of a society that included the teddy bears, the much loved knitted blob from Amelia and the action man, Major Lee the 2nd.

Major Lee the 1st had disappeared in action. She could remember him before he was bought. He stood in the shop window, which they passed when her mother went shopping. He stood to attention in a yellow box with a plastic see-through front. The box had a picture of him abseiling down a rock face. He seemed a good outdoor doll, not the type to be restricted to having tea parties in the house.

She'd pointed to him every time they passed, her mother becoming more dismissive each time. When her mother started to tug her sharply past the shop, she stopped pointing and just stole a secret glance at him.

But he'd turned up in her pile of presents the following Christmas. It was the most magical present ever – just like Christmas presents should be. She got the one thing she had longed for but hadn't expected to receive. She must have looked overjoyed. Her father beamed, all his teeth showing in a smile. Her mother looked flushed and more restrained, but still buoyant, seeing the pleasure in her daughter.

Major Lee was her favourite toy that Christmas. He climbed the stairs, he tunnelled under the tablecloth; fearless, he rode strapped to the back of the dog. Later they both escaped the house to the woods. The streams were not usually so interesting this time of year, with fewer grubs and other life in the cold water. But the tough Major Lee abandoned his clothes and together they went diving for treasure in the sparkling stones at the bottom of the shallow streams. Quartz and fluorspar, Clo informed Major Lee of his discoveries.

The doll went everywhere, and it was for this reason that Alice first banned him from the dining table. Not hygienic to bring the dog-riding, mud-diving doll to the table. She was welcome to bring Cindy who stayed clean indoors. Then he was banned from the sitting room, and gradually from anywhere her mother could see him. And then he disappeared altogether.

A thorough and extensive search was conducted. Clo searched her room. Her father searched the garden and streams, and her mother searched the rest of the house, but he was gone.

'Alice. Where is he?' she heard her father ask.

'For god's sake Edward. She takes him everywhere. He could be anywhere.'

Clo saw Major Lee one more time. She saw him through the condensation on her bedroom window when she looked out early one morning. He was stiff and helpless in her mother's hand, being thrust backwards and forwards as her mother strode towards the back of the bin men's lorry.

A few months later, her father, somehow apologetic, gave her Major Lee the 2nd. She was more careful about showing her affection to this version, but it hadn't been so critical anymore. With the joyous arrival of a new baby girl, who grew up with big beautiful eyes and a penchant for pink, Clo's aberrant tastes were more often overlooked.

It was only when Clo reached her teens that Alice turned her full disapproval on her again and found it impossible to overlook her elder daughter's behaviour.

*

Penny Stratham's mother was on the phone. Penny was in the same year as Clo at school. She sat next to her in French when Penny's usual friends did chemistry or home economics. Penny was quite pretty, quite sporty, quite nice. Clo didn't have any objection to her at all – it would be difficult to imagine anyone objecting to Pen, but they were not great friends. It puzzled her why she sat by Clo in French. In all the other lessons she had her group of friends to sit with, but alone she would turn her attention to Clo.

Clo thought maybe it was because she was good at French. Clo's accent wasn't good, she hadn't inherited her mother's musicality, but she had inherited her father's linguistic aptitude. There was something funny about the questions Penny asked though.

She would ask about which auxiliary verb to use in the past tense. Clo would explain that it was mostly *avoir* and then a handful of exceptions would take *etre*. When Penny didn't seem to understand, Clo explained that sometimes it was just best to think of useful phrases with the verbs. Again Penny didn't seem to take it in.

Clo took Penny's notebook and her fountain pen. She was going to write down her clarification. Penny just smiled at her. Clo didn't think she'd said anything too amusing. Confused, she pressed on. She tried talking through her explanation as she wrote it down, hoping it would find its way into Penny's consciousness.

'There,' she said when she'd finished, looping over the explanation in her neatest handwriting. She offered the notebook back, and Penny accepted it, staring at her with large eyes. She looked like she was holding her eyes open trying to accommodate the weird large pupils.

Clo never told anyone of this strange behaviour, but Penny shared it and more embellished details in a diary.

Clo's mother had her back to her. She was talking on the phone in the hallway and Clo sat and watched from the kitchen table. She could only hear snippets of her mother's halting and curt replies.

She put down the phone and turned to look at Clo. Her face was red and her eyes intense. She was angry, Clo knew that, but there were other emotions mixed in there too, all combined too thoroughly to distinguish. Reverting to a childhood fear, she almost expected a hard slap. But her mother recognised that she was too old for that. Her mother gathered herself and, with purpose, sat down next to Clo at the kitchen table.

Clo had an urge to flee. She held onto her tea, clenching her fingers around the mug. Her mother was silent and reached out her hand to squeeze Clo's arm.

'I need to talk to you about girls,' her mother said.

Clo sat rigid, her muscles tensed hard, ready to spring up and out of the room.

Alice was gathering her thoughts and spoke slowly, like when she was teaching.

'I know it must be tempting, at this age, when you're beginning to have physical urges and want to try things out,' her mother said. 'It is quite natural. God knows, none of us would be here if we didn't have those urges.' She strained a smile, trying to make a joke of it.

'And I know a lot of the boys are still more interested in playing football than perhaps talking to girls, or trying kissing and holding. And you're fully grown and they've barely broken their voices. But you have to be so careful, with girls.' She had turned to look at Clo directly in the eyes for the first time.

'I can see that being with another girl would be so much easier. They know what you look like, they have the same bits and pieces, and it's not as embarrassing as showing a boy who's never seen a girl before. And girls understand you, and you can share things with a girl that boys are never going to understand.

'But that, you see, is the dangerous part. All that emotional bonding, all that physical and emotional understanding is too much. You need a man in there to keep things calm. Do you understand?' Her mother looked at her.

Clo thought she was going to be sick and remained mute.

Her mother turned away, trying to think of another way of getting Clo to comprehend.

'You must see it at school,' her mother said. 'The girls, don't you see them become over-involved, best friends sharing everything, clothes, secrets, getting close and promising to be best friends for life? And then something happens. One of them finds a new best friend, both fancy the same boy...' she tapered off.

'So, when you throw sex in there as well, imagine how destructive that is. Don't underestimate sex Clo. Don't underestimate sex with someone who understands exactly how you work and feel.'

Clo's whole body clenched at the words and she flushed deep red. Her heart was thumping in her chest. It felt like it was about to break out and make a dash for it.

Her mother lifted her hand to stroke Clo's pink cheek. 'You are so pretty, you see,' she said. 'You will break hearts. And female hearts don't mend so well.'

Her mother stood up, their girl talk over, and she was free to go.

After that, her mother had been more watchful of her. Clo had to be more careful in her liaisons as she passed rampantly through sixth form. She was mindful of her mother's warnings about relationships, but her urges, confidence and the abundance of opportunities were too overwhelming for her to take too much notice. They had come back in full force at university though.

9.

'I'm going to drop you here,' said Marella, pulling off Holland Park Avenue. She parked at the bottom of the hill, the white square mansions peering down at them. 'Has Rebecca been thinking sexy thoughts?' she said.

'Oh god no,' said Clo, shaking her head.

Marella frowned.

'I'll be fine,' said Clo, gathering herself and getting out of the car.

'Ring me when she's done,' Marella said.

Clo shivered at the thought of her client being 'done' and watched Marella pull around the corner.

At least she had a hangover. It had the tendency to make her relaxed, sensuous, greedy. This client would be expecting her to perform as part of her expensive enjoyment. She needed her body to work on demand.

A warm breeze flowed down the hill. It breathed around her legs and up her skirt and shirt, caressing her body which she had left free of underwear for this appointment. It raised the shirt around her shoulders and stroked down her back. It made her feel bare and the fine hair at the back of her neck stood up. It should have been a pleasant feeling.

But she felt exposed and vulnerable. She hugged her body, trying to protect herself from the invasive breeze. She thought of Mrs Hamilton, being in her protective arms, feeling the warmth of her body and the softness of her chest below her neck. She imagined being surrounded by her perfume, enveloped in her arms again as she had been when she left the night before. She wished she had stayed longer. She could have stayed all day, and the next.

It was nearly ten years since university she realised, almost a decade without loving affection.

She tried to focus again and bring her mind back to the appointment. She imagined the client waiting for her. She could see the middle-aged woman, waiting in the gloom of her great white house up the hill, waiting to touch her and see her squirm with pleasure. The thought of the client pawing at her and fondling her made her queasy. She was repelled by the prospect of the appointment today.

Come on. She did not have time for this. She realised her tears were starting again. Come on. There was no point in this. She had been affected by someone she would never see again, someone who could never be with her and who could never love her. There was no purpose to it.

She made herself take a step forward up the hill, pushing thoughts of Mrs Hamilton away. She breathed in and put her shoulders back, tilting her chin up slightly. A smile cracked across her face and she walked up to the detached white mansion.

She looked around the quiet street and strode up to the front door to announce her arrival with the weighty brass knocker. She lifted the circular metal but the door was unlocked and opened at her touch. She assumed this was part of today's game and hesitatingly pushed through the doorway.

She couldn't see anyone inside. The large staircase was dim and unlit. The door to her left was shut, leaving her the drawing room to her right as the only option.

She called out. 'Mrs Abrahams? Mrs Abrahams?' No reply. She slowly let herself into the drawing room. The shutters on the windows were closed and she took a moment to adjust her eyes. It was furnished as she remembered – chaise longue, piano, bookcases – except for a lone chair in the middle of the parquet floor.

'Mrs Abrahams?'

She heard the front door close and the locks snap shut. The door to the drawing room was slammed by an unseen person, and footsteps receded in the hallway. It was silent for a moment.

'Do as I tell you, and I won't hurt you, unless it brings one of us pleasure.'

Clo couldn't tell where the client's gravelled voice came from. She spun around, checking the room, behind the furniture and looking for shadows beneath the doorways. The double doors connecting the drawing room and library opened, Mrs Abrahams' figure parting them with outstretched arms.

'Mrs Abrahams?' Clo said with mock alarm.

Her silhouette was neat, dressed in a tight outfit and her grey bobbed hair a dark wedge at the top. It was too dim to see any detail or the expression on her face. Mrs Abrahams took a step into the room, her sharp heels clicking on the floor.

'Turn around,' she barked.

'Mrs Abrahams, I don't....'

'Shut up and do what I say. Get the blindfold,' she ordered.

Clo meekly complied and saw a blindfold and lengths of soft cord on top of the grand piano. Mrs Abrahams' box of toys was open and ready beside them. She looked inside, wondering what the client had in store for her today. She only found a generous dispenser of lube before she was hurried along. 'Quickly!'

Clo heard Mrs Abrahams behind her. 'Now sit on the chair.'

Clo sat down meekly and tied the velvet blindfold around her head. Hands swiftly pulled her arms and fixed them to the chair behind her back. She squirmed in her seat, pretending alarm.

'Now, let's have a look at you.'

She heard Mrs Abrahams begin to walk around her, heels clicking on the hard floor, followed slowly and deliberately by the softer fall of the ball of her foot. She was in front of her. Clo could see around an edge of the blindfold and caught the shining black material of her outfit and a glint of a zip that went all the way through between her legs.

'Naughty,' Mrs Abrahams said. Clo saw teeth snarl in a smile, before the blindfold was pulled up.

Now the blindfold was completely opaque. Turning her head from one side to the other, she couldn't see any light or any shapes changing in front of her.

She stopped turning and waited. She could smell Mrs Abrahams nearby, that distinctive mix of soap, perfume and hairspray she used. Slowly, she became aware of movement closer to her. A cushion of warmer air formed close to her face and she felt moist breath on her neck. She waited in anticipation of a kiss on her neck, could almost imagine soft lips against her skin, when she felt her right nipple being ever so gently pinched. It got the response Mrs Abrahams was after. Clo gulped and flushed as a spark of desire connected her breasts straight to her clitoris. Her whole body became sensitive and heightened to the next touch.

'You dirty girl,' Mrs Abrahams said, knowingly. 'Somebody isn't wearing a bra.' Clo could tell she was smiling. She wondered if she should protest.

'It was hot, I couldn't ....'

'Shhhhh,' said Mrs Abrahams, holding a finger to Clo's lips. The finger ran slowly down Clo's chin, dropped to her chest and, with a deft touch, unhooked her shirt buttons. Her shirt was flipped open, exposing her breasts.

She could hear Mrs Abrahams stand again in front of her. She guessed she was admiring the view.

'Spread your legs.'

Clo obeyed and parted her knees. Her skirt rode up as she spread her thighs further apart. She stopped when she thought Mrs Abrahams would have a clear view.

'Oh, you're beautiful,' Mrs Abrahams breathed out, involuntarily.

Clo could hear Mrs Abrahams' breathing was already heavier, and with a shuffle in front of her, Clo felt her move closer. A soft, moist tongue licked Clo's nipple and a mouth quickly closed around it. The feeling was good, and she arched her back, forcing more of her breast into the mouth. With every pass of the tongue over her nipple, a wave of lust pulsed through her body. Clo began to groan with appreciation.

Mrs Abrahams was kneeling between her legs and Clo squeezed her with her knees. She tried to pull her closer as she writhed in time with Mrs Abrahams' kisses. A hand touched gently beneath Clo's left breast and a fingertip stroked a line from her breast, moved slowly across her abdomen, snaked seductively around her belly button and down to her hairline under the waistband of her skirt.

Clo was fully aroused, swollen and aching. All she could think was that she wanted to be touched. She squeezed Mrs Abrahams tighter, willing her towards her. A finger parted her soaking lips, and she groaned at the unexpected touch. The finger pushed gently inside and then started to slowly circle her lips. She tingled with anticipation from her feet, up her thighs, and her crotch seemed to throb around her clitoris.

'Say it,' Mrs Abrahams growled.

'Touch me,' Clo breathed.

Mrs Abrahams stopped just a millimetre away from where Clo desperately wanted her to stroke.

'Please. Touch me,' Clo begged. She tried again to pull Mrs Abrahams forward.

A soft finger finally stroked around Clo's swollen clitoris. She clenched forward, doubling over, only restrained by the cords behind her back. The finger delicately circled Clo's clitoris, sending glowing pleasure out through her legs and through her body. Her face was hot and she could feel she was already close, her clitoris standing out. She tried to push against the fingers, but Mrs Abrahams drew them away slightly. The fingertip flicked across her, teasing her at the height of her arousal. She could hardly breathe, small gasps coming out with every tantalising touch.

'What do you say?' Mrs Abrahams' voice was stern but strangled.

'Let me come.' She gasped again at another light flick across her clitoris. 'Please let me come,' she begged.

Mrs Abrahams shuffled out from between Clo's legs and Clo heard a zip scrape open. Then Mrs Abrahams was straddling her knee, pressing down her wet cunt, rubbing her lips and wiry pubic hair on Clo. Mrs Abrahams moved swiftly, humping her leg, breathing heavily and grunting.

Clo shrank back with the vivid reality pressed upon her.

Oh god, it wasn't the time to become squeamish. Mrs Abrahams was quickly bringing herself off. It was time for Clo to come.

Think of something sexy. Christ, think of something sexy. A mental collage of breasts, bottoms, arching bodies in the throes of ecstasy quickly filled her head. She desperately tried to pick one that appealed, but she couldn't. Mrs Abrahams was almost there, it was too late. She pushed herself firmly onto Mrs Abrahams' hand and thrust over the fingers as if in the last moments. She breathed heavily with the exertion and hoped that would fool Mrs Abrahams during her loss of awareness as she peaked.

Mrs Abrahams cried out in ecstasy; Clo cried out in stress and anxiety. Both slumped a second or two later after the exertion.

Mrs Abrahams stood up and untied Clo's hands. She heard Mrs Abrahams zip herself up, walk a few steps away and the library doors slammed shut.

Glad to have her hands free again, Clo shook the blood back into them. She took off the blindfold, rubbed her eyes and blinked and looked around the room. She was alone. She stood up and pushed her skirt over her wet knee and buttoned up her shirt, uncertain of what she should do next.

No sound came from the library or from the hall, and she assumed Mrs Abrahams did not desire a post-coital chat today. She headed into the hallway and was about to leave.

'A little off today I think, Rebecca.' Mrs Abrahams' voice came from behind her, out of the darkness. 'I'm not pleased.'

Clo felt light with the guilt of letting down her client and Marella. 'I'm sorry,' she said. 'Yes, not quite on form today.'

She heard the scrape of a lighter and inhalation through a cigarette. A moment later, fronds of grey smoke crept around her head.

'Am I going to have to ask Marella for another?' she asked. 'Would be a pity. You've been a marvellous little whore.'

Clo dropped her head, the earlier sadness returning with full force. Clo didn't know what to say. Her throat tightened.

'I'm sorry,' she said. 'It won't happen again.'

'Make sure it doesn't. Now leave.'

Clo heard Mrs Abrahams' footsteps recede into the house, and Clo stepped into the street.

The breeze cooled her chest and between her legs, chilling her thigh where Mrs Abrahams had relieved herself. She shivered and wrapped her arms around her body, and walked down the street. She stared down at her feet, watching the shoes of another woman clipping over the pavement. Her skin didn't feel like her own, and revulsion crept up her back.

To think that she had held Mrs Hamilton, that this body had hugged someone so special so close. She was revolted by her own body and hunched her shoulders around her head, and wished she could shake it off and shed the repellent skin.

Her face crumpled with grief and she slapped her hands over her eyes. She felt a hand gently squeeze her shoulder, but she couldn't stop the tears this time. She started to sob into her hands, tears and saliva mixing and collecting between her fingers.

'I'm sorry Clo,' Marella said. 'I shouldn't have pushed you today. I think you need a break. A proper break.'

10.

Laura saw Susan's car pull away and watched until it turned and disappeared at the end of the street. She stared at the road for a moment, until the sensation that her house was watching became too much. She turned around and looked over her small home. The windows were dark and she couldn't see Josh inside.

She went in, closing the door quietly behind her, and stood in the hallway, listening. A throaty snore came from the living room, and Laura walked in with small silent steps. Josh was lying on the sofa. He was wearing his boxers and dressing gown, curled over on his side, hugging his arms around him.

She watched his chest expand and collapse, his arms holding himself tight. His mouth had fallen open and a string of dribble connected his lip to his shoulder. His cheeks were saggy and relaxed from deep sleep.

His thinning hair stuck up in tufts. She guiltily wondered how much he had tossed and turned in his sleep, if he'd stayed up until morning and waited for her to come home. She bent down and reached out with her hand, slowly pushing it towards his head. She stretched out her fingers, as if to stroke his hair flat again, but stopped. Her fingers retracted into a fist and she stood up straight again.

She left the room and headed upstairs. The floorboards on the landing creaked as she walked up. She stood still, one foot pressed down on the landing and the other on tiptoe on the stairs. She listened and breathed out when she heard his regular snorts continue.

With one last look around, she went into the spare room. She knelt down by the bed and looked under. An empty suitcase and a grey box of books blocked her view. She pushed them aside and felt with her fingertips across the top of a box of newspapers and another of crockery. She stretched a little further and her fingers touched something cold and smooth, which scraped metallically when she scratched her nails around the edge.

The red McVitie's biscuit tin was dented and scratched. She stroked the lid, her fingers collecting a drift of dust. She felt around its square edge and squeezed. The lid popped off and let in light for the first time in nearly ten years.

Her birth certificate lay on the top: birth registered in London to Kate and David Green. She remembered the phone conversation with the registry office when she'd received the certificate in the post, and panic gripped her belly.

'There's been a mistake,' she said. 'This isn't my original birth certificate. This is the adoption version.'

'We've checked again. That's the only version on record.'

'It must have been lost?'

'I doubt it. Not for that period. I'm afraid that's all we have on record.'

'But they aren't my parents. Kate and David were always clear that they adopted me.'

'I'm sorry. I can't help you any further.'

She remembered standing in the phone booth at the foot of the college staircase, gripping the certificate, and beginning to shake with despair.

*

Laura sat at the kitchen table and sipped from a mug of tea. She stared into the garden through the French windows. Half-focussed, she saw the rectangle of grass outside, sectioned by a sea-pebble path, with black bamboo in the corner and the brushed stainless steel water feature. She tried to replace them with a yellow children's house and small trampoline. She listened for laughter and the sound of bare feet slapping on the stone patio.

She could hear a football bounce, be kicked, and land with a hush in the shrubs at the edge of the lawn. A boy and a girl giggled, and footsteps thudded across the lawn and then slapped towards the patio doors. She looked up expecting to see a small girl and taller boy peering though the window, their hands shading their eyes. The trimmed garden came back into focus through the empty window, and she took another sip from her cup.

Laura looked down at her phone on the table. The garden was reflected in its dark screen and she tipped it up slightly, not wanting to acknowledge this second look. Susan hadn't texted for an hour. Was it her turn to text? She picked up the phone and re-read the last sent message, and remembered again that it was Susan's turn.

She tapped on a new message and typed 'BTW, thanks again for last night. Love L.' She paused, her finger a fraction above the send button. Too many messages. She was indulging in her new friendship too much. She deleted the message and put her phone down.

'Hi.'

Laura spun round in her seat. Josh was still in his dressing gown. He pulled at the belt around his waist and tucked the robe defensively over his chest. He rubbed his head, and the hair stuck up with sweat.

Laura didn't reply and Josh put his hands in the pockets of the gown, his shoulders rounded. He looked down at his feet, rocking from foot to foot, and slowly looked back up at her.

He looked apprehensive. Perhaps he realised he could lose her. His expression reminded her of when he had proposed, kneeling on one knee after celebrating getting her through her first year exams, with a beaming smile that was slowly replaced with worry that he had overstepped her gratitude and the euphoria of the day.

She felt sorry for him, her best friend who wanted children with his wife. Her night's absence had tipped the balance in her favour, showing him she was the one who could walk away. He was waiting for her to dictate terms, and she felt guilty to be putting him through this.

'You've got to let me find them,' she said.

He nodded emphatically, his lips pursed. 'I know. I'm sorry, I didn't realise you felt so strongly about it.' He took a small step forward, but remained separated from her, his weight inclining forward, wanting to close the distance.

'It's never going to go away Josh. I will always want to find them. Please don't try and stop me.'

You will lose me, she thought.

He nodded enthusiastically again. 'Just, can we try to start a family as well?'

Laura felt a chill in the pit of her stomach, but she let him continue.

'It could take years.' He put his hands out defensively, before she could speak. 'And we will look for them, I promise. Just let's do it at a moderate pace, not let it take over our lives completely. Just in case it comes to nothing.'

She couldn't be angry with him. It was a reasonable request from a nice man.

*

Laura turned into the spare bedroom without thinking and looked towards the master bedroom. Perhaps she should be trying to change out of Susan's clothes in there. She listened out for Josh, and heard the scrape of a metal spatula in a saucepan from the kitchen. She could smell onions frying, and she wondered if he was cooking spaghetti bolognese. He knew he was good at that. And she knew it was also an excuse to open a bottle of red wine.

The McVitie's tin was on the spare bed. Had she left it there? She reached down and flicked through the old letters, photographs and notes, trying to remember how she'd left them. Had Josh been in? She hastened through the contents and checked them against her mental catalogue. She piled the photos, separated the letters and held the miscellany in her hand.

On the top lay her only photo of her adoptive parents. She hadn't looked at it since Josh persuaded her to put it away with all the other reminders of her past search.

The white border of the colour photograph was curled and frayed, the veneer of glossy coating cracked in places like dry skin. The colours were too orange for real life. Everything looked washed out and even the sky looked a shade of brown. In the photo, her parents looked towards the camera smiling, and her father had his arm around her mother's shoulder. There was a lake in the background. They were standing on a simple wooden jetty that led out into the water.

In the distance, around the water's edge, were dense deciduous trees, and on the right bank a cottage or farm building made of orange-brown stone. She turned over the photo and read the pencil writing on the back: 'Middle Heyford'. She put the photo back and slid the tin under the bed.

Different emotions and convictions simmered inside as she walked down the stairs. She turned up the hallway, but stopped when she heard her phone beep. Josh shuffled in the kitchen and crossed the view made by the hall doorway. She saw him reach towards the table and pick up her phone. He glanced at it, and then put it back, before crossing the gap out of sight. The sound of stirring metal on metal resumed.

The emotions that curdled inside turned indignant, and she marched into the kitchen. She looked at him, frowning at his back, surrounded by steam.

'You got a message,' he said over his shoulder.

She blinked, surprised at his confession, and picked up her phone. 'Message from Susan'. She wanted to read it. And then she would want to re-read it.

'I think it was from Susan,' he said.

She nodded and discarded the phone, and leaned against the table, trying to show it was of no urgency.

He turned around and picked up a glass of red wine. His face was pink and moist from the steam and wine. He smiled at her like a child. He had a look of remorse, knowing he had been wrong, but wanting to be loved again.

She put her face in her palms and breathed out noisily through the gaps in her fingers. She breathed in and out and her face warmed with her breath. She rubbed her eyes with her fingertips and dropped her hands to the table top.

'I'm sorry Josh. You're right. We should think about having a family. Before I get too old.'

She looked up and saw him beaming. He put down the glass and walked towards her, tentatively looking up at her face, and tried to catch her eye as he cautiously approached.

'That's all I ask. That we don't leave it and forget about it, until it's too late.'

He reached out, resting his fingertips on her shoulder, and pulled her forward when she didn't object to his touch. He wrapped his arms around her. She could hear his breathing, deep and stuttering with emotion. His large hand held the back of her head and pulled her into his shoulder.

'I love you Laura. I would do anything for you.'

He kissed the side of her head, his lips pressing into her hair, and squeezed her.

'We will look, I promise,' he said.

He turned to kiss her, his lips wet on her cheek, and again closer to her mouth. He lifted her head up, his hands either side of her face. He closed his eyes and closed his lips around hers. She heard his breathing become coarse and felt the change in rhythm of his movement. His swaying from foot to foot became more regular, as he rubbed his body against hers. He started to walk her backwards out of the kitchen and towards the sofa, his lips not stopping sliding over hers.

Laura said nothing. She let her husband seduce and kiss her, the way he thought she liked.

But she allowed herself to think of Susan, and what she looked like beneath her dressing gown. She wondered what she felt like, what she smelled like, with her legs open and lips wet. She imagined her warm and moist on her fingers, and wondered what she would sound like if she pushed her fingers slowly inside her. She wondered how her face would look if she circled slowly round her clitoris with her thumb and imagined bending down to kiss her breasts.

As Josh pushed her down on to the sofa, she felt herself pulse and moisten.

Part 3. A Family Affair

1.

Clo pulled the car off the road into a clearing, which overlooked Middle Heyford in the valley below.

'I thought we should call Mum when we were near by,' she said.

Amelia nodded in response.

Clo groped for her mobile in the car door, and stretched to the dashboard to switch off Radio Four. It was quiet. No whirring car rumbling over the road, no chatter from the radio, and no London background hum. The silence made Clo's ears alert and strain in an attempt to hear something in their surroundings. The car began to creak as it cooled and the metal contracted.

They were on a ridge, the highest point for several miles. The patchwork of ploughed earth, yellow crops and green pastures undulated in waves below, criss-crossed with stone walls and broken by small patches of trees. The mercury pool of the lake shone in the afternoon sun. The beech, birch and oak trees had lost their leaves, and a yellow ring of shed foliage surrounded the lake and beside the streams towards the village.

The village looked naked. In summer, only the church spire was visible above the cluster of trees. Only the old yews, smudges of green-black, stood out today and the church and houses were exposed.

Clo rubbed her thumb over the buttons on her mobile. She would rather spend the afternoon with Amelia watching the valley. She turned to her grandmother, and Amelia returned a look that gave away the same reluctance.

Clo reminded herself of the reason for their visit and the necessary thawing of hostilities to a cooler level.

'It'll be nice to see Lottie,' she said.

Amelia nodded. 'And Elly. I bet she's grown.'

Neither moved; Clo glanced once more over the valley. The single carriage road rolled out beneath them, and Clo followed it with her eyes all the way to the village.

'Come on. Let's just get it over with,' said Amelia, squeezing Clo's hand.

Turning the ignition, Clo crunched the car out of the parking space and they started the descent into the village.

*

Clo stared at the biscuit-coloured stone cottage through the car window. The front garden still had the same basic shape: a square of soft lawn with borders, surrounded by a white painted wooden fence. The roses had been replaced with dahlias, past their best now. Her favourite rambling rose had gone. It used to grow up past the sitting room window and climb over the crumbling walls towards what had been her bedroom. She used to be able to reach out of the window and pull the flowers towards her face, a handful of soft, cool fragrance. The memory of the smell made her smile.

The front door was painted a different colour. It used to be her father's favourite blue-grey, the colour they saw on the shutters of French houses on their holidays. She remembered him painting it very carefully and slowly. 'Will remind us of being on holiday every day,' he'd said, smiling down at her.

She heard the latch on the front door rattle and her mother stood in front of it. It was an ordinary navy blue now. Clo waved and helped Amelia out of the car.

'Darling!' her mother said, walking down the path with outstretched hands. She pulled Clo towards her and kissed her with closed lips on the cheek.

Alice looked down at her. 'You're very casual today.' She delivered the negative observation in a way that sounded like a pleasantry.

Clo understood everything the comment implied. She looked unfeminine in those jeans and that T-shirt. Why didn't she wear something other than pumps, Converse, trainers, whatever they called them these days? She shouldn't be so lesbian in front of Lottie. She didn't want Lottie to ask questions about that kind of thing when she was so young.

'Alice,' Clo heard her grandmother say behind them.

They both stiffened at the sound. The back of Clo's head and her spine seemed over-sensitive. Her mother dropped her grip and turned her attention to Amelia.

'Mother,' Alice responded. 'Can I help you into the house?' Her teeth were held tight together and her words hissed.

Clo did not turn around and walked up the path to seek refuge in the cottage. She had to wait a moment after ducking into the sitting room to let her eyes adjust to the change. She put her hands out to balance herself. Slowly the dimness receded around the shapes of the sofa, the bookcase and she found herself in front of Rob, her brother-in-law. She tried and failed to pay attention to him long enough to say hello. Both of them were too diverted by Lottie who sat on the sofa holding baby Elly on her knee.

Lottie still had the extra weight she'd gained from pregnancy, and she had a new mother's face, rosy and plump. She held baby Elly facing towards Clo and Rob. Clo knelt down in front of her sister and leaned over the baby to kiss Lottie's forehead.

'You are looking amazingly well,' she said. Lottie still appeared overwhelmed by the happiness and joy that Elly brought her.

'And how are you doing little sweetheart?' Clo said to Elly. She kissed the top of the baby's head that still had swirls of bleached downy hair. The baby's skin was soft and felt too vulnerable, even for her lips. It was warm and she inhaled Elly's scent when she breathed in.

'She still smells like a new baby.' Clo grinned at her sister. Lottie grinned back nodding. Clo put her hand out to Elly. The baby stared at her with wide blue eyes. She was gurgling and dribbling, and intent on putting her fingers in her mouth.

'Teething, I think, soon,' said Lottie.

Clo tried to tempt Elly by offering her hand, and the baby clung to her finger and spread strings of saliva over her knuckles. Elly gripped her finger firmly and then dragged it inside her mouth. Clo laughed at the baby's persistence at filling its mouth.

'Dad says she looks like you did at this age,' Lottie said.

'Really?' said Clo.

Lottie bounced Elly gently on her knee. 'Are you going to be a bright little girl like your beautiful aunt?' she said in a light voice.

Clo's chest clenched at the compliment from her sister. Lottie would have been too young to understand her disgrace.

Maybe her parents had never told her or explained why her big sister would never be coming home after university.

Clo leaned forward and kissed Lottie on the forehead. 'No. Pretty and bright and happy like her mum.'

Lottie looked into Clo's eyes, gave her a sad smile and then looked up, her mouth falling open.

'Oh! Your father doesn't know what he's talking about.'

Clo flinched at the sound of her mother in the room. Alice swooped down between them and snatched the baby away.

'She's just like Lottie. Or Rob even. Your parents say you were blond when you were little. Hard to imagine you as a little, blond boy,' she said, baby carried in one arm and her other hand pressed onto Rob's chest. Clo's mother smiled, but let her hand linger too long, her palm brushing over Rob's pectoral muscles. The gesture made Clo's skin ripple with revulsion.

Her mother passed the wide-eyed baby to Amelia with stiff arms. Amelia smiled and her cheeks coloured as she glowed at the baby. Amelia pursed her lips forward to say 'Who's the prettiest baby girl then? Who's the prettiest girl?' and Clo laughed, hearing the indulgent voice coming from Amelia's lips.

With her mother distracted, Clo turned to Lottie. 'Is Dad about?'

Lottie dragged her gaze away from the baby and indicated that Clo would find their father in his usual hiding place in the garden.

2.

Clo stepped out of the back door onto the stone patio and walked across the centimetre-perfect grass beneath the fruit trees. The orchard ended in a white fence and a gate led to a narrow strip of land, which twisted out of sight of the house. It was uncut and long, dry grass whispered against her jeans as she approached the wooden summer house, hidden at the end of the garden.

She could see her father through the windows as she approached. He was at his desk, bent over a pile of printed paper – an essay or dissertation. She stepped onto the small veranda and peered in. He'd moved more of his belongings in. There were more shelves and books than there used to be; his novels and newspapers were here as well as his academic textbooks. Behind the desk at the back was a sofa. It looked long enough to lie on. There was a small fridge beside it with a kettle and a cup on top. He must have had the mains connected while she'd been away.

She stepped closer to the window and tapped on the glass. Her father glanced up from a text and peered over the top of his glasses. She smiled at him and opened the door as he stood up to greet her.

'I didn't hear you arrive,' he said, smiling and pulling her into his chest. He squeezed her, not letting go, and rocked her from side to side as she let her head rest beside his chin. She felt him stroke her hair and kiss the top of her head, automatically smelling her hair.

'It's good to see you,' he said, holding her at arms' length, so they could look at each other.

It had taken her a long time to realise how much she'd taken after her father. Her colouring and blond hair had been so obviously inherited from her mother. But she was slimmer, less hour-glass shaped than her mother and Lottie, tempered by her father's slim build and physique.

Her face shape was like her father's. He had high cheek bones and full lips for a man. He was near to retirement, but he didn't seem old enough to be a pensioner. He had aged though. His hair had more grey than its original light-brown, and lines tracked deeply across his forehead and creased to the corners of his eyes. She wondered what he would do if he retired and no longer had an excuse to work in the summer house.

'Sit down,' he said, gesturing to a chair on the other side of the desk. 'You made it OK? Amelia is in good spirits?'

'Yes, she's fine,' Clo smiled.

'And you're both getting by?'

Clo nodded at his habitual inquiry to their finances.

'Good, good,' he said, sitting down. He frowned a little. 'You know I'm always most grateful for you taking care of Amelia.'

Clo shrugged. 'It's no hardship,'

'Yes, you always got on so well.' He paused. 'I just wanted to let you know that I would never have let her go into a home.' He put his hands together and rubbed his entwined fingers across his knuckles. 'But you taking care of her has made my position considerably easier by removing that as a possibility.'

Clo blushed at his candidness.

'You must tell me if you ever need money,' he continued. 'I have funds that your mother is not aware of, and I would have no hesitation about giving them to you and Amelia.'

Clo looked at him, but said nothing, and he waved his hand in the air to dismiss the issue.

He reached across the table, smiled and squeezed her hand. 'It is good to see you. I know Skype and email are good. Nothing like seeing you in person though.'

'I know,' Clo said, trying to hide her sadness.

'You know, I'll be in London more often soon. I've a set of guest lectures at the British Museum. It's a course for members of the public. Make a change to teach people who are interested.'

Clo laughed. 'Can I come and see you?'

'Yes, of course. But I was hoping to pop in and see you and Amelia while I'm down there. Be nice to see you both alone.'

'Please keep emailing though,' said Clo

He nodded, an undercurrent of sadness visible at the sides of his mouth. His expression switched into a smile. 'You've seen Lottie and Elly?' he asked, beginning to beam again.

Clo nodded and grinned back.

'She's all grown up, our Lottie,' he said, still smiling. He sounded relieved.

'Do you see her much?' Clo asked.

'No. Like you, we hadn't seen her since the birth. She must have been busy caring for the new baby. And she's very settled in Edinburgh. Rob's parents are nearby and I think she likes that they can help out and want to be involved,' he said, the undercurrent rippling across his features again.

They both sat in silence, letting the implications of what he'd said settle and then fade away.

'How about a whisky and a cigarette?' he said, grinning almost naughtily.

Clo raised both eyebrows in surprise. He pulled open a desk drawer and threw a packet of Marlboro Lights and a tin of Café Crème cigars on the table.

'Not that I really condone smoking, but I've found that I really do quite enjoy just the one in the afternoons.'

Clo picked out a Marlboro Light from the packet.

'Your mother doesn't like them of course. But she can't really complain if I have them in here.' He shrugged, looking defiant.

He opened another drawer and clinked out two small whisky glasses and bottle of Lagavulin. The cork squeaked and popped out of the neck, and the spirit glugged into the glasses. He passed one glass to Clo and then raised his to chink against it.

'To Lottie,' he said happily.

'To Lottie,' replied Clo.

They both took a sip of whisky. Clo let it sit in her mouth and roll down the sides of her tongue. She let the vapours form in her mouth and rise into her nose. The smell was smoky and peaty, and the concentrated alcohol sent a pleasant warm rush up her nose, behind her eyes and through her head. She closed her eyes to enjoy the sensation.

She opened them again, hearing a click of her father's lighter and leaned across to let him light her cigarette. They both sat back in their chairs. Clo breathed in a satisfying lung-full of smoke, and Edward rolled the cigar smoke around his mouth and puffed out small rings of smoke, like a train.

'Been practising,' he said grinning.

*

'She looks like you,' her father said, after they had been sitting smoking in silence for a while. 'You were just like Elly at that age, but your eyes were even more blue.'

107

'Please don't emphasise that to mum and Lottie though,' Clo said.

He looked confused.

'I don't want them worrying that she'll turn out like me,' she said.

He had a serious and thoughtful expression on his face. Clo was uncomfortable, unsure that he wouldn't, in an uncharacteristic bullish moment, argue with her.

That was their greatest similarity, their temperament: quiet and gentle with a chronic fear of confrontation. She never argued back at her mother. Her father had never given her cause to argue. It was with Sally that she'd first had a serious argument, after her finals.

Leaving the exam hall on the day of the last exam, Clo headed straight for the pub and a couple of pints with the other French finalists. She left early, and cycled home to the terraced house that Sally owned as her landlady. Clo was eager to see her after several days packed with revision.

Sal sat in the living room on the sofa by the window. Clo squinted to see her face, but couldn't make out her expression with the bright light behind her.

'You've been drinking,' she said.

'Just a couple of pints' Clo said, smiling.

'Why didn't you come home straight away? I've barely seen you this week.'

'I left the drinks early to come back. I was just saying goodbye to everyone. It's probably the last time we'll all meet up.'

Sally crossed her arms. 'Would you rather celebrate with them than me?'

Clo frowned, confused that wanting to celebrate with her fellow students was wrong.

'I wanted both I suppose,' she said.

'Is this how it's going to be?' Sally said. 'When you work in London? Are you going to want to go out with your colleagues instead?'

Clo's feeling of warmth and cheer dissipated. All their arguments, no matter how they started, seem to turn to this matter.

'I do want to live with you.' Clo stepped forward. 'I just want to stay with Amelia in London while I settle into the job.'

'The commute isn't bad. Thousands of people do it everyday,' Sal said.

'I know. And I will. But I think I'll be working long hours…'

'Well, maybe this just isn't going to work,' Sal said this time, cutting off Clo's defence.

The statement silenced Clo. She was taken aback by the verbal slap. It felt like the wind had been knocked out of her, and she couldn't force her chest open to breathe. Her eyes had adjusted to the light and she could see Sal's face. It was contorted with anger, and she stared at Clo.

Clo croaked out, 'Is that what you really want?'

In retrospect she knew it hadn't been the response Sally had been aiming for. She'd wanted Clo to beg her to stay with her, realise how much she loved her, cave in to her demands to live with her in Oxford. But Clo had been too naïve back then to realise. She had taken Sally at her word. Why else would someone say something as crushing and final as that, unless they meant it? She'd seen it too many times in other people's relationships since to mistake it again.

'If this is how it's going to be, then yes,' said Sal, inviting Clo to repeal her wish to live in London.

*

Her father shuffled on the other side of the desk. He looked upset, sitting on a mountain of things he wished he could say, but not knowing where to start. Clo looked at him, pleading with her eyes not to start a confrontation. The impasse was broken and the awkward moment diffused by Rob tapping on the summer house window.

'Your presence is required.' He grinned. 'Alice wants you to sort out the lamb.'

Her father got out of his chair, resigned to carving duty. As he passed by the door, he handed over the cigar end to Rob who squeezed her father on the shoulder and took a puff or two as the older man left for the house.

3.

Clo wondered at the size of the whisky that she had drunk when she stumbled back into the house. Lottie was upstairs putting Elly to bed. Everyone else was in the kitchen. She made her way up the stairs and came to a halt in the doorway to Lottie's old room.

The walls were still covered with posters. The pink wallpaper was patched with pop stars, tennis players and horses. Roger Federer grimaced as he punched a forehand, hanging above Justine Henin, biting her lip in a backhand. Lottie's single bed still had the same flowery cover as when Clo had left home. The room appeared ready for her sister to come home after a day at school.

Lottie was sitting on the bed, looking down into a travel cot on the floor. Clo couldn't see the baby's face, but small hands stretched up, swatting the air, reaching for her mother who cooed at her from above.

Lottie beckoned her in. Clo mouthed 'no' and gestured taking a smoke and drink. She didn't think the baby was ready for the vapours of Lagavulin and Marlboro Lights. Lottie rolled her eyes and grinned. Clo blew them both a kiss and turned to go downstairs but glanced into her own room before she did.

There was no trace of her in it. It could have been a different room in a different house. She stepped inside. Her posters of Ellen and Xena wouldn't have lasted long after her departure. Her single bed had gone. Her wardrobe with a built-in desk, where she'd done her homework, had also disappeared. She remembered her maths book in the drawer, hiding the pictures of Catherine Deneuve and Francoise Desmarais. They were patched together with Sellotape after her mother had torn them off the walls.

The room had been turned into another tasteful guest room: a soft cream carpet, a double bed with an oak frame and a matching chest of drawers. She stepped around Rob and Lottie's luggage on the floor and peered out of the window. That was the only thing left of her room, the view.

She turned her back on it and attempted the narrow stairs. She banged into the wall and put her hand out to steady herself. She knocked a photo and the frame scraped against the wall, swinging left and right, coming to rest at an angle with the rest of the pictures. She reached out to straighten it and looked at the picture of Lottie holding a roll of parchment tied in a ribbon. She still wore her glasses at university. It made Clo smile. Lottie looked very studious in them.

She looked down at the other photos. There used to be pictures of Clo and later Lottie from school, glossy portraits with swirling blue and brown backgrounds. They had been replaced by pictures of Lottie and Rob's wedding and professional photos of Rob, Lottie and baby Elly. It was odd seeing the photos, noticing her absence from them. It was as if she had been rubbed out of her own existence.

But they were photos of defining moments that her parents were proud of. She had never gone back for her own graduation ceremony. She had never begun that fast-track career in the civil service. What was there for her parents to be proud of? She had skipped over the rites of passage and had ended up with the job category of sex worker.

She slumped onto the sofa, feeling hazy from the alcohol, and let her head fall back on the cushion. Amelia shuffled through from the kitchen. She was carrying two large glasses of red wine and an unsettling expression. Her face was dark and she shook. Did Clo imagine it or did she hear her mutter 'That fucking woman' under her breath?

'Here you go darling,' she said, forcing amiability through her tight expression. Clo took the swirling glass of wine, before Amelia's agitation spilled it.

Amelia lowered herself next to her on the sofa and puffed. Clo put out her hand to hold Amelia, who squeezed back with a surprising force. They sat in silence. Amelia took a couple of large gulps of her wine and Clo did the same. She hoped the alcohol would make her relax and stop the clenching of her stomach in anticipation of a row between Amelia and her mother.

She heard footsteps coming from the kitchen. She started to rise from the sofa; her heart beat faster and her face flushed. The appearance of her father postponed her flight reaction, and she sank back again.

'Top up?' he said, striding over with a bottle of red wine to refill their glasses. He seemed worried as well. The bottle clinked on the glasses as he poured. He stood back, smiling but his shoulders were tensed.

'So,' he said. 'I believe you went to a wedding recently? Anyone I know?'

Eager to break the silence, Clo answered him. 'Yes, it was Hannah and her partner. You know, Laura's sister-in-law.'

The steps that her words had covered stopped in the doorway, and her mother stood glaring at all three of them.

'A wedding?' she enquired.

Clo coughed, clearing her throat as it seemed to be closing and gagging. 'A civil partnership ceremony,' she clarified.

Her mother looked at the glass and tea towel in her hands and polished the glass. She spun it round, examining it, and rubbed it again.

'Ridiculous trying to pretend two women can have a marriage.' Her eyes were chilly and Clo wanted to hide. 'You know how I feel about this matter,' Alice said.

Amelia spoke more slowly and calmly than Clo would have expected. 'Hannah and Melanie have had a long and stable relationship for eight years now. They are some of the most well balanced, loving people I've had the pleasure of meeting. Having not met them, I can't see how you could have any objection to them being able to marry.'

Her mother had snapped her stare away from Clo and aimed it at Amelia.

'No-one will persuade me that two women are better off in a relationship than with a man,' Alice said.

Clo realised she was beginning to cower and curl up. She peeked through her fringe and saw her father shuffling from foot to foot.

'Yes, there are bad relationships between women…' Amelia said.

Clo's heart beat faster at the conversation turning to specifics.

'…but there are bad relationships between men and women as well,' Amelia went on.

'You know what I'm talking about Mother,' Alice said, raising her voice. Clo thought she did know what she was talking about, and she flushed with the realisation that they were talking about Sal.

'And you know what I'm talking about,' shouted Amelia, getting to her feet.

Clo felt ill. Her head pounded and her whole body throbbed with the force of her heart pumping volumes of blood and energy into her limbs, ready to run from the scene. She swallowed and breathed more deeply. She started to rock. Please don't mention Sally. Not while Lottie's here.

'I cannot stand by and hear you spout this homophobic rubbish any longer,' Amelia was shouting somewhere above Clo's head. 'You've been poisoning Clo for years with your insidious, undermining nonsense. Have you any idea of the damage you've done? The people it's still affecting to this day?' Amelia was almost screaming at Alice.

Clo groaned, wishing Amelia wouldn't defend her. Her position was indefensible and she wasn't worth defending. She had used to think what her mother had told her was nonsense as well. How two women in a relationship were too much. How the feelings that could be unleashed were too powerful when someone who knows you so well, knows how you work that intimately, gets that close to you.

*

She hadn't seen Sally for several days after she had left her house, distraught at the ending of their relationship. She had slept on Laura's floor. Clo needed to pack her belongings for the last time, to spend the summer at home, before starting her London job in September. She left a note for Sally saying when she would call round, so that she could be out if she wanted to. Clo did not receive a reply and went round, wondering if Sally would leave her things outside.

She took a deep breath, fighting back the tears, and strode up to the door. There were no boxes outside and no note. She knocked. She didn't have to wait long. The door was vigorously pulled open by a young woman. Clo recognised her from photos Sally kept in the sitting room. She'd never met Sally's daughter before. She looked down at Clo from the advantage of the step.

'Is Sal in?' Clo asked. 'I need to collect my things.'

The daughter half closed the door again, reaching for a coat from behind. She stepped out of the hallway and brushed past Clo on the pathway.

'Five minutes. You can see her for five minutes. No more. She's in a real mess and I don't want you upsetting her.' She turned and left before Clo could protest that she wasn't the one who had broken up with Sal.

Clo stepped into the hallway. She listened out for movement, trying to determine where Sally was. She couldn't hear anything downstairs. She pushed the sitting room door open and called her name, but there was no reply. She searched the dining room and saw the kitchen beyond was empty. There was no response when she looked out the back door and called down the garden.

She returned to the hallway and stood at the foot of the stairs, reluctant to go up into the bedroom uninvited. She called, cleared her voice, and then called out again, loudly enough for anyone to hear her.

She heard running water. A tap had been turned on. Had Sal been in the bathroom unable to hear her? Despite being naked in bed with her last week, she was embarrassed about the prospect of walking in on Sal in the bathroom. She hesitated. It didn't sound right. The tap running into water sounded too loud. The bathroom door wasn't shut. Sal should have been able to hear her.

Clo felt cold. All warmth seemed to drain from her veins and out of the ends of her limbs. Her legs trembled as she ran up the stairs, taking two steps at a time. She was in full cold panic by the time she crashed open the bathroom door.

Sally did not turn round. She was bending over the basin. Her hair was knotted and greasy, hanging in clumps around her face. Her right hand was covered in wet, bright blood. There was a dark ring around her wrist, streaming blood into the bowl of water below. But the bloodied hand held a razor blade.

As Clo entered the room, Sally held the sharp edge to her left wrist and sliced over her blue veins and artery, letting the skin peel up on either side. She must not have cut deep enough on her right wrist. It was bleeding freely, but it was nothing like the spurts of blood that gushed out of Sally's other wrist.

Clo cried out and rushed towards her. She grabbed both of Sally's wrists and tried to pull her away from the sink. Sally was already drooping with the shock and dropped the razor blade. She slumped to the floor. Clo lost her grip on her arms, her hands slipping in the blood.

Sally's arm oozed blood in pulses over Clo as she tried to get control of Sally's limbs. Clo's T-shirt was wet against her chest and she had a streak of arterial spray across her face, which ran down her forehead and into her eyes.

She squeezed Sally's wrists trying to stop the alarming blood loss. Panic stricken, she realised there was nothing else she could do while she held Sally's arms. She had never heard herself scream uncontrollably before. She was unaware that it was she who was making the noise. It was a cross between a cry for help and a wail of despair.

A passerby heard Clo's horrified scream. He called an ambulance as soon as he saw the scene in the bathroom and Clo waited, clinging onto Sal's wrists and her life. She was exhausted, holding in Sal's blood, willing her to survive. Sally's behaviour was becoming altered and she was cold by the time the ambulance arrived. It pulled in at the same time as Sally's daughter returned home. She jumped in the ambulance with her mother and left the house with Clo sitting exhausted in a pool of Sally's blood.

Clo had no idea how long she stayed there. She was soaked from head to toe. The blood was beginning to dry and crack. When she moved her fingers they were sticky. It was the smell that revived her. The blood reeked. It smelled metallic and the older blood was starting to sour. The smell and sight of it made her want to gag.

Still covered in blood, she phoned Laura from the hallway. She sat on the stairs in shock until Laura arrived. Laura cleaned her up, gave her clothes and took her to the hospital where she waited almost in a waking coma for news of Sally.

They wouldn't let her see Sally and would not give her any news. She was not a member of the family, and Sally's daughter had not left the bedside to relay any progress. Clo sat in the waiting area in front of the A&E desk and waited, staring at the floor.

She noticed how thirsty she had become. Her tongue was dry and her mouth felt furry and tasted unpleasant. She had a headache that felt as if it could crack open her skull. She stood up and looked around. Everyone was rushing around her. No-one had time to show her where to get water.

She wandered wide-eyed around the corridors near the entrance. She was in a state of confusion and half delirious. It took so long to read the signs on doors. She had stared uncomprehending at a sign towards the X-Ray room for several minutes.

She found a door with the familiar silhouette of a woman in a skirt. She drank from the taps from a washbasin. The water was warm and tasted slimy and of chemicals. She slurped several handfuls and then doused her face. She let the tap run, listening to the water, and stared into the mirror at nothing that was reflected there.

It may have been hours again when she returned to the waiting area. She opened the double doors and saw Sally's daughter across the waiting area at the entrance to the ward. She was talking to Clo's parents. Laura must have called her father.

Sally's daughter was pale but angry, and a look of vindictiveness flashed across her face when her eyes caught Clo. Alice followed her gaze and fixed Clo with a stare.

Sally's daughter still talked, facing Clo but talking to Alice. The more the mouth moved, the more disgusted her mother's face became. Clo could only stand and watch, blinking slowly, unable to move and counter any of the accusations. The daughter stopped talking. They both stared at Clo across the waiting area, Sally's daughter with hate and Alice with displeasure.

Her mother turned and walked towards the exit, leaving, and leaving without Clo. Her father stood in the waiting area. He looked sick and ashamed and stared down at his feet. It seemed as if he couldn't raise his head to look at his daughter.

Clo almost cried out to him. But he turned and left the waiting area without glancing back.

*

'You saw what it did to Sally. How can you think that was right? How was that good or natural?' she heard her mother spit across the sitting room.

'Because it was nothing like before. It was completely different,' her grandmother said.

The room had frozen with her sentence. Clo started to come to and dared peer up for the first time. Her mother was leaning forward, staring at Amelia. Her father looked ill. He stared at his feet, paralysed not for the first time by his inability to defy his wife and defend Amelia and Clo.

Her mother stood up straight and collected herself. She put down the glass and crossed her arms.

'Get out,' she said, with a look of loathing. 'Get out of my house.'

4.

Laura only remembered snapshots of Delhi. Her adoptive parents, Kate and David Green, were ex-pats from England and lived there until she was four. She remembered the noise. There was always noise in Delhi: people, cars, cows, machinery on construction sites, horns of the odd small taxis that whirred around. *Tuk-tuks* they were called. It was one of her favourite words. She thought she remembered her mother pointing to them. She sounded like a great clucking hen, 'tuk tuk, tuk tuk', as she pointed to the bug-like car and bike hybrids.

She'd only been in a *tuk-tuk* once, with her father. She remembered being excited by the prospect of it. Her mother hadn't been sure – there were so many accidents on the streets of Delhi and *tuk-tuks* were not safe compared with their old Mercedes. Her father had sat in the middle of the back seat and put her between his knees, away from the vulnerable open sides of the vehicle. She could see his face in the mirror on the front window. He was grinning.

Laura didn't know where they went. She remembered a huge roundabout where there was more traffic than usual. The air was brown with exhaust fumes and dust, and she could barely make out the circle of buildings that loomed over the traffic. They seemed to circle for hours.

Delhi smelled. It could smell nice. An old lady pushed some flowers into her face once, when she was walking with Kate. The woman begged, reaching out to her mother with a toughened old hand, while trying to seduce Laura with the pretty flowers. The petals were soft and cool and caressed her warm face. They smelled clean. Not like a lot of Delhi. A lot of Delhi smelled bad. Soil and animal faeces created dust clouds in summer, and the smell of rotting animals filled her nose and lungs so that she could taste it.

Laura remembered smelling the clean air when they moved away from the city. They moved north into Uttar Pradesh, across the plains and to the foothills of the Himalayas. They had stopped the car when her mother spied a break in the trees. The plains rolled out below them, flat and enormous, into the horizon.

She remembered her mother leaving the car and stretching her arms above her head. She stood on the side of the road overlooking the plains. She was wearing a dark green *salwar kameez* and she put her hands on her hips. Her mother had closed her eyes and made a long noisy inhalation through her nose. Her chest and belly rose, filling with air, and she gasped out through her mouth. 'Smells fresh like England, like the fields of Oxfordshire,' she said smiling. Laura had imitated her. Standing next to her mother in her cotton dress, she placed her hands on her hips, breathed in through her nose and tried to determine what England smelled like.

They moved to an ex-pat farm, as they called it. Her aunt sent her books from England about farms with tractors, green fields, hens, cows, a farmer and his wife. But it didn't look like any of those. It was a complex of wooden houses, a church, a hall and even an outdoor swimming pool. Most of the people there were the families of her father's colleagues. He worked for a civil engineering company, building a huge dam in a valley of the foothills.

Sometimes her dad had to stay away at work for days, leaving her mother and Laura at the farm. She wasn't lonely though. Most weeks she had school and the other children to play with. Then there were the children of the servants who worked in the canteen and cleaned the houses. She wasn't sure why they didn't go to school. They got to cook in the kitchen instead of doing lessons. She liked the kitchens. They smelled of spices, lentils and hot ghee. There always seemed to be a pot of *dhal* on the big stove, plopping and puffing away. She liked the oven best though. It put out an intense dry heat when you went near it, and it smelled of seared kebabs and breads. They ate a lot of Indian food. Even when they ate English food, the food still had a hint of yellow turmeric and fried onions about it.

One year, her mother became very fat and then had a baby. The first she knew about it was her mother and father embracing in the kitchen. Tears were running down their cheeks. He held her face and kissed her tears and eyes. He kept looking at her, holding her face in front of his, laughing and crying and then kissing again.

She remembered them approaching her, standing tall over her. They had their arms linked around each other, fingertips squeezing dents into their sides. Her father had knelt down and told her, 'We're going to have a baby,' as if that was most incredible thing in the world. 'Isn't that exciting?' he said. Laura hadn't known whether it was exciting or not. It was funny how he hadn't said, 'You're going to have a sister'.

As Jenny turned into a toddler, growing hair and beginning to look more like an individual, people remarked on how much she resembled Kate. Laura could see it too. They both had as dark hair as white people got, almost blue in a certain light. They both had sparkling blue eyes, which made the servants' children stare.

'Do I look like my mummy?' she asked one day, as her mother alternated between making dinner and passing pieces of carrot to Jenny in the high chair.

Her mother had turned to her shocked, her face pale. She'd stopped cutting up the vegetables and dropped to her knees. She'd stared straight into Laura's eyes and stroked her hair away from her face. Her mother was too choked to say anything. Her eyes looked over Laura's face, searching from one feature to another. 'I don't know sweetheart,' she said. 'I can't remember.' She pulled Laura close. 'I think it's time we asked your aunt to send us a picture,' her mother said. But Laura never heard anything else about it.

She remembered their last summer in India. She was seven years old. The plains below the farm had turned brown. It was the height of the dry season, and months of heat had scorched the earth. The air was so laden with dust that it burned your cheeks when the wind blew. She remembered chasing columns of dust that magically appeared in the playground, swirling around in pillars that whistled around the buildings.

The dogs and cats sat around in the shade all day, only stretching and yawning, before coming out to play at night. Her father and the neighbour from across the farm stood on the veranda. The neighbour was sweating. Strands of greying hair were slicked back over his red scalp and his usually crisp-ironed shirt sagged with sweat.

'Monsoon's late this year. Doesn't even feel humid yet,' he said.

'No, not a sign of it. Extremely late,' her father agreed, fanning himself with a hat.

Jenny and her mother were inside. Jenny was poorly. Her mother couldn't keep her cool in the heat. She was worried, Laura recognised. She was tired as well. Jenny had woken them all up crying three nights in a row. Her mum joined them on the veranda.

She looked exasperated Laura thought, enunciating the word in her head.

Her mother strode towards Laura and held her hand. She pointed to the neighbour. 'Diane and Philip have made some lemonade and are going to play cards tonight. Would you like to stay over?' she asked her. Laura had said yes straight away.

She loved playing cards with the neighbours. They smiled at her indulgently when she asked if she could stay up late. She sat between them on their rattan sofa while they taught her how to play cribbage. She loved the wooden board and the pegs and holes, and cradled the cribbage board in her arms.

She slept heavily, her mind filled with cribbage terms, while an electrical fault in her parents' home sparked, smouldered and then erupted into an inferno that consumed the tinder-dry house and everyone inside.

*

Laura remembered the British High Commission, waiting in a corridor of cool white stone. She sat on her hands and swung her feet beneath the chair. Her neighbour was talking to a man in a suit who had beads of sweat on his forehead. He kept raising his eyebrows. His forehead creased, resembling a packet of Plasticine, and the sweat dripped into his bushy eyebrows.

'Yes, we've contacted David's sister in England. She knows nothing about her. To be honest, she was surprised that I expected her to know anything. It sounds like they didn't get on particularly. She thought they'd adopted her over here – some poor little Indian girl. Not a clue she was white.'

'Are there any records of her adoption here?'

The man opened his mouth and no words came out. He lifted his shoulders.

'No point even trying?' her neighbour asked.

The man shook his head. 'But assuming she's British, it's more likely that we would have found a record than not, even here, so I think it's more fruitful to search in the UK first.'

Her neighbour turned to her and the sweaty man appeared to pity her. She dropped off her chair, her sandals slapping on the smooth white floor.

'But my auntie used to send me books and birthday presents,' she said. 'She knows my real mummy.'

Her neighbour was sad and knelt in front of her.

'She might have sent you presents sweetheart, but she says she hasn't seen a picture of you and doesn't know where Kate and David adopted you.'

The intense hurt and indignation rose again at the adults who wouldn't listen to her. 'But they said. They said that when we go back to England to live, auntie would be able to give me a present and kiss.'

Her neighbour's throat looked funny, his Adam's apple bobbing up and down.

'Just a minute sweetheart,' he said and he turned away to talk to the sweaty man.

'Is there no way she'll even see her?' he asked.

'No. She swears she knows nothing about her.'

'And no chance she'll take her in?'

The man glanced at her, his face looking saggy, and he shook his head.

5.

Susan parked outside the address Laura had given her. The street lights were turning off and the roads were quiet. She peered out of the car window at the small terraced house. The upstairs curtains were closed but there was a light on downstairs.

She was about to call when the light went off and Laura stepped out of the front door. Laura's shoulders sagged and she frowned as she turned back into the house for a moment. Her mouth moved, talking to someone out of view, and she nodded and closed the door. Susan thought she saw the curtains twitch on the front window, but they remained closed when she checked for sure.

Susan smiled and waved and Laura's expression lifted. She stood up straight and waved back, grinning as she walked towards the car. She began to appear more like the woman Susan had seen with Clo, and who she went running with during the week.

Laura's eyes came alive as she beamed that wide, full-lipped smile and Susan felt her admiration warm in her belly. She was a beautiful woman when she was happy. Susan looked down at Laura's chest that filled her tight shirt. She admired her long legs that had a firmness the handful of years between them gave. She told herself that she looked at her with envy.

'Good morning,' Laura said. Fresh morning air breezed through the car as she got in.

'Morning you,' Susan grinned. She kissed Laura on the cheek, her lips encountering soft warm skin. The contact made her own cheeks glow.

Susan smiled and turned away. She turned the ignition and pushed the car into first. The gears crunched as she forced the gear stick into the right slot. She lifted her foot from the clutch and the engine revved too high.

Susan laughed. 'Sorry, still haven't got the hang of this yet.'

Laura smiled as she clicked in her safety belt. 'Have you not driven a manual before?'

'I have. The first vehicle I drove was a real old army jeep when I was twelve. Dad took me for a test drive around the base. That thing had a brute of a stick shift. Great to learn on. But it was a hell of a long time ago.'

She kangarooed forward and pushed her feet hard onto the clutch and brake.

Laura laughed.

'OK, I can do better than this,' Susan said, patting the steering wheel.

The car lurched out into the road and she settled into her driving. The roads were still quiet when they joined the motorway through the outskirts of London.

'How's Helen?' Laura asked. 'Did you tell her we were going to Middle Heyford?'

'No I didn't,' Susan said, feeling a shiver of guilt. 'She's pretty sensitive about things to do with Mom and I didn't want to upset her. She just wanted me out of the house today, so she could get on with preparing for the party, so she didn't care where I was going.'

Laura smiled and nodded.

'Hey, did you bring the photo?' Susan asked.

Out of the corner of her eye Susan saw her bend to search her bag. An old photo passed into her view, and she held it with a thumb pushed against the steering wheel. Two people stood on a familiar jetty that struck into a lake – an image ingrained in her memory.

'Yes, that's definitely Middle Heyford.'

She passed the photo back to Laura, who carefully put it in her bag.

'Did I tell you that's how I got to know Clo?' Laura said.

'No?'

'We were at the same college. She was a couple of years above me. We were having a staircase party and all our rooms were open and Clo came into mine. She immediately spotted this photo on my notice board.'

'I bet. It's quite distinctive,' Susan said.

'She was very excited when she recognised Middle Heyford and thought she could help.'

'Did she find out anything?'

'In a way.' She saw Laura shake her head. 'It all came to nothing in the end. Clo asked her mum if she'd known them. And I remember now.' Laura turned to her and Susan glimpsed her frown.

'Clo called her mum straight away. And her mum just gave her loads of grief. Things like "who's this girl?", "what are you doing in her room?"'

Susan nodded, listening. 'I guess Clo's mom isn't supportive of her being gay?'

'No. Not at all. Clo was very shaken after the phone call. I saw her mum not long after that too. She was walking with Clo across the quad from my room as I was leaving for a lecture. I waved to them, and her mum just looked me up and down and then walked away.'

Susan wordlessly opened her mouth and stared at Laura, and then laughed. 'Did she think you were Clo's girlfriend?'

'I've no idea. Clo tried to be discreet around college, but she slept with a lot of women, and her mum may have just assumed.' Laura shrugged, lifting her hands, palms up.

'Clo could have said you were straight.' Susan said.

'She could.' Laura replied. 'But I wasn't. Not back then.'

Susan snapped her gaze back to the road. The realisation shot right through her, a streak of embarrassment at her earlier admiration. She glanced down at Laura's body and legs. How different they seemed, now that she knew she might be receptive to her touch. It was difficult not to imagine resting her hands on the soft fabric of her jeans, stroking up her thigh, her fingertips between her legs, feeling the material become warm as she moved her fingers higher. Susan blushed and tried to focus on the conversation.

She rubbed her hand over her face trying to disguise her thoughts. 'You know I'm trying to remember what Clo's mom was like when I was a kid.' The blush started to recede from her face as tiny pins and needles of cold sweat burst on her back.

'I guess I thought she was pretty strict at school.' She looked at Laura, recalling what Laura had said before her distraction. 'Did she ever tell Clo if she'd recognised your parents' name?'

'Clo said she hadn't. Clo was sure that if anybody from the village knew them, her mother would.'

'Sounds right,' said Susan. 'She seemed to be everywhere when I was little. Part of being a school teacher I guess.'

'Clo was going to take me to Middle Heyford, but then Sally…' she lifted her hand.

Susan glanced at Laura, but she had turned to stare out of the window to silently watch the suburbs in the grey morning light. Susan rubbed her thumbs over the steering wheel and wondered if she should ask more.

'Doesn't mean no-one did know them though,' she said.

Laura turned to her with a resigned look.

'I did find someone who knew them. A nurse who worked with Kate at the JR. Kate was a nurse too, and they used to share a lift from a village near Middle Heyford.'

'Did she know anything about them adopting you?'

'No, not a thing. She said she didn't even realise they'd started the procedure to adopt. She said she remembered when Kate left the JR – it was Halloween and she thought she was going straight to India.'

'But you don't think she did?'

'Well I don't know. My birth was registered three weeks later in London and I assume she was there. But then she shouldn't have been on my birth certificate anyway. David was in India at the time, according to his company records, and Kate should have been too.'

'Do you think there been a mistake with the records?' asked Susan.

'I don't know. I don't know what to think anymore,' Laura said. 'It was just so frustrating.'

'I can see why it drove you nuts.'

Laura twitched and Susan regretted her choice of words. She could see Laura's hands gripping her thighs. Susan looked at her wedding rings on her tense fingers and wondered if this was why she married Josh, some stability in the absence of family. It didn't matter, she reminded herself, they were still married. For a moment, Susan was reluctant to reach out and comfort her, not trusting how she would feel at their touch, and then dismissed her own concerns and reached out to hold Laura's hand.

'Sorry, what I mean is…'

'It's OK. You're right. I didn't cope with it well. I'm not as strong as you,' she said.

Susan shook her head. 'Hey,' she said, lifting Laura's hand. 'Maybe you won't find out any more today, but won't it be good to see Middle Heyford?'

Laura nodded and continued to hold her hand.

Susan turned her full attention to the motorway. They were past the suburbs and the London orbital. They climbed up into the hills, through a large white cut in the rise, and then dropped down into the green plains of Oxfordshire. Susan could feel the excitement building in her belly, and a smile of anticipation crept across her face.

6.

Fall in Middle Heyford. The thrill of it prickled in the pit of Susan's stomach. She leaned forward over the steering wheel and peered out through the windscreen. Familiar cookie-coloured cottages slid by on either side of the road. She had remembered the irregular stone cottages, all joined together in a jagged terrace. But she hadn't remembered it being so small.

She turned to Laura in the passenger seat.

'I can't believe I'm here,' she said.

Laura grinned, her enthusiasm becoming infectious. Susan stopped at the crossroads and looked up the street towards a church.

'Is that where Clo lived?' Laura said. 'I wonder how they got on yesterday.'

Susan's memory flooded the street with children, in gingham dresses and grey shorts, carrying sandwich boxes and small leather satchels, and her teacher following on behind them.

'Yeah. That's right. I remember her mom walking down that road on her way to school. This is so weird.'

She looked about the quiet streets.

'The school must be down there,' she said pointing straight ahead. 'And our cottage should be maybe a mile out past there.' She pointed to the left.

She turned the car and headed out of the village. The trees started where the street stopped, and the road turned into a stony lane. The low morning sun moved and blinked through the branches, as the car ground slowly over the track. Susan squinted and shaded her eyes, and caught a glimpse of the lake shining through the trees.

'Look! There it is,' she said.

Their excitement rose further as they crossed a small bridge over a stream and passed several picnic benches spread out under the trees.

Susan could imagine her mother running through the woods, hiding behind a bench and then leaping out. She could almost remember her laughter, coming from behind her. It was so long ago, from when Susan was very small, that she had to concentrate and squeeze the sound from her recollection. Her

128

mother had been happy then, back when she chased Susan under the trees.

Susan pulled over in a small clearing, where the branches grew long overhead and stretched out their tips towards each other. She climbed out of the car and looked up. It was quiet and still. There were few leaves and little wind to rustle the branches. The odd bright yellow leaf fell and floated in the still air, and whispered as it joined the others on the ground.

Susan stepped towards the lake. She slid her toe under the layer of yellow, brown and orange leaves and kicked in the air. And then another rustling kick deeper into the foliage and up. She took a deep breath and filled her nose with the musty smell of the soil and decomposing leaves.

'This is how woods should smell,' she said, and she closed her eyes and let the smile light her face.

She turned around and looked at the cracked skin of the oak trunks, the tough smooth bark of the beeches and the silky white birches. 'It's just how I remember it,' she said. 'Smaller though.'

She got down on her knees and looked at Laura. She must have been around the height her mother had been. The trees looked right from this angle. She laughed loudly. 'Yes, that's better. Everything's the right scale now. Come on,' she said reaching out her hand. 'Let's go to the lake.'

Susan pulled up on Laura's hand. They followed the dry mud path through the trees, Laura matching her long strides beside her.

At the edge of the woods the ground turned to rough stones, which crunched and scraped under foot. Closer to the lake, the stones became quieter, embedded in wet sand and her feet began to sink where the water had recently licked up the shore. She stood next to Laura and gazed over the lake. The water appeared viscous in the still air, shivering and wrinkling in patches with a passing breeze and then relaxing again.

Susan picked up a flat pebble and rubbed it with her thumb to clean away the dirt. The feel of its coarse gritty texture dislodged another memory and she crouched and spun the stone across the water. It bounced in three large loops and then stuttered with several more, until it plopped into the calm water.

'Seven I think,' she said

'Did your dad teach you to skim stones here?' Laura said.

'No, my mom.' She stood up straight with her hands on her hips. 'We used to hang out down here for ages, hiking round the lake, playing under the trees. I think Mom used to go jogging round the lake. She loved being outdoors.'

'Like you,' Laura said.

Susan smiled and nodded. 'Yeah, in a lot of ways. I thought she was great letting me be a bit of a tomboy. I used to wear dresses when I was really young, and I was just covered in grazes. And she said "OK Susie Sue, trousers for you". And I loved it.'

She saw Laura frown and look away.

'What?' she said. 'What you thinking?'

'I was just wondering how your dad was about you being gay,' Laura shrugged. 'If it was strange for him, you being so like your mother?'

Susan frowned and breathed out. 'Yeah, it wasn't great to start with. I came out to him when I was eighteen and at college. He just didn't want to know. Really in denial.'

The memory of her father's reaction intruded on the idyll; sitting in his armchair in their army house on the base, shaking his head vigorously, forbidding her news. She breathed it away.

'It was pretty hard. Being away from home and him not wanting to talk. That was a couple of tough years. But you know, later on he was really good. He came round.' She looked at Laura. 'He once told me that I needed to be true to myself otherwise I'd end up getting hurt and hurting other people. And for a hard-core army guy, that was pretty enlightened.'

'He sounds like a nice dad,' Laura said.

Susan nodded. 'Yeah, I think so. Basically he was a good guy. I'd like to think I'm like him in a lot of ways. Sure I look like my mom, but I think my outlook and personality take a lot after Dad.'

More sensible, more considered, more stable. Susan stared at the lake and Laura did not ask any more questions. She watched Laura pick up a pebble, clean away the sand with her thumb and spin it across the lake, counting the bounces out loud.

'Seven,' she said.

Susan laughed. 'Pretty good. Who taught you?'

'Oh I just picked it up from the other children in India,' Laura said.

*

Susan looked around the lake. The trees circled its edge, their advance cut off abruptly by the water. The rows of trunks were broken by an old farm building on the far side, under a green pasture that covered the hill above. A path from the hill contoured round the green fields and then sloped down into the trees, worming its way through the undergrowth, to join the path round the water's edge by the jetty.

She stared at the wooden structure, the only break in the smooth lake, stretching out to nothing in the middle of the water.

'Come on,' she said. 'Race you to the jetty.' She tugged at Laura's elbow and started running.

'What?' Laura shouted.

Susan stopped and turned around. She breathed in and out sharply. 'Let's race to the...'

Laura laughed loudly as she sprinted past her. She grinned as she turned back to Susan.

'Hey!' Susan shouted. 'You're cheating!' But Laura did not stop.

Susan started into a run and accelerated along the beach. Her steps were muffled by the sand and her shoes sank into the ground. She turned up into the trees and onto the path. She leapt over a branch and chased along the path, as Laura zig-zagged ahead, in and out of the trees. Susan turned her gaze and saw the jetty. She watched it leaping up and down in her vision, getting closer as she ran around the lake. Trees hid it for a moment before becoming revealed again as she sprinted past.

Her quiet thudding steps turned to sharper sounds as the path joined the lane to the jetty. She could hear the boards rattling ahead with Laura's steps. She looked up and saw Laura slow her pace and stop a few metres from the end.

Susan thumped onto the jetty. She breathed deep quick breaths and her face burned as it filled with blood. Sweat gathered and ran down her face in the still air and she felt her back moisten and drip. She stopped beside Laura and they both stared at the familiar scene.

'You won, but you cheated,' she said, panting. Laura laughed, it was a good sound. They looked about them.

It was a vivid colour version of Laura's fading picture of her parents. The perspective was identical, and the tree line and old farm building in the background hadn't changed, but there was space and too much sky where Laura's parents had stood.

Susan could see the disappointment in Laura's face.

'I don't know what I expected,' Laura said. 'It looks wrong without them standing there.'

Susan put her arms around Laura's shoulder and urged her down. They sat with their legs hanging over the edge of the jetty. Susan squeezed Laura's hand and stared down into the water. She could see yellow stones at the bottom of the lake, with green strands of algae anchored to them and reaching up to the surface. She refocused her eyes and saw their reflections in the water. Their hair hung around their faces and she couldn't see the detail of Laura's face. They looked the same in the dark reflection.

'You know it's strange being here for me too,' Susan said. 'I feel like I should be going home for tea in a few minutes. I can picture ham sandwich triangles and those little square colourful cakes with icing swirls on top.'

'French Fancies?'

'Yeah, those are the ones. I feel like I'm going to go home with Mom, have tea and play until Dad comes home, when I have to go to bed.' She shivered. 'So strange being here without them.'

Susan looked towards the end of the jetty. 'I can almost feel them here, you know. It's creepy. Like ghosts. I think I remember a time when we all stood here and had our photo taken. Just like the one of your folks. Mom was wearing some flowery dungarees, quite flarey ones, and Dad,' she laughed, 'Dad had a perfect ironed shirt and his combats on.'

She'd been happy then too, hadn't she? Her mother's smile in the photo wasn't forced. Her head was tilted back in a laugh. Her arm was wrapped around her father and her other hand held Susan's shoulder in front of them. How old had she been then? Not yet at school. Perhaps four years old. Had she been too young to detect her mother's sadness?

She shrugged away her doubt and got to her feet. 'Come on,' she said, stretching out her hand. 'Let's have a picture.' She pulled Laura to her feet and into her side. She could feel the

132

warmth of Laura's body where their hips and breasts met and under Laura's arm that stretched around her shoulder. Susan held the phone in front of them.

'A new start,' she said, and she kissed Laura on her cheek.

The phone clicked and she turned it over. Susan's eyes were closed and her lips were pursed against Laura's cheek in the image. Laura's face was flushed and she was smiling, that beautiful expression when her eyes shone and she opened her full lips wide, just how a smile should be.

'Gorgeous,' Susan said.

7.

Susan led Laura away from the jetty. They followed a narrow path along a stream, their legs scuffing dried grass and brambles that hung over the edges. They joined a lane that took them away from the village.

'There it is,' Susan said. 'That's our house.'

She jogged towards the thatched cottage that stood on the outskirts of the village. She stopped at a wall that separated the lane from the garden. She pulled on the top, and the biscuit-coloured stone crumbled under her fingers as she peered over.

She blinked at the view, trying to reconcile it with her memory. The lawn around the house was the same shape, the rectangular cottage sitting in a bigger rectangular lawn surrounded by a stone wall. It still blurred into currant bushes, fruit trees and longer grass at the back, but the flower borders around the house had changed. They were more regimented than the scattering of meadow flowers her mother grew. The window frame was painted National Trust green. It wasn't quite right, but she couldn't remember the colour it had been and the hazy memory nagged at her.

Laura came up beside her. 'What a beautiful garden,' she said.

Susan frowned. 'It's almost the same,' she said, unnerved by the subtle differences.

'We used to put a red tartan picnic blanket on the grass,' she said, pointing to the lawn, 'and have lunch out in summer. I remember Helen used to chase me around the trees at the back and play hide and seek.'

She squinted down the back of the garden, trying to see if the old stone shed, her favourite hiding place, still existed. It was there, but the roof had sagged and collapsed.

'They used to have other people over too. They were quite sociable I think.' Her memory filled the lawn with couples, young men in uniform and women with smiling faces. She had trouble making their faces distinct and could not attach names with certainty.

'I guess they would have been friends of Dad's from the base, and maybe some of Mom's friends from when she worked. I don't know though. They were just more adults.' She frowned, dissatisfied with her memory.

She walked along the wall and let her hand brush over the stone. She tried not to peer into the window in the side of the house. The lights were off, but an empty cream sofa and lifeless flat-screen TV caught her eye.

'We just had a black and white portable TV when I was little,' Susan said.

She stopped and stared into the sitting room. She remembered sitting on a sofa. She could almost feel the rough material on her palms. She sat on the edge of the green-brown cushion watching *Rentaghost*. Her mother had turned the TV up loud, but she could still hear them in the kitchen.

Metal saucepans clattered on the cooker and plates scraped carelessly on the kitchen table. She could hear them both shouting, but couldn't make out what they said. A saucepan lid crashed onto the floor, ringing round as it settled. The shouting became higher pitched and louder and she saw her father's shadow cross the doorway. The front door slammed a moment later.

The house went quiet, the manic laughter from the children's programme the only sound. Her mother came through from the kitchen, her face turned away. She sat down beside Susan quickly, so that she couldn't see her face. Her mother put her arm around her shoulders and stroked up and down firmly. 'How are you Susie Sue? Is your programme good?' Susan nodded and carried on watching. Her mother stayed with her, staring at the TV, sniffing every few seconds.

Susan blinked and tried to clear away the memory. She tore her gaze away from the living room and walked more cautiously around the front of the house. The cottage had two windows with the front door in the middle, painted the same green. She remembered now. It had been green before, just a dark green.

She recalled the door being open and her mother standing in the doorway. She could see her tears this time. Her mother kept snatching up her hand to wipe the tears across her face, but all it did was make her eyes redder. She was trying to smile. The corners of her mouth twitched up for a second, before being dragged back down. Her chin was pitted with tense and wrinkled skin and it trembled.

Her mother waved with her hand up high, shaking her hand at the wrist with strained enthusiasm. Susan remembered waving back. Her mother touched her belly, perhaps trying to quell her deep grief, and covered her mouth as Susan was pulled away in her father's firm grip.

Where were they going? She turned up the road. Where had they been going, leaving her mother so upset? They got into the car parked on the side of the road. Her father opened the door and Susan jumped in. She usually sat in the back when her mother came with them, but the back seat was full of suitcases and boxes.

Her father started the car and they pulled away. She looked around to wave to her mother again, but the front door was shut. The car began to roll past the house. She wound down the window quickly and leaned out and saw the dark shape of her mother in the sitting room. She was standing looking out of the window, her hands raised to her head, squeezing handfuls of hair.

'You OK?' Laura said. She was holding Susan's arm.

Susan stumbled; she felt light and dizzy with the shock of the memory. She bent down, supporting herself with straight arms on her knees, and concentrated on her breathing. She closed her eyes, but lost her balance and Laura grabbed her shoulders to stop her from tumbling.

Laura knelt beside her, peering up at her, concerned.

'I'll be OK in moment,' Susan said.

She took a deep breath and stood up straight, pushing on Laura's hand for support. She breathed in again, trying to ready herself to explain, but she was reluctant to give her thoughts that much order. They were leaving. They were leaving her mother and she didn't remember them coming back.

The memory flooded back of the hotel where she heard that her mother had died. She looked at the room with fresh eyes. It was huge. Her father couldn't afford a hotel in England with rooms that size. Her father was sitting on the bed. The bed could have slept three of him. She tried to look around the room for more clues, but all she could remember was the swirling pattern on the generous expanse of floor.

Could she remember what was outside? She strained her memory, trying to make it focus on the scene through the window. She was sitting on the bed, too small to see anything on the ground outside. But she could see a tall sign a few metres away. It was a motel sign. Why were they in a motel in the States when her mother was still in England? Why had her dad taken her away? She remembered Helen's voice on the phone, a curdling mix of anger, blame and grief. 'She's killed herself Robert. She's killed herself.'

Susan put her hand down, chippings from the road bedding painfully into her skin, and slumped to the ground. She strained her eyes wide, trying to focus. She put her hand over her mouth fearing she may vomit.

'Oh god. Dad left her,' she said through her fingers.

8.

Laura lifted the brass knocker on the front door of Helen's house. The sound resonated in the quiet London street and then it became silent. The chatter of people inside the house was audible. She peered through the sitting room window without shame, hidden by the darkness outside. The lights were dimmed, but she could see a handful of people in dinner jackets and cocktail dresses. She held her clutch bag tightly in front of her, prepared to be welcomed by Helen. The front door opened and Laura had to look down. A young waitress opened the door and stood aside to let her in.

Her heels sank into carpet as she walked along the hallway and then clipped on the parquet floor of the kitchen. More guests lingered around the dining table and in the kitchen, the conversation at a polite early evening level.

She stepped outside through the patio doors. Strings of small white lights lit the edges of the walled garden, and candles in lanterns around the lawn flickered warm light across the guests. A group of tall people hung around informally at the end of the garden. Two identical young men with two children each, two boys and two girls, appeared incongruous, whirling around and throwing the children in the air while dressed in their tuxedoes.

Helen broke away from the middle of the group and walked towards her. She had her hair tied up and more makeup than when Laura had first seen her. She held a champagne glass in one hand and stretched out the other to greet her.

'How lovely to see you again. I'm so glad you could come.'

Their fingers entwined and they kissed each other once on the cheek.

Helen looked at her and frowned. 'Your husband not with you?'

Laura shook her head. 'He's late from work. He said he'd catch up later. I'm sure he'll be here soon.'

Helen's face relaxed into a smile. 'Good. Good. I look forward to meeting him.'

Laura blushed and turned away, realising that she didn't want to introduce Josh.

Helen held her arm and stood at her side. 'You look very nice by the way.'

Laura self-consciously smoothed her dress. The cut was more revealing than she was usually comfortable with, low across her cleavage and with little spare material over her breasts. 'It's new. I treated myself for this evening,' she said.

They glanced up at the same time, when a child squealed.

'I doubt you'd recognise them from the photo, but those are my boys,' Helen said, holding her glass out and pointing. She laughed. 'And those monkeys are my grandchildren.' One of the boys screamed and giggled as he was spun around in the air.

Laura smiled. One twin continued to hold the boy, turning him upside down and swinging him by his feet, while the other twin was assaulted by the three remaining children, all pleading for the same treatment. Two women sat on the swings, holding glasses of wine, smiling and talking to each other. Helen's eyes were glazed, staring at her family. She came to and turned to Laura.

'I'm sorry, you haven't got a drink have you. Give me a moment, and I'll get one of the waiters to serve outside.'

Laura watched Helen go into the house and caught sight of Susan as she turned. She was standing in a small group of men and women in dark clothes. Susan stood out in a white linen dress, cut close around her body and long legs. Her dark hair was loose around her shoulders and her feet were bare. She held a pair of high heels in her hand. The sight made her want to smile, except Susan appeared distracted. She stared at nothing in front of her, her cheeks and jaw tense, while the others chattered.

Laura tiptoed across the lawn and gently curled her fingers around Susan's arm.

'Hey you,' Susan said. Her face lifted when she focused on Laura.

'You OK?' Laura asked, smiling.

Susan nodded and put her arm around her shoulders as they moved away from the group.

Laura slipped her hand around Susan's waist. Her bare arm came into contact with Susan's naked back, exposed by her low cut dress. The initial touch and its pleasure made her start, almost making her remove her hand. She held her palm still. She could feel the muscle down the sides of Susan's spine move as Susan turned towards her into a hug. Laura held her close a moment too long, enjoying the pressure of Susan's breasts against her own

'You sure you're OK?' she said.

Susan forced a smile across her face. 'Yeah, I'm fine. Just struggling with the memories. Should have known that going back there would stir things up.'

Laura held her hand. 'Have you talked to Helen yet?'

Susan shook her head. 'No, not yet. I didn't want to spoil her evening too.'

'You sure you're going to be OK?'

Susan nodded 'I can cope,' she said.

A genuine smile spread across her face. Her eyes widened and her eyebrows started to rise. Susan dropped Laura's hand and she started to wave in the direction of the patio door.

Susan shouted, 'Oh my god. You look amazing!'

Laura snapped her gaze around. She saw Clo coming towards them. Her hair was dark blond, slicked back over her head. She wore minimal make-up, just enough to highlight her shining eyes and draw attention to her full lips. Her silvery green dress flowed about her legs, clinging to her toned stomach and wrapping around her breasts. It was hard not to admire her body through the fine sensual fabric that caressed her legs as she walked towards them.

Laura took a short sharp intake of breath. But it was not a response to the sensual vision of Clo, rather jealousy stirred in her stomach and made her feel empty and sick. The jealousy kept leaping and snatching at her heart. Susan was holding Clo's hands, kissing her.

'My god. What a change,' Susan said. 'You're a complete knock-out.'

Laura watched Clo respond with poise and charm, thanking Susan for the compliment and smiling at her. Laura's heart tugged again. The possibility that Clo and Susan could be attracted to each other was like a cold slap.

She tried to interpret Susan's feelings. Susan grinned at Clo, flushed cheeks and eyes wide as she spoke to her. The physical reaction was unmistakeable.

'Is Amelia with you?' asked Susan.

'Yes, she's inside talking to Helen.' Clo frowned. 'They looked upset when they saw each other.'

'Were they getting on?' asked Susan.

'Oh yes. Not in that way. Just…' Clo stopped.

'Brings back the memories about Middle Heyford and Mom?'

'Yes.' Clo nodded. 'I think so.'

Laura stepped forward, the pins and needles of jealousy still tingling through her body. She swallowed, her jaw taut with tension.

'How did things go yesterday at home?' she asked, her voice sounding strangled.

Clo's forehead wrinkled in distress. 'A bit shit really.'

Her jealousy evaporated and she held Clo's shoulder. 'Oh no, what happened?'

'To be honest I don't know. We'd been there a while. I'd had a bit to drink with Dad and it got a bit hazy. But Amelia was already annoyed when I came in to the house. And everything just blew up between Mum and her.' Clo stared in front of her. 'It was horrible. She told us to leave.'

'What? She threw you out?' said Laura.

'Yes. I was too drunk to drive anywhere. We ended up sitting in the church yard for hours, until I was all right to drive.'

'I'm so sorry Clo,' Laura said. She drew Clo into her arms. 'I thought it was a bit optimistic going to stay.' She rocked Clo back and forth. 'I didn't think it would go so badly that quickly though.'

'Neither did I.' Clo's voice was muffled, her face buried in Laura's chest.

Laura lifted her hand and stroked Clo's hair. 'I'm so sorry.'

'Me too,' Clo said. She had closed her eyes and had her arms around Laura's back.

'This is a great dress by the way,' Clo said, her voice still muffled in Laura's cleavage.

Laura frowned and grabbed Clo's shoulders. She pushed her out of her chest and held her at arms' length. 'Clo! Do you mind?' she said, finding it difficult to stop the smile from breaking through her affront.

Clo shrugged and smiled at her. 'Well. You look great.'

Laura checked Susan for support, but she was staring at her chest. When they made eye contact, her eyes were as dark as when she looked at Clo.

*

They sat on the cast iron chairs on the patio. A lantern flickered on the table between them and Clo's dress sparkled in the light.

'Where did you get that dress?' Laura asked.

'I was going to ask the same. It's amazing.' Susan said.

'I borrowed it,' Clo said. She was already beginning to slur and she tipped another half glass of Champagne down her throat.

'You know,' said Susan, 'I was window shopping in Bond Street and I swear it's just like one in Christian Dior.'

Laura laughed but noticed Clo blush.

'Not sure where it's from,' Clo said, and she looked away.

'Does she always look this stunning when she goes out?' Susan asked her.

Laura smiled. 'Yes she does,' she said, regretting her friend's appeal. 'You wouldn't think it from how she dresses most of the time would you?' Laura laughed, 'and she has got it horribly wrong from time to time.'

Clo looked clueless and Susan intrigued.

'Well,' Laura said, 'Clo and I were invited to a wedding of someone we knew at college, a girl from a well-off family.'

'Weren't they all,' Clo chipped in.

'Apart from us,' Laura said. 'I was a house doctor at the time, so I hardly paid any attention to the invite before the wedding. I was either sleeping or working or both.'

Susan smiled and nodded sympathetically.

'Clo just kept badgering me about what I was going to wear. Clo usually just turns up looking great, even if it's just a T-shirt and jeans,' she gestured towards her for the evidence. 'So I didn't know why she was getting so worked up about it. I finally asked her what all the fuss was about. And she pointed out that the wedding was fancy dress.'

'Fantastic,' said Susan. 'What a great idea.'

'Well,' said Laura, less sure. 'Clo had sorted her costume and wanted to make sure that we weren't dressed the same. By this time, it was way too late to sort out anything for me and Josh. We just had to turn up in black tie and the usual. Pretend we were James Bond and Miss Moneypenny or something.'

Clo tried to be indignant but was starting to giggle.

'Turns out,' Laura continued, 'on closer reading of the invitation, it said "Dress code: fancy"'

'Oh,' said Susan, in an exaggerated look of understanding.

'And by that,' Laura continued, 'they meant "really very smart"'

'Not fancy dress.'

'Not fancy dress,' Laura confirmed with a shake of the head.

Susan and Laura were both starting to laugh.

'And it was the most expensive, formal wedding I think I've ever been to,' Clo said. 'They had the ceremony in Winchester Cathedral. She was from quite a religious family.'

Susan had covered her mouth, trying to hide her laughter, and asked through her fingers 'What did you go as?'

'Catwoman,' Clo replied.

Laura and Susan collapsed together leaving Clo attempting to appear unamused.

'When did you notice that no-one else was in fancy dress?' Susan asked.

'I was running late,' said Clo. 'I was the last one to arrive as they were closing the doors. I just dashed in and sat at the back.'

'Oh yes I remember now,' Laura said, 'I turned around to see what the noise was. I was expecting to see the bride and her father, I suppose everyone was. But I looked over the rows of god-fearing relatives to see Catwoman running into Winchester Cathedral.' Susan and Laura collapsed again, convulsing with laughter.

Clo shrugged. 'Everyone wanted their photo taken with me.'

'Oh yes, the group photo had you curled up at the front didn't it,' laughed Laura.

*

They picked at a small plate of canapés in the middle of the table. A waiter poured more Champagne into Clo's glass and Susan sat staring into the middle of the table.

'Are you having a good time?' Laura asked her quietly.

'Not bad,' she said.

Susan took a sip of Champagne and dropped her gaze into her lap. Sadness fell across her face. Laura reached under the table to squeeze her knee and Susan held her hand. A tingling sensation thrilled up her arm as Susan's fingers entwined with hers and tickled her palm. Susan lifted their hands to her mouth and kissed Laura's knuckles. Susan's breath was warm and moist on her fingers.

'Hey you!' Josh's voice was loud above her, and he clasped her shoulders with both his hands. She started under his grip, snatching her hand away from Susan's. Her shoulders rose and became tense under his pressure.

'Hello Clo,' he said. He sounded as if he were trying to be jovial. He sounded drunk. Clo lifted her glass to him and grinned dozily.

Laura stiffly turned round to face him. 'How long have you been here?'

'Actually about an hour,' he said. 'I bumped into Toby Wilkins on the way in. Do you remember him from college? He works in Harley Street apparently. He and his wife are here. They've a couple of great kids and another one on the way.'

He reached down and gripped her around her wrist, pulling her up and away from the table.

'Come and meet them,' he said.

'Wait a second. I should introduce you to Susan.'

Susan stood up and offered him her hand. 'Great to meet you, Josh.'

Josh took her hand and shook it once, before dropping it and grabbing at Laura's wrist again.

'I'm sure we'll get a chance to talk again later,' he said. He walked away pulling Laura with him. She stumbled as she got to her feet and tried to match his pace. Josh didn't look back. He pulled her towards the patio door and through the kitchen.

'There they are,' he said.

He pointed to a man in the wide hallway, smoking a cigar and talking to another couple. His wife, heavy with pregnancy, was being pulled in two directions by a small boy and taller girl, one on each hand.

Laura looked back to see her friends sitting at the table. Susan's back was towards her and she couldn't see her face. She could see Clo. She was smiling at Susan, looking too beautiful.

Laura was nearly into the hallway and they were about to disappear from view, when Susan turned around to gaze after her.

9.

Laura leant against the doorframe to the sitting room. She clutched her champagne glass and swirled the wine. The glass was warm in her hand. Josh slurred and swayed between the wall and the stairs, and his conversation with Toby was becoming louder. Toby's children clattered up and down the stairs, as his wife quietly begged them to calm down. Josh was swearing and his face was pink. Laura noticed his rented dinner jacket was too big.

She tried not to think of Susan and what she might be doing with Clo. The look on Susan's face as she watched Clo enter the house kept leaping to the front of her mind. Laura stared down at her glass and swirled it faster. She had no right to be jealous. She should be happy for Clo that someone so attractive appreciated her.

'Really? What a surprise? I thought she moved to America,' she clearly heard Helen's voice say.

Another voice said something that she could not make out. She stepped back and peered into the sitting room. Helen was sitting next to Amelia on the nearest sofa, facing away into the room.

'Well how was she?' Helen said.

'Not good. Not good at all, I'm afraid.' Amelia's well-spoken voice came through.

'I took her rather by surprise. She wasn't expecting to see me at all and I brought back all the old memories.'

'So she hasn't got over it then?' Helen said.

'I'm afraid not. She'd moved on with her life of course, remarried, took on some television work and tried to make a career in America. But now that has started to fall apart, I'm afraid she is back at square one again, after all these years.' Amelia sounded sad.

'Please remember me to her,' Helen said.

'Yes of course. I would like to give her your phone number if I may. As a friendly voice while I'm away in France.'

'It would be my pleasure,' Helen said.

They were quiet for a moment. Helen crossed her legs and sipped from a champagne glass, Amelia from a china cup.

'Does it send a chill through you, seeing them together?' said Helen.

'I know what you mean my dear, especially with Susan's likeness to Isabelle.'

'But Clotilde looks so very much like her mother too.'

'Do you think so?' said Amelia turning to Helen. 'I can't see it myself. Perhaps the colouring.'

Helen went quiet.

Amelia put her hand on her knee. 'She's an incredible girl. Very gentle, very warm, honest. She can be infuriating, but you'll not find a malicious thought in her. Nothing like her mother.'

Helen looked away and took several sips from her glass.

Laura felt a shiver of apprehension. The compulsion to leave the house and check on Susan and Clo grew. But what would she do? Hold them apart? Tell Susan to stay away. She stood torn between the conversation, her attraction to Susan and her obligation to her husband.

'Susan seems so very different as well,' Amelia said. 'She's quite a mature girl. Responsible I think. I suppose she had to grow up quickly without her mother there.'

'Yes. I'm still so annoyed with Robert for taking her back to America. I think having us near could have been a great source of comfort, and I never forgave him for it.'

Josh reached out and grabbed Laura's arm. The sensation of his hand on her bare skin shocked her and made her squirm. 'I said they're leaving,' he said loudly.

Laura looked up and saw the back of Toby's wife gripping an arm of each child. Laura was about to raise her hand to say goodbye, but Toby shut the door on his family and walked towards her with a drunken grin on his face.

'Right, let's start drinking properly,' he said, rubbing his hands together.

'Let's go and sit down, mate,' said Josh. He stumbled, as he attempted to slap his friend on the shoulder. Laura followed them into the sitting room, but lingered behind Amelia and Helen.

'Oh dear,' Helen said. 'It's still all rather a mess isn't it.'

'Well, yes it is. And this is part of my reason for leaving. It has brought it home to me how little Clo has moved on since her business with Sally. And without some encouragement, she may never have a normal life. And I'm almost completely to blame for that. I didn't do enough to counter her mother's toxic lies and, of course, I thought the truth would be too much for everyone to bear. And if she hadn't been caring for me, I think things may not have dragged on for so long.'

'When do you leave?' Helen asked.

'A fortnight on Tuesday; I'm taking Eurostar and then the TGV to Avignon. Should be frightfully quick and painless.'

'Does Clo know about your plans?'

'Not yet. I don't want to give her too much time to dissuade me. Of course we've talked about me going to winter with Barbara and Bernard before, but no, she doesn't know that my mind is made up. She really must have a chance to get on with her life, get a job she enjoys and a girlfriend too, without me holding her back.'

Laura's chest was heavy. Her shoulders slumped as she followed Josh and Toby further into the room. She could feel tears threatening and she blinked to keep them back.

Her progress was stopped abruptly by Josh who stood in front of her. 'Will you get us some drinks?' he slurred. 'Some beer would be good.'

His eyelids were drooping and he stared fixedly at her nose. Another drink and he would pass out. He didn't wait for her to speak and he turned and dropped onto a sofa next to Toby. She grabbed two glasses of Champagne from a forgotten tray and handed them over. Josh smiled gratefully, having already forgotten his request, and she walked out.

Clo was sitting by the dining table, slumped over her arms, her eyes closed, deep and noisy breaths coming from her mouth. A small string of dribble ran from her lips to her arm. Laura smiled and reached out and stroked her hair. Her grief and panic began to recede, spared the sight of Clo and Susan together.

She looked around the kitchen and stepped out into the garden to find Susan in the garden with her cousins. The children were starting to cry.

'I'm sorry,' said one of the twins. 'It's way past their bedtime. We really should go.'

Susan smiled and reached up to kiss him. 'Yeah, you must if you need to. Thank you so much for coming and staying so long.' She looked at one of the children. 'Come here honey,' she said, reaching down and picking up the little girl. She lifted the child onto her hip and smiled at her. The girl looked at her, her face dark and lower lip protruding. Susan swung her hips round, gently rocking the child, talking quietly to her. The girl's lip began to relax and her arms slid around Susan's neck. Susan continued to gently swing the girl and hold her. She could have been her own.

Laura was locked to the spot. She couldn't take her eyes from Susan holding the girl. Her long brown arms cradled the child with ease. Her hair flowed around her shoulders, blending with the girl's long hair.

Laura's heart thudded. She saw everything she wanted in that instant, and grief and longing clenched her chest. She wanted to join them, put her arms around both of them. The feeling was so powerful, she forgot to breathe and she stared at the scene of her longed-for family.

The girl rubbed her face and giggled.

'Is my hair tickling your nose?' Susan asked.

The girl grinned and nodded emphatically and threw her arms back around her neck.

'Do you want a hand with these guys?' Susan asked her cousin.

'No it's OK. You enjoy your party,' the twin said.

Susan lowered the girl to the ground and kissed the top of her head. 'Goodnight you guys. Sleep tight.' She waved to the children and her cousins as they walked across the lawn and disappeared into the house.

Susan's shoulders slumped as soon as they were out of sight. She stared at the ground for a moment and then looked in the direction of the house. Laura walked towards her and placed her fingers in her palm. Susan turned to her with exhausted eyes and a weak smile. Laura could not speak.

'I'm going to turn in,' Susan said. 'It's been a tough day.'

Laura slid her hand through Susan's arm. She still couldn't talk. She led her forward, not taking her eyes from her face. Laura saw her properly now. She took in the shallow creases around Susan's eyes, her long eyelashes surrounding deep green irises. She recognised that her façade was cracking and falling apart and saw the confident American drained by her memories, but still leaving a woman who could respond so naturally to an upset child. Laura could not leave her side.

*

149

Laura led her up the stairs to her room. They entered without turning on the lights and stared out of the window. The edges of the garden were drawn below them in strings of small white lights, and the lawn flickered with moving shadows of people in the torchlight. Laura looked at Susan, her face a dim glow from the lights.

'You holding up?' she asked.

'Struggling.'

Laura could hear Susan's voice cracking. 'Come here,' Laura said. She pulled her close, resting Susan's chin on her shoulder. She stroked Susan's hair and pressed her face against Susan's cheek. Susan clung to her and shuddered in a sob within Laura's encircling arms. She breathed out quickly. 'Sorry,' she said.

Laura held her tighter in response. She could hear her breathing out sharply, trying to keep her composure.

'I've had too much to drink, and it's been an upsetting day,' she said lifting her head from Laura's shoulder. They stood holding each other, their faces close enough to touch.

Laura could feel Susan's warm breath on her lips. She was breathing deeply, holding her breath between long inhalations, trying to calm herself. The breaths were loud, but became quieter and shallower. As her breathing became more regular, it grew warmer, moister, on Laura's lips. Her chest rose less violently, shallower breaths lifting her chest so that it gently touched Laura's.

Susan let her hand slip along Laura's spine. The soft touch sent pulses of pleasure through Laura's body, radiating warmth through her torso and down the front of her body. She breathed out in a gasp.

Susan's eyes became dark and wide with shock and attraction, but she didn't move. For a moment, they stared at each other. Laura was vividly aware of where their bodies touched. Susan's naked arm around her bare neck, her soft breasts stroking against Laura's as they breathed, their thighs that brushed tantalisingly close. Laura tentatively pulled Susan closer and their breasts came together. Susan tilted up her head and a quiet gasp escaped her open mouth. Laura pulled her closer so that they touched down their bellies and thighs, their bodies sealed together. They both breathed quicker, their breath mingling in their closeness.

Laura bent her head forward a fraction at a time, slowly closing the gap, until her lips delicately touched Susan's. The feeling of Susan's soft tender mouth on hers released all of her longing, the sensation flooding through her in an instant. Susan closed her mouth around hers and they began to kiss frantically, moist lips slipping over full, swollen, greedy lips. Susan held her face and Laura closed her eyes as Susan's warm, succulent mouth enjoyed hers.

Almost unaware, she grabbed at Susan's dress, pulling it up. Her hand found soft, delicious skin and Laura squeezed Susan's thighs, unable to get enough of the first touch of a woman she'd had in ten years. She ran her hand up higher, her fingers squeezing naked female flesh, softer and warmer the higher she felt. She ran her palm over Susan's buttocks and tugged at her underwear. Susan moaned and Laura could feel her underwear was moist as she pulled down on the fabric.

She could smell her. It was intoxicating – the fresh sweat and moisture from between a woman's legs turned on by her touch. Her head buzzed, basic desire controlling her. She pushed Susan towards the bed, kissing across her cheek, and took large mouthfuls of her neck.

She lay on top of her. They were both breathing heavily as she lowered herself down Susan's body. She pushed up Susan's dress over her chest and the sight of her naked breasts made her groan. Her head was drawn down and she ran her lips over Susan's nipple. It stood pert, tickling against her lip, and she heard Susan murmur as she started to gently draw it into her mouth.

Susan reached out to Laura's arm. 'I want to touch you too,' she said in between breaths. Laura let Susan pull her hips closer and Laura turned to continue kissing greedily down Susan's body.

She tasted and smelled addictive. Laura could not take enough of her in. She lingered, kissing around Susan's taut belly. It smelled the most pure here, where no perfume had reached. But she could not resist going further. Susan's soft hair stroked her cheek as she moved lower. She could feel the wet and heat against her lips. The scent was overwhelming and her breath rasped with anticipation.

She could feel Susan tense and surge beneath her, trying to encourage her lower. Laura moved her hands beneath Susan's hips, angling her up and towards her. She kissed slowly down the soft crease of her legs. She could hear Susan groaning. She was stroking her hands uncontrollably over Laura's back and down her legs trying to pull Laura onto her face.

Her arms shaking, Laura tentatively lapped between Susan's lips. A single, delicious lick. The remembered and long-missed taste was overwhelming. She couldn't stop. She hungrily licked around Susan's lips, driving her face into her. Susan groaned and tensed and tried to push herself closer into Laura's face. Laura lapped at her again, feeling her spasm in time with the movement. Her own arousal made her dizzy as Susan whimpered.

Laura could not keep Susan waiting any longer and slowly moved her mouth over Susan's clitoris. Susan had stopped shaking and was paralysed beneath her. Laura let her breath tease her for a moment, breathing warm air over her, to let her know how near she was. Laura opened her mouth and then slowly slipped her warm lips around her.

Susan tensed beneath her. Laura let her spasm, keeping her lips locked around her clitoris and her tongue stroking, as she held Susan to her. She began to kiss and lick her deeper and faster. Laura was losing control, pushing herself further into Susan, moisture covering her face.

Overwhelmed by the taste and pleasure, Laura only half registered Susan pulling her hips over towards her. She was lost in Susan, when she felt the stroke of hands over her buttocks, pulling her down onto Susan's face. Laura cried out as Susan's lips enveloped her clitoris. Her hot mouth sucked Laura in and ripples of pleasure coursed through her body. The pleasure spread out in waves through her skin, as far as the top of her scalp. Her skin prickled in ecstasy across her back and down her limbs.

Uncontrollable, they devoured each other, forcing each other even closer. The realisation that Susan was going to come made Laura shudder with arousal and the rush in her groin was intense. She felt Susan start to curl up in tension beneath her and she sucked her quicker to take her over the edge, just as Susan did the same for her. They rocked taut together, holding each other tight to each other's mouths as they tensed and pulsed and moaned.

*

'Susan?'

They both looked up towards the door. Laura recognised Helen's voice.

'Susan?'

They both scrambled from the bed, pulling up straps on dresses, retrieving knickers from the floor, and smoothing material down their legs.

'I'm in bed,' Susan shouted.

'You OK?'

'Yes, sorry. I was very tired. I'm sorry I didn't say goodnight.'

'That's all right my love. Just checking you were OK. Good night.'

They both stared at the door. Laura prayed that Helen would not come in. She saw a shadow move across the strip of light under the door. Muffled footsteps slowly receded, but she couldn't tell in what direction. She crept closer to the door, turning her head to listen. Her ears throbbed and she strained to hear above the blood rushing through her veins. Her whole body pulsed with her strong heartbeat, panicking with the fear of discovery.

She opened the door a fraction and squinted in the light. She couldn't see anyone on the landing or down the stairs as she stepped out. She turned back to Susan. She looked pale in the glow from the landing. Was she shocked at what they'd done? Did she regret it?

Laura heard a noise behind her, echoing in the bathroom. She snapped her head towards the noise and saw Helen's reflection in the bathroom mirror. She held lipstick to her lips, her mouth open wide, but she was staring at her.

Laura blushed deeply and twirled around. Her stomach felt light as she dashed across the landing. She pulled up her dress and ran down the stairs and didn't dare turn back.

10.

Susan woke alone. Early morning light came around the edges of the curtains and the room began to take on a grey shape. She stared at the ceiling, astonished at her encounter with Laura.

Laura hadn't come back. Susan had heard Helen on the landing after she'd fled, but ignored her quiet request to come in. Laura texted later to say that Josh had passed out. She was in a taxi on the way home and she wanted to see her again this morning.

Susan could smell her. Her moisture had filled her mouth and nose and she could still taste her. The memory of Laura and feeling her lips around her own clitoris made her gasp, and she trembled with longing and arousal.

She sat up and swung her legs off the bed and shook her head. She tried to think how they could be together, but there were too many reasons and principles in the way. She buried her face in her hands. The smell of Laura was stronger as she breathed through her fingers that had enjoyed her the night before.

She could never have her again. Her stomach clenched with regret and her body ached, wanting to be touched and sealed against the perfect fit of Laura's body. She stood up and put on her jogging pants, T-shirt and hooded top, and left the room, unable to face her feelings.

The staircase creaked under her feet. The house made no other sound. She looked down the hallway. The sitting room smelled of stale alcohol, from dregs of Champagne in abandoned glasses. She checked the kitchen, but there was no sign of Helen.

Susan stepped out of the front door into frosty air. The cold stopped her breath until she became used to the change and then she started into a jog. She squinted in the low sun and headed up the hill towards Hampstead Heath.

*

Laura stood on top of Parliament Hill. She was hugging herself, facing away across the fields towards the City skyline. Susan stopped and the grief flooded through her again. Tears began to fill her eyes and chill in the cold morning air. She doubted her resolve and was about to turn away when Laura saw her.

Laura's entrancing smile beamed from her face and she walked towards her.

Susan froze, her arms crossed in front of her. She opened her mouth but did not say anything. Laura slowed and her expression changed. Her smile sagged and contracted into a closed mouth. She shook her head.

'Don't tell me that was a mistake. You can't tell me that was a mistake.' Laura stopped a couple of paces away and stared at her.

Susan swallowed. 'It can't be anything,' she said.

'I haven't felt like that about anyone for a long time. I don't think I've ever felt like that. You can't tell me that didn't feel right to you.'

Susan's stomach clenched, grief gripping her insides. She breathed heavily, struggling to say the words that betrayed her feelings. She took in a deep breath.

'It was passionate. We were both drunk…'

'I wasn't drunk by then.' Laura fixed her with a stare.

Susan rubbed her head. 'You've got so much going on. Your parents, starting a family with Josh. I can't mess that up for you.'

'You wouldn't be…'

'I'm sorry. I can't be the one to break up a family. I'm sorry I slept with you. It caught me by surprise.'

Laura's mouth was closed and pursed with grief.

'Do you not find me attractive?'

Susan looked at her. She knew what was underneath Laura's sweatshirt, how her breasts fell without a bra, what she felt like and how she tasted, how they fitted together so exactly. Tears glazed her eyes and her eyebrows rose in despair.

'Was it just sex?' Laura asked.

Susan shook her head. Her chest was imploding with the longing to be with Laura. She forced herself to make another excuse.

'I've got some sorting out to do of my own too. This thing about Mom still being alive when Dad left has really thrown me. I've got to get my head round that.'

'Let me be there for you,' Laura said. 'You've been there for me.'

She wanted her to be. She would have loved it.

'You can't. I've got to sort this out. Talk to Helen. My head's a real mess right now.'

'I'll wait,' said Laura.

Susan put up her hands.

'No, don't make me do this. I can't split you and Josh up. It's just not right.'

'Don't you think I'm the better judge of that?' Laura said. She looked angry.

'I don't think you're thinking straight this morning. Don't mess up your life on a whim.' Susan turned, knowing her resolve was wearing thin.

'This isn't a whim.' Laura's voice rose, breaking with despair and anger.

Susan started to walk, concentrating on her feet as they moved along the path.

'Please don't walk away from me,' Laura said. Laura's fingers dug into her arm and she spun around as Laura dragged her back. Her expression was a mix of fear, anger and desperation. Their bodies joined together and Susan felt instantly aroused by Laura's chest softly pushing into hers.

Laura pulled Susan's head forward and kissed her. Her cheeks and nose were cold against hers, but her lips were hot. Susan's body reacted quickly, remembering how it felt the night before. She felt a twinge between her legs and started to push her body into Laura's, running her hand down her back and pulling her hips into her own. She kissed her deeply, feeling the heat intensify where they joined.

A loud wolf-whistle startled her and they fell apart. She looked around, shocked at her surroundings, and saw two young men jogging by and laughing. Laura tugged at her, trying to pull her back into an embrace

'No. Stop it!' Susan pushed at her and held her at arms' length. Her tears started to fall freely and her face contorted in grief. 'I can't have you!'

Susan turned and started to run. Laura shouted after her, but she couldn't make out the words above the thud of her feet on the ground. She thought she could hear Laura running after her and she put her head down and sprinted down the hill.

Part 4. A Reunion

1.

'You can still change your mind,' Clo said.

Amelia peered out of the bay window into the mews, waiting for the taxi. She didn't reply. Clo cleared her throat and Amelia turned around and smiled.

'I won't change my mind, darling.'

'Will Barbara be able to take care of you if your arthritis is bad and you need help to wash, go to bed, get off the loo?' Clo said.

'My dear, they've hired a lovely French girl who is going to help around the house, and who is more than capable of helping me if I require it.' Amelia tilted her head and gave her a kind look.

Clo stared down at her bare feet and rocked from the heel to the ball of her foot and back again. 'I don't want you to think you're getting in my way,'

'I know sweetheart. But the truth is I have been stopping you getting on with your life.'

'But I like my life just the way it is,' said Clo, holding her hands up.

Amelia frowned. 'Really? Wouldn't you like for once to plan ahead, rather than having to be ready to cancel everything on my behalf? Wouldn't you like to get a job that you love and meet new friends, maybe have a girlfriend one day?'

'I have a job, friends…I'm happy.'

Amelia looked at her without blinking. 'Then why did you come home in despair that night?'

Clo blushed and looked back at her feet. She tried to think of a protest.

'I don't see many happy people drinking themselves into oblivion either,' her grandmother continued. 'And I don't think you're that happy secretly meeting colleagues under the archway.'

Clo's cheeks inflamed. Amelia's hands lifted her face and she was forced to look at her grandmother.

'I have held you back my dear,' said Amelia. 'It's been too long. You've more than done your duty. You've cared for me like no-one else could. But it's time you gave yourself a chance at being truly happy.'

Clo blinked, and tried to look away.

'Please just try while I'm away. And when I come back, let's see how things are.'

*

Clo watched the taxi driver from the window. He filled the boot of the cab with Amelia's suitcases. Amelia lurched over the cobbles and opened the car door. She turned around once and smiled and waved. As the taxi pulled away, Amelia's grey hair was visible through the back window.

Clo sat on the sofa. She listened to the silence of the house. London hummed outside but it was unnaturally quiet indoors. There was no Radio Four playing in the kitchen. There was no sound of Amelia moving around the lower floor, or making a cup of tea, shuffling the newspaper or turning the pages of a novel. There was nothing to respond to. No Amelia to ask how she was. No guest of Amelia to make tea for, or lunch or dinner. Clo's ears rang in the silence, making a noise in the absence of any from the house.

She cringed, remembering Amelia's reference to Marella. She was grateful her grandmother had not humiliated her by pushing the subject, but knowing that Amelia suspected made her nauseous. She got up from the sofa and paced around the living room, trying to dispel the unpleasant feeling that clung to her. The nausea began to wane but her restlessness did not. What was she meant to do? She had signed up to more shifts at the patisserie while she took a break from Marella's appointments, but they were not going to fill much of her time. There was no-one to cook for, no-one to check on, no-one to keep company, no-one to tell when she found a programme on the television that they might find interesting.

And there was no safe, emotionally numb sex either. She would miss that.

There were no clients to think of. No new ways to concoct to keep them intrigued, no mental preparation required. She wouldn't have to give that extra thrill to Mrs Marchant, or indulge in post-coital conversation about opera with Mrs Abrahams. There was no need for exercise to keep her body firm, no daily routine of moisturising, trimming, filing and clipping to keep her presentable.

Clo could lie in bed, growing her armpit hair, and no-one would notice.

*

She got a haircut.

She sat in the chair and looked in the mirror at the teenage girl who stood behind her with a pair of clippers and a scared expression on her face.

'Give me a grade one,' Clo said.

'Are you sure?'

Clo smiled. She was thrilled that she did not have to make any concessions to the tastes of her regular clients. 'Make me look like a hard-ass dyke,' she said. 'No soft finish. Just a grade one all over.'

The girl appeared hesitant and afraid.

'Please,' Clo said, and she smiled.

The hairdresser, slowly at first, began to mow into her locks. It looked so satisfying, stripping away lanes of hair, and then she was alarmed when longer than expected pale clumps floated down onto her hands. It was cold with almost no hair. She felt stupid for not envisaging this. She reached up and stroked her scalp when the last strip of hair had been removed.

The hairdresser brushed away the debris from her shoulders, and her hair resembled a strange blond animal curled around the bottom of the chair. The hairdresser fetched a mirror so Clo could check the haircut for herself. The hairdresser tilted the mirror to present the back (bald), the left hand side (bald) and the right (also bald).

The hairdresser rubbed some product on to the remnants of her hair. 'This should soften it a little, give it some shape,' she said. Clo was perplexed, but it seemed to make the hairdresser happier.

'You actually have a really nice head shape,' the girl said, looking Clo over. 'I thought you were going to look really butch, but actually, if anything, you're more feminine. It makes your neck and face look more delicate,' she said, reaching out and stroking Clo's scalp.

Clo sank in her chair with disappointment.

*

Two o'clock. Six hours until she was meeting Laura and Susan. She hadn't seen them since the party. They'd kept cancelling, telling her their shifts had changed, and she was desperate to see them now Amelia was gone.

She had a shower and washed away the itchy detritus of her hair. She discarded her dressing gown and walked around the house naked, trying to enjoy the freedom from having to be presentable for Amelia's friends.

What else? She put on some trance music and turned it up loud. The neighbours on either side were at work, and Barbara and Bernard opposite were away. She opened the curtains, and bright sunshine blinded her and flooded into the sitting room. She turned the volume up again and stretched her hands up in the air. She felt more naked than usual with almost no hair on her head. Her trimmed pubic hair was slightly longer.

She made herself a cup of tea, dancing from cabinet to fridge, to kettle, to work top. As the music thumped she indulged more and closed her eyes as she moved to the rhythm in the middle of the room. Head from side to side, more and more, until the beating crescendo made her want to jump up and down.

Coming down from the music's high, she noticed an anomalous ringing, out of time with the beat. The red light of the telephone by the window attracted her attention and she snapped off the music.

'Hello?' she said, out of breath.

'Hello darling.'

'Amelia,' she said, grinning. She flopped onto the cushions of the window seat.

'It's just a quick call my dear. Just to let you know that I'm alright. I'm in Paris and I've met up with Barbara and Bernard who are taking the train with me the rest of the way.'

'How's the weather?' Clo asked.

'Wonderful. Getting warmer and drier with every mile.'

'That's great,' said Clo, smiling.

'How's everything there?' asked Amelia. 'Are you OK rattling around the house by yourself, or have you had the girls over already?'

'No, just me and I'm absolutely fine.'

'That's good. Oh I forgot to say before I left that the lady who was staying for a few days at Barbara and Bernard's has signed up for the winter. So don't be alarmed if you see someone over at their house.'

'What?' said Clo.

'There's someone renting the house opposite,' repeated Amelia.

Clo stood up and snatched the curtain around her. She put her face close to the window pane and peered through the rays of sun. The extreme squinting was not enough to gain a view and she put down the phone to shield her eyes with her hand.

To her distress the tenant was home. The bay window opposite was open and a woman was sitting on the window seat. She was smoking a cigarette, and puffed plumes of smoke into the cobbled space between them. Furthering Clo's distress, she was a very elegant, older woman, perhaps in her fifties. She sat sideways, her long legs crossed in a skirt. She wore a soft v-necked jumper over a full chest and she held her cigarette aloft in graceful fingers.

She had short hair in a forties style, but with a natural relaxed curl. Grey streaks curled at her forehead. She was wearing large sunglasses, the kind that movie stars wore in photos when they were snapped while out doing ordinary things, like shopping.

Clo gulped and stared at the attractive woman. She looked like an older version of Francoise Desmarais. The woman tapped the ash off her cigarette into a wine glass and turned to face Clo. She raised an eyebrow and smiled.

Clo's mouth dropped open, rendered dumb by the beautiful woman and her smile. She slowly lifted her hand in a wave to acknowledge her. The woman smiled at her, in a way that made Clo feel pleasurably funny inside, and she disappeared into the darkness of Barbara and Bernard's sitting room.

Clo retrieved the telephone. 'Yes, I've seen the neighbour,' she said.

'Oh that's good. Bernard was worried you'd be running around the house starkers if you thought that no-one was around.'

Clo blushed and clutched the curtain tighter.

'He's a funny man at times,' Amelia said.

2.

Four o'clock.

She could catch her father's lecture at the museum and have a coffee with him before walking over to Soho. She took the tube to Russell Square and walked across the small park to the British Museum.

She peered through the glass panel of the fire door to the lecture theatre. He stood on the stage in front of perhaps fifty students. They all leaned forward, their heads following him around the stage. Clo watched his silent mouth moving, his arm gesturing energetically. She pushed at the plate on the door and settled in a seat at the back.

'Now Aristotle, Plato's student, was a polymath.'

Her father's voice reached her, loud and confident. He turned and walked up to the screen. He thrust his arm towards marble-carved images of Plato and Aristotle. They had pale grey faces and odd opaque eyes beneath solid ringlets of hair.

'He had an interest in all subjects studied at that time, from what we'd term botany to rhetoric, ethics…'

He threw his shoulders and arms out wide, showing the breadth of the world view he was explaining.

'Isn't it said that he was the only person to know everything there was to know?' asked a young man in the front row.

Her father smiled and strode towards the man. He pulled out a chair and twirled it around on one leg. He sat astride the chair, leaning on its back, and looked intently at his audience.

'Perhaps the last person to know everything that was known at the time. But how would we know? And then wasn't there less to know in the Dark Ages?'

The audience laughed.

'And of course the works are attributed to Aristotle, and many were completed by students over a number of years…'

It was strange seeing him in another setting, being another person. The young man was leaning on his elbows, holding his face in line with her father's, attentive. Her father was the centre of everyone's attention.

She blushed. It was a shocking contrast between the charismatic professor and her diminished parent, and she was embarrassed, spying on this part of his personality. He was confident, inspiring, a full-blooded human. And he looked happy, for more than just a moment.

She moved back towards the door, hoping he would not catch sight of her. She didn't want to infect this separate world with a reminder of the rest of his life. He was still talking to the young man when she slipped through the door, and her heart gave a twinge of regret at being denied the company of her father.

*

She started to drink. She sat by the bar in Beck's and gulped her third pint of strong lager. The liquid was cold as she swilled it down, making her insides chill and shiver. She bounced her feet on the bar across the bottom of the high stool, nervous at her lack of company. She hadn't had a conversation with anyone since the morning, and she dreaded the prospect of returning to an empty home without Amelia.

It was getting late, already past nine. The bar was starting to fill and there was no sign of Susan or Laura. The downstairs bar and dance floor were open and the music thudded through the floor and pulsed through her hands on the bar. Groups and couples of women filled the tables and congregated around the pool table at the back. People gathered behind her, queuing for the bar, and the air was humid and began to smell of perspiration.

She stared down at her drink. It was joined on the bar by a pair of breasts, squeezing out of a tight top. She looked up at their owner, a young woman, perhaps still a teenager, who stared back at her. She had long, dark wavy hair, freckles and a smile.

'Hi,' the young woman said. 'Can I get you a drink?'

Clo held up her half empty pint. 'I'm OK thanks,'

'Oh I'm sure you'll guzzle that down in no time. I've been watching you.'

Clo stared at her with an open mouth.

'I'll get you another,' the girl said. 'You're drinking this right?' She pointed to the tap of German lager and Clo nodded, not knowing how to refuse.

They were quiet while the girl ordered a bottle of blue WKD and Clo's pint. The girl's chest nudged into Clo's arm as she paid and retrieved the drinks. She drew up a bar stool and brushed her breasts past Clo's face as she sat down. She leaned an elbow on the bar, her other arm propping up her chest, so that her breasts looked as if they might tumble out.

'I'm Kerry,' she said, smiling and looking into Clo's eyes.

'Clo.' She kept both arms on the bar, keeping her chest to herself.

'I like your new hair,' Kerry said.

Confusion and a pang of fear occupied Clo's thoughts and she stared at the girl.

'I've seen you in here before,' Kerry said.

Clo nodded slowly. 'Yes, I come in here quite often.'

'Don't worry, I'm not stalking you or anything,' Kerry laughed, a bit. 'You're hard to miss though. Me and my friends have spotted you before.'

Clo looked around automatically, hoping to see a group of girls about to take Kerry away. 'Are they here tonight?' she said.

Kerry took a swig of WKD and shook her head. 'No, not tonight. They're all paired up at the moment. Just me tonight, all on my lonesome.'

Clo shuffled in her seat and glanced towards the door. 'I'm waiting for a couple of friends,' she said, pointing her thumb over her shoulder. She could feel her eyes widening at Kerry.

'I'll just keep you company until they get here then.' Kerry smiled, leaned closer and put her hand on Clo's knee.

Ten o'clock. Clo ordered the next round of drinks, to settle her obligation, and looked over her shoulder towards the doors. She checked her phone for the time and found a missed call and two texts. Neither of them were coming. Susan claimed a late shift change and Laura a cold. She pocketed her phone and started to panic at the lack of company, apart from her present companion.

'You been stood up?' Kerry asked. She took another swig and peered at her down the bottle.

Clo nodded. She swayed to the side, disoriented by the alcohol and wobbled back on her stool. 'Friends can't make it.' She had to concentrate. She knew she was slurring, her tongue slow and twisted in her mouth.

'You can hang out with me then,' Kerry said, holding her hand. 'Come on. Let's go and dance if they're not coming,' she said, slipping off her stool.

Clo swallowed and stared at the outstretched arms, resisting.

'Oh come on,' Kerry said. 'Just a dance.'

The air became more sweaty and moist as they descended the stairs. It was darker and couples lurked, joined together, in the corners of the bar. Kerry dragged her towards the main room. The waves of music thumped them as she opened the door. Clo could see a dark, heaving mass of people moving and dancing on the floor.

Kerry pulled her into the crowd and Clo was instantly surrounded by hot, moist bodies, rubbing up behind her in rhythm. Kerry pulled her close and put her arms around her neck. She moved her hips to the beat and rubbed into Clo's groin. She smiled and grabbed Clo's hands, winding them around her behind, and squeezed her fingers into her buttocks as if to pin them there. She replaced her hands around Clo's neck and looked at her with dark eyes.

Clo was tense, unable to relax into the movement. She held Kerry's behind as if it was infected, her shoulders rising in panic. Kerry looked desperately at her and drew her face roughly towards her. Clo felt Kerry's lips, sticky and sugary, press into hers. The smell of alcopop made her nauseous. She tried to pull away, but Kerry's hands locked around the back of her head and she was forced to slide her lips over Kerry's face to break free. She dipped out of their embrace and pushed through the throng. She clawed her way to the bar, not wanting to look back.

Clo spilled out into the small corridor by the toilets and felt a thump on her back. She tripped into the women's loo, pushed by a hand from behind. She stumbled and was pulled back, catapulted around to see Kerry's dark face. Clo blinked at her, her head spinning, and her thoughts took a moment to catch up. Kerry looked ugly in the harsh fluorescent lights. Her expression was unkind.

'What the fuck's up?' Kerry said. She had her hands on her hips.

Clo shook her head, and her brain felt sluggish. 'I don't want to dance like that.'

Kerry laughed. 'That's OK. We don't have to dance.' She stepped forward and put her arms around Clo's shoulders. She opened her mouth wide, wet lips taking huge mouthfuls of her neck. Clo could feel her teeth gnawing her skin. Kerry's hands were sliding down her back, pinching her painfully.

She struggled in Kerry's arms, the grip becoming tighter the more she pushed.

'Stop it!' Clo said. She pushed Kerry away and the girl stumbled back, a hurt expression on her face. She leant back against the sinks and crossed her arms.

'What's your problem?' Kerry said, her expression sulky.

Clo put her hands up. 'Look, I'm sorry,' she slurred. 'I just don't do this. Not relationships.'

Kerry thought for a moment. 'Who said I was after a relationship?'

Clo swayed and put her arm back to support herself on a loo door. 'I can go home with you, shag you, no problem. But I don't think that's what you want. It's never, ever, what people want.'

'Why don't you try me?'

'Believe me, I've tried before.' She looked at the floor, which blurred as her head swayed from side to side. She saw Kerry's feet move under her gaze and her body move closer to hers.

'But you haven't tried me,' Kerry said, slowly. She lifted Clo's chin up and kissed her hard on the lips. She moved quickly, sucking in her skin painfully. She avidly kissed down her neck as Clo squirmed and tried to push her away. Her teeth sank into Clo's flesh hard, as Clo tensed her shoulders and tried to haul herself away.

'Ow. Fuck. That hurts,' she said, clutching a hand to her neck. She took it away, dabbed it again and checked for blood. Clo stared at Kerry and started to circle around her, as far as possible out of her reach. The girl turned with her, looking sorry.

'I'm sorry. I won't do that again,' she pleaded. 'Just give me your number and we can meet up when we're both sober.'

Clo shook her head. She didn't take her eyes off Kerry, as she backed into the door and pulled it open.

'Just give me your fucking number,' Kerry snarled, and Clo lurched out into the corridor.

She swam through the darkness, between the bodies in the bar, the sweat of others soaking through her clothes. She pulled herself through to the stairs. She didn't turn round and couldn't hear if Kerry shouted above the music. She dragged herself up the steps and stumbled out of the bar into the cold air of the street.

It was late. She stared at a building across the road, trying to stop the street spinning. She couldn't force her brain to remember where the night bus stopped and she began to stumble home. She passed a small newsagent that sold everything you needed when everywhere else was shut. She bought a half bottle of gin and tripped out of the door with it in her hand.

She had to think hard to walk in a straight line. It was a relief to concentrate. It distracted her from reliving the encounter with Kerry. It made her panic every time it flashed into her head. It was a long, cold hour home, even with the gin for sustenance.

She fumbled around in her jeans pocket, groping for her key. She held herself up, palm pushed against the door, as she tried to focus on the keyhole. Her hand gripped the key, as she swayed left and right, uncoordinated across the door. She breathed out, collected herself in a stumble, and leaned her chest and face heavily against the door. She slid her arm up the panel, closer and closer to the lock. The key scraped and trembled over the lock but slid in.

Relieved, she stood up and twisted the key. It turned half way round, but became stuck. She pushed it to twist it back, her usual remedy, but it wouldn't move. She pulled at it and tried to twist it the other way, but the key was firm. She tugged it hard, and she fell backwards into the mews.

'Fuck.' She looked up and checked the windows. They were all shut.

She staggered against the door, letting the feeling of hopelessness wash over her, and slumped onto the step. She sagged as if someone had removed her bones. She lifted the gin bottle from the ground and with relief found that there was half left.

Gin was cold. It flowed and chilled down her throat and made her a sombre drunk, not a warm, happy drunk like whisky did. She glugged swallow after swallow and began to fade.

'I'm not doing too well on this fresh start thing,' she said to the absent Amelia.

She was half way through the half when she felt a cold drop on her bare scalp, then another. It began to rain persistently. Large, cold raindrops ran into each other and streamed down her scalp. Unimpeded by hair, they trickled round her ears, down her neck and down her back and chest. She looked at her feet and allowed her tears to merge with the rain.

She closed her eyes, water tickling over her eyelids and streaming down her nose. It was almost relaxing, as the water softly ran over her, and stroked and gently massaged her scalp and face. She drifted for a moment. She must be tired, falling asleep on a cold wet step. She swayed and jerked awake, and she opened her eyes to try to rebalance herself.

There were two feet in front of her, two well-heeled feet, some nice legs and a skirt. Clo looked up and blinked away the rain from her eyelashes. The rest of the neighbour towered over her, holding an umbrella above them both. The raindrops seemed to fall like needles around her, streaks of water lit up in the white street light. But the woman stood protecting them.

'Do you know who I am?' she asked down to Clo.

'Yes,' said Clo, swallowing to clear her voice. 'You're the pretty lady from across the road.'

3.

Clo woke up in pain. Her neck was stiff and her knees had seized. She opened her eyes and found she was lying on a sofa, one which was a couple of inches too short to accommodate her full body length. Her neck was bent and her head rammed into the cushioned arm.

She was covered with a duvet that she did not recognise: light, washed-out denim blue with large wooden buttons in a row across the top. She felt exposed, even though she was covered. She lifted up the duvet and saw she was dressed in a T-shirt and a pair of knickers that she did not recognise. The grey T-shirt was baggy and the lacy knickers were loose and airy around her legs.

She sat up and a wave of nausea hit her throat. At the same time, pain hammered inside her skull. She moaned and squinted through the pain and tried to swallow away the nausea.

There was a bay window by the end of the sofa. It looked like the one in her sitting room, but she was definitely not at home. It was disorientating. Had she woken up somewhere completely different, it would have been less disconcerting, but it was like waking up at home in the wrong decade and someone had redecorated. She groaned with confusion and at the effort it took to move.

She unwound her legs off the sofa, stretched up her arms, lengthening out her limbs and stomach muscles, and dropped her hands to her head to straighten out her hair. She panicked for a moment when she found none, and then remembered that she'd had it chopped off.

She stood up, wobbling a little, and crossed over to the window. Opposite she saw a more familiar window, a more familiar sofa, with a kitchen in darkness at the back. She was staring at her own house. The strangeness and disorientation made her dizzy and she put her hand out to steady herself.

Her outstretched fingers encountered an oak mantelpiece on the wall opposite the sofa. A bowl of potpourri clinked against the wall as she knocked it. What was she doing in Barbara and Bernard's house? She rubbed her aching head and crumbled sleep from her eyes. She opened her eyes again.

There was a group of photos on the mantelpiece: a black and white photo of Sidney Lumet, Gene Hackman and Francoise

Desmarais, all grinning with other people that Clo recognised as actors. Francoise Desmarais had her forties hair style, the same as in the film *Remembrance*, and Clo smiled, thinking how good she looked.

But then the photo also triggered a bad feeling, a rising sense of dread. Remnants of a conversation were becoming clearer in her memory.

The next photo also featured Francoise Desmarais. She was with another woman of a similar age who resembled her, a version that did not work so well. They were in a group with two older women.

Clo began to recall saying repeatedly 'Do you know that you look just like Francoise Desmarais? Really you do.'

More snippets of drunken ramblings occurred to her. She remembered slurring 'Do you know who she is? Most people don't. But you really, really, look like her. And that's a huge compliment. Because I think she is the most beautiful women in the world. Seriously. And you look so like her. It's so bizarre.'

She scanned down the line of photos. Francoise Desmarais stared out from the next photo, and the next. Clo felt the panic intensify. She spun around. Where were her clothes? She did not remember getting undressed. She doubted that she would have bothered getting undressed if she'd been by herself. And where was the neighbour?

She heard the click of heels over the cobbles in the mews and rushed over to the window. The neighbour was returning, carrying a shopping bag, and it was too late for Clo to run. She heard the front door downstairs open and click shut. There was a shuffling, perhaps of shoes being removed in the hallway, and then soft footsteps on the stairs. Clo turned around and sat on the window seat, pressing herself as far away from the sitting room door as possible. The door handle turned, and the neighbour came into the room and stood before Clo.

The neighbour smiled, that same knowing smile that Clo had seen yesterday. It did not make her feel so good today. The neighbour put down the bag of shopping on the kitchen surface and sloughed off her coat. She looked at Clo, perhaps expecting some kind of response. There was none. The neighbour stepped forward until she was close enough to reach out a hand in greeting.

'I wondered if introductions would be necessary again,' she said, haughtily. 'Fran,' she said.

Clo reached out a hand. She took a moment or two before she could articulate her own name. 'Clo,' she said, through a phlegmy throat. 'Ahem. Clo.' Fran gave her hand a firm single shake and dropped it.

'Oh I remember you,' she said, laughing.

She turned away and Clo stared after her. It was strange seeing someone in three-dimensional detail who was so familiar on a two-dimensional screen. There was much more flavour to her. The way she moved, the different angles she took in. Clo had most often seen her from the front in stills or long close-ups in films. She was more interesting in the flesh, much more character than in touched-up photos.

She was older than in the films, but she was one of those women who looked better older. She looked more like herself, all the character and face shape finally showing through now the puppy fat had gone.

And she had a very nice bum. Clo watched Francoise Desmarais' bottom recede into the kitchen and shook her head, chastising herself. Really must not be lustful. Really must not lech after Francoise Desmarais, especially when she's in the same room. She shook her head in disbelief.

It was novel to be lustful for no reason, not to schedule or in readiness for an appointment. And what could be safer than lusting after one of the most beautiful, unobtainable women in world? What could go wrong with admiring one of the world's most attractive, heterosexual women?

4.

'Would you like some breakfast?' Fran turned towards Clo. 'I believe a full English breakfast is one of the best hangover cures.'

'Yes please,' said Clo, still in disbelief. She smiled, catching a hint of a French accent as Fran spoke.

'Come, sit down,' Fran gestured towards the breakfast bar. 'It won't take long and I'll get you a coffee.'

Clo started towards the kitchen. Standing up, she remembered her headache and that she was still wandering around in a T-shirt and an oversized pair of knickers.

'What happened to my clothes?' she said.

'They're still drying I'm afraid,' Fran said over her shoulder. 'They were soaking wet. I had to peel them off you.'

Clo blushed. 'Oh. Did I need help with all my clothes?'

Fran laughed. 'It would have been a cruel sport to leave you to yourself. You were very drunk. And I had already seen you naked earlier yesterday anyway.'

Clo shrugged, used to exposing herself, and sat down at the breakfast bar and watched Fran making breakfast. Fran poured them both a coffee and placed a cup in front of Clo.

'Don't worry,' Fran said, 'you were well behaved last night. Although, you did warn me that you might be unbearably horny in the morning, if you had a hangover.'

Clo dropped her head onto her arms. 'Oh god,' she said, muffled by the breakfast bar. Fran laughed.

*

'Voila. There you go.' Fran announced the breakfast, pushing a plate in front of Clo.

She almost dribbled, looking at the food, smelling the bacon under her nose. It was browned and crispy at the edges but had a succulent bite to it. The saltiness was intense on her tongue, which had dried and become numb with her hangover. She cut into a roast tomato. The tangy juice oozed in her mouth, refreshing and invigorating her tired taste buds.

'Nyom'. It was just what her jaded mouth needed. 'Ooo. What have you put on these?' she asked as a flavour that came through. 'Is it celery salt and a bit of Worcester sauce?'

'Yes it is,' said Fran smiling, eating her breakfast opposite.

'That's really nice,' said Clo, taking another mouthful. 'I suppose that's what you'd mix in a bloody Mary isn't it, but I hadn't thought of adding it to roast tomatoes. It's lovely,' she said, digging into the rest of the food.

The fresh orange juice, the salty bacon and fatty, filling rosti were turning Clo human again; from waking up her mouth to warming and settling her tummy.

She stared at Fran as she ate her breakfast in a more restrained manner. She was pale, thin around her face, perhaps. It was surprising for someone who could cook such a breakfast.

'Are you always a good cook?' asked Clo, with half a mouthful.

Fran looked up, raised an eyebrow, and dabbed her lips with a napkin before speaking.

'No, I must admit that I don't cook very often. But I find that I can't live without an English breakfast.'

'That's odd, being French,'

'Yes,' replied Fran, and she looked away.

Clo stared at her eyes, watching Fran's long eyelashes leaping and falling as she blinked. She had dark eyes. They must be a very dark brown. Clo strained forward trying to determine their real colour.

'Would you like to use the phone to call a locksmith after breakfast?' Fran asked.

Clo's mind went blank.

'Your key was stuck?'

'Oh,' said Clo, deflating. 'Yes, that would be very handy, thank you.'

The hangover had made last night seem a long time ago. Remembering it brought back her nausea.

'I'm sorry,' said Clo. She realised that she must be outstaying her welcome. 'Meeting you, just a bit distracting, made me forget where I was. I'll go phone now.' She got down from the stool.

'I didn't mean for you to rush your breakfast,' Fran said behind her, as Clo walked over to the phone.

Clo flicked through the Yellow Pages, and tried A. Locksmith. She turned away from Fran and persuaded the locksmith to come and break into her house. She put the phone down and stared out of the window. Her evening and encounter at the bar were coming back to her, and a wave of nausea swelled in her stomach.

'Everything OK?' Fran asked.

Clo turned around and tried to smile. She remembered being bitten and snatched up her hand to cover her bare neck. It would surely have made a visible mark.

Fran looked at her with a straight face, over her coffee cup. 'An interesting night?' she asked.

'No,' said Clo. 'Not really. I just misunderstood someone's intentions, again. And they didn't take "no" very kindly.' She shuffled between her feet uncomfortably and tried to change the conversation. 'Do you mind if I wait here a bit longer? The locksmith said he'd be about an hour.'

'Of course,' said Fran more warmly. 'Your clothes are still wet, so unless you fancy waiting on the streets in my underwear, I think you should wait here.' She smiled again.

*

'What brings you to London, and to Barbara and Bernard's house?' Clo asked, amused at the dichotomy of a French grande dame renting the room opposite.

'Working,' said Fran, concisely, finishing her coffee and taking a copy of *Le Monde* from the shopping bag. She picked up her glasses case and snapped it open in the same action as Clo's grandmother. It was odd thinking of her doing something as mundane and indicative of the shortcomings of other mortals as having to wear glasses. She put on the glasses, pushing them up her nose with her index finger, and then spread out the newspaper on the worktop.

Clo smiled in admiration.

'Is there something wrong?' asked Fran.

'No,' said Clo. She tilted her head to the side. 'You look really attractive in glasses though,' she said, grinning.

Fran appeared amused, but also irritated, and flicked through the paper in response, settling on a page with the crossword and sudoku.

'Are you doing the crossword?'

'Yes,' said Fran, not looking up.

'Do you want some help?'

'It's a French crossword,' said Fran, looking over her glasses. 'You said your French was very rusty last night.'

Clo frowned, unable to recall saying it. 'My verbal French has always been poor, mainly an atrocious English accent apparently. But my written French is still pretty good.'

Fran frowned and then nodded and pulled out another stool beside her.

Clo shuffled up next to her, from where she had a good view of Fran's cleavage. Her jumper was filled with two large breasts and it was impossible not to look down between them where they squeezed together. They pushed up as soft inviting mounds, perfect for dropping your face into. The perfect shape and size ….

Fran tapped the crossword irritably with the pencil. 'Are you looking at the clues?'

'Muh?' said Clo, lazily taking her eyes away from Fran's chest. 'No, I was just trying to work out what cup size you are.'

Fran whipped off her glasses and turned around to examine Clo. 'That's a terrible excuse. Are you always like this?' she asked.

'It's partly the hangover. I suppose I'm still a bit drunk actually. But it's mainly the quality of the breasts. Although I would be more subtle about looking at them, if I were completely sober.'

Fran laughed and shook her head. 'You're very honest.'

'In general, I think I probably am, but…' she was at a loss for words and looked guiltily at Fran.

'Oh we all have secrets,' Fran said. 'That's not the same thing. I meant that you have a very open manner. You are very clear when you are telling the truth, and very clear when you don't want to tell the truth. And besides, you have a very expressive face that gives you away.'

Clo looked at her, not knowing how to take what she said.

'I mean it as a compliment,' Fran said seriously. 'I don't meet many people that are particularly genuine.'

Clo remained silent and Fran turned back to the crossword.

*

175

'So what you working on?' asked Clo, recovered and grinning again.

'You're not a great help with this crossword are you,' Fran said, glancing out of the corner of her eye.

'Is it a film?' Clo persisted.

Fran pretended she had not heard her.

'Is it a war film?'

'No,' said, Fran laughing. 'Why do you ask that?'

'Because you had that same hairstyle in *Remembrance*,' Clo said.

Fran looked at her more seriously. 'Yes I did. But no, this is not a war film.'

Clo fidgeted, restless beside her. 'I've got to ask you,' she started. 'In *Remembrance*, when I watched it when I was little, I saw a scene that I couldn't find in later editions on video. There was a scene where you walk through a forest, and you approach the guy, I think, and you say "you've got the most incredible eyes."'

'And that's it?' said Fran, staring at the crossword.

'I just remember it so vividly. More than any other part of the film.'

Fran became closed and frozen. 'I don't recall that scene,' she said. 'But then it was a long time ago.'

Clo realised that she was sounding like a fan and dropped the subject. She watched Fran fiddle with her pencil, twisting it over the clues, but not crossing any out. She seemed distracted.

She had a striking profile, a slightly long face. It added to the haughty look she sometimes turned on, regal at times.

'So who's in the film with you?' she asked, grinning, unable to keep from chipping away at the frosty veneer of Francoise Desmarais.

Fran growled in mock frustration, which made Clo smile more. Fran turned to her, dropping her pencil.

'You're not going to let me do this crossword are you?' she said, mock exasperated. Clo could only shake her head.

She looked at Clo, more serious for a moment, and dropped her eyes and breathed out.

'OK,' she said. 'You've got my attention. What do you want to know about this film?'

'Everything!' said Clo.

5.

Clo crossed her arms outside in the cold, tiptoed from foot to foot on the cobbles, and regretted not accepting Fran's coat and pair of shoes. She had recognised the coat as Yves Saint-Laurent and didn't want to wrap it around her body, which was still sweating alcohol.

The locksmith was kneeling in front of the door. 'Won't be a second, love. Then we'll get you inside.'

Clo nodded and looked away up the mews.

Marella appeared under the archway. She hesitated, perhaps waiting for Clo to signal that it was acceptable to approach, and walked slowly towards her. Clo felt ridiculous, tiptoeing barefoot on the cobbles dressed only in a T-shirt and French knickers, which were not even her own. Marella began to smile as she came closer.

'Is this a bad time to call?' she asked.

Clo blushed. 'I've broken the lock, but we'll be in soon,' she said.

'I can come back later. I was only calling round to drop off some paperwork and see how you are.'

'That's OK,' said Clo, hugging herself tighter.

Marella watched her, with that feline smile, a small flicker of concern interrupting her expression as her eyes dropped to Clo's neck.

'Did you run into trouble last night?' she asked.

'No,' said Clo. 'I stayed with a neighbour.'

Clo hunched her shoulders more, wanting to hide. She wished Marella hadn't called. She looked incongruous next to Clo, dressed in an expensive long black coat and suit. Her skin crawled on her back as she willed Fran not to look out of the window and wonder who Marella was. She was too obviously not a normal friend. Clo tried to quell her paranoia and continued to hop from foot to foot.

'There you go my darlin'.' The locksmith stood up. 'You get inside and I'll get this fixed up.'

*

Clo drew up her legs and hugged her feet to her bum on the sofa. Marella sat opposite, her legs in black tights, crossed over her knees and exposed by the slit in her skirt. She held her hands with fingers entwined comfortably on her lap, composed and opaque.

'How are you?' Marella said, smiling a little.

Clo hugged her knees and rocked backwards and forwards, nervous with energy from meeting Francoise Desmarais and having Marella call. Clo did not know what to say. She knew what she wanted to say. She wanted to leap up and down with excitement and tell someone that she had met Francoise Desmarais. Francoise Desmarais, that actress who she always talked about. That she's called Fran by her English friends. She's shooting a film in London at the moment. It even has Daniel Johnston as her co-star. How's that for a comeback? Because she hasn't been in a film since she left the UK and that was at least twenty-five years ago. And she looks amazing. And Marella knows that Clo does have a tendency to admire the older woman, but this time you really would have to agree. And she's living over the road. And she made her breakfast. Francoise Desmarais made her breakfast.

But Clo said, 'I'm OK. Things are OK.'

Marella glanced above her eyes and back again. 'Your clients might not like your new haircut. Mrs Abrahams will have something to say about it, I'm sure,' she said.

Clo lifted her hands to her head, rubbing her palms back over the short hair. 'Yes, I imagine she will.' Mrs Abrahams was used to having her own way, especially as Clo's most frequent client. Yes, she would detest the more androgynous image. Clo looked away from Marella and out of the window. 'I just fancied being myself for a while,' she said.

Marella nodded and they were silent.

'I've got last month's results by the way,' Marella said, taking a white envelope out of her inside coat pocket. She rested it on the arm of the sofa. 'They're all clear.'

Clo nodded, relieved more than usual, and went back to hugging her knees.

'If you're going to have more time off,' Marella said, 'I have a proposal for you.' She had tilted her head to look at Clo. 'I would like to talk to you about some catering business.'

Clo frowned, confused.

'I would like you supply some cakes for an afternoon tea,' she said.

'From the patisserie?'

'No. I thought you could supply them yourself, and I will pay you directly. You're an extremely good cook and baker, more than good enough to compete in business, and I thought you might welcome the money at the moment.'

'I suppose I could.' Clo replied. 'Would you like to tell me a bit more about the afternoon tea? What did you have in mind?'

'It's for me, two clients – a female couple – and an escort. They want to meet whoever I assign before a full appointment. I did initially have you in mind. They're a little nervous and need some hand holding and convincing that it's not as sordid as they fear. I thought you would put them at ease. But,' Marella raised her hands. 'I will try to find someone else.'

'When's the meeting?' Clo asked

'They're on holiday at the moment, so it will be in about a month's time, the afternoon of the fourteenth. Tell me the cost nearer the time.'

'Did you have particular food in mind? Sandwiches, petit fours, more classics like scones?' asked Clo.

'Whatever you think suitable,' said Marella.

'Is the afternoon tea just something to put them at ease, distract them?'

'No, not necessarily,' said Marella, smiling.

'Who are the clients?' asked Clo. 'What kind of people are they?'

'Well off,' said Marella, staring towards the ceiling, 'I'd say they look like they enjoy their food.'

'More the kind of people to blow out on clotted cream and chocolates than small morsels and delicacies?'

Marella nodded. 'Towards that end, yes.'

'Do you want them to be pleasantly incapacitated, or do you want more of a taster type menu, just to excite their taste buds and seduce their palates?'

Marella thought and slowly replied, 'Between the two I think. Indulgent and generous, yes, but I want to leave the option of an immediate appointment open. So perhaps don't fill them up too much.' She almost laughed.

Clo frowned and concentrated, half focussing on Marella. 'So, sensuous, warm, body temperature, moist, light, tempting…' Clo stopped, leaving the list hanging.

Marella was smiling at her. 'This is why you're my best employee,' she said, and her smile dissolved into a sadder expression.

*

'I brought you something else too,' said Marella, bending to retrieve something from her bag. She passed a gossip magazine over. 'Page twenty.'

'I didn't know you read these,' said Clo, laughing.

Marella shrugged. 'Sometimes useful. Good to know who some of the new clients are.' She smiled, tight-lipped.

Clo turned open the magazine to where it wanted to fall apart. There was a photo of Fran. She was walking down a street with her co-star Daniel Johnston. She looked tired. Daniel was holding her arm and pointing to something out of the picture. The caption suggested an intimacy between the soon-to-be-divorced mature film actress and her younger co-star, in a non-libellous way.

The association gave Daniel more credibility in Clo's eyes. She thought that he would be the type of actor to attend film premieres with a young blonde on his arm, not someone with substance like Fran. She nodded with surprise and increased respect.

The relationship seemed credible from Fran's point of view. Daniel was a handsome red-blooded male, an ego boost for a woman going through a divorce. Although she hadn't detected any preference from Fran when she had mentioned her co-star. There had been no hesitation or unexpected warmth at the mention of his name, or any hint of diverting the conversation to cover up her attachment.

'Well?' said Marella, expectantly.

Clo looked at her blankly.

'It's Francoise Desmarais,' Marella said. She watched Clo, her expression hard to read.

'I hadn't seen a recent photo of her,' Marella continued. 'She's in London. Interesting that she should return now, don't you think. She's doing her first film for over twenty years.'

Clo stared back, her mouth slightly open, wondering what Marella was getting at.

'I thought you'd be more excited,' Marella said, tilting her head to the side. 'Are you not a fan?'

'Yes, yes I am,' said Clo smiling. 'I was just wondering whether they really were an item,' she said holding up the photo.

'I wouldn't believe everything you read in there,' Marella said, smiling knowingly. 'I'm surprised she's in there actually. She was never a big star here was she? I suppose it's only because of Daniel Johnston.'

'Yes. I suppose so,' said Clo. She was almost bursting, wanting to tell Marella that Fran was just across the mews right now; that if they spoke any louder, she would probably be able to hear them with the windows open. That if they watched for long enough, maybe they would see Daniel Johnston call round.

'I didn't know she was getting a divorce,' she said instead.

Marella shrugged. 'Well that might be true. It would be easy enough to verify.'

A silence descended. Marella still studied her and Clo fidgeted. She thought she knew what Marella was trying to ascertain.

'I'm just not ready to come back yet,' Clo said.

Marella smiled. 'I know.'

*

From the window, Clo watched Marella leave, checking that Fran did not see her. She walked back to the kitchen and picked up the magazine from the kitchen surface. It was nice to have a recent photo of Fran, even though it was not a good one. She looked drawn, unhappy. Daniel must not have been doing a good job of revitalising her that day. But then Clo had found Fran so difficult to read, even face to face.

She could not decide whether Fran liked her or not. She was amused by her. She had laughed at Clo's state of health more than once, and sometimes she had verged on affection with her amused comments. But then she would close up or turn away.

Clo shook her head. She was over-analysing. Meeting Clo was not the same calibre of event as meeting Francoise Desmarais. Beyond clearing an additional set of breakfast dishes after Clo had left, she suspected that she did not linger further in Fran's thoughts.

　　She saw her just before bedtime though. Clo peered out of the window and saw the opposite attic room light up. Fran appeared in the window, her arms stretched out to close the curtains. Clo grinned and waved madly. Fran look displeased for a moment, but smiled before returning a single wave of her hand. She closed the curtains and Clo bounded across the room and jumped on the bed, letting her body bounce and feel elated.

6.

Fran sat in the makeup trailer next to Daniel Johnston. He was reading the sports section of the newspaper, and held his ankle on his knee, clutching it with a tanned hand. He wore a T-shirt, tight across his broad chest and revealing arms that looked like they could bench-press a car.

She turned her gaze to the faded version of herself in the mirror. She looked and felt fragile. She was at her lowest in the mornings. Her hair was no longer as flowing and shining as it once was. It was iron grey, brittle and weak and ready to snap. Better to admit defeat and keep it short like this. No point trying to grow that straw hair.

She rubbed moisturiser into her face, to try to inject some suppleness, some youthful life into a skin that cracked and flaked. It was so dry. She felt like she might disappear in a cloud of dust if a gust of wind should blow. She imagined herself crumbling away like a sand sculpture in a dry desert wind. She was pale, grey, barren. How did she get to be this old? All those years that had gone by. Years of half-living in luxury, New York, California, walking around numb. The world had moved on around her, while all she had done was age.

London had been a sharp slap around the face. It had woken her from her stupor, opening all the old wounds and memories. And here she was in England again, alone, in pain, just older. She felt like a cold, hollow, empty shell.

The film was not helping, playing the same character she saw before her. They were shooting the early scenes, of the despairing widow, not yet revitalised by meeting Daniel, her young lover. She wasn't a widow, but she was leaving a very dead marriage.

The makeup woman appeared in the mirror. 'I'll be with you in a minute love,' she said. 'Just popping out for a ciggie while we give the moisturiser a chance to sink in.' The woman wrinkled her nose and nodded, and disappeared out of the trailer.

She heard the woman's lighter scrape.

'How's she doing?' asked the director's voice. 'Go easy on the shadowing today,' he said. 'I need her to start looking more alive for these scenes.'

'Love, every day I put less shadowing on. She looks bad enough without it,' the makeup woman replied.

'She's looking thinner to me,' said the director.

'She's just turning into a bag of bones, I tell you. I don't know how we're going to make her look attractive for the later scenes.'

Fran did not know either. How were they going to make her look like a convincing older lover of Daniel Johnston? Her weight had plummeted on her diet of cigarettes and red wine. She did not look or feel well.

'Want to know a secret?' he whispered. 'I'm going to be a dad.'

She snapped around her gaze and saw he was grinning with teary eyes. A wave of emotion rose up her chest. She covered her mouth with her hand and blinked as her own eyes watered.

He grinned wider and nodded. 'Don't tell anyone. I don't want the press following my wife everywhere.'

She squeezed his arm. 'Of course not; I'm so happy for you.' She pressed praying hands to her lips. 'Oh come here,' she said, straining her arms around his shoulders.

'I'm so happy,' he said. His sonorous voice reverberated through her.

He wiped his eyes and smiled when she released him.

'Is this why you're doing the film?' she said.

'Yes, in part. I wanted to stay in London for my wife. And a good art-house film makes a nice change for me.'

She nodded, looking at his toned upper body.

She turned away and let her smile drift and the euphoria swell and subside. She knew how she would feel soon, the emptiness that would be left behind. She watched her smile fade in the mirror and her cheeks sag.

'You'll be fine,' Daniel said.

She looked at him in the mirror.

'You're still beautiful,' he said.

Fran smiled, not believing him.

'And besides, your sexy French accent is back,' he said flicking the newspaper straight. 'You had an American influence for while, but it's gone now.'

*

The day was long. The scenes had needed several takes with the introduction of pages of edited dialogue. Playing the raw grief of a woman in mourning, over and over again, had exhausted her.

She walked slowly over the cobbles of the mews, holding herself with crossed arms. Her phone buzzed in her pocket. She took it out and saw her divorce lawyer's name flash across it. She could not face him today. She'd played too many crappy scenes to have the energy to deal with her crappy reality.

'Fran!'

She looked up to see Clo, smiling out of the window.

'Fran. Wait,' the youth called down to her. She bounded out of the building like a big ball of sunshine.

'Would you like some dinner?' she said, holding Fran's claws in her warm youthful hands. 'To pay you back for a wonderful breakfast and for inconveniencing you.'

'I'm terrible company,' Fran said, fading. 'I wouldn't want you to make an effort, not for me tonight.'

'It's no effort. I'm just about to put a casserole on anyway. It's beef and Guinness. A real comfort dish.'

She knew which dish she meant. The thought of it warmed her.

Clo led her into the house and to a sofa by the window.

'Sit down,' she said.

Fran sat limp on the sofa, without enough energy to resist.

Clo slipped off her shoes and placed them carefully by the sofa. She gathered several cushions behind Fran and patted them. 'Now lie down while I get you dinner. Come on,' Clo said. She picked up Fran's ankles and swivelled her around onto the sofa.

Clo poured a glass of blood temperature red wine. Velvety, fruity, down-to-earth Cotes du Rousillon. Tasted like home. Clever girl.

'Relax while I make you dinner,' Clo said. She dimmed the lights to a warm comforting glow that suited Fran's mood. She put on Bach.

'From Amelia's collection,' Clo admitted. 'Easy to lose yourself in a glass of wine and Bach. Dance music,' she grinned. 'Close your eyes and let it take you anywhere you want.'

The sixth Brandenburg concerto. The one that takes you away before you even realise it has started. Fran relaxed her head into the cushions and watched Clo moving around the kitchen, frowning in concentration as she chopped, stirred, and fried. Fran's cheeks were beginning to glow with the wine and the warmth of Clo's regard. Was it wrong that Fran basked in that light? She began to drift and Clo disappeared in a blur of drowsiness. She began to dream and remember her that night.

Fran had watched Clo from her window. She watched her fall into despair, soaking in the rain. Clo had been polite and gentle, even while too inebriated to stand.

'I'm OK, thank you,' she'd said, when Fran suggested she come in from the rain.

Fran persuaded her to come indoors, slowly leading her in. 'I'm sorry. I'm really wet. I don't want to get your house wet,' Clo said, her deep creamy voice slurring.

She obediently held her arms up high, while Fran peeled her T-shirt from her body. She put her hands on Fran's shoulders to hold herself steady while Fran unhooked her bra.

Her body was like a sculpture, a perfect shape that you could not help wanting to run your fingers along, touching the smooth soft curves, letting your fingers discover the rougher clefts and grooves. Fran had not let herself but instead had wrapped Clo in a towelling dressing gown and pulled her close, trying to warm her through.

'Thank you. That's nice,' Clo said. She clung to Fran, and hid in the curve of her neck.

Fran dabbed her shaven head dry and lifted up her face. She could not keep her cheeks dry, no matter how many times she pressed the soft towel to her skin. Tears would not stop flowing in the two steady streams down her face.

Clo looked at Fran, her drunken eyes slowly focussing. Her eyelashes pinched together in wet glistening points. She blinked her eyes, not understanding. 'You look like Francoise Desmarais,' she said, smiling a sad smile.

'I used to be Francoise Desmarais,' Fran said.

Clo had not understood. 'Francoise Desmarais is the most beautiful woman in the world,' she said, matter of fact.

Once she lay down, she only took a few seconds to fall asleep. Fran watched her for many more. In the mono-colour street light, she looked like the young woman she had first met. Only the hair length was different. She reached out tentatively to touch her head. It felt fine and soft as Fran stroked over her scalp. She knelt by the sofa and bent down to press her cheek to Clo's head. It felt almost downy, like a baby's head. It was so intimate that Fran blushed, embarrassed at her inappropriate gesture.

Fran wondered if Clo had any idea how grateful she was, how pathetically grateful, for how Clo had lusted over her yesterday. How refreshing it was to be so unequivocally desired. Clo really did seem to like her breasts, but Fran had known that already.

7.

'Morning,' said Clo. She grinned as she stepped out of the front door and found Fran leaving her house across the mews

'Hello again,' Fran said. She raised her eyebrows and tilted her head, an expression of amused displeasure on her face. She was all made up with full eyeliner and eye shadow and deep red lipstick. She was wearing a checked Yves Saint-Laurent coat open over a low-cut black dress, and when she put on a large pair of sunglasses she looked the complete movie star.

'You look nice,' said Clo, walking over to her.

Fran smiled and Clo admired the creases it made in little semi circles in her cheeks. Clo gazed at the full, deep red lips and licked her own.

Fran coughed. 'Was there something you wanted?'

'Oh. No. I was just going for walk,' Clo said smiling. 'How about you?'

'I was going into town,' Fran said.

'Would you like some company?' Clo asked, grinning and bouncing on her toes.

'Are you hung over?' Fran asked.

'No. You're safe today,' Clo grinned.

'I don't believe a word of it,' Fran said, and she smiled.

They walked out of the mews and along beside the tall, white terraced houses of the residential road. Clo put her hands behind her back and walked awkwardly. She felt funny about being next to Fran in full movie star mode. Fran looked at her around the side of her glasses and Clo gave her a rosy-cheeked smile.

'Is there something on your mind?' Fran asked.

'You look particularly good today,' Clo said.

Fran frowned, but with a smile on her lips. 'Do you ever stop flirting?'

'Oh, sorry. I didn't realise that's what I was doing.'

Fran raised her eyebrows in despair and tutted.

'Does it bother you, me flirting with you?' said Clo.

Fran frowned. 'No. I was only joking. Why would I mind? It's flattering.'

'Because I'm a woman.' Clo shrugged. 'Some women might find it uncomfortable.'

'Have you ever found a woman not welcome your admiration?'

Clo thought for a moment. 'Actually, no.'

Fran shrugged. 'Exactly. It's very flattering, so long as it's done well.' Fran smiled and raised an eyebrow, and Clo blushed as her tummy went light.

'Besides, I've had women flirt with me before.'

'Have you?' Clo would have been unable to hide her interest and did not attempt to.

'Of course. I'm an actress and I've met a lot of people over the years. It's a liberal profession, so naturally I've had women approach me.'

Clo stopped and stared at Fran, open-mouthed. 'Were you ever tempted?'

'I wouldn't say tempted. Perhaps curious. When I was younger.' She started to walk again, but Clo stared at her, fixed to the spot.

'You'd like me to tell you more?' Fran asked.

Clo nodded.

Fran breathed in trying to recall. 'Well. I was young, perhaps eighteen, doing one of my first films in France, *Avant Qu'elle Parte*. Do you know it?'

Again Clo could only nod.

'It was the woman who played my mother in that film. She was quite taken with me.'

Clo looked at her. 'And….'

Fran laughed. 'You really want to know the details? OK. We shared a trailer when filming and she flirted with me almost every day. When it came to the wrap up party, I'd had a little to drink, so I asked her if she wanted to kiss me.'

Clo looked at her and put up despairing hands. 'And…'

Fran looked at her, her mouth creasing in one corner. She stepped forward and took off her glasses and hooked them in her cleavage. Clo followed the descent of the glasses and her mouth fell open as she stared at the tops of Fran's ample breasts. They were tanned and beautiful with the odd freckle that Clo could barely resist reaching out and stroking.

Fran's fingers touched her gently under her chin. Fran lifted her face and Clo gazed at her, mesmerised by the darkest hazel eyes and long eyelashes. Clo's gaze wandered to her plump lips, and she felt a slight tingling between her legs as Fran licked her lips with the tip of her tongue to moisten them before she spoke.

'She held my chin softly in her hands like this.' A tickling lightness filled Clo's body as Fran cupped her chin in her hand. The energy went from her limbs and she rested her head in Fran's hand, like a small adoring puppy.

Fran tilted her head to the side to match her and lowered her voice. 'She leant in, and very, very gently, pressed her lips in the corner of my mouth.' Clo's face tingled and came alert as Fran gently touched the corner of her mouth with her fingertip.

'Then she slid her lips gently along mine.' The tingling sensation shot across her mouth and down her body as Fran stroked her finger delicately over her lips. Clo's face flushed and her lips ached to be kissed. She breathed out a long and silent 'oh'.

'And then she kissed me quite slowly and firmly.' Clo closed her eyes and leant in as Fran pressed her fingers gently to her lips, closing her mouth. Clo's mind went blank and she murmured an appreciative 'mmmm'.

'And that was that,' Fran said abruptly, and took her hands away from Clo's face.

Clo tipped forward and blinked back into reality. She stared at Fran who was smiling a little at her.

Clo coughed to clear her throat. 'And?'

'That is all,' Fran said, flicking her gaze down and up again.

'But did you like it?'

'Boff.' Fran shrugged her shoulders and flicked her hands in the air. 'It was all right.'

'All right?' Clo said, her eyes wide with disbelief.

'Well, I suppose, it felt nice. She had soft skin which makes it more pleasant.'

'But that's it?' Clo said, incredulous.

'I didn't fancy her, so why should it have been extraordinary. I've kissed men that I didn't fancy and felt less. So….' She shrugged and turned to walk again.

Clo stared after her, unable to move. Fran reached back and hooked her arm beneath Clo's, tugging her forward.

'Of course,' Fran said. It doesn't mean that I wouldn't like kissing another woman if I tried it.'

And Clo said something that was neither in French nor English.

*

They stepped up out of the tube station at Tottenham Court Road, the close dark air turning into a light breeze as they emerged into the chattering street. Fran put on her glasses and Clo watched as people stole a glance at her as they passed. She smiled, proud to be in her company.

Fran swirled around to face her. 'I have to see my solicitor, but I'm early. Perhaps you fancy a coffee?'

Clo nodded enthusiastically.

'Any recommendations about where to go?' Fran asked.

Clo glowed and rose on her toes. 'Where's your appointment?'

'Just behind Cavendish Square.'

'Shall we walk along Oxford Street? We can always have a coffee in Selfridges if we don't find anywhere on the way.'

'That sounds perfect,' said Fran, and she looped her arm through Clo's, who beamed and led the way.

Buses and taxis growled by on the street. Shopkeepers shouted out, selling hats, music players, London sweatshirts and souvenirs. Sharp, tinny music in English, Hindi and Arabic cut across their path.

Clo's awareness of her surroundings blurred as she stared at Fran's hand hooked over her arm. She loved the long, elegant fingers that rested lightly on her arm, and forgetting herself, she placed her hand over Fran's. She felt the warmth of her skin, and she squeezed Fran's hand as if checking she was really there. She felt a cool ring on the little finger and took her hand away to look. There was an indent on her ring finger and a stripe of paler, bare skin. She squeezed Fran's hand again and looked away down the street.

'You haven't asked why I'm going to see my solicitor,' Fran said.

Clo hesitated. 'I'm afraid I assumed it was about your divorce.'

Fran stiffened beside her. 'Oh, so you do know about that.'

191

'It was in a magazine and an article in the paper.'

'Yes, I suppose I should have guessed that you'd see it in your British press.'

She heard Fran laugh through her nose. 'I'm surprised you didn't ask about it though,' Fran said.

Clo shrugged. 'I didn't want to pry.'

Fran stopped and Clo was pulled back. Clo turned and saw Fran staring intently at her, her lips thin and tight and her cheeks knotted. She opened her mouth to speak, but shook her head.

'You are such a bewildering mix of forwardness and reticence.' Fran said. 'You surprise me at every turn.' Her eyes, beneath her sunglasses, switched between Clo's as if trying to fathom her thoughts. 'And sometimes you are painfully acute and read people so well, then another moment you can be so naïve that I could mistake you for being stupid. You are an intriguing mix of opposites.

Clo blushed. 'Sorry.'

'On the contrary. I find it no bad thing.'

Fran set off again and pulled Clo gently with her.

'I think I should tell you a little about my husband, however,' she said.

Clo didn't understand Fran's compulsion to tell her, but didn't want to stop Francoise Desmarais confiding in her.

'I met him in the States. He was a senior lawyer. Never marry a lawyer. He was working for the studio, where I was making a terrible little series that I hope you haven't seen and wish you never will.'

Fran rested both hands around Clo's arm and Clo listened, hooked on her words.

'We kept bumping into each other, at work and at some work-related parties and he invited me out for dinner. I found him a quite predictable man, even though he kept the company of a lot of interesting friends that we had in common. He was handsome, however, and he wasn't entirely without charm and he was well off – we had a comfortable life and marriage.'

'Why do you want to leave then?'

Fran turned to her and raised her eyebrows. 'Why leave a predictable loveless marriage?'

'I've never had a very long relationship and that doesn't sound so bad to me.'

Fran laughed. 'You don't strike me as someone who would settle for something so average.'

Clo blushed, not knowing whether she would or not.

'Anyway.' Fran said. 'Something happened that made be realise that I couldn't settle for it.'

Fran turned to look at her, holding her eyes with an expression Clo couldn't fathom. She blinked, wondering which way Fran's expression would go. A frown played across Fran's brow but her eyes looked wide and intensely interested in Clo's reaction. Then Fran blinked and turned, and the interest passed.

'I realised that I'd been using him to hide away from myself. He had also been unfaithful.'

'Oh I'm so sorry,' said Clo. Her heart grieved and her eyes began to smart in sympathy with Fran. She gripped Fran's hand on her arm and looked at her, trying to reach out with some comfort.

'Oh, boff, don't be sorry. It was a blessing in many ways, and it has given me an incredible amount of bargaining power.'

'Does he want to carry on seeing the other woman?'

Fran shook her head. 'No. I suspect he's far too worried about the association. And that is all there is to say about him.' She turned and looked at Clo. 'Unless you have any questions.'

Clo shook her head, her mind quite blank, and she smiled at Fran.

'Good,' said Fran, who lifted her chin and swept Clo along the street. 'There are other things I should tell you, but let's sit down first.'

8.

Susan parked the car on the street, up the hill from Helen's house. The early morning sun shone through the windscreen and she rested a moment, her eyes closed, and basked in the heat. The sunlight glowed bright orange through her eyelids and they started to warm. Her head nodded and twitched and she opened her eyes wide. She was exhausted from the night shift and she felt sick with fatigue, her body confused by the brightness of the early day.

She checked her watch and grabbed the rucksack from the seat. If she was quick she would catch Helen before work. They'd been passing each other in the house for days.

Her phone fell from her bag and bounced on the seat. She'd missed another call from Laura while she was driving home. Her phone displayed the photo of them by the lake, Laura beaming at her, overjoyed. Her chest clenched and she gulped down the longing. She closed her eyes, but her mind involuntarily pictured Laura holding her, comforting her, so that she could feel her arms around her shoulders. She could still remember her smell.

'Stop it.' She put her finger over the delete button next to the photo. She hesitated and stroked her finger over Laura's smile.

'Shit.' She couldn't delete the photo, but she couldn't cope with the constant reminder. She stepped out of the car, annoyed at herself, and strode home.

*

She could hear Helen in the kitchen. Crockery scraped in harsh rapid sounds. Susan cautiously entered the kitchen and saw Helen packing her bag for work and drinking hastily from a cup of coffee.

'Morning sweetheart,' she said, swallowing a last mouthful. 'I'm afraid I'm just dashing to a clinic. Are you around this evening?'

Susan nodded. 'Yes. And I really need to talk to you.'

Helen tilted her head to the side and looked sympathetic. 'I know you do darling. It's been written all over your face for days.'

Susan took a moment to respond, dazed with exhaustion and confused by her aunt's knowledge.

Helen frowned. 'It's about Laura, isn't it?'

'Oh god no,' said Susan. She shook her head. 'No, there's nothing going on there.'

Helen smiled and raised her eyebrows. 'Really?'

'Honestly no.'

'I can spot a walk of shame you know.'

'I don't know what you're talking about,' said Susan, angrily.

'I saw her come out of your room.'

Susan blushed. 'That was a mistake. It won't happen again.' She snapped out the words, wishing them to be true.

Helen nodded. 'Probably for the best,' she said. 'I can see you're hopelessly attracted to each other, but she is married. And you, she and her husband, and god knows who else, could get horribly hurt.'

Susan nodded. 'I do know that. That's why I'm staying away.'

Helen smiled. 'OK.' She turned and picked up her bag, flicking through the contents to check everything was there. She walked towards Susan with a smile on her face and reached out to put her arms around her shoulders.

'Look, it's Dad I really need to talk to you about.' Susan spat out the reluctant words.

Helen froze and her smile fell from her face. Her hand lingered in the air for a moment and then dropped to her side.

'What do you want to know?' she said.

'Why he left Mum.' Susan could feel her eyebrows rising and her lower lip curl downwards, quivering with emotion.

Helen blinked and couldn't look at her. 'I didn't think you remembered,' she said.

'I didn't,' Susan said. 'I went to Middle Heyford and saw our house. I remembered leaving in the car, and I don't remember coming back.'

Helen covered her mouth and looked away from her. Susan reached out to touch her. Helen grabbed her hand and squeezed it hard, but she wouldn't meet her eyes.

'It's complicated,' Helen said. She looked like she was about to say more, but kept her lips tense and shut.

'I'm not little anymore. I will understand.'

'I know. I know.' Helen glanced up, her eyes glazed with tears. 'They were such different people. It didn't surprise me that things went wrong.'

'Was it Dad's fault?'

'Yes I think it was. Not solely his fault, no, but he should have let Isabelle go back to work when you went to school. That's when it all started. She wasn't happy just being the wife back home. She loved you both, but she was a fantastic GP. She had such a natural sympathetic manner that people loved seeing her and she loved helping them.'

'They used to argue,' said Susan. 'I can't remember what about, but I didn't think it was about work.'

'Of course there were issues. What couple doesn't have issues? But if he'd let Isabelle work, I'm certain none of it would have happened.'

'None of what?'

Helen twitched back and blinked. 'The split,' she stuttered. 'I don't think they would have split up.'

Susan looked at her unable to tell what Helen was thinking. 'Will you talk to me more about them?' she said.

'Yes, I will. Later though please. I need to go now, and I need to think it through.'

'But please talk to me,' Susan said, squeezing her hand tighter. 'There's so much Dad didn't tell me. I know it's painful and that's why I never pushed it with Dad, but I've remembered things and I don't know how to put it all together.'

Helen nodded, a tear running down her cheek. 'Yes, I promise.' She held Susan's hand in both of hers and kissed her fingers. 'I'm sorry, I need to go now.' She dropped her hand, picked up her bag and hurried out of the house without looking back.

Susan rubbed her forehead, circling round her eyes. She had another shift that night and she needed to sleep. Her phone rang, muffled inside her bag. She unzipped her rucksack and the ringing blared out. Laura's photo shone at her again. She let it ring in her hands, more and more tempted to answer it, to hear a friendly sympathetic voice. She imagined seeing her, holding her hand and pulling her into a close, comforting embrace. She could imagine Laura's soft hair against her face and her warm skin against her cheek. She shuddered with the mixed emotions, longing, anger and frustration all festering in her chest.

She stood up and threw the phone back in her bag and walked out of the house.

*

Oxford Street was noisy and soothing. Susan walked in the direction of Tottenham Court Road, her hands in the pockets of her thick coat and her shoulders hunched around her neck. She walked slowly and people streamed past and towards her.

She passed a man selling *The Big Issue* to a group of tourists. Two women, with skirts shorter than their knickers and sporting fluorescent hair, clicked by. A woman with pinched lips and neat square paper bags from Liberty caught her eye. The woman turned her hollow cheeks and heavy eyes towards her and walked on by into Selfridges.

Susan let her eyes focus on the middle distance and the swarming people blurred into a colourful haze. She smiled, the chatter of thousands of voices calming her. Her eyes rested on an indistinct face with large insect eyes. She blinked and a middle-aged woman with large sunglasses came into focus. The woman was walking towards her, slower than the rest of the crowd, dressed in a checked coat that looked like it was straight off the cat walk. Her distinct red lips parted as her jaw dropped, leaving a gaping mouth.

'Susan!'

She stopped and looked away from the woman. A waving hand above the crowd near the woman caught her eye.

'Susan.'

The voice and wave came closer and she stared at the young woman with no hair.

'Oh my god, Clo.' Susan laughed. 'I didn't recognise you.'

Clo grinned at her.

'It's quite a change isn't it?'

Susan reached out and stroked the top of Clo's head, feeling the short blond hair tickle her palm.

'It's gorgeous. Really suits you.'

'Thanks.' Clo turned around. 'Sorry, I must introduce you to…'

She stopped and turned away, and Susan looked in the same direction. The middle-aged woman was gone. She saw the checked coat flash between pedestrians in the distance and then it disappeared.

'Clo?'

She turned around and her face was pale.

'You OK?'

'I was with someone. I was going to introduce you.' Clo frowned at her. 'But she's gone.' She looked confused and upset and she turned back to stare along the street.

'I'm sorry. I don't know what happened.'

Susan tugged on her arm. 'Do you want to sit down? You don't look great.'

Clo turned back and Susan thought she would refuse. Clo looked at her, eyebrows raised in distress. 'Yes, I would.'

*

They sat down with their coffees in the roof-top café in Selfridges.

'Do you think she was feeling OK?' Susan asked.

Clo shook her head. 'She was fine as far as I could tell.'

'Have you known her long, your neighbour?'

'No, we met just last week, but I've seen her every day since then. I've perhaps been too familiar. Overestimated how much she wanted to know me.' She looked away.

'I'm sure she'll explain when you next see her,' Susan said.

Clo turned towards her. Susan looked into her eyes, which reminded her of sparkling white sand through tropical water. She stared too long and found Clo looking right through her.

'And how are you?' Clo said.

Susan blinked. She was going to say fine but hesitated. 'Actually, I'm a bit of a mess.'

Clo waited, her expression warm, and Susan continued. 'I don't know if you knew that Mom killed herself,'

Clo shook her head. 'I'm sorry, no I didn't. Amelia just said she'd died when you were very young.'

Susan nodded. 'Yes, I was about six when she died.' She swallowed and tried to order the thoughts that were tangled and pulling in every direction in her head.

'I've been remembering so many things since I arrived in England. Like I always thought Dad and I went back to the States after she died, but she was still alive when we left. I remember it clearly now. Dad's dead and I can't ask him about it. Helen hated Dad and sometimes I'm too afraid of what she'll tell me. I just don't know what to think at the moment.'

Clo met her eyes, but didn't speak.

'Dad was real touchy about things to do with Mom when I was growing up. I didn't like to push it. I always thought it hurt him too much. Like there was this one time,' she said leaning forwards, 'I remember Mom being fat when I was little. It was at Helen's house in the garden. She looked so sad and I remember it clearly, like a photograph. But it was only when I was about eleven or twelve that I suddenly realised she must have been pregnant. I asked Dad about it and he started to cry. That was real shocking for my Dad. Course I didn't want to upset him and all he ever said about it was "she died".'

'Do you think that might have something to do with why they split up? Or why...'

'She killed herself?' Susan completed Clo's sentence. 'Actually I don't know. I don't know when it was. And I'm kicking myself for not pushing things with him.'

'Your mum wasn't pregnant when you left the UK?'

'No, I don't remember her being big when we left the cottage.' Susan frowned, her brow heavy and tired with the concentration. She sat back in her chair and breathed out. 'God, I just don't know. Maybe that's when it started. Mom could have been depressed because of losing a baby.'

'Can you ask Helen?'

Susan nodded. 'Yes. Although she'll have a different version to what Dad might have said, and he's not here anymore to defend himself. Dad was the only parent I really knew. It's not long since he died and I can't cope if Helen rips him apart.' She looked away. 'God, everything's so complicated and difficult at the moment.'

She turned back and looked at Clo who had tilted her head to the side.

Susan blushed. 'Sorry. I'm in a state. I met someone recently. Someone I like very much, but must not get involved

199

with, and that's just got me in a mess as well. I'm all over the place at the moment.'

Clo smiled. 'That sounds like a nicer mess to be in.'

'Oh it would be. But I really mustn't go there.' She looked at Clo. 'How about you? Anyone complicating your life at the moment? Are you seeing anyone?'

'Oh, in my dreams.' Clo laughed. 'Actually I did meet someone. Someone very lovely indeed.' She frowned. 'Married.'

'Typical.' Susan laughed.

'Then there's my incredible neighbour. Another stunning, unobtainable woman.' Clo breathed out through her nose. 'You wait a lifetime for someone perfect... Like buses.'

9.

Susan sat up in bed. She rubbed her eyes and looked towards the window. The sun had gone down, but it was still light outside. She checked the clock. She'd had four hours sleep. She swung her legs out of bed and headed for the kitchen. She yawned and stretched as she went down the stairs. She peered out of the glass panes at the top of the front door as she passed, seeing the street bounce up and down through the frames.

She froze on the penultimate step. Outside, on the opposite side of the street, was Josh. He was staring straight at her. She didn't move or blink. He stood in the street, a phone in one hand, staring at the house. Her eyes started to seize, strained wide open, and they prickled as they dried.

Josh looked away and she blinked rapidly, trying to remoisten her eyes. She ducked down the stairs and grabbed her phone out of her dressing gown pocket.

She had a text from Laura. 'I must speak to you. I'm coming round.'

She used the number and listened to the ring. She didn't answer. 'Laura, this is Susan. What's going on? Josh is outside the house. Call me, OK?'

She went into the living room, her arms shaking. She crept along the wall up to the window, and peered out from around the edge. He was still there. He looked up the street and across at the house, and sat on the garden wall of the house opposite.

'Shit.'

She showered, dressed and packed her bag for hospital, and waited in the shadows of the sitting room for him to leave. He paced short distances up and down the road and checked his phone, ringing a number and angrily putting it back in his pocket. She watched him kick the wall and stride away down the hill

She stepped out of the door and looked down the street. Josh's head, with a small pale bald patch in the middle of his dark hair, bobbed above the cars. Susan locked the door and hurried up the street, her hand tight around the straps of her rucksack. She was breathing heavily and didn't hear the footsteps behind her until she felt a hand grab her arm. She whirled around ready to strike out, but stopped her blow when she saw Laura holding on to her.

'Jesus. You scared the crap out of me.'

Laura looked shocked at her reaction, but still clung to her arm.

'I'm sorry,' she said. 'Please, can we talk?'

She looked tired, grey under her eyes, and her hair was unwashed and tied back.

'I was going to knock on the door, but Josh followed me here.'

'I know. He's down the bloody road.' Susan pointed angrily down the street. 'What do you think you're doing?'

'I would have talked on the phone if you'd answered,' Laura said quietly. 'I'm sorry. This was a last resort.'

Susan took a deep breath. 'Yes, I should have called back. I'm sorry.'

Laura looked hurt. 'Have I really got this badly wrong? Do you not want to be with me at all?'

Susan shook her head. 'It doesn't matter what I want. You're married. You've got a lot of things going on. I can't get involved.'

Laura stared intensely into her eyes. 'Am I just not tempting enough? You can tell me if that's what it is.'

Susan tried to turn away and Laura moved with her, trying to look into her eyes.

'I'm mad about you,' Laura said. 'I can't stop thinking about touching you. I keep smelling that dress I wore at the party because it's covered in you.' Laura squeezed her hand. 'I will leave you alone, if you don't feel like that. But please don't push me away if you do.'

Susan shook her head. 'It just doesn't matter. It doesn't matter how I feel or what I want.'

'Does it matter what I want?'

Susan breathed out. 'We both know what you want. You want to find your folks. You want to have kids and get on with your life.'

Laura opened her mouth and then nodded. 'You're right. I do. But not with Josh.'

Susan couldn't reply.

'I saw you pick up your cousin at the party,' Laura said. 'I don't think I've seen anything more beautiful. I couldn't take my eyes off you. You looked so natural with her. I could imagine you with loads of kids running around, picking them up and spinning them round, cuddling them when they fell over.'

Susan looked away.

'I don't even know if you want kids. But it made me realise that I do, but I can't do it with Josh. When I saw you at the party, it was like a switch. I would have taken you and that girl as my family at that moment. I don't care if I have children, or adopt, or you have them. I know it doesn't matter to me now. I just don't love Josh and the thought of having kids with him is repellent.'

Susan put her hands over her face and spoke through her fingers. 'Don't say that. You can't do this to him and I don't want you to regret it later.'

Laura's fingers gently curled around hers and pulled her hands away from her face. She held onto one hand. 'I won't regret it. I love you. And I think you love me. I'm not expecting you to say yes straight away, and I'm not expecting you to want exactly the same as me. But I want a chance. Please.'

Susan looked at her and felt her heart cave in. Tears collected in her eyes. She shook her head. 'It still doesn't matter. We can't do this.'

She turned and walked up the hill towards her car, tears flowing down her cheeks.

'I've left him,' Laura shouted. 'And I won't go back. You wouldn't be splitting us up.'

Susan kept walking, knowing if she lost momentum she would turn around pull her into her arms.

Laura didn't follow. Susan didn't hear any footsteps. She reached the car without being impeded and quickly got in. She drove down the hill, trying not to look for Laura as she drove by.

She saw Josh first, striding up the hill along the pavement. He intercepted Laura as Susan drove past and she heard Laura shout 'Leave me alone'. Susan glanced in the mirror. He was trying to hold Laura, grabbing at her arms and pulling her down the street. Laura was bending away with her full weight, unable to escape his grip.

Susan braked and turned to look out of the rear window. Laura was trying to kick him and scratch at his face while he gripped her wrists. She landed a kick between his legs and he folded, his face twisted and red. He still did not let go and he pushed her roughly on to the pavement, forcing her hands against her chest and neck, his full weight behind them.

'You're hurting me Josh. Stop.' Laura's shout was curtailed by his hands at her throat, but Susan heard it clearly.

Susan thrust the gears into reverse. The car screamed up the hill as she floored the accelerator. She fell back into the seat as she braked sharply, and threw open the car door.

'Get your hands off her, or I call the police.' Susan grabbed her phone and held it out for him to see as she dialled 999.

He let Laura go and tried to stand, still hunched over in pain.

Susan reached across and held the passenger door open as Laura struggled from the pavement. Laura limped across the road, holding her arm, and got in the car.

Susan turned to Josh. 'And if I see you around the house again, I also call the police. You got it?'

Josh did not speak or nod. His face was still contorted with pain or anger, she couldn't tell. She pressed her foot to the floor and they sped down the hill. She looked in the mirror and saw Josh hobble into the road staring after them.

She reached out her hand across the car. Her fingers shook as they came into contact with Laura's. They both turned to look at each other, their eyes wide with shock.

10.

Clo walked along the mews carrying a bag of pastries and cakes in one hand and rubbing her eyes with the other. Her knuckles felt grainy on her eyelid and she drew away a floury hand. It was grey early morning and she had finished her shift at Vincent's patisserie.

She looked up at Fran's window. The curtains were drawn on the sitting room and the floor above. She hadn't seen any movement since leaving the house yesterday. When she'd returned from meeting Susan, the curtains had been closed and it was dark and, for the first time since meeting, they hadn't waved good night through the attic windows.

She stopped beneath Fran's window and looked up. A light, perhaps from a table lamp, glowed behind the curtain. Should she call round, and check Fran was well? She lifted her hand to the door, ready to knock, and then withdrew it. She didn't want to impose, and turned to cross the mews.

A window creaked open behind her and she saw Fran leaning out and looking at down her.

'Morning,' Fran said. She was fully dressed and made up, but she looked tired and her voice cracked as she spoke.

'Hi.' Clo hesitated. She stared at her, trying to discern Fran's feelings. She looked hurt, but Clo didn't know why.

'I'm sorry I…'

'Would you like some…'

They both stopped.

Clo stepped forward. 'I wondered if you'd like some pastries. I brought these back for you,' and she held up the bags.

Fran tilted her head and smiled at her, her eyebrows raised in sadness. She disappeared from the window and opened the door a few moments later.

'For you,' Clo said, and she stretched to hand over a paper bag while remaining at a respectable distance.

Fran untwisted the top of the bag of pains au raisin and croissants and held her nose over the top. She smiled. 'I love the smell of fresh pastries. Thank you,' she said. 'Would you like to come up? Have one of these with me? I was about to have another cup of coffee.'

'Oh no, it's OK,' said Clo. 'It wasn't a ploy to get invited to breakfast, and I'm dirty from work,' she said, glancing down at her floured trousers.

Fran shook her head. 'That doesn't matter. Please, come and have one of these with me.'

Clo sat on a stool at the breakfast bar and laid out the bags on its top. She sat, tense, wondering if Fran's mood might change.

'Would you prefer a cup of tea?' said Fran, turning away from the cupboards. 'I know you usually have tea at home, so I bought some leaves.'

Clo grinned, too much, and elation seeped back into her body at Fran thinking of her when they were apart. 'I would love some, thank you.'

Fran glanced over her shoulder. 'What's in the other bag,' she said.

Clo dragged over the larger bag and frowned. 'I was experimenting with some recipes at the patisserie. I've got to prepare an afternoon tea in a couple of weeks for…for a friend and I'm a bit worried that I'm going to let her down.'

Fran sat down opposite with the coffee and a pot of tea. 'Why would you let her down?'

Clo tried to work out if Fran was really interested. She was nervous about talking freely to her this morning, not knowing how she had offended her on their walk in Oxford Street. She shrugged with resignation and smiled, deciding to enjoy Fran's company.

'Well, I promised my friend indulgent but not fussy food, but I just haven't quite found the right things yet. I've been working on some chocolate brownies, and I think I've got the texture and taste nearly right, but I want to bring in your sense of smell too. I tried adding a tiny amount of orange oil, but it was too much. So I've gone with some very fruity plain chocolate which is more subtle.'

'Do I get to try one?' Fran asked.

'If you like.' Clo smiled at Fran's interest in her food. She reached into the bag. 'You see, it's got to be just the right size. Here's a piece, just right to pop in your mouth.'

She held up the morsel to Fran's lips.

Fran tilted her chin, her eyes closed, and slowly opened her full red lips. She stuck out her tongue a little to lick in the offering.

Clo carefully placed the cake on her tongue, her fingertips gently catching on Fran's lips.

Fran closed her eyes and began to chew. 'Mmmm,' she said. 'Yes, that works for me.' She licked her lips and swallowed and opened her eyes. 'Do you have any more?'

Clo shuffled restlessly in her chair. 'Do you want to try something else?'

'What have you got?' said Fran, smiling.

'Now this I'm quite proud of,' said Clo, reaching into the bag. 'They're probably just the right temperature. I took them out of Vincent's oven before the end of the shift. They need to be warm to work.'

She held out a sphere of dark cake. 'Open wide.'

Fran closed her eyes and took in the cake. 'Mmmm!' she said, and her eyes opened wide.

Clo grinned. 'They're mini treacle toffee puddings with the sauce inside.'

'That's incred…' Fran raised her fingers to her lips and wiped away the sauce that she was dribbling. 'That's incredible. Mmmm!' she swallowed. 'That really is something quite special. Have you done anything else?' she said, leaning forward and trying to peer inside the bag.

Clo hesitated. 'I'm not sure about these,' she said. 'Essentially it's lemon meringue pie, but with the flavours and textures enhanced.'

She held out a small rectangle of layers. 'It's shortbread base made with icing sugar, for that melt in the mouth sensation, an extra lemony layer above and hard meringue…'

Fran took the morsel from her, before Clo could finish speaking, and popped it into her mouth. She started to chew the cake and lick her lips. She frowned as she pushed her tongue into her cheeks.

'I think that's possibly the best one yet. Perhaps because it's tart after the very sweet, what was it called, treacle toffee pudding?'

Clo began to bounce on the stool. 'Yes, that's what I thought. That's brilliant. I'll have to get you to taste the other recipes.'

'Yes please,' said Fran, smiling. 'You know, you should sell these at the patisserie.'

Clo shrugged. 'Vincent's not interested. Not in keeping with a French patisserie. I can understand his point. But.' She stopped and blushed. She felt foolish admitting an idea, a dream, she had.

She looked at her new friend and relented. 'I really wanted to get the place next door with Vincent and set up an English cake shop. Have classic English and French cake shops together and then have a shared area between them for tables and chairs and serve tea and coffee.'

'It sounds like a fantastic idea,' Fran said, smiling. She reached into the bag and pulled out another treacle toffee pudding. 'I really think these would sell like...' She looked confused.

'Like hot cakes,' said, Clo smiling.

'It is hot cakes isn't it?' Fran shook her head. 'I forget English phrases sometimes.'

Clo smiled at her. Her English was almost perfect. She thought she detected the remnants of a French accent sometimes, now that she had heard her voice for many hours. The only time that she noticed English was not Fran's native language was when she became unstuck on idioms, stupid lazy phrases that would embarrass her and trip her up.

'Anyway. I think they would sell very well,' said Fran.

'I think they would. But Vincent's not that interested again. So.' She shrugged.

'Would you make me a cake?' said Fran after a moment.

Clo sat up straight. 'I'd love to. What did you have in mind?'

'I would like to take a birthday cake for Daniel next week. I would pay you for it of course,' she said.

Clo sank back on to her stool.

Fran had looked away at her watch. 'I'm so sorry. I must leave for work. I'm going to be late,' she said. 'I must get ready.'

Clo hid her face, while she collected the bags from the surface and got off the stool.

'*À plus tard*,' Fran said.

'*À plus*,' Clo said and turned away.

*

From her sitting room window she watched Fran leave. Fran's shoes clicked over the cobbles, and Clo watched the high heels as her legs stretched back out of her skirt. Fran swirled a cream coat around her shoulders and swept out of the mews.

Clo dropped onto the sofa. It was the first time Fran had mentioned Daniel in a while. When did they carry on the affair? Was that why she was so contrary with Clo? Had she said something stupid?

Fran seemed to be at home most evenings. If she was not being fed by Clo, she would often be sitting and reading with a glass of wine. Clo could see her from her window, sitting on the sofa with her feet up, looking studious in her glasses. She liked seeing Fran in her glasses. She always wore contact lenses to work and it was a treat seeing the real Fran, out of hours, relaxed and no longer playing a character.

She reminded Clo of Mrs Hamilton. The thought surprised her. It was the perfume. They wore a very similar perfume. But also, the way she laughed. Clo felt elated when she heard Fran's laugh, when she caught her off guard with a joke or flirtation. She loved the lack of artifice at those times.

She wondered what she was like with Daniel. Was she the same? Was she seeing the real Fran? Or did she see someone she wanted to see, superimposing another personality whenever she appeared to warm towards her.

11.

Clo was going to the studios to deliver Daniel Johnston's cake. She'd spent a day covering the cake. It had a crisp chocolate biscuit base, a firm milk chocolate mousse and raspberry filling, and was coated with tempered chocolate of twelve varieties, a different variety for each slice of the cake.

She finished it with minutes to spare and placed the cake in a white box. She looked down at her clothes. She was wearing jeans covered with patches of flour and chocolate, and a T-shirt with two women kissing on the front. Would she cause Fran embarrassment arriving as she was, a small, chocolate-covered dyke asking for Mme Desmarais? But she had no time to change.

The guard at the security gate was talking to a young woman with short hair and a leather necklace, and Clo waited behind her.

'Can I help, love?' the guard asked over the woman's shoulder.

Was she meant to leave the cake here? Had Fran invited her in? She didn't want to overstep the mark again. 'I've brought a cake,' Clo said.

'Aw you shouldn't have,' said the guard.

The woman turned around, and opened her mouth to speak. She stopped and looked down at Clo and the cake box.

Clo smiled. 'It's a cake for Francoise Desmarais.'

The woman coughed and raised her eyebrows and smiled. 'I'm here to meet you. Fran was expecting you. But you're not like any baker I was expecting.' She laughed. 'Would you like to follow me?'

The woman led her into a huge grey box filled with scaffolding, cables, lights, cameras, people and clothes racks. In the centre was a well-lit area containing a domestic room where she could see Fran and Daniel. Everyone was watching them, and the cameras were pulled in close. Someone shouted 'Positions please' and the woman held her finger to her mouth and drew Clo nearer to the scene.

Clo could see Fran's face clearly. She stared up into Daniel's eyes. Her lips were tense and her eyes narrowed, concentrating on his face.

'We've got to stop,' he said.

210

Fran blinked. 'Why?'

'I'm sorry, I can't do this anymore.'

Fran didn't let go of his face, her eyes casting around his. 'But why? I don't understand. Yesterday you were talking about leaving her.'

Daniel shook his head. 'I can't now.'

'Have you changed your mind? Do you need more time?'

Daniel hesitated. 'She's pregnant,' he said.

Fran's face flickered. Her eyes widened and the frown melted away from her forehead. Her cheeks slowly dropped. Would she cry? Would her eyebrows slowly bow with grief? Clo waited for her shoulders to shake and Fran to collapse into him.

Fran slapped him across the face. The sound cracked across the studio and Clo stepped back in surprise. Fran held her hand across her chest, the follow-through frozen. Her face was a mixture of hurt and venomous anger that thrilled and frightened Clo. Her eyes were glazed, but there were no tears of grief. She stood stiffly, unapologetically staring at Daniel. There was no sound and no-one moved.

'Cut!' The director shouted across the stage and Clo breathed out. People started to move and chatter.

Fran relaxed her shoulders and laughed. 'I'm so sorry,' she said. She reached her hand up to Daniel. 'I thought you were going to move away.'

The woman elbowed Clo gently in her side. 'She's incredible, isn't she?' she said quietly.

Clo looked at her and smiled.

'I think I'm smitten,' the woman said. 'But then, unfortunately, I think she is too.'

Clo frowned and turned back, ready to observe Fran's behaviour with Daniel and gather the evidence of their attraction.

She was too late. Fran had seen her. Fran's face lifted in a smile that made Clo's heart beat quicker. Her face was suffused with blood, giving her a happy glow. Clo could feel herself growing in height on the spot, and her weight lifted.

Fran stepped over the cables and walked over to her.

'You made it,' she said. Her eyes were wide with pleasure. 'You look nice today,' she said intimately. She was near to Clo, her head leaning to the side, and she smiled, admiring her. Clo's whole body warmed with the compliment and she smiled back, mesmerised by the expression on Fran's face.

'Ladies!' a voice boomed behind them. 'I believe you have a birthday cake for me.' Daniel strode up behind Fran, making Clo leap out of her trance.

He stood beside Fran and put his arm around her shoulder. He was taller than Clo expected. The screen did not do justice to his physique.

'I'm Daniel, and I believe you are Clo?'

She smiled and nodded and opened the box to show him his gift. 'I hope you like it,' she said. 'Fran said you love chocolate and raspberries so I've improvised with this.'

The cake resembled segments of chocolate marquetry.

'My god,' he said. 'That's a piece of art, not a cake.' He stared into the box.

Clo set the box on a table and put a slice of cake on a paper plate for him. 'This piece is coated with Tanzanian chocolate, a little more vanilla flavour to it than some of the others. I think this is the best piece,' she said, lifting the offering to him.

He took the plate without speaking and took a small, tantalising mouthful.

He chewed, working the cake around his mouth. He looked as if he were really appreciating it, letting the chocolate melt in his mouth, feeling the tangy raspberry slice across the tongue, almost enough to make his eyes water.

He swallowed, and turned his attention to Clo, opening his mouth ready to speak. No words came. He stared at her instead. His mouth dropped open more and he looked to Fran and then back to Clo.

'I don't know which I'm more amazed by, the cake or the colour of your eyes,' he said, blinking.

He rubbed his hair with his spare hand and coughed. He took another mouthful from his plate.

'It's the cake,' he said. 'By a fraction I think it's the cake. This is incredible,' he said, digging in for more. 'I can't believe how luscious this cake is.' He licked his fingers. 'That is a cake to seduce someone with. It should come with a certificate, 18 and over,' he said, pointing at the box and then looking at Fran.

'Seriously, I've been seduced by less.' He put his arm around Fran's waist and pulled his fingers into her hips, drawing her closer to him. 'Food to round a woman's hips and warm her heart,' he said, grinning.

Clo looked at them both. They made a handsome couple.

Fran blushed. She folded her arms and dug the point of her shoe into the side of his foot. Daniel laughed and let her go.

*

Fran walked her to the door of the studio, their arms brushing together. Clo could feel her warmth through her sleeve. She looked at Fran's face and saw the glow still there.

'I wondered if you would like to come to a piano recital,' Fran said, smiling. 'It's next week at Wigmore Hall.'

'Oh yes. What pieces?' Clo said.

'Brahms I believe. It's a friend of Daniel's who's playing and he's arranging tickets.'

'Oh,' said Clo confused 'Is Daniel going too?'

'Yes,' Fran answered, as if this was obvious.

'OK. Yes, that would be nice.'

They continued to walk towards the door.

'I've a long day,' Fran said. 'But can I see you later?'

Clo smiled and nodded.

'Would you like to come over for a drink?' Fran said, close to her. 'I'll still be here for dinner but home by nine. Unless you're busy,' she added.

Clo shook her head. 'No, that would be lovely.' She couldn't take her eyes from Fran or stop the silly smile on her face. Fran was looking the most beautiful she'd seen her. Whatever Daniel was doing, she was thriving on it.

'Don't worry if you change your plans,' Clo said, imagining Fran being tempted by Daniel.

'Oh, I'll definitely be home,' Fran said. She stopped and pulled Clo round to face her. 'Later then,' she said.

Fran leaned forward and kissed her on the lips, the way that French friends do, and Clo couldn't help but linger that second too long.

12.

Fran heard the doorbell. She had slept in too long, on her first day off in several weeks. She came out of the bathroom, washed and wearing her dressing gown, naked without her makeup. She was not ready for Clo to see her blank old face. She was enjoying Clo's admiration too much to see it disappear when confronted with what was underneath. Too late. She could not keep Clo waiting.

She threw the keys down to Clo from the window and tried to ready herself. She sat by the breakfast bar, facing the door, and waited with a clenched stomach to see Clo's disappointment.

Clo frowned. 'You feeling OK?' she said.

Fran's stomach sank. 'I'm fine thank you. I just haven't put any makeup on yet.'

Clo shook her head, 'I meant that you're not ready for work. Are you ill?' she asked, sitting opposite her.

'I've got the day off.'

'You should have said. Did I wake you up? You could have had a lie-in,' said Clo.

'I don't like sleeping in too long anyway.'

'Amelia's like that. Although that's more because of her aches,' said Clo. 'I could lie in all day I think.'

The sadness lingered in Fran's belly. She was like an old woman, closer to a grandmother than to Clo.

She watched Clo settle, putting her bag on the floor and arranging the pastries in front of them. Clo looked up into her eyes and smiled. She watched Clo's eyes move around her own, taking in their bareness and surveying her pale cheeks and unpainted lips. Clo blushed and dropped her gaze and then raised it again to look her in the eyes.

'Not such a movie star without the makeup?' Fran said.

'No,' said Clo, a smile lifting her face. 'That's not what I was thinking. I thought that you looked naked without your makeup. It's nice.' She raised her eyes to Fran's again. 'You've got a streak of grey on your top eyelashes,' she said, leaning in closer to study them. She smiled in admiration.

Fran automatically lifted her hand to her eyelid. She usually covered that streak of grey with mascara.

'You look like you should be doing an advert for some age-defying product,' Clo said giggling.

Fran raised an eyebrow. 'So I look as if I need to use age-defying products.'

'Of course not.' Clo laughed. 'You're the after, not the before. You're just one of those women who looks their age but looks good on it,' she shrugged, then she remembered her news. 'Hey, Vincent might be interested in extending the range at the patisserie. He's asked me to put together some samples and then we'll see how it goes,' Clo said, excitement bubbling up.

'That's fantastic,' Fran said, and a pulse of teary joy rose through her chest. It shocked her how Clo's emotions played with hers. Seeing her smile made her feel overjoyed. Seeing her despair was overwhelming. She had never mirrored another adult's feelings to this extent before. The sensation was both thrilling and terrifying.

'What are you up to today then?' said Clo, biting into a croissant.

'I was wondering if you would like to come for a walk,' Fran said. 'It looks like it's going to be the first sunny day in ages and it's a wonderful and frosty morning.'

'Sounds good, although I might slump a bit,' said Clo, swallowing a mouthful. 'I need to get some sleep at some point.'

'I'll bundle you into a taxi if you drift off,' Fran said.

'Or if I get a bit dull,' suggested Clo.

'That too,' laughed Fran.

*

They sat in St James' Park, surrounded by the city. The morning sun hadn't yet burned through the mist, and it smoked around the frosted grass and lake.

They sat on a bench by the side of a path, clouds of vapour swirling around their heads in the soft light, their breath mingling around them. Fran had her hands deep in the pockets of her long, thick coat, but she lifted her head back to let her face take in the weak warmth of the sun.

'I love sunny days in autumn,' she said. 'I don't have to worry about getting a tan and causing a continuity headache for the director.'

215

Clo didn't say anything.

Fran turned to her. 'My grandmother's Algerian, so I tan very easily,' she explained.

Clo smiled and nodded.

'Did you know that?' said Fran, laughing.

Clo blushed. 'Yes, I'm afraid so. I did tell you I'm a bit of a fan. Does that freak you out?'

'No it doesn't.' Fran raised an eyebrow. 'Perhaps I know things about you too,' she said.

Clo frowned and turned away. Fran was about to apologise.

A young woman was jogging in their direction, her pony tail swinging behind her head. Her head faced straight ahead but her eyes looked sidelong towards Clo. Clo still stared away from Fran, and she assumed that she looked at the woman too. The jogger's eyes tracked Clo, as she ran past with an expression of pleasure on her face. Fran waited for Clo to turn round, to follow the knowing look of the runner, but she continued to look away.

'Did you not notice the woman running past?' Fran asked.

Clo turned around. 'Sorry?'

'That woman jogging by. She really looked at you.'

Clo looked past her to the jogger. She shook her head. 'No. Do you think she knew me?'

Fran sat up straight. 'How are you single?'

Clo stared at her blinking, but didn't respond.

'When was the last time you were involved with someone?' Fran asked.

'A long time ago. Ten years.'

'Why?' said Fran, shocked.

Clo shuffled uncomfortably. 'I don't... I don't get on so well in relationships.' she said, struggling to get the words out.

'Who does really?' said Fran. 'Haven't all but the last failed in some way?'

'I seem to be worse than most,' Clo said and she turned away. Fran could see her gulp, a ripple flowing down her throat in a beam of sunlight.

'But that shouldn't stop you trying,' said Fran, confused.

'I did, once,' she said. 'But she tried to kill herself.'

Fran felt cold. She feared that she had inadvertently uncovered a familiar personality. She shivered unpleasantly with fear.

'Why did she try to kill herself?' Fran asked flatly.

'Because I didn't love her enough. I was always one step behind her. She was just that bit keener, that bit more in love.' Clo paused. 'It makes people think and feel terrible things when they are always yearning and rejected by the person closest to them. And I didn't know that at the time.'

'Did you promise her things you couldn't give? Try to keep her interested?'

'Do you mean did I string her along?' Clo asked, turning around. Her eyes were red and watery.

'Yes,' said Fran.

'Not intentionally. I liked her. I didn't realise I was meant to like her a lot more.'

'Did you leave her?' Fran asked, still frigid with revulsion.

Clo became more agitated. 'She asked me to leave,' she said, shakily. 'I didn't know that she meant stay. I was young and I didn't know that I was meant to plead with her to stay. I thought she had finished it, and I was gutted. We weren't getting on well. I was surprised she wanted to end it so abruptly, but it wasn't so unexpected that I shouldn't believe her and insist on her taking me back.

'Look, I don't understand the rules of relationships,' Clo continued. 'I'm less naïve than I used to be, and I can read people's behaviour better, but as soon as love goes wrong I don't understand people any more.'

Fran blinked and Clo came back into focus. She was upset and it was because Fran had goaded her. Fran felt dreadful. She picked up Clo's hand and looked down at it.

'I'm sorry. Forgive me,' she said, shaking her head. 'You hit a nerve. I can explain.' But she could not. Her mouth was dry of words. She put her arm round Clo's shoulders. 'I'm sorry.'

Clo was breathing heavily beside her. 'That's OK. It was a horrible time,' she said, wiping her eyes. 'My parents hated me because of it. I could see the disgust on Mum's face at the hospital. And Dad, he looked so ashamed. So I know, it was my fault. OK? But I paid a heavy price for it.'

Fran clutched her forehead, agitated by her pushing at Clo, her cruel questioning.

'I'm sorry,' is all she could say over again. No other words, no better explanation would come out.

Clo sat back, breathing out heavily. 'No, I'm over-reacting. It's me,' Clo said. 'I just saw my parents again recently, and I'm still a bit sore from that,' she said reaching out to hold Fran's hand.

Fran grabbed for the lifeline Clo had thrown her. 'You've still not made up with them?' she asked.

'No. And I don't think it's going to happen now,' Clo said. 'I still get on with Dad. I always have. It's just what happened back then and Mum that comes between us,' she said, frustrated. 'But Mum? I always used to think that we would sort it out. That in the end we would be a happy family, all issues resolved. But I don't think it's going to happen anymore. The last time was just awful. Amelia and she went at each other so violently; just detested each other,' she said, shaking her head.

'But you get on with Amelia?'

'Oh yes,' Clo said, turning to her, smiling so that the old tears were squeezed from her eyes and ran down her cheeks. 'I'm really lucky to have Amelia. I wish you could meet her,' she said, looking into Fran's eyes. 'I think you would like her. I think she would like you. She speaks French and she's an amazing lady,' Clo's eyes flicked between Fran's excitedly.

Fran wanted to smile. She shuffled uncomfortably next to Clo. She had so much to tell her. Some things she wanted to say, some things she should. All the things she had needed to tell her that day in Oxford Street, but she did not know how to begin. She opened her mouth wanting to say 'I'm sorry'. She thought how she would explain, but it would mean telling her everything, from the beginning.

But that was the most painful memory of all, what she had been trying to recover from all these years. She rocked forwards and backwards, trying to force herself to tell Clo the truth. Her chest clenched, resisting the breath necessary to make the words. She had to force out her stomach to let the air in.

'I had a child. I had a son. He died.' She was taking deep heavy breaths, gasping for air between her sentences. 'He was knocked down. Killed straight away. He was only three.'

She had to force out the words. It felt like she was painfully throwing them up. Her body pulsed, her aching heart beating hard and fast. A rushing noise deafened her. A wave of intense grief gathered in her belly, rose up her chest, and threatened to overcome her. The despair filled her. How could she have turned away? Why had she not stopped him from walking towards the road?

She thought she might black out with the pain of divulging her secret. She was unaware of where she was. She couldn't see. She wasn't sure if it was light or dark. She felt the old wounds. As if a massive claw had reached out and gouged her insides, leaving them open and screaming raw with pain. She heard herself howl. She did not know if it was a memory, or if she howled at that moment. She was rocking over her empty insides, clutching that hollowness that never went away. No matter what she did, there was always that sickening loss.

She was aware of warm tears, flooding down her cheeks. Streams and streams of them, as if someone was pouring warm water over her face. She was clinging to someone. She had her head on a shoulder. She was rocking slowly with them. They stroked her hair and held her tight. They were warm.

Clo was holding her upright, squeezing her tight. Fran could feel her soft warm cheek against hers. Time had passed, she had no idea how long. She opened her eyes, surprised to see bright sunlight over Clo's shoulder. She blinked, and the world came back into harsh focus. She saw people walking around the park, walking their dogs and chatting with friends. It seemed so odd how everyone carried on with their lives around her. She was cold, exhausted and exposed, an oddity in the world.

'Take me home,' she murmured, not wanting to be seen. She did not want to be exposed to anyone except Clo.

*

She was shivering. Clo tucked a duvet around her on the sofa. She put pillows behind her head and made her warm, sugary, alcoholic coffee. Fran felt drained. She tried to focus her mind. She had only just begun her story. She had so much to tell yet. But she shook whenever she tried to gather her thoughts together.

Clo laid a soft hand on her face, stroked her cheek and gently kissed her on the forehead. Fran drifted off.

*

'He would have been about your age,' she said later. 'It's strange when I think of it like that. I've been missing a little boy for over twenty-five years. It makes it seem unreal when I realise that. Like my grief can't be real, because he wouldn't be how I imagine him to be, how I remember him.

'He would have been a grown man, perhaps with a family of his own. I start to picture how he might have looked: tall, dark hair, smiling and laughing. I imagine his wife and his family, like they're on a video.

'And then I realise that it's all made up. That I will never know if that's anything like it would have been. And then the image fades and disappears and I feel numb inside. Until the next time, when it seems like it only just happened, that I just turned my back and I have lost my child again.'

She could not say anymore, not right now.

13.

Clo stared at herself in the bedroom mirror. She was meeting Fran straight from work at Wigmore Hall, and she wondered if she had dressed appropriately to accompany her.

Clo had kept her hair short after the initial shearing. Today she brushed it flat, parted and slicked to the side. She wore a cream suit, which she had found in the charity shop, similar to one she used to wear for Marella's work. She knew she looked best in that. She wore a fine merino jumper next to her skin, cut so low that when she buttoned her jacket it appeared she was naked beneath. She added a silver necklace with a long pendant that rested in her cleavage. The look was respectable, but androgynous.

She applied some eyeliner, mascara and lipstick. The effect was immediate. Much more heterosexual, but she did not wear it comfortably today. She wasn't dressing for a client. Her eyes and lips were ludicrously big and she looked like a cartoon version of herself. She wiped off the lipstick, leaving a trace of eyeliner. She was herself again and she hoped Fran would approve.

It was dark when she arrived in Wigmore Street. She walked along the orange-lit pavement towards the hall's entrance with its ornate metal and glass awning. Men and women in long, dark coats politely shuffled in from the street, holding open the doors for each other. She spotted Fran waiting a little way from the entrance. She wondered if she was hiding, meeting Clo in secret and waiting until everyone had settled, before creeping in at the last moment.

Fran looked nervous. She held her clutch bag with both hands, glanced up and down the street, and paced across a few squares of the pavement in her black high heels. A small crowd hid her for a moment. Clo walked towards the entrance and strained her gaze over the queue of people. The men and women streamed in and disappeared, leaving her face to face with Fran.

Fran's lips parted and her mouth dropped open when she saw her. Fran stepped forwards. 'You look stunning,' she said.

Clo could not take her eyes from Fran's. Her eyes were dark and wide, her admiration complete and unrestrained. Clo was too shocked to blush.

'Thank you,' she said.

'Daniel and his wife are downstairs in the bar. Shall we join them?'

'I didn't know he was married,' Clo said

Fran nodded with a single bow of the head and turned to be by her side. She took her hand, and Fran's eyes did not leave hers for a second.

'Are you feeling all right?' Clo asked, worried about Fran's state from the day before.

'Perfectly,' she said. Fran stroked her soft fingers beneath Clo's chin, turning her face towards her. Fran bent her head and gently pressed her lips against Clo's in a greeting.

Clo shut her eyes and felt her bottom lip slip between Fran's and let herself enjoy the sensation of enclosing her mouth. She felt Fran touch her cheek, cradling it in her hand, and her head began to lighten as if drifting off to a most pleasant oblivion. She couldn't tell how long they stood there, melting together. Her lips slowly, deliciously, slipped over Fran's, the sensation thrilling every nerve in her body. She fell back slightly, as her lips closed and she came back to earth, hazily, blinking with heavy, drugged eyes and a smile on her face.

Fran looked at her, absorbed, and without taking her eyes from her, led her into the hall. Clo grinned and felt as if she floated beside her.

They descended to the bar, which was heaving with blue, beige and black-clad men and women, drinking Champagne and single malt whiskies. Clo could smell the peat from the whiskies and hear the glasses chinking in between the chatter and polite laughter.

Faces turned towards them, looking at Fran with flickers of recognition and admiration and then to Clo. She expected Fran to drop her hand, but Fran held it firm and Clo could not help the smile that stretched across her face as she basked in the approval. They found a space at the end of the bar and Fran scanned over the crowd on tiptoes.

'Will you wait here?' Fran said, her voice deep and quiet. 'I'll try to find Daniel and bring them here.'

Clo nodded, willing to do anything that Fran asked, and watched her disappear into the crowd. She leant against the wall, still trembling and high from the kiss and her acceptance by Fran. She felt warm and light inside and clutched the bar in a daze.

'Rebecca. What a surprise.'

The warm, light feeling was instantly replaced by a cold flood of fear, which plunged through her body as she recognised Mrs Eleanor Abraham's gravelled voice. She spun round to see her just steps away.

Sharp and angular in her black suit and grey bob, she cut through the crowd to sidle up to the bar. Clo could smell the cigarette residue on her as Mrs Abrahams pushed her body up to Clo's. Mrs Abrahams clawed at her arms that she held protectively against her chest.

'Relax my dear, or you'll attract attention to us.' Mrs Abrahams grinned, showing her yellow teeth.

Clo dropped her arms, but took a step back, recoiling from her client.

'Well, I see you're back at work. That's good. And how much does it cost to have you for an evening out? Marella never said that was an option.'

Clo stared at her, dumb, only capable of wishing her away.

'Well? I'm genuinely interested. It's been too long Rebecca, far too long.'

Clo couldn't speak, and she stood frozen, staring at her predator.

'I like the hair by the way. I wouldn't have thought it, but I do. It makes you look younger. Very sexy.' Clo stared at the woman's mouth as it hissed and licked over the words. Mrs Abrahams lifted up her claw to Clo's face, stretched out a finger and stroked across her cheek. A long fingernail scraped down her skin. 'Yes, beautiful and youthful,' she said. 'Is that what your other client likes?'

She thought she was with a client. She would think Fran was a client. Clo backed into the wall and looked nervously around Mrs Abrahams, scanning the crowd in a panic. Fran would be back any second.

'I have to go,' she stuttered.

Mrs Abrahams' eyes narrowed. 'What's the matter? Not done to intrude on someone else's time?'

Clo pushed her hands out. 'I must go.' She pushed away from her to head towards the door. Mrs Abrahams' fingers dug sharply into her arm and pulled her back.

Mrs Abrahams glared into her eyes. 'I want you,' she hissed, 'I don't care what it costs.'

'Let me go, please,' Clo said. She tried to tear herself away, urgently searching the room for Fran. She couldn't bear that she might see them together. And no-one must see Fran in her company for a second longer. The thought that anyone would think she was a client made Clo feel ill.

Fran emerged from the bodies at the bar. She stopped just a few metres away and stared at Clo and then Mrs Abrahams. A slight frown and look of confusion rippled across her face. She looked at Clo with an expression that Clo could not distinguish.

Clo choked, filled with despair. 'I'm sorry,' she mouthed. She gave Fran a desperate look of regret and turned, snatching her arm from Mrs Abrahams, and fled the room. She ran up the stairs, her chest aching and her heart breaking, as tears poured down her face.

'Clo!'

She heard Fran's voice behind her. She ran faster up the stairs and sprinted towards the entrance.

'Clo! Please wait!'

She was out on the empty street, but still Fran pursued her. She turned under the dim street light and saw Fran emerge from the doorway. Fran saw her immediately and started to walk towards her.

'Please stop. You can't be seen with me,' Clo shouted. She shook her head violently. Her voice broke as she shouted. 'Please, you must stay away.'

Fran slowed her walk but still approached her.

'Please,' Clo whispered. Her face was heavy with sadness, her brow despairing and her mouth weighed down in grief. 'You mustn't be seen with me.'

Fran stopped, her face imploring Clo to stay. 'Please, you can tell me you know. Please don't be afraid,' she said.

Clo wished she could explain and the lump in her throat choked her. The hopelessness of her position and her past weighed heavy around her heart. Her head bowed, and all optimistic feeling drained away.

'I'm sorry. I must leave you alone.' And she turned and ran up the street.

*

Clo sat in darkness, by the window, the curtains open. She hugged her knees, her head bowed. Tears and dribble continued to roll down her face and drop onto her chest and stomach. She felt the full weight of her grief, and her skin and flesh were leaden on her frame. She could not lift her face from her knees.

From the corner of her eye, across the mews, she saw the light come on. She saw a silhouette at the window. It waited for perhaps ten minutes and then slowly receded. The light went off.

Clo knew what she wanted to think, but she didn't want to say it clearly in her head. 'I don't want to lose her.' Saying those stupid words, as if Fran could ever have been her lover. She was stupid, so stupid.

She had become infatuated with Francoise Desmarais. Like all those people who fell in lust with her. Falling for her beauty and deliriously in love with her, without any regard for how she might feel or whether they could ever think of being together.

'I love her and I don't want to lose her.' The thought was clear and insistent. She closed her eyes to try to stop the overpowering thoughts, and squeezed yet more warm tears from her eyes.

She would have done anything for Fran, anything to have her, but there was nothing she could do. The chance – but inevitable – encounter with Mrs Abrahams suddenly made it clear to her that she couldn't be someone else or change her past. She needed to stay away and never be seen in public with Fran.

She realised how much she would miss the sound of Fran's voice. She loved the way she sometimes dropped the letter 'h'. She would miss having breakfast with her every day. She loved that Fran loved food and that she made fun of Clo and raised her eyebrow. She loved watching films with her. She loved laughing at the same things and laughing at Fran when she found something hysterically funny that Clo had not. She loved that she kissed her goodnight. She loved that when she looked out of the bedroom last thing, Fran was always there to wave to her. And the thought that it would never happen again overwhelmed her, and she began to sob without restraint into her knees.

14.

Clo watched Fran leave for work in the early morning twilight. She watched from the darkness of the living room, as Fran walked up the mews towards the studio car waiting under the archway. Her head was bowed and she walked slowly. The driver held open the back door for her, and as she turned she looked up towards Clo, almost directly into her eyes. Clo's heart clenched as she saw the expression on Fran's face, drained and tired. The compulsion to rush out to her and comfort her was overwhelming, but she gripped the window ledge and forced herself to stay.

She had slept badly, waking and panicking that Mrs Abrahams might have approached Fran after Clo had fled. Tears welled up whenever she pictured Fran being told of her secret life. She'd given up on sleep at four o'clock in the morning and got up to bake for Marella's afternoon tea.

She thought it would distract her, but all she could think of was how she had enjoyed baking the treats for Fran, and her heart lurched again at the loss.

Late in the afternoon, she rang the bell on Marella's Kensington business flat with difficulty from behind a stack of white cardboard boxes. She could see the top of the door open above the boxes, but her view was obscured. She heard Marella laugh.

'I assume that's you under there Clo. Come in.'

Marella's hand guided her in through the door, along the wide hallway into a kitchen that overlooked the garden square. Clo set down the boxes on the table in the middle of the room and lifted the lids on each.

Marella peered into the open boxes and walked her fingers over the morsels, a smile on her lips.

'These look delicious,' she said. 'What are they?' She held up a small sphere of mini treacle toffee pudding.

Clo took the pudding from her, gave it ten seconds in the microwave, and handed it back. Marella bit into it. Her eyebrows lifted. She closed her eyes, chewing and appreciating the small pudding and clotted cream and caramel that oozed from the centre.

'That,' she said with uncharacteristic indelicacy, her mouth still full, 'is genius. They are going to love these.'

Clo smiled. It was an effort, and her tired face ached. She turned back to unpacking the cakes and arranging them on a tiered cake stand. Marella kept glancing towards her, their eyes meeting for a moment, before turning back to the cakes.

'You look tired,' she said, quietly.

'Bad night's sleep,' Clo said.

Clo continued arranging the cakes, but Marella stepped back and studied her closely. She leaned against the table and crossed her arms.

'I had a phone call from Mrs Abrahams this morning,' Marella said.

Clo dropped the small ball of cake she was handling and watched it roll across the kitchen floor.

'Oh,' she said.

'She wants to arrange an appointment.' Marella tilted her head, trying to catch Clo's eyes.

'Are you ready to come back?' Marella asked. She sounded unsure even questioning her.

Clo stood still, her arms by her sides, and stared at the cake on the floor. Her limbs were heavy and her head sagged. She couldn't think of a single reason not to go back. Her week's work at the patisserie couldn't keep Amelia and her as comfortably as a session with Mrs Abrahams. She would never find someone who would cope with her background, least of all the only woman she had ever truly loved, and whom Clo couldn't risk exposing to ridicule.

'Perhaps,' she said, not lifting her head.

She saw Marella's foot moving on the floor. She tapped her foot from the tip of her high heel to the ball of her foot. Clo met her gaze. Marella was analysing her.

'I think I'm ready,' Clo said, trying to sound confident.

Marella nodded and looked away. She breathed in deeply and then out through her nose in a laugh.

'You know, I heard some gossip the other day that might interest you,' she said. She was staring at her own foot that still tapped the floor. 'Rumour has it that your favourite film star's a dyke,' she said.

'What?' Clo shook her head, confused about who Marella referred to.

'Francoise Desmarais. Rumour has it that she's a dyke,' she repeated.

Clo frowned. 'But it's not true,' she said. The word 'dyke' sounded nasty when applied to Fran like that, in the context of gossip.

'No really. It's from a source that's likely to be accurate,' said Marella.

'That's rubbish. Who's the source?' said Clo.

'I heard it a few days ago, through a friend of a friend, admittedly. But it comes from someone on set, apparently.' Marella looked at her without flinching. 'She's had a constant companion while she's been in London.'

Clo was on the verge of refuting it again, when her own defence dawned on her. Fran did not have time to have a constant companion with her busy shooting schedule. When would she fit someone else in? And besides, she saw her at breakfast time and most evenings. Clo had even seen her most weekends too. Clo would have noticed, being in her company constantly. And indeed, at last, she did.

'But,' she stuttered, struggling with the realisation. 'It might just be a friend.'

Marella smiled at her. 'Are you not pleased? '

'I just don't think it's true,' she said, dazed.

'Well, the companion is apparently way too attractive to be just a friend,' said Marella, laughing.

Clo blushed.

'Apparently the photographer doing the stills was around the day she called in on set,' Marella continued, 'so there may even be a photo of her.'

Clo chilled inside. Her hands began to shake and her stomach churn with nausea. She was too late. She had already been associated with Fran, seen by too many people with too much inclination to gossip. The thought of Fran being ridiculed for having a prostitute for a companion was unbearable. She thought of how upset Fran would be by the humiliation.

Clo could not think straight. She knew she was tired, but her mind was teeming and confused. She kept imagining Fran's expression at being associated with a whore. She would be angry at Clo selfishly allowing Fran to befriend her while knowing she would be a source of gossip and ridicule.

'Oh god,' Clo said.

'Are you OK?' said Marella.

'Tired, so tired,' was all she could say.

'I'll call you a taxi,' said Marella, worried.

Clo's head buzzed with competing thoughts. She strained to think clearly. She must warn Fran. Such a noise in her head and sorrow clenching at her chest; it made her gasp, the strength of it. What time was it? She had to squint at the clock on the taxi dashboard, struggling to make her mind concentrate enough to take note of the time. Fran would nearly be home. She must keep her heart from breaking and her head from screaming until then. It took an effort to contain them.

She knocked on Fran's door. 'Oh god,' she muttered aloud. The thought of having to tell the last person she wanted to know about her past made her feel ill. Her head reeled and grief plunged in her chest. Stop it, she tried to think. Fresh tears sprang hot in her eyes.

Fran opened the door. The happy expression she had been wearing to greet her quickly dropped away. 'Come in,' she said. 'Come and sit down.'

She drew Clo gently by the hand up the stairs. Clo felt limp and horrible, wishing Fran would not touch her. Fran sat Clo on the sofa and sat on the window seat to attend to her. She tried to hold her hand.

'Don't,' said Clo. She shook her head, drawing away the hand that would soon repel her. Clo stood up, trying to avoid the intimacy that was about to vanish.

'You can tell me what's wrong,' said Fran.

Clo breathed in and squared her shoulders, preparing herself for what would inevitably come. 'I heard some gossip today,' she said, 'about you and me.' She swallowed.

Fran smiled. 'I think I've heard that rumour too,' she said. 'I think that naughty Daniel may have started it.'

'But you can't be associated with me,' said Clo, the pain and panic breaking through again.

'Why not?' shrugged Fran. 'I'm a middle-aged actress way past my prime. What do I have to lose? I've had silly gossip about me before. It will pass.'

'You don't understand. There are things you don't know about me…There are things…'

Fran stood up and stretched out her arms to comfort her, but Clo stuck out her hands to keep her away. 'Don't come close to me. Please don't be nice to me.'

Fran stopped and frowned. 'There are things I haven't told you as well. Things I should have told you. Things I've known.'

Clo shook her head. 'Please.'

'I should have told you weeks ago,' Fran continued. 'I knew this would be painful, but I was too much of a coward to tell you.'

'Please let me tell you.'

'I was too embarrassed to start with…'

'Please be quiet!' Clo shouted.

Fran froze in front of her. Clo saw her through blurred tired and teary eyes. She saw the silhouette of Mrs Hamilton against the window, nervously holding her hands crossed in front of her.

Clo collapsed to her knees and burst into wracking sobs.

15.

Clo knelt before Fran, with her hands held protectively around her head. Fran got down on her knees and tried to peer through the arms and fingers. She could see her breathing deeply, convulsively. Clo's ribs expanded and her body rocked as her lungs forced her to expand and then collapse again. Her tears had stopped, but she didn't speak. Fran felt numb, her consoling touch rejected. She was isolated, unable to comfort Clo and mend the thing she had broken.

Clo's breathing was becoming quieter, more controlled. She uncurled her head from her hands, her face red. She pushed herself away from Fran, leaning back against the armchair. She drew up her knees in front of her, a defence between them. Her eyelids were swollen, pink and sore. She swallowed hard, trying to regain her speech.

'I don't understand what you want,' she said.

Fran smiled, relieved that Clo had begun to talk.

'I think you are attracted to me in some way,' Clo said, looking up at her. 'But I think I also disgust you. You're repelled by me at times.'

Fran shook her head. 'It's not that. I could never find you disgusting.' A wave of sorrow flooded through her for the way she had equivocated over how she felt about Clo, the effect this must have had on her, pulling her in and then pushing her away. Fran had not meant to toy with her.

'I can understand why you would be disgusted,' said Clo. 'I don't have a past that's easy to deal with. My job isn't pleasant to think about.'

'I don't have a problem with that,' said Fran. 'I know you play a role. And I knew what you did when I met you. It would have been stupid of me, unfair, to pursue you if I'd had a problem with that. As long as you can give it up.'

'Then I don't understand,' said Clo, her eyebrows creasing up again, her eyes wide with despair. 'Is it that I'm a woman, that I'm the first woman you've been attracted to? I could understand that. I've known plenty of women who were unsure at first,' she trailed off.

The words stuck in Fran's throat again. She could explain, but it was not her story to tell anymore. Not only her story.

'What do you want from me?' said Clo.

Fran smiled, breathing out a half laugh. 'Isn't it obvious?'

'No,' said Clo, raising her voice in exasperation. 'Do you know how many feelings I have for you? I have had a crush on you since, since I can remember. You were this wonderful, beautiful ideal woman while I grew up. I had pictures of you on my wall and hidden in my school books.

'And then,' she gulped, 'I met Mrs Hamilton. The first person in a very long time I've had feelings for. That was the first time I understood what people meant when they said they instantly knew someone is for them. I don't think I really believed that before. And then I felt so bad about myself, realising how far away I was from having someone wonderful like her.

'I felt lost that morning, coming home. I wanted to stay, and kiss, and hold…' Clo swallowed, 'I had never felt that strongly about anyone… And then I meet you,' she said laughing through her tears. 'And I fall for you,' she said, despairing. 'I had a crush on Francoise the film star, I fell for Mrs Hamilton and I'm in love with you,' she said, shaking her head. 'How many times do you have to make me love you?' She shook herself, almost angry.

'Do you know how humiliated I feel?' she said. 'How stupid you must have thought me. How stupid was I? A real Lois Lane level of stupidity,' she said.

Fran's lips twitched in a smile, but she said nothing.

'And so,' Clo continued 'through all that, I can't tell anymore, never could, what on earth you want with me.'

Fran smiled, unable any longer to hold back her adoration. As bewilderment clouded Clo's face, she wanted only to take her into her arms and hold her. She looked at Clo, trying to gauge if her touch would be welcome.

'Could you love me? In time could you love me?' Clo asked.

Fran swallowed away the rising joy and sorrow. She nodded, 'Yes I could.'

'Could you love me, physically?' asked Clo.

'Oh good god yes,' said Fran.

Fran moved closer, unable to tell if Clo would still reject her touch. She slowly put out her hand and reached for Clo's face to tentatively touch her cheek. The caress was thrilling, that first touch after feeling isolated; cold dejection to feeling the heat of another body, accepting now where before it was rejected. Clo held Fran's hand to her cheek. She squeezed it and turned her face into it, kissing the palm hopefully.

Clo's lips felt luscious against her skin. Fran's arm tingled, coming alive at the sensation that ran through her limb and down her body. She lifted her hand to Clo's head, stroking over her hair, pulling her closer. She kissed her head, her soft hair, her forehead, across her eyebrows, her still wet eyelids, her soft, warm, salty cheeks, moving hungrily towards the corner of her mouth.

Clo turned cautiously to meet her mouth. Fran's lips swelled with the anticipation of her kiss. She kissed tentatively, dabbing her mouth on Clo's. Her lips moistened as Clo's lips moved over hers. Her soft, delicious lips slid and teased her mouth. Fran kissed her deeply, taking more of her in, unable to get enough of her taste. She ran her tongue around the inside of Clo's lips, melting into her.

They knelt up in front of each other, not wanting to lose contact with each other's lips. Their hands grabbed at each other urgently, not knowing what to touch next but wanting so badly to touch. Fran kissed across Clo's face in large greedy kisses. She kissed down her neck to the delicate curves and caves of her shoulder and collar bone.

Clo fumbled with Fran's shirt, pulling the front apart and tearing buttons off where it would not yield. Fran dropped her hands down Clo's back and dragged at her T-shirt, unable to remove it quickly enough. She pushed away at her own shirt sleeves as Clo pulled at them.

Fran slid her hand down Clo's smooth back, unhooking her bra as Clo did the same to her. They parted slightly, letting their clothes drop away, and then slowly, deliciously, pushed their breasts together. Fran breathed out. A tear threatened to spill at the sensation of being held close. She squeezed Clo into her, wanting to feel her body against her own.

Clo started kissing her, down her throat and down her chest, kissing large mouthfuls of her skin. Clo tugged at the fastening of Fran's skirt. Fran let her go, and put her hands behind her back to help unhook the skirt while Clo fed on her breasts. Fran's mind went blank. Waves of sensation pulsed through her body as Clo closed her mouth around her nipple and swept her tongue over it. Fran tried to tug at her skirt zip but could not coordinate her thoughts and body as Clo satiated herself on her breasts.

Clo pushed down Fran's skirt and her knickers. Fran could feel she was already wet as they slid moistly past her thighs. She blushed with embarrassment at her body's full, overflowing reaction to Clo's touch.

Shaking, Fran ran her fingers around the waistband of Clo's jeans and pulled at the buttons, popping them open. She dragged the jeans and knickers down in one movement, stroking her hands over Clo's buttocks. She pushed Clo gently to the soft rug and pulled her jeans away as she leant back. She lay beside her, looking down the body that shuddered in anticipation. Fran stroked Clo's chest and circled her smooth breasts. Clo tensed, her body clenching with every tantalising circle. Fran moved her fingers closer to the erect nipple.

She looked at Clo's face and saw her eyes were dark and fixed on hers. Fran gently teased her nipple between her fingers. Clo was breathing quickly and Fran could hear the rasping excitement of her breath as she squeezed her gently, massaging her breast at the same time. Clo looked at her, her face and lips flushed and full but her eyebrows crinkled and raised, as if helpless in pain. Her mouth quivered. She was unable to speak. It was the most arousing thing that Fran had ever seen.

She ran her finger down Clo's stomach and watched her muscles tense in rhythm, pushing her body closer to Fran's touch. Fran pushed her fingers through Clo's hair, seeing the ferocity of her clenching increase, and teased her, circling her fingers above her clitoris, touching gently at the curly hair. Clo moved, almost agitated, beneath her. She put her hand out to Fran and pulled her body closer, parting her legs.

Fran stopped her circling and slowly moved her fingers lower. Clo stopped moving and gave her one last pleading look. Fran moved her fingers, slipping into the lubrication between Clo's lips, and Clo cried out and curled tense beneath her.

Fran thought that she might black out with the pleasure she felt at the way Clo reacted to her touch, arousal taking over her body. She moved her fingers quicker, feeling Clo become bigger and move more urgently against her.

Clo pulled her closer, moaning frustration at not being able to reach her. And then Fran felt the softest, gentlest touch between her own legs. Soundlessly she tensed. Her mouth opened, wanting to cry out, but the spasm made her mute.

'Oh,' she finally breathed out, the first spasm receding. And then 'Oh' with every circling touch that Clo made. Just a few more touches, she thought, stroking Clo more firmly and pushing herself onto Clo's hand. Overcome and out of control they made each other come hard, writhing tightly together, crying out at the release of the weeks of tensions.

*

They lay entwined on the sofa under the duvet. Fran watched Clo snoozing as her head rested on Fran's arm. She looked at every curve and plane of her face, taking advantage of her first opportunity to savour her up close. Clo looked less perfect asleep. Her cheeks sagged, relaxed and unconscious. Her mouth had opened, her lower jaw relaxing. She looked more real. Fran glowed with the warmth she felt towards her and could not help smiling at her sleeping face.

Clo closed her mouth and her cheeks rose back into place. She pursed her lips together and then one eye, and then the other, popped open. She opened and closed her lips again, trying to wake her mouth.

'Sorry. Have I been asleep?' she said.

'Yes, you have,' said Fran laughing.

Clo raised her eyebrows high, trying to keep her eyes open. 'I'm so sorry. That's unforgiveable isn't it, just drifting off to sleep.'

Fran smiled. 'Not at all,' she said reaching up to stroke her face with her free hand.

Clo blinked and blinked again, trying to focus on Fran and then she let her face settle at last, fully awake.

'Is my face a mess?' asked Fran. 'Is my makeup everywhere?'

Clo smiled a sleepy happy smile, 'Yes it is.'

And Fran laughed.

'I still can't quite believe you want to be with me,' said Clo. 'After that?'

Clo flushed. 'You know what I mean.'

'I do yes,' said Fran. 'I think I wanted you from the first moment I saw you,' she added.

'When I fell into your breasts?'

'No,' said Fran laughing again. 'I saw you from the window. You were helping some American tourists. I heard your voice. It's very seductive. I could listen to it all day.'

Clo smiled, perhaps too conscious of her voice to talk at that moment.

'Yes. I think that probably was the moment.'

'Did you follow me home?' asked Clo at last.

'Yes I did,' said Fran. It was still painful remembering the shock, being overcome by seeing Amelia after all those years, and realising who the wonderful young woman that she had fallen for must be. She was frowning, she realised. Too quiet, too abrupt an answer.

'Will you tell me some day?' asked Clo.

Fran nodded.

'Will it change the way I feel about you?'

Fran shook her head. 'No, I don't think it will.

Part 5. A Revelation

1.

Laura sat on the bench in front of the grand piano. Helen had said she could play while she stayed, but she'd felt too awkward to try while Helen and Susan were at home. Susan was on another night shift and Helen was not yet back.

Laura lifted the fallboard and stared at the keys. They looked more yellow than her cheap Yamaha keyboard. She touched the key for middle C and gently pressed it, feeling the difference in weight between the grand piano and the keyboard at home. The note rang out perfectly. Helen must have had the instrument tuned.

Laura sorted through the sheets on the music holder and found Debussy's *Girl with the Flaxen Hair*, generously scored with pencil marks to indicate change in tempo and dynamics. She spread out the sheets and hesitantly started to play, checking her fingers across the keys and glancing up again at the music. She played the piece through slowly, getting used to the keyboard, then again with confidence.

'That's beautiful.' Helen's voice came from the doorway. She smiled and walked towards her.

Laura pulled her hands away from the keyboard and placed them in her lap. 'I'm sorry. I didn't hear you come in.'

Helen stopped by the piano. 'I came in quietly,' she said, smiling. 'I could hear you from the street. It was wonderful.'

Laura stuttered. 'I'm just getting used to the instrument. And I'm a bit rusty too.'

'It was slower than Isabelle used to play it, but beautiful nonetheless.'

Laura was embarrassed, caught by Helen at her sister's instrument. She was nervous of overstepping Helen's hospitality and risking her disapproval.

Helen put her hand out. 'I didn't mean to stop you, by the way. Please carry on.'

Laura swallowed and stretched out her fingers over the keys, reluctant to refuse the request. The blood had left her hands and her arms felt full of nerves. She looked up at the music but couldn't focus on the notes.

'You're shaking,' Helen said, grabbing Laura's hand and holding it in hers. She sat down on the bench next to Laura and held her hand on her knee.

The apprehension spread up Laura's arms, through her chest and up her neck so that her voice trembled when she spoke. 'Sorry. I feel bad about staying and the trouble I've caused.'

'Oh no, you mustn't.' Helen squeezed her hand tighter. 'You are welcome here. I've put some of your boxes in the second floor bedroom.' She smiled. 'I know you two will want to sleep together, but everyone needs their own space, so you've got your own room too. I wouldn't have invited you if you weren't truly welcome.'

'I wondered if Susan had persuaded you.'

Helen nodded. 'Yes she did. But you are still very much welcome.'

Laura still shook. She gripped Helen's hands and tried to control her trembling. 'I don't think Josh knows I'm here. You shouldn't have any more trouble with him hanging around.'

Laura blushed, remembering the scene in front of Helen's neighbours, when Josh pushed her to the ground and screamed at her, before Susan took her away.

'Have you heard from him?' Helen asked.

Laura shook her head. 'I've told him to only contact me by email. It upset him too much when we talked on the phone, and he just became angry.'

'Does he believe that you've left him now?'

'I think so. He's stopped pleading with me to come back. He's mainly angry.' She tentatively looked towards Helen who held her hand to her chest. Helen smiled at her, but her eyes were analysing her.

'I didn't mean for this to happen,' Laura said. 'I just love her.'

Helen smiled at her sadly and dropped her hands into her lap. 'Yes, I'm afraid that was clear when I first met you.'

Laura blushed and turned away. 'I absolutely adore her,' she said, emotion rising in her chest.

Helen breathed in next to her. 'Are you sure you've left Josh for good?'

Laura nodded emphatically. 'Yes. I would never go back. I care for him and I feel painfully guilty. But I don't love him. I can't have his children. I can hardly be in the same room as him.' She clutched her stomach feeling the nausea swell as she imagined being physically close to Josh.

'Has it been like this for long?' Helen asked.

'Always. I never loved him like that. He was my best friend at school. We did the same subjects and helped each other get to Oxford.'

She turned to Helen, who was frowning in concentration.

'I was so motivated to get to Oxford, because I thought my family might have been from the area. When I got there, I became so absorbed in searching for them that I got behind with my lectures and lab sessions. When I reached a dead end and Clo left, Josh helped me scrape through my exams. We stayed in Oxford together over the summer to catch up for the following year. We went out and had too many beers one night…' She looked away.

'And you slept together.'

She nodded. 'I was going to tell him in the morning that it was a mistake. I mainly slept with women at the time, and he knew that. But he was so happy. He asked me to marry him, and I stupidly didn't think I could refuse.'

'Did you think you needed to be grateful?'

'Yes I did.' Laura nodded guiltily. 'But it wasn't just that. We got on so well. People say your partner ends up as your best friend anyway. I didn't think I was doing anything wrong.'

Helen squeezed her hand. 'But it's left you vulnerable to someone you could love.'

'Yes.' Laura gulped. 'I've never met someone like Susan. She's beautiful, intelligent, and she's so strong. I can't believe how she's coped without Isabelle. I can't help but admire her.'

Helen squeezed her lips together and tilted her head. 'You're not as weak as you think you know. And Susan's possibly not as strong either.' She laughed. 'You have a sympathy that would do her good. In fact I think you complement each other wonderfully.'

Laura stared at Helen, not quite believing her. 'Do you really think that?'

Helen nodded again. 'I do. You're like Isabelle was. She had a gentle, loving manner. I suspect you make as good a GP as she did.'

Laura was still unconvinced.

'Oh I know Susan is very capable and has learned to stand on her own two feet, but she could do with someone supportive and nurturing. She's had too long without it.'

Laura blushed, embarrassed by the compliment but also glowing with Helen's approval. She cleared her throat, and wondered if she should risk ruining her approval. 'She needs you as well though,' Laura said.

Helen looked at her, not understanding.

'She needs to talk to you about her parents. She's been desperate to talk to you since the party, and I've got in the way.'

'I know,' said Helen, glancing down. 'I've been avoiding it, which I know is wrong.'

'She's been remembering things about her parents.' Laura took a deep breath. 'We went to Middle Heyford and it really shook her.'

Helen looked up at her with an expression of shock and contorted pain. She turned away quickly to hide her face. 'I didn't know that. No wonder she's started to ask questions.'

'She's very tense. And I know a lot of that has been my fault, but she's confused about what happened. She said she'd talked to you, but she still doesn't understand why her dad took her away.'

Helen stared at nothing and Laura wondered if she'd heard. She thought she'd already gone far enough and didn't want to repeat what she'd said.

'I don't know how to explain to her,' Helen said, still staring in front of her. 'I can't explain to her.'

Laura reached for the older woman's hand and squeezed her fingers. 'Perhaps she just needs to hear more about them, rather than explanations. Then maybe it will begin to fall into place for her.'

Helen looked up at her and frowned.

'It's just a suggestion,' Laura said. 'I'm sorry if that's not appropriate.'

Helen shook her head. 'No, I think it's a good one.' She smiled and sniffed. 'You've quite turned the tables on me.' She laughed. 'It's been a while since anyone's done that.'

Helen stood up, more herself again, and reached a hand to Laura. 'Come on,' she said. 'Let's get some dinner.'

Laura stood up and took her hand and Helen looped it through her arm. Helen patted her hand. 'I think I will enjoy having you here. You know, the name Laura is a family favourite. It was my mother's name. I think you'll fit right in.'

Laura glowed at the approval and relaxed by Helen's side. They walked arm in arm to the kitchen, and Laura felt the most at ease and accepted in a long time.

2.

Laura half opened her eyes. It was still dark. She heard Susan shuffling and removing her clothes before sliding under the duvet behind her. Susan nuzzled into her neck and Laura moaned quietly, bending her head into the pillow to let Susan bury her face into her. She felt Susan's warm breasts touch her and her belly fill the hollow of her back. Susan's hair tickled her behind and she sleepily registered the tingling between her legs.

She kept her eyes closed and Susan began to kiss the back of her neck, slowly taking in mouthfuls of her skin, a gentle nibble at a time. She covered Laura's neck and then teased along her shoulder in delicate kisses.

She felt Susan's hand curl under her breast and the tip of one finger gently stroke her nipple. She opened her mouth, her breathing becoming heavier. She started to turn over, lifting her arm across Susan, wanting to touch her, but Susan took her hand and guided it between her legs. Susan was already warm and moist between her swollen lips and Laura's fingers slipped in easily.

Susan pulled her closer, squeezing her breast tight, and then reached and ran her fingers down Laura's belly and slowly between her legs. They touched each other slowly in the dark, Laura still not fully awake. She began to peak and felt Susan clench behind her. They breathed hard, Susan's face resting in the crook of her neck, and they tensed in time, breathing out in long, powerful spasms.

They slowly relaxed together and the warmth and glow of the orgasm spread over them. Laura felt a smile melt her face and she drifted off to sleep again, her hand still between Susan's legs.

*

It was light around the curtains when she woke once more. Susan was still curled up into her back, her arm over her legs. Laura carefully lifted the arm and rolled out of bed. She wrapped a dressing gown around her shoulders and quietly went downstairs.

Sun was streaming through the kitchen skylight and she squinted as she stepped into the room. It was warm and she stretched out her shoulders and arms and yawned pleasurably.

'Sleep well?'

242

She opened her eyes wide, trying to focus through the morning blur, and saw Helen sitting at the table, reading a paper, a cup steaming in front of her. Helen tilted her head and smiled a lop-sided smile.

Laura dropped her hands by her side and blushed. She nodded, a little embarrassed, but with the smile still on her lips. 'I'm just going to get a coffee', she said, wanting to turn away and hide her red cheeks.

Helen smiled and flicked the newspaper out and pretended to read.

Laura stood next to the coffee machine. 'I thought I'd unpack my stuff today,' she said.

Helen folded the newspaper. 'Good idea. It will be nice to see you settle in properly. The back bedroom is a bit smaller, but it's quieter overlooking the garden.'

'Thank you,' Laura said.

'Are you planning on staying in tonight?' Helen asked.

'As far as I know.'

'Good. It's the first time we've all been in and awake, so I thought it would be nice to have dinner together.'

'Yes. That sounds good.'

'Well hello to you as well,' said Helen, looking towards the door.

Susan walked in, rubbing her eyes.

'Sorry, did I wake you?' Laura said. She went to cross the room towards her and then felt reluctant, sensing Susan's mood.

Susan shook her head. 'No I woke up early. Couldn't get back to sleep properly.' She frowned, but tried to smile, her lips pinched in the corners. The smile failed to make her eyes shine and she turned and walked towards the patio door and stared out of the window. Laura could see she was tense, her arms crossed and her shoulders hunched.

Helen looked towards her for guidance, but didn't speak. She fidgeted with her coffee cup on the table, slowly spinning it around in her fingers. It scraped on the table, the only noise in the room.

Laura picked up her own cup, realising she needed to leave. 'I'm going to make a start on the unpacking,' she said, excusing herself. Susan nodded and Helen looked at her, but neither spoke.

Laura turned and walked out of the kitchen, feeling the tension creep over her skin as she turned her back to them. Her bare feet padded over the carpet and she heard Susan break the silence.

'You've got to talk to me, but you've got to be fair about Dad,' she said.

Laura turned at the bottom of the stairs. She couldn't help peering along the corridor and through the kitchen door. She could see Susan by the window. She was facing Helen and her arms were still crossed defensively.

Helen took a while to respond. 'I know darling. I will try. I know you must have so many questions about Isabelle. Robert was reluctant to talk about her, I know that.'

Laura could see Susan's face was rigid and upset. 'Could you tell me about my sister then?'

'What?'

'I remember Mom being pregnant. I asked Dad about it, but all he'd say was that she died.'

Laura tried to see Helen. She could make out her hands around her coffee cup but no more. Her fingertips were pale, pressed into the sides of the cup.

'She did die yes.' Helen's voice sounded strained.

'But when?' Susan dropped her arms and leaned onto the table. 'I don't remember Mom giving birth. And I don't remember her being pregnant when dad left. What happened?'

Helen was slow to respond. 'She was pregnant when Robert left. She probably wasn't showing by then.'

'Did he know?'

'Yes.' Helen's response came slowly.

'And he still left?'

'Yes.'

Susan stared towards Helen. 'Did he think it was somebody else's?'

'When he was at his worst, yes.'

'Mom was having an affair?' Susan stood up, back from the table, her eyes wide.

'The baby was his Susan. I don't doubt that.'

'Then how could he leave?' Susan shook her head, bewildered, and raised her hands.

244

Laura heard a chair scrape and Helen's shoes clip on the kitchen floor and saw her walk across to Susan. She held Susan's arm and looked up at her with sympathy.

'I know it's difficult to understand. But their relationship was a mess by then. I can see why he was angry.'

Susan stared at her. 'But you don't think he should have left.'

'No. But I wish more that he'd stayed than think he should have done, to be fair to him now.'

Susan shook her head. 'But how do I remember Mom being pregnant? I don't remember Dad bringing me home.'

'He didn't. He came back to London to sort out divorce proceedings. I persuaded him to bring you here. Isabelle stayed here after Robert left. I didn't want her alone in that cottage in Middle Heyford.' She spat the words and Laura could see an expression of distaste on her face.

Susan's mouth hung open. 'She was here?'

'I tried to keep an eye on her, but I had the twins to care for. They were just a few months old and I couldn't think straight with the sleep deprivation. I wanted her to see you as much as possible, because I could see her withdrawing.'

Susan turned around and stared out to the patio. 'That photo,' she said. 'She's pregnant in that last photo isn't she? The one where she's sitting out there.' She pointed towards the iron chairs and table outside.

Helen nodded and stood beside her, holding Susan's arm. 'Yes, she was.'

'Is that why she killed herself?'

Helen stared at her, but didn't reply.

Susan looked at her. 'Because she lost the baby?'

'It's complicated,' Helen said.

Susan shrugged off her arm. 'Oh come on Helen. You've got to tell me.'

Helen shook her head. 'Being pregnant didn't help. It's a powerful cocktail of hormones, especially after having the baby. She was in an extremely bad way when your father left and the pregnancy undoubtedly took its toll. Post-natal depression at that stage could well have pushed her over the edge.'

Susan crossed her arms. 'Do you think, if Dad had stayed, that Mom would still be alive?'

'I can't really say, but yes.'

'Did Dad leaving make Mom lose the baby?'

Helen had covered her eyes with her hands. Laura could see her mouth open with grief.

Susan was shouting. 'Would Mom and my sister still be alive if Dad hadn't left?'

Helen shoulders shuddered, and Laura heard her cry. She nodded her response and Susan turned and strode out into the garden.

3.

Laura hurried up the stairs away from the kitchen and the sound of Helen sobbing. She ran past Susan's room, up another flight of steps, and turned into the bedroom at the back. The curtains were closed and it was dim inside, her pile of boxes and suitcases making an angular shape on the floor by the bed.

She opened the curtains and peered down into the garden. Susan was pacing along the path. Laura felt nervous about the encounter she had just witnessed and about seeing Susan distressed. Her stomach shrank and fluttered as she strained to think about what she could do.

She watched Susan walk quickly into the house. Laura turned around to the door, hoping Susan would come to her.

She heard Helen shout. 'Susan, please.'

Susan's voice came up the stairs louder. 'Leave me alone. I don't want to talk anymore.' And the front door slammed.

Laura snatched the phone out of her pocket. She stroked the screen to Susan's number, but hesitated, her finger paused over Susan's image. Should she let her cool down, give her time to think? She was torn by the inclination to comfort her and the feeling that she should leave Helen and Susan alone. She held the phone in both hands for a minute then forced herself to put it back in her pocket.

She left the room and stood on the landing, wondering where Helen was. It was too awkward to go down and comfort her and she felt trapped. She returned to her new room and slumped onto the bed.

She looked around in the bright daylight. It had been a guest bedroom, with an ensuite bathroom. An empty wardrobe stood against one wall and botanical paintings decorated the other. There were no family photos in this room.

Resigned, she unzipped the suitcase she had been living out of and hung her shirts and skirts in the wardrobe. She'd only brought her new clothes: her blue jeans, tailored shirts, skirts from department stores and shining new shoes. In her haste she hadn't sorted her old belongings. She'd left her cheap clothes behind with Josh.

She peered into the small ensuite bathroom. There was a loo, shower and set of shelves, but she had nothing to put on them.

All her makeup, toothbrush, toothpaste and deodorant were already living downstairs with Susan. She turned around. The bedroom looked too bare, too much like a hotel. She reached down and opened a cardboard box and looked over the contents. She slid her finger over the spines of her books: *The Secret History* recommended to her by Helen and the cracked spines of some comfort reads she'd hastily packed at home.

She put *The Secret History* on the bedside table and arranged the rest on the shelf above the bed. She pushed the books together, but they tipped over and slid along the shelf, too few to fill it.

At the bottom of the box, she found her tin of photos and documents from the search for her parents. She sat on the bed and scraped open the lid. The photo of Kate and David looked at her from the top of the pile. She took it out and held it, seeing it afresh. The photo had captured Kate's real smile, the one where she was laughing and her eyes were creased and shining. David had his arm around her shoulders. His lips were closed, but Laura could see he was about to break into a grin. Kate was turned towards him beneath his arm, her hand resting on his chest.

She felt longing inside and wished she could see them again. Guilt mixed in with her feelings as she remembered how much she had loved them. She hadn't thought about them as her parents for so long. She'd been too distracted by her attempt to find her biological family to have missed them as she should have. She touched the photo to her face and kissed their picture, the way she used to when she stayed the night at their neighbours' house in India.

She placed the photo on the bedside table, propping it up against the book. She could leave it out, displayed, now that Josh was no longer there to brush away her past and its temptation. The thought of seeing her parents' photo whenever she liked comforted her, and she reached out and stroked her finger across their faces.

The stairs creaked outside the room, and she glanced up expecting and hoping to see Susan. The footsteps slowly came closer and Helen appeared. She looked hesitant and held her hands in front of her, as she came to a stop in the doorway.

'How are you doing?' Helen asked. Her voice sounded worn and her eyes were tired.

Laura smiled. 'Very well; it's a lovely room, thank you.'

Helen nodded. 'It's yours for as long as you need it.'

'Come in,' said Laura. 'Please come in.'

Helen stepped in and walked towards her. She breathed out and settled onto the bed next to Laura, holding her hands in her lap.

'Did you hear us?' she asked, looking at Laura from the corner of her eyes.

Laura nodded.

'I'm afraid I made a mess of talking to Susan,' said Helen. 'It's difficult making myself remember what happened and trying not to hurt Susan. Isabelle was my sister, and I really struggled with her death.'

Laura put her arm around Helen and pulled her close. 'I think Susan does know how hard it is for you, but I think it's taken her by surprise how coming back to England has made her feel. She'll come back and be more calm, I'm sure.'

Helen relaxed against her chest and Laura heard her breathing out, trying to maintain some control.

Helen put her hand on Laura's knee. 'I hope so,' she said.

She gave Helen another squeeze around her shoulders, but felt her stiffen. She wondered if she'd squeezed too hard at first, but Helen's fingers dug into her thigh. She drew away trying to see Helen's face. She looked pale and was staring past her at the bedside table.

'Are you OK?'

Helen didn't reply. Her mouth was open and her eyes wide. She slowly lifted her hand and pointed. 'Where did you get that?' she said.

Laura looked around to the bedside table and the book. 'I bought a copy,' she said. 'Because you recommended it.'

'The photo,' Helen said desperately. 'Where did you find that photo?' Helen started to rise and reach out to the photo of Kate and David.

Laura laughed, unable to understand Helen's fright. 'It's mine. It's a photo of my parents,' she said.

Helen stood up, the photo in her hands, and stared at Laura with alarm. 'But you were adopted.'

'Yes, they're my adoptive parents,' Laura said. 'They died when I was young. She stood up and reached out for the photo, but Helen snatched it away from her.

'But they can't be,' Helen said.

Laura held her hand frozen in mid-air, beginning to feel a chill coursing through her at Helen's reaction.

Helen stared at her, horrified. 'Kate and David Green can't be your adoptive parents.'

Laura nodded, moving her head only a fraction, her neck too stiff to move any more freely.

Helen blinked rapidly, 'Where did they adopt you?'

Laura hesitated, beginning to feel paralysed by Helen's reaction. 'I don't know,' she said. 'That was why I could never find my biological parents. There was no record of it.'

'Do you know when you were you born?'

'My birth certificate says November twentieth, but that could be wrong as well.'

Helen stiffened more. 'In London?'

'Yes, it was,' Laura said stepping back. 'Why?'

'Oh my god.' Helen lifted her hand to her mouth. Her eyes were wide. 'They said you died. They said you were dead.' Helen stepped towards, trying to reach out for her.

Laura moved back, afraid of the change in Helen. 'What are you talking about?'

'The reports from India; they said you all died. Kate, David and their daughter.'

Laura put her hands up to keep Helen away. 'They did die. They had a daughter, Jenny. She died in the fire.' She'd been too young to feel her omission in the papers, how they had neglected the surviving, adopted daughter. The papers had not covered the inferno that swept away her family with much accuracy.

'But the Greens couldn't have children.' Helen said. 'That's why they wanted you.'

Laura froze, her face numb. She couldn't speak for a moment. 'How do you know this?'

'You're alive. Oh my god, you are alive' Helen was reaching around her, trying to hug her. Laura thrust out with her arms to push her away, her stomach curdling at what Helen seemed to be saying. Helen was pawing at her, clinging onto her shirt front as Laura tried to pull away. She dragged the older woman with her.

'Stop it,' she said. She pushed Helen back. 'How do you know this? How do you know my parents?'

Helen stood up, her mouth turned down and her eyes distorted with grief. She dropped her hands by her sides and stood up straighter. 'I'm your aunt.' She had to swallow. 'Isabelle was your mother. She wanted the Greens to have you.'

'You're my aunt?' Laura stared at her. 'But they contacted David's sister. They thought she was my aunt, but she said she knew nothing about me.'

'I don't know David's sister, but I definitely knew about you. The Greens were Isabelle's best friends. Kate stayed here in the weeks before Isabelle killed herself.'

Laura felt light and dizzy and couldn't concentrate on Helen's words. She staggered back, her arm flailing behind her for support. Helen moved towards her. 'I'm so sorry,' she sobbed. 'I wanted to keep you. But I was so overwhelmed with the twins. And when Isabelle killed herself, I couldn't cope. I agreed that Kate should take you.'

Laura felt the doorway to the bathroom behind her. She gripped the door frame, feeling dazed.

Helen stood in front of her, hunched over and pleading with her.

'I'm so sorry. I tried to stay in touch. I sent you presents, books. They said they were only going to stay in India until David's contract ran out, and I could see you again when you came back to England.'

Laura shook her head, backing into the bathroom. She was disoriented with the thoughts and images that flooded and swirled in her head. She blinked, trying to make sense of it and make it all fit together.

Helen was still pleading with her and reaching out to her. 'I'm so sorry. Oh my god, you're alive.'

'Stop.' Laura shouted. 'Stop it.' She put her hands out to keep Helen away. She was shaking from her fingertips, up her arms and through her chest. She drew her hands to her mouth and felt her lower lip trembling against her fingers. She was cold and weak and could only stare at Helen.

Helen backed away and stood up straight once more. She breathed in and out and tried to talk more calmly.

'Your mother was Isabelle. She killed herself after you were born. Your father was not in a state to take care of you and raise you. He was struggling with Susan and would not have looked after you properly, not a newborn.' She shook her head.

Laura stared at her, incredulous.

'He agreed that the Greens would take you.' Helen continued. 'They were such kind people. And they were leaving to start a new exciting life. But I wished I could have looked after you.' Helen reached out to Laura's hand, but Laura snatched it away.

'Kate registered you as her own child. It was the quickest thing to do at the time. I trusted them and we kept in touch. They sent me news and sent me photos of you. They were good like that, reassuring me that you were OK. But we lost contact for a short while when they moved from Delhi. I was on sabbatical that year and we lived abroad. Our letters must have crossed. The next I knew was that they had died in that terrible fire. We thought you were dead. We all thought you were dead. Amelia, Robert, we all thought you were dead.'

Laura could only stare. Her legs felt weak and she fell back against the doorway

'I have a photo of you,' Helen said, urgently. 'Give me a moment. I'll get it from my room.' She hurried out of the room, turning back to say something to her, but Laura could no longer hear what she was saying. The sensation and the news were unreal.

Her clearest thought was how Susan would hate her. She felt ill. Susan would detest her. If what Helen was saying was true, the thing Susan had been loving was her own flesh and blood. And it was the flesh and blood that had caused her mother to commit suicide, inflicting the post-natal depression to send her over the edge.

'Here,' Helen said. 'Here you are.' She placed a photo in front of Laura of her younger self.

Laura stood at hip height to Kate and David, in a gingham dress. Her hair was caught up in pigtails. She remembered that dress. She felt terrible remembering that dress. Helen's story was starting to become real and vivid, backed up with evidence.

What had she done? She felt numb, not able to take in the discovery of her family and its cruel immediate loss. Stabbing through her numbness, she realised that she was going to lose Susan, the woman she loved more than anything in the world, and a woman she had been trying to find her whole life. I'm going to lose her, she thought, and there was nothing she could do about it.

Laura's belly clenched. 'Oh. God.' The nausea swelled up and heaved from her stomach. She turned and fell towards the

252

toilet and vomited. She clutched the seat in her arms as she threw up in successive waves. The grip wouldn't let go and she retched until only saliva dribbled from her lips.

Her face felt swollen and she was deaf from the pressure of vomiting. She rocked back on her heels and slumped onto the floor. Her stomach ached from the spasms and she held her belly, breathing hard and noisily. As she recovered, she became aware of voices. She lifted her head and tried to listen above the thumping pulse in her ears.

Her heart leapt as she recognised Susan's voice. She was in the bedroom, shouting angrily. She began to shake, anticipating Susan's reaction, but couldn't resist getting to her feet and turning round. She felt dizzy and grasped at the door to pull herself up. She covered her mouth, and her stomach gripped again.

Susan was staring at Helen with an expression of horror and pain on her pale face. Helen turned to look at Laura and Susan followed her gaze. Laura shivered when their eyes met and her stomach clenched. The expression on Susan's face darkened and the hate that Laura saw, as she turned and vomited again into the toilet, seared into her memory.

4.

Clo woke up smiling. Fran had left for the studio, but Clo could still smell her perfume on the pillow beside her. She rolled over sleepily, hugging the pillow, and breathed in the scent that lingered. She loved the perfume Fran wore. It was made for her by a perfumier in Paris who worked for Chanel. He must have been a little in love with her too to keep making up the distinctive cocktail all these years.

Fran had been ready to leave for work, but Clo had been persuasive that she spend more time in bed in lieu of breakfast. Clo giggled aloud, remembering taking Fran by surprise the evening before as well, and rolled around with the pillow, euphoric in the memory.

She had been constantly smiling these past few days. The permanent grin was making her cheeks ache. She felt high, drunk, but she had not had a drink in weeks. She did not miss it. She would not want to dull these feelings with alcohol.

Fran had left some breakfast in the kitchen, Clo noticed when she went downstairs. She sat down at the breakfast bar with a cup of coffee and absently took a bite out the croissant that remained. The phone rang in the bay window and Clo strolled over and idly answered it.

'Hello?'

'Hello darling.'

'Hi Amelia. How are you?' she said, recognising her grandmother's voice.

'It's just a quick call. We're just about to head out for the day. But could I ask you one thing quickly?'

'Yes?'

'Have you seen Laura recently?'

'No I haven't actually. We arranged to meet up a couple of times since the party, but she had to cancel. Why?'

'It's just I had an email from Helen,' Amelia said. 'Laura's left Josh and…'

'She's left Josh?'

'Yes, and there's been the most dreadful mix up. Helen really needs to talk to her, but Laura won't see her. She won't even see Susan.'

'I had no idea. Shit. Sorry Amelia. But shit. I really didn't know. When?'

'I assume a few weeks ago,' said Amelia.

'Weeks ago?' A wave of guilt washed through Clo. She had called Laura a couple of days before with no answer, but she had been too distracted with Fran to pursue it.

'My darling, Helen wonders if you could talk to Laura,'

'Yes of course. Where's she living if she's left Josh?'

'Helen did have the address. Hopefully Laura hasn't moved on from there. I shall email it through. You know, I think I will be coming home soon,' said Amelia.

Clo rubbed her forehead. Different scenarios for Laura leaving Josh rushed through her head. 'Sorry, did you say you were coming back?'

'Yes my dear. We'll talk later.'

'OK. Speak to you soon. Oh, Amelia?'

'Yes?'

'Did you know that Fran...Francoise Desmarais is staying at Barbara and Bernard's? She's their lodger.'

'Really my dear? How lovely.'

'You do know who I mean?'

'That film actress you like?' Amelia said.

'Yes.'

'Yes, well how nice for you.'

Clo frowned, not knowing if Amelia fully understood. She opened her mouth about to explain further, but wondered what she should tell her. She had no idea where to start.

'OK. Speak to you soon,' she said instead, and they hung up.

*

Clo ran up the stairs and showered quickly. Her mind was already constructing likely scenarios that would lead to Laura leaving Josh and which somehow involved Susan and Helen. Amelia had not been clear about why she mentioned them, and Clo disliked the scenarios her mind created. She would rather she was told the truth, not have time to fabricate something perhaps worse.

Laura did not respond to her calls, on her mobile or her direct work number. Clo checked with the surgery reception, who confirmed she was on leave, but they could not say anything more. She set off to the address Amelia had emailed.

Clo pressed the buzzer for a third time on the front door of the flat and waited. She turned around, wondering what to do next. The street was not in a good area. The Victorian terraces were run down, some boarded up with secured metal barriers. Someone desperate enough had bent away the barrier on the house opposite, leaving what looked like dried blood streaked down the side of it. The alleyway to the side of the building smelled of urine. Laura must have been in a hurry to have rented a flat here. She pressed the buzzer again. Laura's car was parked in the road and Clo was convinced that she was inside.

Ten times she counted, until Laura answered the door. She heard the chain being slid back and a deadlock clicked open. Laura let the door swing open and gestured for Clo to come in and close the door behind her. Clo could only see her back in silhouette as she followed her down the dim hallway. It smelled damp and mouldy. She followed Laura into the sitting room. It was brighter, the sun flooding in through a bay window bare of curtains. There was only an old sofa in the room, standing on bare floor boards.

Laura turned around to her at last. She looked ill. Her hair was lank and unwashed. She was very pale. Her eyes appeared bruised and dark from lack of sleep. They were glassy and fractured by jagged, thin veins. Clo refrained from saying anything; there was little point telling Laura how bad she looked.

'What happened?' Clo asked quietly and as gently as she could.

'I left Josh,' Laura said, more calmly than Clo expected. 'I left a couple of weeks ago. I'm sorry I didn't tell you. There's just been a lot going on.'

'Christ, don't say you're sorry to me,' said Clo. 'Are you OK? No you're not OK. How are you doing?' she said, groping for the right question.

'I think I'm doing all right. Josh wasn't doing so great, but I think I've persuaded him that I'm not going back, and that it's for the best. I didn't love him and couldn't stay with him,' she said, looking away, still managing to control her voice.

'And Susan?' Clo asked tentatively. 'Amelia said Susan and Helen wanted to talk to you?'

'Susan and I… aren't getting on so well,' Laura said, her voice starting to wobble. 'She… We've found out…' She gulped. 'We've found out that we're sisters,' she said, her voice weakly rising higher in despair.

'Really?' said Clo, trying to restrain a surging feeling of joy for Laura, that she had finally found some biological family.

Laura could only nod, and swallowed convulsively.

'Oh my god,' said Clo unable to restrain herself. 'That's incredible. I thought, Oh god, I thought you two were involved or something…' she had started blurting out, ashamed of the story that had constructed itself in her head.

Laura looked at her with an expression of such sorrow and loss mixed with fear and shame. Her eyes could barely hold Clo's. Laura held herself, her arms wrapped around her body as if she would fall apart if she took them away. She started to shake and shiver, losing control.

'Shit,' said Clo. 'Shit, shit, shit,' realising her terrible mistake. She stepped forward to support Laura, who was on the verge of collapse. Clo strained to take the weight of the tall woman, who did not have the strength to support herself anymore. They both sank to the floor, Laura suspended around Clo's shoulders.

Laura started to sob, large inhuman howls that had no vestige of control left to hinder them. She wheezed and gasped, straining to get the air into her lungs, past the tears and saliva that dribbled from her open mouth as it contorted with grief. She cried out in wails that would not stop when she breathed in and out; a terrible sound that made Clo shiver.

Laura clutched at her stomach, bending forward. Clo, recognising Laura's classic response to grief, quickly looked around for a bowl. She was too late. Laura was on all fours, facing away from her, gripped by spasms of nausea. Nothing came out. She retched and retched, but only groaned with each painful wave. She could not have eaten for days Clo realised, holding her shoulders and rubbing her back.

Exhausted, Laura sat back over her heels, wiping her mouth and letting her lank hair hang down and hide her face, and sobbed.

5.

'I couldn't stop thinking how humiliated I was in front of Helen,' said Laura. 'She must hate me.' A wave of painful embarrassment overcame her again. She felt ill when she thought about Helen knowing how physical Susan and she had been, what they had been doing with each other in her house. Laura broke into a sweat. She clutched at her belly, trying to stop the unbearable convulsions.

How disappointed her aunt must be in her. What must she think of that young girl she had cared for so much, and how she had turned out? The person she would most like to have impressed and won over must now find her vile.

'And then I'd remember how Susan looked at me,' Laura said. 'She hated me. I don't think she could stand the sight of me. I couldn't stay looking at their faces a moment longer. They were both repelled by me and I couldn't get their faces out of my head, even when I ran away from the house

'I stayed at a hotel. I didn't sleep for two days and I was starting to see things. I really thought I saw both of them in my room, Susan hating me and almost ready to attack me. I took some pills to make me sleep and I woke up calmer. I wasn't hallucinating at least.' She pinched at her arms. She still felt repulsive. The skin on her body was cold and clammy and did not seem like her own.

'I had to stay another night,' she continued. 'I remembered Mum and Dad and how Helen had said they were good people.'

She had kept her parents in a box for so many years. They came bursting out now, laughing and smiling, running out to pick her up and spin her around in the air. She saw her mother in the Indian sunshine, smiling down to her and holding her tiny hands. How she had missed them and yearned for them to comfort her. The memories would not stop coming, more colourful and vibrant than ever before: her father coming home eager to see her, being carried on his shoulders, being held upside down and laughing uncontrollably, her mother brushing her hair before going to school, kissing her small cheeks, holding her into her soft belly, Laura's arms unable to stretch all the way around her mother.

'Then I thought how I'd lost Susan. And that was like a knife, a really sharp pain. Not the pain that I felt yearning for Mum and Dad. I was so frustrated at her hating me. I wanted to scream at her to stop.' Laura was breathing heavily. 'I wanted to shake her and tell her to love me again,' she said covering her mouth. 'And then I would remember what we'd done, what her aunt knew and I would feel horrible again.'

Round and round the thoughts and images had gone, pulling her in every direction, humiliation turning to grief and yearning turning to desperate loss, unrelenting and spinning in an exhausting cycle.

'But she hates me. And I ran. I'm not sure how long ago that was,' Laura said hazily.

*

Clo went to fetch food. She brought bread and cheese and made cups of tea. She made Laura sit on the sagging sofa and made her attempt to eat something, anything. Laura could barely comply. Her stomach and mouth almost rejected the food, unused and shrunken from her involuntary fast. She nibbled on a chunk of mild cheese and white bread, having to chew it to sludge before she was able to swallow it.

The tea was good; hot, sugary, comforting tea. Laura began to feel warmer and almost human. Her cheeks were hot with the blood rush from the caffeine. Her limbs prickled. They were still heavy, but it seemed that they were coming alive again. She was thirsty too. Her occasional handfuls of tap water had not been enough and her own smell reminded her that she had not washed for days.

She looked at Clo, able to focus on her at last. She noticed that Clo was watching her, concerned. Laura tried to smile at her.

'You amaze me,' Clo said. 'I don't know how you've coped.'

'I haven't,' Laura said, shaking her head. 'I've been taking sleeping pills to make me sleep, so that I could stop going over and over it in my head, at least for a couple of hours'.

'I'd probably need sedating for a good month if it were me,' said Clo.

Laura looked at Clo. All she saw were expressions of concern and affection from her friend. 'Thank you,' said Laura, 'for not hating me.'

'Of course I don't hate you,' Clo said. 'You didn't know. How could you have? And, I'm genuinely not bothered by it anyway,' she said shrugging.

'How could you not be?' asked Laura, straining to believe her.

Clo sat back, analysing her thoughts. 'I think it's because there's been no abuse, no abuse of a position of trust or authority. You're both equals.' She frowned. 'No-one's been taken advantage of. And there's no reproduction, no risk of becoming pregnant with a child who might suffer physically. So, why would it be so terrible? Aren't those the reasons it's a taboo?'

'What if it had been you and Lottie?' Laura asked, unconvinced.

Clo looked taken aback. 'Yes, I see what you mean,' she said. 'That does make me feel ill. But it's not the same,' she argued, leaning forward enthusiastically again. 'I grew up with Lottie. We had a relationship at home that you and Susan never did. And even though we've both left home, she has a family even, I could never think of her as anything other than my little sister. It's not the same.'

'I can't think of Susan as a sister,' Laura admitted. 'I can only think that I've lost my perfect lover.' She pictured Susan and how she used to look at her before that day. She tried to morph her into a sister who she should love, but not passionately. The image only turned into the woman who hated her.

'I keep thinking that I should be grateful that I've found them,' Laura said, 'but I can't. They're Susan's family. Helen is Susan's aunt. Her parents are dead and they're not real to me.'

'Have you spoken to Susan or Helen?' Clo asked.

'No. I haven't heard from Susan. Helen has called, left messages…' she said, shaking her head. 'Would you phone her for me?'

'Helen?' Clo asked.

'Yes. I want her to know I'm OK,' said Laura. 'I couldn't face seeing her, but I don't want her to worry. She was so upset and then so overjoyed when she told me that she thought I'd died.' Laura started to shake again.

'Of course.' Clo reached across to take her hand and reassure her.

'I think I would like to talk to her some day. I liked her. I think I could see her as family, if she could forgive me, if she could stand the sight of me…' Laura trailed off. She started to slump again, her head bowing as the thought of Susan's hatred began to grip her chest once more. She felt Clo's hand squeeze hers.

'Look, how about this to make you feel better about yourself,' Clo said, grinning at her. 'I've been working as a prostitute for the past few years.'

'What?' said Laura. She lifted her head, her mouth and eyes open wide.

Clo cleared her throat, nodded and fidgeted in her seat. 'I've been working as a prostitute. Quite a specialist, lesbian prostitute. For richer, older women if you must know,' she added, looking uncomfortable.

'Clo?' said Laura incredulous, her mouth still open

Clo shrugged in response.

'Clo! Well fuck me,' said Laura in disbelief. 'Fuck,' she said staring at Clo. 'No fucking way.'

Clo had to shrug again.

Laura burst into hysterical giggles and Clo could not help but catch them too. They both laughed until tears ran from their eyes, looking from one to the other, each creasing up more violently as they saw the loss of control in the other.

Laura gripped her tired stomach, trying to stop it hurting with the unexpected bursts of laughter. She reached across the space between them, to hold Clo's hand.

'Shit,' said Laura recovering. 'How did we get here?'

'Are you disgusted with me?' Clo asked.

'No,' Laura said. 'I'm not.' She shrugged.

They looked around the room, at where they had ended up.

'You can't stay here,' said Clo. 'Stay with me for a few days while you find a better place. You can have Amelia's room.'

'I'm OK here,' said Laura, shaking her head.

'No you're not. This place is horrible. It's pretty scary during the day. I'd hate to think what it's like at night.'

'It's not great,' admitted Laura. 'Just a couple of days, then. Let me get sorted. Find a better place,' she said.

'Good. Hopefully you can get a decent night's sleep and some food down you. You might like to have a shower too,' Clo said, grinning as she wrinkled her nose.

6.

Clo sat on the sofa, put her feet up and wriggled her bottom to bed herself in. She held a hot mug of tea to her chest, prepared for a quiet night in. Fran was doing an interview and Clo found herself oddly anticipating seeing her on television in lieu of meeting her this evening. She wondered if Fran would seem different, less of a film star, now that she had spent time with her, doing everything from the mundane to the ecstatic.

Laura had gone out for the evening to meet a friend from work, the first time she'd been out by herself all week. Laura had been sleeping most of the time since she had come to stay. Clo had not seen much of Fran. To Laura, she invented a dozen reasons for late-night shopping, so that she could catch Fran to kiss her and hold her and tell her how much she missed her. Tonight she hoped that Fran would leave the television studio early, so she could see her before Laura came home. Clo's body was starting to yearn acutely for her. She ached when she thought of Fran.

On the TV the show was starting. She shuffled her bottom again and made herself comfortable, ready to spend some quality time with Francoise instead. But the lock on the front door clicked twice making her jolt. There was a quiet shuffling of a person in the hallway, removing coat and shoes.

'Only me!' she heard Laura shout up the stairs.

Clo cursed quietly, wondering whether she was about to miss the show.

She heard the now familiar sound of Laura's footsteps on the stairs.

'You OK?' Clo asked.

'I just couldn't face it,' Laura said, shaking her head. She looked drained as she walked across the room, her shoulders hunched, and she dropped on to the sofa to stare at the TV.

'Cup of tea?' Clo said more brightly than she felt.

Laura nodded, still staring at the TV.

Clo switched on the kettle, grabbed cups from the cupboard and rinsed the teapot, her ears straining to hear if Fran had yet appeared on screen. The kettle started to bubble and hiss and the broadcast voices became indistinct. She peered across to see the screen. The kettle clicked off, steam sighing from the spout as the show's entrance music blared across the room.

'Oooh. Clo. Clo!' Laura was pointing at the television. 'It's that woman, that actress you used to like. She's on the telly. What's she called? Francoise… Francoise something.'

'*Francoise Desmarais*!' the television host announced loudly. Clo edged into the room and saw the male presenter leap up to meet Fran. The camera caught her striding across the stage, accompanied by polite applause from the audience.

'She looks fantastic,' said Laura, open-mouthed. 'Did she look this good in those films you used to make me watch?' she asked.

Clo smiled at Laura, shook her head in mock despair, and walked over to join her. Fran stepped up onto the set, tall and confident, as if she could brush anyone aside by force of personality alone. She wore a tight, crisp shirt, which her breasts seemed desperate to leap out of. She was glowing, with full lips painted in shining red lipstick, and her sparkling dark eyes making her appear somehow predatory. Clo thought she looked fantastic.

The host was too eager to greet her, too flirtatious. He held her hand too long, and tried to guide her to sit down close to him. Fran fluidly moved beyond him to offer her equal greeting to his wife and co-host.

Laura giggled. 'I like that she's cosied up to the wife instead. I wonder if she likes women.'

Clo tried to give her a disapproving look, but Laura was too taken with Fran to notice. Clo sat down next to Laura, slightly irritated at having to share the television.

'*You're here in London filming with Daniel Johnston,*' the male presenter was eagerly telling Fran.

'*I am, yes,*' Fran said, smiling at the host's wife.

Fran sounded more French on the telly, Clo thought. Perhaps she was playing up her French persona for the public. As the interview went on she flirted with both presenters. She bent forward, holding her arms protectively across her chest, but in a way that displayed her bosom to full advantage. She was concentrating especially on the woman, Clo noticed, smiling. And the hostess seemed to be warming to Fran, despite the initial freeze after her husband's fawning welcome.

'She has a wonderful cleavage,' said Laura surprised. 'I mean a really wonderful cleavage.'

Clo blushed and grinned. 'Well you've perked up,' she said.

She had been thinking the same thing though. Fran was extraordinary on camera. She was blooming. She seemed real enough to reach out and touch, she looked so vivid. The film editor seemed to have warmed to her too. The camera lingered on her, cutting away the presenters as superfluous to the interview. Clo made an almost inaudible 'mmmmm' sound, losing herself in a close-up.

'I can understand what you see in her now,' said Laura.

Her admiration was starting to make Clo feel uncomfortable. It was strange enough drifting off with dreamy feelings for Fran while Laura was here, without her friend lusting after her too.

'We've got a clip from the film, I think. We're very lucky to have this by the way. It's from an early cut of film you're finishing I believe. Take a look at this.'

The softer, more subtle lighting showed Fran even more becomingly. She looked to the side of the camera. She was walking slowly towards someone she desired. The camera held her, loved her. It closed into her face, intimately, showing just her shoulders and head. She loosened her coat, stroking it off her shoulders, and let it drop to the floor. She touched down her throat, finding her shirt collar and started to ease the buttons undone, one by one, all the while bearing down on the audience, getting closer and closer.

'Wow,' said Laura.

'Yup,' said Clo, her mouth having difficulty with the gibberish her brain was sending it.

On the screen Fran looked down, fixing her target from beneath her long eyelashes. She smiled so seductively, lifting her eyebrow at the same time, that Clo felt a jolt of desire pulse right through her. She knew that look so well. She covered her mouth, afraid that she had gasped. She held her breath, trying to hide her feelings, but Laura was too mesmerised by Fran to notice.

Fran's image began to blur as she came close, lifting her hand to the audience's face, her full lips parted. The clip finished and the audience burst into enthusiastic applause. The studio camera focused on Fran, who smiled and looked pleased, and then panned out to show all three.

The male host shuffled uncomfortably and his wife slumped back in her chair and breathed out, fanning herself with both hands.

'*My goodness*,' said the hostess. '*I think you could have seduced me in that clip*,' she said, her eyes wide with surprise.

'She's not joking,' said Laura. 'I bet there's not a dry seat in the house,' she giggled.

'Ew,' said Clo, grabbing a cushion and swiping it at Laura. 'What?!' asked Laura, smiling.

'Just, just, that's beneath you,' said Clo, struggling to defend her discomfort at Laura finding Fran so alluring.

'*Ladies and Gentlemen, Françoise Desmarais*,' the hostess said enthusiastically, standing and beginning the applause that grew into an ovation from the audience to send Fran offstage.

Clo got up. She was hot and sweating. She wiped her forehead and ran her hands through her hair. Her still short tufts stuck up with the perspiration.

'Oh,' said Laura deflated 'She wasn't on for long enough,' she added slumping back onto the sofa. 'Do you have any of her films still?'

'No,' said Clo, lying.

'That's a shame,' said Laura, sounding sad again. 'We could have watched one.'

Clo felt bad. She did not want to close Laura down if she showed any enthusiasm. 'Let me take a look,' she said.

She found her video of Redemption. She did not want to watch it though. She had loved the film, but since Fran had closed up when she mentioned it, she felt guilty about having it. She dusted it down with her shirtsleeve after retrieving it from its hiding place at the back of the shelf. The cover showed Fran almost as she remembered her in the missing clip, but not quite right. To Laura's delight she slotted the film into the machine and found a packet of popcorn to microwave. They settled into the darkness to watch the last film Fran had completed before her early retirement.

*

'Shit,' said Clo, jumping from the sofa. Laura stirred beside her sleepily. Someone had knocked loudly on the front door. It could only be Fran, back from the post-show drinks.

'Turn it off,' Clo said. Laura stared at her, blankly, so that she had to grab back the remote and stab it at the video to stop the

266

film. She rushed down the stairs, forgetting to switch on the light in the stairwell, and opened the door.

Fran broke into a smile that glittered in the street light as she caught sight of Clo, her eyes moving over her with desperation and longing. Clo's heart lifted at seeing Fran. She had not seen her properly for too long. Fran stepped forward to her urgently, pulling Clo towards her.

'I've been thinking about you all day,' Fran said, making Clo immediately react to her, becoming fluid in her arms.

'But…' Clo tried to speak. 'Laura's back early,' she failed to say.

Fran kissed her forehead, her cheeks, down her neck. She massaged her back, caressing her, desperate to touch her. Fran tugged at her T-shirt, impatient to touch Clo's soft skin. Clo started to drift and her mind blurred as Fran ran her hand up her spine and started to stroke around to her breasts.

'I could hardly wait to see you,' Fran said, breathing heavily.

Clo made a sound, but it didn't form any words.

The hall light blinded them, harsh after the semi-darkness. Fran tensed, but did not let go of her. Clo felt Fran lift her face away from her own to peer up the stairs.

'You appear to have a guest,' Fran whispered in Clo's ear.

Clo blinked in the light. 'Sorry,' she said, trying to come to.

Fran stood up straight and turned Clo around and under her arm in a brisk, neat movement. They stood beside each other and stared up the stairs. Laura stared back in wide-eyed shock. Clo blushed, but Laura was not looking at her.

'Are you going to introduce me to your friend?' Fran said cheerily, clearly more alert than anyone else.

Clo put her hand out to gesture to Laura. 'This is my friend,' she said, unable to offer anything more helpful.

Fran looked at Clo fondly, smiling, and kissed her forehead affectionately. 'Not one of your fortes, introductions, are they?' she said laughing.

Fran ran up the stairs and Laura backed into the sitting room, her eyes wide.

'*Enchantée*,' said Fran, shaking Laura's hand and kissing her on both cheeks. Laura stared at her, lipstick marking her cheeks like two mouth-shaped blushes.

'I'm Fran.'

Laura seemed unable to respond as Clo appeared behind Fran.

'This is Laura, a friend from college, who's staying a few days,' she managed.

'Ah yes. Good. Clo has told me a little about you,' Fran said.

Laura partially recovered. 'Hi,' she croaked, shaking Fran's hand again. 'Yes, I'm Laura. You don't live across the road do you?' she said, suddenly looking amused.

'Yes, as a matter of fact I do,' said Fran.

Laura smiled more, nodding. 'I had noticed that Clo was very neighbourly these days. Taking pastries out every morning and shopping every few minutes. We've been stockpiling pints of milk you know. I suppose you must be the reason.'

'Yes, I suspect I am,' said Fran grinning.

'You should have said something,' said Laura, looking at Clo at last. 'I wouldn't tell anyone. And you could have stayed the night. I'm OK here by myself. I won't do anything stupid.'

Clo just felt relief that she could spend the night with Fran again and that she no longer had to hide her from her friend.

Part 6. A Resolution

1.

Fran stumbled from her house into the mews, blinded by the low morning sunlight. She felt dazed, filled with the scent and taste of Clo. Hormones made her blood rush and her thoughts stray in a cloud of voluptuous fog.

Fran did not know why she had ever worried about how she tasted. She had wondered how men had brought themselves to kiss women. It seemed so messy and dirty. She no longer wondered. Remembering Clo's distinctive smell made her smile and lick her lips, remembering her savoury taste. The memory made her clitoris clench and pulse and she felt weak and dizzy. It was almost too arousing. She grabbed back at the door, steadying herself.

This was going to be a bad day. She was too distracted, unable to concentrate. She needed to focus on her appointment with the solicitor and then pack to go away for a night's shooting on location. Daniel would notice this new level of intoxication. He had looked at her knowingly earlier in the week.

'What?' she had said, irritated, unable to think what gossip he had found or manufactured about her now.

'Nothing,' he said, full of something.

'Come on Johnston. Out with it,' she had said, pulling herself up into full grande dame hauteur.

'Oh, just that I think someone's getting the best sex of her life,' he said smiling. He started to hum, pretending not to notice Fran turn an intense scarlet.

He laughed. 'I think it's great,' he said, more genuinely. 'She has fed you up, loved you up and you're looking ten times better than you were.'

Fran was looking better. Even she could see that. Her cheeks had a lush rosiness to them. Her eyes were clear and sharp. Her bust was bursting out of her shirts. She had managed to keep the rest of her body under control from Clo's cuisine, by daily trips to the swimming pool; otherwise she would have caused real continuity problems for the film. She glowed on camera, especially on the days where she was desperate to rush home to Clo.

Clo filled her head, visions of her, the smell of her, her touch and taste. The thoughts were overwhelming this morning, making Fran close her eyes and step back against the door. She could not stop thinking about Clo. Images would snap into her head at any time of day. The thought of her face while she came would make Fran's heart and groin clench, overwhelmed.

In the read-throughs of the rewritten scenes, she had drifted off spectacularly. She had almost groaned out loud remembering Clo going down on her the night before. She could see her soft, pale pink tongue, lapping gently between her legs. The memory made her blush now. There was still something so wonderfully forbidden about such a beautiful woman enjoying her taste and eating her out. It was overwhelmingly arousing.

'Fran?' said a voice, a soft familiar male voice. 'Francoise?'

She snapped open her eyes but was blinded by the sun's rays. She shaded her brow and saw a silhouette of a slim, older man walking towards her. He came closer, his shape blotting out the sun when he was almost before her. He stopped close enough to shake her hand.

'Dear god. Edward?' she said, embarrassed to be face to face with the father of the woman she was having such arousing thoughts about.

'I thought it was you.' He smiled kindly at her. He put out a hand to greet her. She stared at it wide-eyed, keeping her hands away from him and pressed to the front of her coat. This was so wrong. She was still aware of the juices of the previous night's activities. She could not touch this man.

'You're early,' she said alarmed.

'Yes,' he said, confused. 'I took an earlier train. I was looking for my daughter, Clo,' he said.

'She's still asleep,' Fran blurted out, pointing towards her own house. She blushed at her intimate knowledge of Clo's state and her location in the wrong house.

'Oh,' he said, clearly wondering what to do next. 'I should have called,' he continued, more to himself than to Fran. She continued to stare at him, frozen like a rabbit in headlights, unable to decide which way to go.

'I suppose I could get a coffee and wait at that little patisserie around the corner,' he said. 'Would you care to join me? It would be nice to catch up.'

Fran checked her watch and nodded, careful to walk a good yard away from him, terrified that he could smell what she had been doing with his daughter.

He had aged well, she thought, as she watched him ordering a fruit tart and coffee for them both. He was slim, not a sign of a pot belly. He seemed happier than she remembered. He had the lightness in his expression that belonged only to the carefree.

He settled across the table from her. She could see where Clo got her bone structure. She saw the bulkier male version of it before her. She shook her head. She did not want to find any other trace of Clo in him, no other trace of the delicious woman who she couldn't stop thinking about.

'So how are you?' he asked.

A memory of being between Clo's legs appeared in her mind. She was holding Clo's soft buttocks, pulling her ever closer to her face.

She tried to cover the gasp at the memory. 'Good,' she said, blushing. Good god, she couldn't concentrate. 'How have you been?' she managed to drag out of her head as a sentence one should say at a time like this.

Her body was sensitive, tingling with the stimulation it had received from Clo. She did not think there was a part of her body that had not been caressed, licked or kissed by her. She was aware of every inch of it. It was if her body had been asleep all these years and now had been pleasurably and irrevocably woken.

Clo had turned her into one large erogenous zone. And when she had straddled her; Fran closed her eyes, overcome with that memory. She had straddled her, their legs intertwined, and Clo had slowly worked her hips between Fran's, pushing their lips closer and closer together for the most succulent, delicious kiss of all. The intimacy of it had made Fran almost cry. They had joined together, fused, both almost incapacitated by the arousal it gave them.

'And I'm doing a bit of my own research now I've retired,' Edward continued.

Fran had showered afterwards, hoping to make an early start in the morning. She came back to bed, Clo unabashedly watching her as she moved across the room, smiling at her, in admiration and lust. Clo looked at her body in such a lascivious way that Fran almost felt embarrassed, almost tempted to hide it away beneath the sheets so that Clo would stop seducing her with her eyes.

'Turn over,' Clo had said, in that voice that made her melt in compliance.

Clo sat astride her. Fran could feel her soft hair tickling her buttocks. Clo leant down, her breasts gently stroking her back. Clo kissed her neck, moistly squeezing her with her tender lips, enticing every bit of skin to respond. Clo worked her way behind her ear, along her hairline, down her neck. She kissed and gently nibbled away at the muscle between Fran's neck and shoulder, sending warm, glowing shivers down her spine. Clo lifted Fran's arms and kissed and caressed the sides of her breasts.

She kissed down her spine, licking every dip between every bump. She kissed and grabbed and mauled her buttocks in a way that made Fran laugh with pleasure. And then Clo licked her in a way that made her blush now and had taken her by surprise then. 'Oh,' Fran had exclaimed. 'Oh,' she said with the pleasure it gave her.

'So I've been in the reading room all day yesterday,' Edward said.

Fran blushed deeply at the things she wanted to do to this man's daughter, blushed at what his sweet daughter had been doing to her. All the incredible, impolite things she had done to her.

'I'm in love with your daughter,' she blurted out. And she has so utterly and wonderfully fucked me that I cannot understand a single word you are saying, she could have added.

He sat back in his chair, clearly startled. 'Well I had gathered that, I think,' he said at last. 'I was more wondering whether it was such a good idea,' he said considering. 'Do you think it's healthy, given the past?'

She stared at him. This bright man was already two steps ahead of her. She felt foolish and exposed now the warm thoughts of Clo had been driven from her head. She felt suddenly sober. Perhaps she had been fooling herself. Perhaps the past would change how Clo felt about her. Had it been an unhealthy thing to do? She did not think it was. Quite the contrary, she had not felt this good, alive, or at peace with herself in a long time.

She looked at Edward, calm enough to speak at last. 'Good idea or not, there's nothing I can do about it. I'm sorry. I couldn't give her up.'

He looked at her seriously. 'Does she feel the same way?'

It seemed arrogant to assume that Clo felt as consumed by her as she was by Clo. But Clo had always been easy to read, which made seeing all the love flooding out of her all the more wonderful to experience.

'Yes, I think she does,' she said with as little presumption as she could manage.

He smiled. She thought he approved. He then looked away and sighed. 'Well. We have a problem then I assume,' he said. 'Does she know already?' he asked.

'No. I couldn't tell her. Not without agreement from you and Amelia,' she said.

'I think you're right,' he said, after a moment's consideration. 'It would be best to consult with Amelia I suppose. She knows her best. So,' he said, smiling again. 'Are you happy? Are you and Clo happy?'

'Yes I am. Yes we are,' said Fran laughing. She covered her mouth, conscious of how much she was grinning.

2.

'Do you want to make a start?' the therapist asked.

He looked at Susan with that impassive face, with only objective thoughts behind his eyes. Susan seethed. This wasn't her idea. Helen and Laura had decided this neutral ground was best.

She had been angry since Laura had fled from Helen's house. Susan saw the world through a veil of hate, which tainted her perception of everyone and everything around her. She drove through a red haze, her eyes feeling as if they could burst from her skull with the pressure of her rage.

She nodded. 'Yeah.'

'We can always start again if Laura arrives.' The therapist smiled a little. Laura hadn't made it to the first appointment.

'How have you been feeling?' he said, his head tipped to one side.

'Well, angry,' Susan said. 'What do you expect?'

The therapist said nothing, and blinked slowly. It was irritating.

Susan clenched her jaw. It ached and her teeth felt like they would crack with the strain. She stared down at her hands; her fingers were entwined and tense.

'I can't think about my dad without going into a rage.' She breathed quicker, imagining him preaching to her about having to do the right thing all those years. 'He was a fucking hypocrite. He left Mom when she was pregnant and took me away from her. No wonder he shied away from talking about her. I always assumed it was the pain of her leaving us, but the bastard left her.'

She took a deep breath and noisily blew it out of her mouth.

'I used to feel so guilty, when I was young, about wanting to ask about mom. I wanted to know why she left us. How could someone I remember loving me so much, and being so much fun, decide to kill herself rather than being a mom to me? He must have known that I would think that. He wasn't stupid. And he just let me. And all the time it was his fault.'

She rubbed her eyes with her fists.

'But then I still don't understand. I don't remember Mom clearly when we left. I mean, to kill yourself straight after having a baby? I just don't get it. If she had lost me already, why wasn't she desperate to keep this one and be her mother? Post-natal depression? Was it really that quick?'

'Could Helen help explain?' the therapist said.

'I can't talk to her,' Susan dropped her hands, and clasped them together again. She started to twist them, her fingers bending painfully. 'I can't face her. She should have told me everything a long time ago. She should have said that I nearly had a sister. There were times when she could have done that.'

She spat out the words and stared angrily at the therapist.

A memory flashed in her head of Helen joking about Laura and the noise they made when Susan came home late at night. A wave of hot humiliation flooded through her.

'But I can't face her,' Susan said, and she lowered her gaze.

'And Laura. Do you want to talk about her this time?' the therapist said.

She went cold. How was she meant to feel about a sibling who might have caused her mother's death? How did she feel about the sister she had been fucking? What did it feel like to see the woman she loved being sick at the sight of her? She had no idea how to order her thoughts and feelings. But she wasn't about to tell some random fucking counsellor about her anger, loss and humiliation. It was bad enough being here at all.

The door opened, pushing through a cushion of air and noise, and made Susan and the therapist turn.

'I'm so sorry I'm late,' said Laura.

Susan grabbed the arms of the chair, ready to stand and greet Laura, automatically wanting to be near her. But Laura did not look at her. She stared only at the therapist as if Susan wasn't there. Laura seemed drained and fragile. She was thinner.

Susan tried to catch her eye, to see if she could find Laura in her eyes, but she resolutely looked away. Laura circled around behind her chair and sat down next to Susan so that they faced the counsellor in parallel. Susan felt the full chill of her frost.

'I'm afraid I've been busy. Being back at work...' Laura trailed off.

The therapist nodded, with an understanding smile on his lips that made Susan's skin crawl.

'I've been trying to sort out things with Josh too,' Laura said.

'You're going back to him?' Susan couldn't hide her surprise.

She saw Laura blink, but she kept staring ahead at the therapist.

'I don't know how much Susan has told you,' Laura said. 'But I split up with my husband recently, and I've been trying to divide up our belongings. We had a house together and he needs to start getting on with his life without me.'

How very considerately and properly she treats her husband, Susan thought. Susan detested Josh. She detested Laura for spending time on Josh and the divorce, but not with her.

'It's been exhausting,' Laura said, looking down. 'So I'm sorry, I'm not well prepared for this.' Susan heard Laura gulp beside her.

The therapist nodded. 'That's fine. Susan's told me the bare bones of your situation. Let's start by establishing what you are both hoping to get out of these sessions.' The counsellor looked at each of them serenely.

Susan saw Laura look down and she was silent. The therapist stared at Susan and she opened her mouth expecting to say something. But her mind had gone blank. Susan was here because Helen had told her to be. She had expected that one or either of them would break down in tears, and that they may find the whole thing cathartic, and then be able to move on and start acting like sisters, or something like that. She did not know. What the hell was she meant to want from this? What the hell was a good way forward? It was all pain and humiliation as far as she could see.

Her mind swelled with her thoughts and feelings, unable to tell what she wanted. She focused on what she thought was the right thing to do, cutting through the noise to a considerate outcome.

'I guess,' she found herself saying, 'that I would like us to get to a point where we might be a family.' She was nauseous hearing the words. 'I'd hope that we could start talking at least.'

'Have you not talked at all since…?' the counsellor asked.

'No,' said Susan.

'And you would like to help involve Laura in the family in some way?' the counsellor asked.

Susan found herself nodding sagely, sickened at her complicity in this session.

Laura fidgeted next to her. Why could she not sit still? Laura's breathing was agitated and she gulped noisily.

'And you Laura. How about you? Do you feel the same way?' the counsellor asked.

Laura was turned away from Susan. She could not see her face. She was frozen, hiding from Susan.

'I can't do this. I'm sorry I can't do this right now,' Laura said, standing up. She picked up her bag from the floor. 'Perhaps another time,' she said and she hurried from the room.

Susan looked around, shocked. She shouted after Laura. 'You're the one who wanted these sessions.' But Laura didn't look back.

Susan stood up and raced out of the room after her. 'Where do you think you're going?' she yelled after Laura.

Laura appeared to wave a hand at her dismissively without turning around.

'I thought you were the one who wanted these things, to move on and be family,' Susan shouted, furious that after all that effort to be civilised, to say the right thing, Laura had walked out on her again.

Laura said something inaudible. Was she crying? Susan could not tell. Laura was still walking away from her, down the corridor, out through the double doors.

'What did you say?' Susan shouted into the noisy cold air outside. Laura was hurrying away from her, around the side of the building, down an alleyway, towards the car park.

Did she say, 'Please leave it? Not now?'

'Look, I've made a hell of an effort coming here today, again,' Susan yelled. 'Have you any idea what it's going to take to think of you as my sister?'

Laura stopped dead ahead of her, but did not turn round. It took Susan by surprise. She slowed her pace, coming to a stop a couple of steps behind Laura. She waited.

'Well what the fuck do you want?' Susan asked. 'I'm telling you that I'm here. That I can be your sister,' she said unconvincingly, the horror evident in her words.

Laura turned around. 'Well I don't want to be your fucking sister.' The ferocity of Laura's riposte took Susan by surprise. She felt chilled for a moment, Laura's response a bucket of cold words thrown over her.

'I don't want to sit in that fucking room,' Laura shouted, 'with you and that fucking counsellor talking happy fucking families.' Laura strained her neck forward, her eyes wide with anger.

Susan knew she was leaning backwards, unbalanced, Laura's ferocious words forcing her to retreat.

'I can't even begin to think of you as a sister,' Laura said, her eyes blazing.

She thought she saw in Laura's eyes rejection, desperate despair and loathing.

'Well OK. That makes two of us,' Susan said. 'Of course I don't want you. Why the hell would I?' she said, nastily.

'Fuck you,' Laura shouted and she launched herself at Susan. Laura pushed her back hard against wall. Taken by surprise, Susan cracked her head on the brick wall of the alleyway. Laura held her by her shirt, pushing her fists roughly into Susan's neck, pinning her against the wall.

'I don't want anything to do with you either,' Laura screamed at her. 'I wish I'd never met you.' She dropped her hands as suddenly as she had grabbed at Susan and turned and walked away.

The pain in her skull inflamed her and the sight of Laura walking away again was too much. Susan became incensed. Her legs felt no fatigue as she chased Laura down. She was light and strong as she caught up with her, her heart pumping adrenaline through her veins.

Laura must have heard her footsteps. She turned around, prepared and ready to launch her own assault. Laura swung at her. Pain exploded inside Susan's mouth. She could taste the iron in her saliva. Instantly, she retaliated, swiping the back of her hand hard across Laura's face, the rings on her fingers smashing across Laura's mouth.

Laura spun away with the strike and bent over. She held her face, dribbling dark red from her mouth. Her lip looked as if it had split. The injury did not seem to diminish her rage though.

Laura ploughed into her belly, winding her and driving her back. Susan's legs slipped and stumbled backwards as Laura pushed at her. Her legs buckled and lost contact with the ground and she was held in the air for a moment, light and unable to push against anything solid. Then she dropped. She fell on her arm first, felt her humerus bend, trying to take the strain, and then snap. And then nothing.

Susan woke. Her head hurt. She was lying on the path. How her head ached, all around, blinding pain. She wanted to get up, but she could not lift her head. It was too heavy. She could not understand how she could ever have lifted her head before.

She drifted and woke again. She felt sick. Laura was speaking somewhere near, speaking urgently and loudly. She could not see her. She could not tell who Laura was talking to. They didn't reply.

3.

Clo was looking well, thought Edward. It had been a long time since his eldest daughter had been so relaxed in his company. Perhaps it was the surroundings, seeing her in her own home rather than at her mother's. He was about to correct himself, in their house. But his initial thought had been more accurate, he mused. He should have visited Clo before. He should have visited a long time ago.

She looked older, more mature. Perhaps it was what she was wearing: a dark grey v-necked jumper and pale trousers, instead of her T-shirt and jeans. She had made an effort for his visit and he smiled at why she should feel she had to.

She poured a cup of rose-coloured pale tea.

'It's white tea,' she said, smiling and passing him a cup on a saucer. 'I've made it with spring water so the chlorine won't spoil its flavour.'

She offered him a pale finger of shortbread, almost white. It crunched pleasingly in his mouth and then dissolved it was so short. Creamy and buttery vapours reached his nose.

'Perfect,' he said. He frowned, staring at the remainder in his fingers. 'I honestly can't see how anyone could improve on that shortbread.'

He wasn't hungry. He realised that the sublime apricot pastry he had ordered in the patisserie must have been made by her as well. She had chosen for him better than he had, however. The floral delicate tea and biscuit had been much more to his taste.

'These are really quite extraordinary,' he said, another nibble crumbling and dissolving away. 'Quite how you've turned something as mundane as shortbread into something so exquisite…'

She smiled, her eyes wide with enthusiasm at seeing her efforts so well appreciated.

He took a sip of the aromatic tea, which resurrected the butter flavour in his mouth and sent subtle rose-scented vapours to his nose.

'Gosh. That tea does rather complement it well.' He took another sip. 'Really quite a treat,' he said, surprised by the way the two offerings played on his senses. She grinned, pure joy.

'You're looking well,' he said, recognising the same glow in her face that he'd seen in Fran's. She smiled and averted her eyes and remained quiet. He wished he could ask her about that glow and tease her.

'Have you heard from Amelia?' he asked instead.

'Yes I have, although only a short phone call recently,' she said. 'She says she might be coming back early.'

'Really? Did she say why?'

'No, actually she didn't, and I'm surprised she is. I think she wanted me to get used to living without her.' She blushed and went quiet, halting her conversation where it might have naturally turned to new friends and acquaintances.

'I've been doing more shifts at the patisserie and doing a few private orders,' she said. She sat on her hands and rocked backwards and forwards and was silent again.

He filled the silence. 'I was thinking of moving to London, a few days a week to start with,' he said. 'I've taken a lighter timetable this year, and I will retire the next. I'm planning on doing some of my own research, something I've had in the back of my mind that the university wouldn't particularly like.' He smiled and put his cup back on the saucer, feeling the excitement at the freedom retirement would give his work and personal life. 'I should be able to pop in more often,' he said.

Her agitation increased, and she stared down at the table and kicked her feet under the chair.

'I've started seeing someone,' she said, holding her breath and waiting for his reaction.

He hesitated. He wanted to ask her leading questions, to enjoy her revelation.

'I love her,' she said. 'I really, truly love her.'

He asked the academic question, 'Does she love you in return?'

'I think she does,' Clo said, looking straight into his eyes. She appeared incredulous with the admission. The good fortune to be loved back by the person so adored seemed too much to believe. She took a deep breath.

'I don't think I can hurt her. Not the way I hurt Sally,' she said.

His chest clenched, realising how much she had been haunted. It had taken a decade and someone as exceptional as Fran to break through to her.

'Do you believe me? Do you think it will be all right?' she pleaded with him.

He put his cup and saucer on the table and urgently reached out for her hand. 'Of course it will,' he said. 'Millions of people fall in love without a second thought. You were terribly unlucky with Sally. It wasn't your fault.'

He saw her flinch and he felt cold to see the way it still affected her. 'You weren't cruel to her,' he said. 'You didn't try to hurt her. I don't think you should blame yourself for it, certainly not by now.'

He tried desperately to engage her full attention. 'I'm so sorry I didn't tell you this at the time,' he said. 'I…'

He felt sick remembering his humiliation and inability to overcome fear for the sake of Clo. But he would not have changed the decision he made that day in the hospital, where Clo watched her parents walk away from her. He had to stay with his wife. He could not have thrown down an ultimatum that day. He needed to stabilise the family home, stay with his wife for the sake of their teenage daughter Lottie.

'I know Dad. You don't have to explain,' Clo said. She looked at him with devastated understanding and allowed him to take her hand.

'Please don't tell Mum though,' she said. 'I couldn't bear it if Mum found out.'

He frowned at her, seeing her overtaken by fear. He breathed in. 'I've been a coward, Clo, a terrible coward.'

She stared at him.

'I owe you an apology,' he said, and grimaced as soon as he heard the words. 'God, it's so much more than an apology. I've failed you in the past so many times.'

'Dad, you don't have to say this,' Clo said, looking horrified.

'No, I'm afraid you are wrong, my dear daughter, quite wrong. I've put myself above you. I've put Lottie above your needs. And since Lottie left home I've been complacent and lazy, leaving Amelia to support you when I should have done my very best to make things up to you. '

Clo shook her head, refusing to listen. 'Dad, please don't. It's all in the past.'

He looked at her, seeing a familiar fear. It was his weakness too, this aversion to confrontation. It had allowed Clo's mother to dominate.

'Just please don't tell Mum,' Clo said.

4.

Clo ran up the stairs and peered out of the bay window. She watched her father walking away up the mews, his head bowed in thought. She shaded her eyes and desperately tried to see into Fran's living room. Had she already left for filming on the coast?

She saw a light go off and a few moments later Fran appeared at her front door. Clo's heart leapt, desperate to say goodbye to her. She wanted to run downstairs and to hold her one more time before she left.

Her father loitered under the archway waiting for the taxi. She watched as Fran carried her suitcase up the mews and away from her. Clo willed the taxi to arrive and take her father away as she saw Fran drop her suitcase next to him and stand to wait for her ride. Clo held her breath, hoping her father would wander away, and then her mouth fell open as he turned and talked to Fran.

It wasn't a casual conversation. Fran didn't check her watch. She didn't glance up at the sky to agree about the weather. She nodded and said something without a smile and reached out and squeezed his arm. Clo's couldn't move. Her eyes were wide, and her cheek was cold against the glass. Her lips felt numb as she gaped at her father and Fran.

A car pulled up and the driver leapt out and came to take Fran's suitcase. She chatted to Clo's father as the driver packed her luggage in the boot of the car. Clo banged her head on the window when Fran gestured for her father to get in the car with her. Her father helped her in and followed her and closed the door, shutting both of them out of sight, and the car pulled away.

Clo stumbled away from the window seat. Her body and mind were numb, and she stared towards Fran's house across the mews, unable to comprehend how the two should be familiar. She waited, expecting anxiety and doubt to start corroding her insides, but they didn't come. She stood paralysed, her hands prickling by her sides.

Her bottom buzzed. Her mind was blank and all she could think of was the sensation of her phone in her back pocket against her buttock. The ringing interrupted her blank mind and then it stopped and Clo's mind was empty.

Her bottom buzzed again and she snatched the phone out of her pocket, realising it could be Fran. Laura's name flashed across the screen and she tapped the answer button.

'Hi?'

'Clo,' Laura said quietly. 'I've hurt Susan. She's in hospital.'

'What? What happened?'

'We had a fight and she landed very badly.'

'Is she going to be alright?'

Laura's voice was shaky. 'I think so.'

'Do you want me to come?'

'Yes. Please.' Laura said.

'OK. OK. I can be out of here in a few minutes. Tell me where you are.'

*

It was early morning and still dark outside the hospital window. Susan was talking in her half-sleep. Clo sat by Susan's bed and watched her stir again, mouthing something inaudible. Susan had started to wake yesterday, but she had surfaced in agony. She had pressed her morphine drip up to maximum and passed out again. Clo held the hand that was free from plaster, letting her know someone was nearby should she surface again.

Laura had been treated, her lip stitched and glued. Her mouth was swollen and she looked as if she had been caught on a monstrous hook like a fish. Laura had given up trying to speak and she lingered around the entrance to the room, hopeful of hearing Susan's recovery.

Susan still looked pale, thought Clo, casting her eye over her. Susan was muttering and her eyes moved beneath her eyelids. She breathed in sharply and coughed. The dry cough heaved her body, dislodging her arm painfully.

Clo stood quickly, putting herself into view.

'You've a morphine drip. Here,' she said, putting the control in her hands.

Susan ignored it and coughed painfully again.

'Water? Do you need water?'

Clo clumsily poured lukewarm water from the bedside jug into a paper cup and handed it to Susan. Susan sipped it awkwardly, unable to sit up, and it spilled over her mouth and down her cheeks onto the pillow. A nurse came in from the corridor, sweeping Clo aside, and tilted Susan's bed into a gentle incline so that she could swallow more easily.

'There we go,' said the nurse, pushing Susan's pillow to support her. 'Good to have you back again. Let's get you on some of these tablets as well as that drip now,' she said, checking the tubes that ran into Susan's arm. She helped Susan swallow two large white tablets with a well-practised movement. The nurse departed and Clo tentatively approached the bed again.

Clo sat beside her, avoiding a direct line of sight, so that Susan did not have to look into her eyes. Clo lifted Susan's limp fingers and held them. Susan twitched at first, surprised at the touch, but let Clo take her hand.

'If you don't want me here, if I'm making things worse, then I can go,' Clo said quietly. 'Just say and I'll go,'

Susan turned, ready to speak, but coughed again at the effort. She grimaced at the movement, but did not release Clo's hand.

'You've been in and out over the past twenty-four hours,' said Clo. 'I don't know if you remember.'

Susan rolled her head to the side.

Clo hesitated, wondering where to begin.

'You've broken your arm quite nastily,' she said. 'It was pretty unlucky. I'm sure the nurse or doctor can tell you the details. It's likely that you're concussed too, so they've been keeping a close eye on you.' She didn't know if Susan understood, but she tried to reassure her. 'Helen will be here soon.'

Susan groaned and rolled her head with distress.

'She's very worried and you'll need her when you're discharged. You took quite a knock to your head. You were dizzy and altered before you blacked out in the alleyway apparently. They don't want to discharge you after that degree of concussion without someone to take care of you.'

Susan became calmer and cleared her throat. 'OK. I understand,' she said, half in whisper, half breaking into voice.

Clo helped Susan take a few more sips of water, and held her hand again. Clo felt deflated and exhausted. She found it hard to believe how badly relations between Laura and Susan had deteriorated. The passion and anger of their feelings had shocked her. She felt disjointed, as if she was not in tune with the world. She squeezed Susan's hand again, to comfort herself.

'Laura's being treated here as well,' Clo said.

Susan twitched away her hand and her face coloured with a flood of anger. Clo sat rigid and forced herself to brave Susan's response.

'She wasn't as badly hurt,' Clo pressed on, 'but her lip was quite nasty.'

For a moment, Susan appeared remorseful, and her eyebrows trembled with sorrow. Her eyes glazed over with a sheen of sadness. She tried to blink it away, so that it would not gather into tears. Clo watched as Susan tensed, collecting herself, then the anger returned to her brow.

Clo shuffled on the chair, uncomfortable.

'I think I need to say something,' she said. 'I'm not sure how you'll take this, but I think it needs to be said.' She swallowed. 'It won't make you feel any better; it may make you feel worse. But I can't see you or Laura moving on without it.' She breathed in deeply and exhaled as much as she could.

'More than anything, it's losing you that has hurt Laura most.'

Susan made an unconvinced noise, a quiet snort of a laugh.

Clo continued, trying not to lose her nerve. 'I think she's finding it hard to face you, because she can't bear losing you as a lover.'

Susan shook her head, slowly, surely.

'You may find that hard to believe, because of her initial reaction.' Clo paused, hoping that she was right. 'She said that she felt sick when she realised who you were. But that was because she thought you would hate her. She thought your mother died because of her, and you hating her for it was too much to bear.'

Clo gathered herself. 'I think you mistook her reaction as being disgusted by you and the thought of you two being together. And yes, god, she's confused about that, but she is far from repelled by you.'

Clo gulped again, exhausted from expressing her assumptions.

Susan took her hand away. Clo feared that Susan's anger would be turned on her, or that she might freeze and shut her out. Clo's heart thudded in the moment waiting for Susan's reaction.

Susan made a noise. It could have been a mocking intake of breath or a sharp uncontrolled inhalation of grief.

Susan raised her hand to her face and covered her eyes. Her mouth was contorting, pulling down unhappily at the corners in despair. A tear ran down her cheek and the rising grief made her body convulse with pain.

Clo was about to comfort her when someone else entered the room. It was Laura. Clo wondered if Laura was about to chastise her, but Laura only looked at Susan with an expression of sorrow and love and Clo knew that she should leave. Clo backed away, letting Laura come close to take Susan's hand.

Laura leant forward trying to say consoling words through battered lips and stroked her cheek against Susan's.

*

Clo breathed out with relief that she hadn't been wrong. She ran her fingers across her hair and then pushed and massaged around her eyes with her fists.

'Is everything OK?' Helen was walking along the corridor towards her, tight concern on her face.

'Susan's awake. She seems better,' Clo said. 'Laura's in there with her.'

Helen looked alarmed.

'It's OK,' said Clo. 'They were crying when I left, but they were OK.'

Helen went to peek into the room. She returned with an emotional look of relief on her face.

'Thank god,' she said bending over, her hands on her knees to support herself. 'Oh thank god.' She pulled up straight and breathed out noisily.

'Do I have you to thank for that?' she asked, smiling at Clo.

Clo blushed. 'You might not have liked what I said, but I think it has made things better.'

Helen put her hand on Clo's shoulder. 'Thank you,' she said.

Helen wandered back to the doorway and peered in on Susan and Laura. She leaned against the wall and quietly watched over them. Clo came up to her side.

'Is it OK if I leave? Are you happy looking after Laura too?'

Helen smiled and nodded. 'Much more than happy.'

Clo shuffled next to her, her own needs starting to nag at her. 'I think I need to talk to my dad,' she said.

Helen frowned. 'I think you do too.'

Clo looked up at Helen, but couldn't read anything from her expression.

Helen crossed her arms. 'I need to tell Susan and Laura some things about their mother. I can't hold back. It's done far too much damage as it is. Unfortunately it's not limited to our family. Since Amelia isn't back, I think you should ask your father.'

Clo stared at her. 'Can I ask you a weird question?'

Helen mouth flickered and she nodded.

'Do you know the French actress Francoise Desmarais?'

'Fran?' Helen said, without emotion.

'Yes.'

Helen nodded again, and Clo's mouth dropped open.

'Fran lived in Middle Heyford for a while,' Helen said, her jaw tense. 'I believe she stayed in the area after finishing a film. She wanted to spend some time with her family.' She looked away. 'I think it's about time your father told you the rest.'

5.

Clo turned at the crossroads in Middle Heyford and drove towards the lake, the low sun close to blinding her. The car crunched over the frozen puddles and she parked in the clearing by the water, well away from the house and her mother's view. She walked up a white, sparkling path beside one of the streams she used to play in. She tried her father on his mobile, but he still didn't reply.

Clo avoided the front of the cottage and walked up the lane that ran alongside her parents' garden. She leaned on the frosty stone wall and tried to glimpse her father. It was sunny but bitterly cold. She could feel crystals of frost on top of the stone wall.

She spotted her father moving around in the summer house. He was packing several cardboard boxes on his desk. He was arranging volumes, inspecting each carefully and either packing them or putting them on a shelf behind his desk. She could see his breath clouding in the chilly air.

She circled around the stone wall and clambered over to the summer house. She tapped on the glass window, wanting to alert him to her presence. He did not smile when he saw her. He dropped the book he was inspecting and relaxed his shoulders and tried to make his lips spread into a welcoming smile.

'Come in, come in,' he said, opening the door and taking her by the hand. 'Shut the door. It's cold today'.

He drew her close in an awkward welcome and held her to his chest. 'I was half expecting you,' he admitted, sighing. He drew a chair round to sit her next to him at an empty corner of the desk.

'Drink?' he said, rattling at the drawer in the desk.

Clo shook her head. Her father frowned as he drew out the whisky bottle and two glasses from his desk.

'I'll pour you a glass anyway,' he said. 'I may well drink both.'

The smell of the whisky was enticing, perfect for a frosty day. But she wanted to keep her head clear.

'What are you doing?' she asked, pointing at the upheaval in progress.

He seemed cheered at the distraction, a postponement of the inevitable. 'I've found a small flat in London, actually in

Bloomsbury. I'm going to spend a few months at least there. Very handy area,' he said. 'I'm looking forward to it enormously.'

He looked bright at the prospect. It would have been good to see him so full of hope and energy at any other time.

'Are you leaving Mum?' she asked. Her father seemed too cheery at the prospect for his plans to involve her mother.

He stopped and considered his response to his daughter's question. 'In a way,' he said. 'We haven't talked. We've not discussed the matter. I'm simply moving out for a few months, and neither of us has any objection to that. Being the coward that I am, I'm quite happy with that approach,' he said frowning. He looked at her, waiting.

'I want to ask you about Fran,' she said.

He found it difficult to hold her gaze. He took a large gulp of whisky and looked away, collecting his thoughts.

'I was hoping Amelia would be home for this,' he sighed. He had finished his glass and poured another. 'I would recommend a drink, you know.'

*

'I wouldn't say your parents had the best of marriages, but it was far from the worst,' Helen admitted. She sat on the side of the bed holding Susan's hand. Laura sat in the chair, her head in her hands.

'Your mother was a wonderful person,' Helen said sadly. 'Isabelle had so much energy, and she was a lovely mother to you.' Helen squeezed Susan's hand. 'But things changed when you started school. She wanted to go back to work at the JR in Oxford, part-time at least. Your father wasn't keen. Robert was a more conservative person than Isabelle; a very kind, responsible man but quite traditional. I think he had become used to Isabelle being the carer, of him and Susan.

'Middle Heyford's a small place to spend so much time by yourself, day after day, especially for someone with so much life as Isabelle.

Helen paused for a moment, gathering herself. 'She started an affair,' she said, audibly swallowing her emotion. 'I didn't know for a while. She was acting strangely, more evasive and impetuous. We hadn't been to stay as often when I was getting closer to giving birth to the twins, and I was too distracted to make much of it at first.

'I remembered later that she seemed very up and down. She was so erratic, elated and glowing happy one time and then deflated and fatigued the next. I wish I'd asked her,' she said.

'One weekend, she came down to stay with us by herself. She was particularly down. She said that she and Robert were expecting another baby. I thought she would be happy. She so loved having you. I didn't know why she seemed distressed by it. I tried to comfort her, but she closed up.'

Helen was more affected now, her voice was beginning to break.

'I found out later that she had admitted to her lover that she was pregnant with Robert's child, and that had been the breaking point of the affair. This was despite them agreeing that Isabelle should stay with her husband, and that they should not endanger their marriages. What did she expect?' Helen said angrily. She clutched at the material of her trousers, squeezing it with frustration.

'They had been planning to go away for the weekend,' she said, agitated still. 'They met down by the lake in the clearing. Isabelle was ready with the car, but she couldn't leave without admitting her state. She was beginning to show by then. It wasn't something she could hide much longer, not from a lover.

'They argued, nastily. I suppose these things could never happen any other way. But I think I know who I blame for making it needlessly traumatic and more destructive than it should have been.' She said it with an angry expression on her face.

'Isabelle started the car, wanting to get home to you and Robert as soon as she could, regretting every single moment of that affair. She said that she raced away from the clearing, along the lane through the woods. She was crying and she could hardly see.

'She was nearly at the edge of the woods when she saw a blur of colour out of the corner of her eye. She looked, trying to focus on what it was. She started to steer off the road in the direction that she was looking, and too late she saw Fran. She was screaming at her. Isabelle didn't have time to understand what she was shouting before there was a bump at the front of the car.' Helen paused, looking blank and drained.

'She said she tried everything, but she had killed Fran's son instantly. He was only a small boy, about three I think. His head was the same height as the bonnet of the car. The headlight struck his skull hard. He had an aneurism. He would not have suffered, at least.'

Helen paused, checking to see if Susan and Laura could take any more. They stared at her, their eyes wide with shock, but nodded for her to continue.

'She was distraught and confessed everything to Robert. I sometimes wonder if she could have lived with herself if she had kept the affair secret,' she shook her head.

'Robert didn't take it well.' She paused again, swallowing hard. 'I can't blame him. He was hurt very deeply by the affair. He didn't understand how she could risk their family like that, which is how he saw it. They tried to continue together but, and I'm sorry to say this about your father, he was a very stubborn man at times, stubborn and traditional. I don't think he could even try to forgive your mother.'

She smiled sadly at Susan. 'He wasn't able to see past the affair in the end and he left, taking you back to the States. I don't know if he thought it was a permanent move at the time. He said he needed time away, at home on safe ground, he said.

'Isabelle found it hard without you and Robert. Without the distraction of something good in her life, she couldn't help but fixate on what she had done to Fran. I could see her, reliving that moment, killing Fran's son, over and over again.

'Isabelle stayed with me for several months. She was heavily pregnant with you by that time,' she said, looking at Laura. 'I tried to distract her, but I was so tired and busy with the twins that I couldn't be with her always. I wasn't who she needed anyway. She needed you and Robert to live for.

'She didn't go out. I brought her food, which she dutifully ate to feed you both. But she just sat in the garden and stared out at nothing most of the time. She held you, her hands on her stomach, muttering to you. She even sang to you sometimes. But she hardly said a word to me those last few weeks. She was only making herself live long enough to give birth to you.'

Helen began to cry, finding it difficult to relive what had turned out to be her sister's last few days. 'I'm sorry,' she said, sniffing and wiping her eyes. 'I haven't talked about this in a long time.'

Laura put her arms around Helen's shoulders and kissed the top of her head.

'She gave birth to you at home.' Helen continued. 'Your uncle was there that day and Isabelle insisted she wanted me to deliver you. She was very calm. She said that you were on your way, and that she'd like for you to be born in the family home. It was actually a straightforward birth, just a couple of hours,' she said, raising her eyebrows.

'I had such hope after that. She took you in her arms and she looked happy, exhausted but happy. I remember her saying, "We've done it," congratulating you and herself for getting through. And you were a beautiful baby. I think you would have warmed any mother,' Helen said, looking up at Laura with affection.

'I didn't even realise she'd gone out. She'd swaddled you in the Moses basket and left you asleep. I heard you crying and went up to comfort you and couldn't find her.

'I had a phone call from the hospital late in the evening. She'd taken herself to the morgue, lain down on an empty table and pumped herself full of potassium chloride and anaesthetic. She would have been unconscious within a few seconds and been oblivious when her heart stopped.'

Helen's voice broke and she wept into her hands.

*

'Fran was inconsolable, as you can imagine,' said Edward.

He looked pale, but Clo did not want to stop his remembering.

'I can't imagine what she must have felt. I don't want to imagine what she felt,' he said, shuddering. He leant forward to squeeze Clo's hand.

'It was a terrible time,' he said, looking ill. 'I was working upstairs when I heard the ambulance go past. Your mother had left for the weekend, she wasn't around. I looked out and saw the ambulance turn off towards the lake so I knew that something must have happened nearby.

'I rushed out. Amelia was staying with us that summer to help out, which was fantastic for me and you,' he said, nodding towards her. 'It gave me a bit of time to catch up on work, and you had Amelia to take care of you. It was a relief to see you with Amelia, you know,' he said smiling a little. 'She and you responded to each other so much better than your mother. You even spent some time with Fran and her little boy that summer. Fran lived in the village with her first husband and Amelia and she got on very well. Do you remember?' he asked, hopefully.

Clo shook her head indicating she did not, more shocked with every revelation. But she did remember Fran. The memory had become distorted with time, merging with other images and scenes from her films. But she did remember her. An image that had been burned into her mind: that missing scene from *Remembrance* that she had never been able to find.

'Unfortunately,' he said, frowning, 'having Amelia here to take care of you also gave your mother a lot of spare time.'

He shook his head and continued with his story. 'I followed the track where the ambulance had gone. I had a dreadful fear that something might have happened to you or Amelia. You both liked spending time in the woods down by the lake.'

He shuffled his feet, visibly affected by his recollections. 'I saw his small, pale body on the floor of the woods. It was obvious even to me that he was dead. He looked so odd, that pale little body on the mud in the yellow leaves. The ambulance man was trying to revive him. He was putting a mask around his face and unpacking a resuscitation kit.' He shook his head, remembering the futility of the paramedic's efforts.

'I saw Isabelle next. She was on all fours a little distance away from the body. She had been throwing up, but was then just staring at the ground in front of her.

'Fran was being held by the other paramedic. She was…' he convulsed in a cough. Clo could see that he had difficulty getting the words past the lump in his throat to describe the level of pain he saw in Fran at that moment. He frowned, concentrating on regaining his composure, his eyes out of focus and staring just beyond her.

'Then your mother came through the trees,' he said, still staring into space. 'I was confused. I thought she had already left for the weekend, to see a friend of hers.' He trailed off.

'Fran flew at your mother as soon as she saw her. It took both the paramedic and me to hold her back.'

He fell silent. He blinked himself back into focus and rubbed his eyes. His attention returned to his whisky glass. He refilled it and swallowed the spirit in one gulp.

'Fran blamed your mother as much as Isabelle for her son's death, you see. She heard them, one day by the lake. She knew of their affair. She had heard them having one of their arguments.' He looked up at her, almost shy with the confession. 'Your mother is not a nice woman at times. She can be most vindictive and manipulative. And while I'm not a man who would ever be described for strength of character, I have always managed to walk away for the sake of my sanity when she was at her worst. I don't think Isabelle could.

'I don't think they had known each other long enough for Isabelle to realise how contrary, erratic and unfair your mother could be. That, together with your mother's abhorrence of any relationship beyond what she considered the norm, made what I imagine was a very destructive relationship.

'Fran had heard them arguing about whether they should carry on their relations with their husbands.' He gulped. 'Your mother wanted to keep her heterosexual relationship you see, she just didn't want Isabelle to as well. Most unfair. She was most unfair to Isabelle,' he said, shaking his head.

Clo stared at him in astonishment, her mouth open. He looked up at her tentatively, ashamed of his admission. She felt herself pushing back in her chair and away from him.

'I cannot tell you how sorry I am for not protecting you from your mother. I was at best unaware of the poison she told you, and how she made you pay for her own mistakes. At worst I was a coward,' he said emphatically.

'It was a dreadful, humiliating time. It took me years to recover from her having an affair. We never recovered our relationship. I only managed to recuperate enough to keep living the rest of my life. And I'm sorry to say that, because she had an affair with a woman, I found it all the more difficult.

'It was a very different era in many ways,' he said, his eyes pleading for understanding. 'At the time, I thought it so much more excruciating for her to have been with a woman. And I'm afraid that humiliation persisted for a long time. It gave her an intolerable amount of power in our relationship. So much that it deterred me when I should have protected you, when you needed me at the hospital for Sally.'

6.

He had let her go. Clo ran from the summer house unimpeded. She sprinted away from the house, through the woods, as fast and as far as she could, until the lake blocked her way. Her lungs were raw, sucking in the frosty air. She wheezed with the effort and bent over a fallen tree trunk. She could see clouds of her breath billowing from her mouth and swirling around her. She shook; she could not tell if it was with shock, rage or sorrow. She tried to breathe more evenly but her breath shuddered and spluttered out of her as her entire body trembled.

Her mind did not know where to begin. She felt all at once pain and sorrow, and hatred and rage. She could not have stayed with her father in that state. She had too many mixed feelings and she felt his rejection all over again. All those times he could have defended her, she now realised that he should have done so. He had stood by, paralysed by his weakness and the shame of his wife betraying him in a way painfully reflected by his daughter.

She saw him again, all those years ago, at the hospital after what happened with Sally. He had looked ashamed and she had thought it was because of her. She realised now that it was his own guilt that he had been feeling. She saw him, swallowing down his humiliation and obediently following his wife away from his daughter, out of the hospital.

Clo knew that he had to choose Lottie then, but he should have protected his elder daughter much earlier than that. She pushed herself to a standing position, hurting her arms with the force of the movement. He had stood by and let her mother's aversion to Clo's sexuality go unchecked, because of the wounds that defending it would open. He should have been braver.

She wanted to run back to him and scream at him in frustration. She wanted to shake him and yell that he should have done something. What he should have done, she didn't know. She could not hate him. Beyond the alternating feelings she had for him, she knew that she would come to terms with him.

Her feelings for her mother were much simpler. Clo's face flushed at the thought of her mother. She felt her mouth curl and her nose wrinkle in a grimace of distaste. She felt the angry force of the blood in her face as she thought of her mother's life-long

298

hypocrisy. She found her mother's affair and her disapproval of her own daughter's behaviour too intolerable to reconcile in her head.

Clo had always believed it was her fault, this rift between mother and daughter and the problems it caused the rest of the family. Despite Amelia's reassurances, she thought that the arguments between her mother and grandmother had been caused by Clo's sexuality.

She pictured them, Amelia and Alice, mother and daughter, set against each other with her cowering away. She saw her father looking on ineffectually. She saw her mother hate Amelia, abhor her daughter and accuse her husband.

Clo felt sickened. She remembered the time her mother had slapped her at the children's party where the other girls took their knickers off. Her mother had struck her viciously. She had been so young, unquestioning and vulnerable to her mother's behaviour. Fury flashed through her, flushing her skin. She fumed that no-one had been there to defend her. She almost pictured herself in the scene as her grown self, driving her mother away from her, protecting her young self from her mother.

Clo wanted to run back to the house. She wanted to tear through the garden and kick through the borders. She could almost feel the weight of the ornate plant pots as she imagined picking them up and hurling them through the windows. She wanted to hear the satisfying smash of the glass and the crack of the wooden window frame. She wanted to walk up to the house and kick in the smart navy blue door. She wanted to rip off the brass lion door knocker and throw it through her old bedroom window. She would march into the sitting room and up the stairs. She would tear down the sanctimonious family portraits that excluded her.

Clo thought of Lottie in the photos and her father in the house. She felt cold, the heat and energy of her anger dissipating, realising she would hurt her sister and father. She clenched her fists by her sides and beat her rigid cold thighs. Clo hated her mother, but she could not reject the rest of the family she loved. She shouted. She shouted a list of the harshest words she could think of.

*

Clo's head was quieter and she was aware of feeling cold. She walked out from beneath the trees to the water's edge by the jetty. Clo walked, with her head down, along its old planks that creaked under her feet. The silvery water rippled through the gaps in the shrunken timbers. She felt weary.

She closed her eyes and the air chilled her moist eyelids. She trembled with exhaustion. She had run through her hate towards her mother and her despair at her father, and was becoming numb to her feelings.

She would not do anything, she decided. There was nothing she could do. There would be no argument with her mother. There would be no screaming about her hypocrisy, no clash of hands or words. The family home would be left intact. She simply would not see her mother again. A threshold had been breached and Clo had no intention of seeking reconciliation. She felt coldly sure about it, her mind quiet and clear with the realisation.

She had room for other thoughts and feelings now. She did not want the thoughts or the feelings to come, but she knew they would. With a sinking heart she wondered how she was ever going face Fran again.

7.

Clo peeked through the archway, trying to see if Fran was home. The rooms were dark and none of the windows were open. She didn't think Fran would be back yet. Clo hoped she was not back yet. She still couldn't think what she would say to her.

She walked to her own front door, staring up at Fran's sitting room window, wary of seeing Fran's smiling face appearing above her. She was so busy trying to detect life in the building opposite, she had not noticed that her own home was occupied. She entered the front door and stopped instantly, stunned at the open door to Amelia's bedroom. Two suitcases propped it ajar and she stared at them, confused.

'Clo? Is that you?' her grandmother's voice called down from the sitting room.

'Amelia!' Clo broke into a smile and ran upstairs. She turned into the sitting room breathless, eager to see her grandmother. Amelia was sitting at the breakfast bar with a cup of tea and smiling at Clo, her arms outstretched towards her.

'Clo my darling,' she said, shuffling off the stool towards her.

Clo enveloped her grandmother in her arms and squeezed the fragile woman as hard as she dared. She could not have hoped for a better welcome home.

'It's so good to see you,' Clo said, tears of relief and happiness streaming from her eyes. She unwound her arms from Amelia and stood back to see her properly.

'You look really well,' Clo said, smiling through her tears. Amelia had a slight tan and she appeared taller and relaxed, her chronic pain absent.

'When did you get back? How did you get back? How long for?' Clo delivered her questions in rapid fire.

Amelia chuckled. 'I got back this morning,' she said. 'Although I'm too late, it seems.' Amelia held Clo's arms as she looked at her. She smiled but her eyes were full of concern. 'Your father wanted me to be here when you found out, but he tells me that I'm a little late.'

Clo snatched her arms away from Amelia at the mention of her father. The reflex was involuntary and she felt sorry for her reaction.

'Let's sit down,' Amelia said, gently pulling at her hand to encourage her towards the sofa. They sat beside each other and held each other's hands. Clo opened her mouth, but remained speechless. The frustration she felt towards her father had resurrected inside. She tried to find the words to adequately explain to Amelia why she felt so ambivalent towards him. She squeezed Amelia's hands in concentration but still didn't know how to communicate her feelings. She closed her eyes and growled her frustration, lifting their hands up.

'I know,' Amelia said, understanding. She released her hand from Clo's and stroked her granddaughter's head in sympathy.

'I don't hate him,' Clo said. 'I'm just…' she tensed again. 'I'm just really fucking annoyed with him.'

Amelia laughed and stroked her hair more vigorously. 'I know. Oh believe me, I know that feeling when it comes to your father,' she said.

'I will get over it,' Clo said, looking into Amelia's eyes. 'I will be able to forgive him, but it's going to take some time.'

'Good,' Amelia said, smiling. She sighed too and held her breath in a pause for a moment. 'Did you see your mother?' she asked.

Clo's body froze. She had reservoirs of vitriol that she could pour out to Amelia, but she did not see the benefit of underlining her mother's faults to her grandmother. They both appreciated what a poisonous woman her mother was.

'I don't want to see her,' Clo said, her tone steady. 'I don't ever want to see her again. I'm not saying that because I'm angry. I've thought it through and I don't think she would ever be sorry about her attitude or what she's done, and I just don't want to have anything else to do with her.'

Amelia was quiet for a moment, considering her own response. She started to nod, in resigned agreement. She pulled Clo's head towards hers and held it against her lips for a moment.

'I think you may be right,' she said, letting go of Clo. 'Before I went away, I had almost come to the same conclusion.' She patted Clo's hand, restless at her uncomfortable thoughts. 'I nearly told you everything that day at your parents'. I nearly screamed it at your mother. If Lottie hadn't been there…' She trailed off and looked away.

'What time did you get back?' Clo asked, eager to talk of more pleasant things. Amelia turned back to her. 'Not long ago at all. It's wonderfully quick on the train,' she said, smiling.

'You should have told me,' Clo said. 'I would have come to fetch you. I hope you got a taxi from the station.'

Amelia squeezed her hand. 'I was fine. Fran met me at the station and helped with my luggage.'

Clo blushed and was unable to hold Amelia's gaze. Amelia held her hands firmly, not letting her get away. 'She seems very well,' Amelia said softly. 'Very well indeed.'

Clo frowned, hoping that the rising feeling of sadness would subside if she concentrated. 'She must hate me,' Clo said, shaking her head. 'She must hate the lot of us.'

Amelia's arm returned around Clo's shoulders. She touched Clo's back, trying to reassure her.

'She is a long way from hating you,' Amelia said. 'She's had time to come to terms with who you are, and to become acquainted with our family again. I will admit that she was very distressed at first. It must have been a painful shock to confront her past so suddenly.'

Clo twitched, uncomfortable at her grandmother's knowledge of the evening and the thought of Fran's horror when she realised who Clo was.

'She followed you home, after your appointment,' Amelia said. 'I looked out of the window after you came in and saw her walk into the mews to find you. It took me a few moments to recognise her. I may not have if she had not so obviously recognised me. I'm afraid she broke down almost instantly. I think she had been holding back those memories for too long, far too many years.' Amelia fell quiet.

Clo turned back towards her, unable to resist asking more about Fran.

'Did you look after her?' Clo asked quietly.

Amelia smiled at her. 'Yes I did. I'm glad you went to bed straight away.' She squeezed Clo's hands to reassure her. 'I took her to Barbara's across the road. She was not in a good state. I can imagine she felt a horrible mix of pain and awkwardness at an assignation with my granddaughter.'

Clo twitched again and blushed.

'She had been immediately taken with you, though,' Amelia said, smiling at the memory. 'She could admit that later. And why shouldn't she be?' she said, reaching up to stroke Clo's hair affectionately. 'I did reassure her that you were nothing like your mother. I'm afraid I said all that I could to encourage her attachment to you. Although I think the food that I took over, which you'd made, was probably more persuasive,' Amelia said laughing.

Clo looked up at her grandmother and smiled, pleased to hear that she had done something to bring Fran some comfort in those first days.

'But she's almost a different woman now,' Amelia said, sitting up straight. 'Quite, quite different. Amazing how restorative falling in love can be,' she said, smiling broadly at Clo.

Clo would have blushed had she not heard familiar footsteps in the street below. She had looked up eagerly at the sound of sharp heels confidently striding over the cobbles. She turned longingly towards the window and then nervously back to Amelia.

'Go on,' Amelia said, releasing her hands. Clo sprang to her feet and across the room to the window. She saw Fran opening her front door, step inside and disappear from her gaze. She waited for her to appear in the sitting room and squinted, trying to see Fran in the darkness at the back of the room.

Fran entered the room hurriedly. She removed her coat, throwing it over a sofa. She was searching for something. As she approached the window, Clo could see her more clearly. Fran was frowning, concentrating on her search, but did not seem otherwise distressed. She came closer to the window, casting her eyes from one side of the room to the other, making a pass across the floor, another scan back across the window seat, until she caught sight of Clo across the mews.

Her expression changed. Her features relaxed and her eyes became wide with obvious and intense pleasure at seeing Clo. Fran looked almost tentative; her lips were curling into a smile.

Clo found the smile and the response to seeing her infectious. Her fears disappeared. She began to feel light again. She felt a warm, wonderful feeling fill her body once more. She could feel her own eyes widen, reacting to Fran avidly and with pleasure. She saw Fran's smile broaden still further. Clo felt her own mouth begin to stretch into a smile that was close to ecstatic. She could not help but grin and laugh she was so happy to see Fran again.

Clo started to back away from the window, not taking her eyes from Fran. Across the mews, Fran mirrored her movement, retreating into the darkness to get to the door. Neither of them wanted to lose sight of each other until the last moment. And then they both turned away in the same instant and rushed down the stairs, eagerly pulling at the front door, to run to meet each other in middle of the mews.

Acknowledgements

I'm incredibly grateful to the following for their help with After Mrs Hamilton: Diana Simmonds for her generous time, encouragement and severe words when I needed them, besides telling fabulous stories and being wonderful company on the other end of the computer. T.T. Thomas curbed my worst excesses. Kiki Archer gave generous feedback and encouragement. Liz West was a willing guinea pig. Anonymous persons were inspiring. Jayney got me started writing and has been having to live with it ever since. Not all advice was heeded, and any remaining issues are my own.

About the Author

Clare Ashton grew up in Wales and lives in Oxfordshire with her partner Jayne and their toddler son Joe.

She is the author of Pennance and likes to write fiction featuring strong female characters and more than its fair share of lesbians. She loves to mix suspense, intrigue, romance and darker elements too.

Also by Clare Ashton

Pennance

Find more at:

Blog: http://rclareashton.wordpress.com
Facebook: http://www.facebook.com/pages/Clare-Ashton/327713437267566

31871875R00173

Made in the USA
Lexington, KY
28 April 2014